*Their Love Knew No Boundaries
in the Empire of the Heart . . .*

"You saved my life, Rashid. I have promised that you will be well paid for your services."

He gave an odd laugh. "Perhaps. But tonight I find myself in need of other rewards." His words were no more than a breath of sound against her mouth. He brushed his thumbs against her eyelids, closing them, and a moment later she felt his lips cover hers in a gentle kiss.

At the touch of Rashid's tongue against hers, a wave of excitement swept through her body. He kissed her again and again, until even her innocence could not protect her from the knowledge of how deeply the passion had begun to blaze within him—and within her . . .

Books by Jasmine Craig

THE DEVIL'S ENVOY
EMPIRE OF THE HEART

EMPIRE OF THE HEART

JASMINE CRAIG

CHARTER BOOKS, NEW YORK

EMPIRE OF THE HEART

A Charter Book / published by arrangement with the author

PRINTING HISTORY
Charter edition / April 1989

ISBN: 1-55773-184-5

Charter Books are published by The Berkley Publishing Group,
200 Madison Avenue, New York, New York 10016.
The name "Charter" and the "C" logo
are trademarks belonging to Charter Communications, Inc.

PRINTED IN THE UNITED STATES OF AMERICA

10 9 8 7 6 5 4 3 2 1

"How can a small Power like Afghanistan, which is like a goat between these lions, or a grain of wheat between two strong millstones of the grinding mill, stand in the midway of the stones without being ground to dust?"

Abdur Rahman Kahn
The Life of Abdur Rahman, Amir of Afghanistan
(London, 1900) Volume II, page 280.

EMPIRE
OF THE
HEART

PROLOGUE

Afghanistan, June 1875

About twenty miles out of Kabul, Miss Lucinda Larkin decided that she totally despised camels. Their smell was disgusting, their temper evil and their swaying gait seemed calculated to induce nausea in the sturdiest British stomach. At the caravan's present speed, she estimated it would take two more days to reach the ancient, fortified city of Jalalabad.

Lucy wasn't sure how she would bear another forty-eight hours in intimate partnership with her camel. So far, she and Belzebub had ridden less than five hours together, and her throat was already rasped raw with grit and dust, while her posterior had long since passed into a state of advanced rebellion.

No wonder there had been a gleam of malicious humor in the Amir's eyes as he offered to replace the weary horses of the British trade delegation with fresh and sprightly camels from his own stable. Amir Sher Ali might owe his precarious hold on the throne of Afghanistan to the goodwill of the English government, but Lucy doubted if he felt any obligation to deal honestly with his allies. She was willing to bet large, unladylike sums of money that his camels would all prove spavined long before the trade delegation reached British territory in India.

Unlike her dear papa, who would undoubtedly find good in the devil himself, Lucy knew that she viewed the world with a

1

deplorable streak of cynicism. Lady Margaret, her stepmother, often cited this unbecoming characteristic in the lengthy list of reasons why Lucy had attained the advanced age of one-and-twenty without receiving an offer of marriage.

"My dear Lucy," the long-suffering Lady Margaret had remarked. *"English ladies learn to ignore the little foibles of their friends, particularly their gentlemen friends. Kindly remember that ladies are never witty, especially at the dinner table."*

Lucy wondered if it was only her cynical view of the world that had made her so suspicious of Amir Sher Ali's lavish hospitality. Her father's advisers, men of considerable experience in Eastern affairs, had all been delighted with the Amir's willingness to sign a trade agreement. They had seen nothing questionable in his desire to put on a good show for the visiting English. Only Lucy had suspected treachery behind every bowing servant and intrigue behind every smiling dignitary. What's more, her feeling of unease continued to grow even after the delegation had left Kabul in a shower of rose petals and good wishes. The crafty old Amir was up to something, she was sure of it. She wished she could believe the substitution of mangy camels for spirited horses was the full extent of his planned mischief.

Her camel belched loudly, then bent its head and began to chew its knee with leisurely indifference to the animals colliding to a stop behind it. With commendable self-control, Lucy resisted the urge to tell the beast exactly what she thought of its temperament, its owners and its heritage. After two or three minutes of battle and many encouraging shrieks from the camel drivers, she managed to convince Belzebub that he wished to walk forward at the same sedate pace as his fellow camels. Sweating and exhausted, Lucy wondered why in the world she didn't stay home and embroider sofa cushions like any other self-respecting English lady. She knew the answer, of course, and it could be expressed in two words: her father.

As if summoned by her thoughts, Sir Peter Larkin, head of Britain's trade delegation to Afghanistan, jostled his camel into position alongside Lucy's.

"Hello, dearest, time for our luncheon," he called, smiling cheerfully.

"Thank God for small mercies!"

Sir Peter's eyes twinkled. "Can it be that my own intrepid Lucy has finally found a mount she cannot master?"

"A camel is not a mount," she retorted grimly. "It is a fiendish instrument of torture devised by the Eastern mind to persecute naive Westerners."

Sir Peter laughed. "Ah, Lucy, sweetheart, forget about your camel for a moment. Breathe in the freshness of the air! Look at the mountains and see how the snow sparkles on the peaks! Listen to the sound of the river singing as it makes its way down the hillside! Who can worry about a little physical discomfort when such grandeur is all around us?"

"Dearest Papa, somehow I find it amazingly easy!"

He chuckled but didn't reply, except to cup his hands around his mouth and bellow out the command to halt in execrable Pashto.

The warmth of her father's personality seemed to have worked its usual magic, for the camel drivers, often reputed to be as surly and uncooperative as the animals in their charge, immediately set about the difficult task of persuading the camels to stop and kneel so that their passengers could dismount.

Lucy gazed affectionately at the rotund, bouncing figure of her father as he climbed down from his camel. She swallowed over a sudden lump in her throat as she watched him hurry about, offering help and encouragement to the aides, translators, guides and general hangers-on of the delegation.

He is so kind, she thought, so *good*. Plenty of successful businessmen talked loudly about their service to the community, but Sir Peter didn't waste time boasting about his generosity. Four years ago, he had simply sold his profitable business and set sail for India. Since then, he had spent half his fortune building schools and hospitals in the remote frontier regions of the Indian Empire. Lucy admired him almost as much for his energy and efficiency as she loved him for his kindness.

Servants were arranging provisions for a picnic luncheon beneath two hastily erected awnings. Ignoring a malevolent, cross-eyed gaze from her camel, Sir Peter extended his hands and helped Lucy slide stiff-legged to the ground. She jumped aside just in time to avoid Belzebub's final, vicious swipe at the skirt of her riding habit.

"Huh, fooled you that time," she muttered.

Belzebub closed his eyes disdainfully, then returned to belching and chewing his knee.

Sir Peter gave an absent-minded pat to the camel's hump and somehow managed to avoid getting his hand bitten off. "I think I want to wash the dust from my face far more than I want to eat," he said, "How about you?"

"Mmm. Much more." Lucy shaded her eyes against the sun. "Where do you suppose all the camel drivers are running off to?"

"Their luncheon. They're probably afraid we'll ask them to do something if they stay too close at hand. Look, Mahmud's waiting by the stream with soap and towels. As always, he seems to have anticipated our needs perfectly."

They strolled down to the water in companionable silence, and by the time she'd removed all the travel dust from her face and hands, Lucy felt almost human again.

She returned the towel to the servant and smiled teasingly at her father. "Now that we're thirty yards away from Belzebub, I'm prepared to admit that the view of the mountains is spectacular. I shall miss seeing them when we're back in the Punjab."

"Will you? Then you've enjoyed this trip to Kabul?"

"Of course! Papa, surely you have not been taking my grumbles seriously? I wouldn't have missed this experience for anything."

"My conscience has troubled me somewhat. Your mama warned me repeatedly that this was not a suitable journey for a young lady. Certainly, the Afghanis seem to have little respect for women, either their own or other people's."

"Mama does not enjoy travel," Lucy said neutrally.

Sir Peter hesitated for a moment before speaking. "You are quite right. Your mama, in fact, feels that her health is suffering in this part of the world. She wishes to return to England, and so does your sister."

Lucy bit back an inelegant snort. Lady Margaret, the daughter of an earl, had never concealed her dissatisfaction with the limitations of life in colonial India, so Lucy wasn't surprised by her father's announcement.

"But what about the school you are building in Guirat?" she asked, choosing her words carefully. "And the new medical office in Lahore?"

"Your mama has rightly pointed out that I am not irreplaceable. There are many others who could oversee those projects. Besides, Penelope will soon be eighteen, and she is entitled to experience the pleasures of mingling with a more cultured society than Lahore can provide."

In other words, her stepmother and stepsister were bored, which wasn't surprising since their interests lay exclusively in the latest ladies' fashions and gossip about the London social scene. Lucy suppressed a useless little spurt of anger. She was a realist and knew that if her stepmother had decided it was time to leave India, then the rest of the family might as well start packing their trunks. Sir Peter's generosity would never withstand the onslaught of his wife's ruthless determination to move.

Lucy turned sharply away, not wanting to betray the bitterness of her thoughts to her father. He didn't need to have her sulks added to all his other problems. His wife and stepdaughter were quite enough of a burden for one man to bear.

The rat-tat-tat-tat of sound exploding out of the mountainside was totally unexpected. Lucy covered her ears, whirling around just in time to see her father fall to his knees. His hands were clasped around his waist, as if he suffered from an acute bellyache, and brilliant red liquid seeped horribly between his fingers.

"Papa, what is it?" She threw herself onto the sand beside him, calling for Mahmud, scarcely noticing the cacophony of shouts and cries echoing throughout the camp. Tears gushed down her cheeks, although her conscious mind hadn't yet permitted her to acknowledge why she wept.

"Papa, what's wrong?" she whispered urgently, cradling his limp body against her breast.

"Keep . . . your . . . head . . . down. Shot."

"Shot? Shot?" she repeated wildly. "No, you can't be shot. You mustn't be shot. It's only thunder. It *must* be thunder."

Sir Peter closed his eyes.

"Mahmud!" she yelled over the ricocheting noise. She pulled feverishly at the buttons of her father's tunic. "Bring the medical kit to the *sahib*!"

Her father opened his eyes. With a visible effort, he raised his bloody fingers to caress her face. "God bless you, Lucy. I . . . love . . . you . . ."

"No!" Her voice rose into a scream of mingled terror and disbelief. "No, Papa, you mustn't die!"

His body slumped backward and she fell across him, feverishly patting his cheeks and chafing his hands.

"Oh God, where are the servants? Why does nobody come to help me?"

The screams that were her only answer gradually faded away, and the barrage of rifle fire ceased. The agonized cries of dying humans were replaced by the jangle of harness as terrified camels and pack mules struggled against their tethers.

Slowly, Lucy raised her head and looked around. Bodies.

Everywhere bodies. And blood. The camel drivers were coming back, she noted with a strange sense of detachment. Crawling out from behind the rocks and boulders where they had hidden themselves in anticipation of the attack. The Amir had planned this treachery all along. She had been right to suspect him.

Realization of what she had lost changed her apathy into a momentary burst of fury. She scarcely noticed when a small troop of Afghani tribesmen rode into the camp and began looting the bodies of Great Britain's trade delegation. With the enamel bowl Mahmud had used to hold their washing water, she scrabbled in the soft sand of the river bank, digging with maniacal energy until she had scooped out a shallow pit.

She paid no attention at all when half a dozen of the tribesmen gathered around her, hotly debating her fate. With the last of her strength she rolled her father's body face down in the grave—that way the vultures would not find his eyes so easily—and covered his blood-stained back with sand.

When every inch of his scarlet diplomatic uniform was covered, her anger drained away, like the last scoop of sand trickling through her fingers. Her body hollow and her mind utterly blank, she sat primly beside the mound she had made, hands crossed in her lap, waiting.

An English lady never makes a spectacle of herself. Stepmama would be proud of her for remembering the rules.

The tribesmen closed in upon her with threatening gestures. Lucy adjusted her skirt so that the buckles of her riding boots were no longer visible.

An English lady never displays her ankles. She frowned. Why mustn't ladies show their ankles? She couldn't remember.

She didn't resist when one of the men pulled her roughly to her feet and tossed her over his shoulder. He stank of sweat and garlic and murder, but she wouldn't give him the satisfaction of screaming or begging for mercy.

An English lady doesn't converse with the natives, even when she is about to meet a fate worse than death.

Had stepmama really said that? What an odd thing to say, even for stepmama.

The tribesman carried her to his horse and slung her carelessly across his saddle.

Miss Lucinda Larkin blinked. She was staring at the heaving, foam-flecked withers of the bay gelding which last week had belonged to her father.

Nausea swelled ominously within her, and she felt herself begin the rapid, spiraling descent into full-fledged hysterics. Closing her eyes, she took refuge in the ultimate sanctuary of every well-brought-up young English lady.

She fainted.

CHAPTER ONE

Kuwar village, Afghanistan, May 1877

Lucy wrung the icy water out of a black headshawl, then placed it in the basket alongside her newly washed *kamis* and faded red pantaloons. Six bitterly cold winter months had passed since she'd last been able to do laundry in the mountain stream, and she eyed her fresh-smelling clothes with satisfaction. Sometimes she thought that being constantly dirty was the worst thing about life as one of Hashim Khan's slaves.

She wiped her hands on the tattered edge of her *kami*, scarcely noticing the twinge of pain as a coarse thread of wool caught in the open chilblain on her finger. Pain, she had learned during the past two years, was always relative and could often be ignored.

The sun felt good on her shoulders, warm but not yet burning with the fierceness of high summer. She sat down on the bank of the stream and dipped her feet into the water, gasping as the melted snow swirled in bursts of dazzling foam around her ankles. When her feet tingled with cleanliness, she stood up and stretched, easing the cramped muscles of her thighs. Her English body still rebelled occasionally against the endless hours spent squatting or kneeling. She tugged her baggy trousers back into place, trying to remember what it had felt like to sit in a proper chair, but the image refused to come into focus. She had forgotten how to summon up any memory of softness or comfort.

Lucy shrugged, a touch impatient with herself. Nowadays she rarely wasted time in remembering. Checking to make sure her *chadri* was pulled low on her forehead as modesty demanded, she looped the free end across the lower half of her face and held it firmly in place with her teeth. She swung the heavy basket of laundry up onto her head, balancing the load with the ease of two years' constant practice. If only her stepmother could see her now, she thought wryly. Lady Margaret's lectures on the need for a lady to keep her head up and her shoulders straight would take on a whole new meaning.

The earth beneath Lucy's feet felt warm, and tiny clouds of dust puffed up between her toes as she walked down the rock-strewn path to the village. The ground, in fact, seemed unusually dry for this early in the year. If the summer ended in drought, Lucy had no doubt she would be blamed for the lack of water, just as she had been blamed for the blizzards and bitter cold of the long winter. Keeping her head attached to her shoulders was becoming more and more of a challenge as the days passed.

She had learned to be sensitive to every nuance of mood among her captors, and as soon as she reached the outskirts of the village, she realized something momentous had happened during the hours she had been away. A camel kicking his master in the teeth perhaps, or somebody giving birth to twins.

One little boy, too young to understand the foolhardiness of his action, toddled up and tugged at Lucy's *chadri*, babbling the news in baby talk until his older sister pulled him away, scolding loudly, her voice quivering with fear.

Lucy walked on, her gaze fixed on the ground straight ahead. She didn't dare say anything reassuring to the little boy. She dare not even look at him, in case he sickened and died—a frequent occurrence in the filthy conditions of the village, but one for which she would certainly be blamed.

She knew she ought to be able to laugh at the ridiculousness of it all, but today she couldn't summon a smile. Being an evil *jinn* was a lonely business. Her vision suddenly blurred, and she rubbed her eyes, then stared at her fingers in astonishment. Why were they wet? She touched her eyes again, feeling more wetness trickle down onto her cheeks. Good lord, she thought, I'm crying.

She dashed the tears away, angry at her display of weakness, quickening her pace as she approached the white-washed, mud-brick walls of Hashim Khan's palace. Miryam would be furious that she had taken so long over a task everybody else considered unnecessary, and she couldn't afford to offend the old woman. Not only was Miryam Mistress of the Khan's Female Slaves, she also was one of the few people who had no fear of Lucy's magic powers.

Most of the villagers were convinced Lucy was a *jinn*, a paramour of the Great Satan himself. How else had she killed three fine men, brothers of the Great Khan, without leaving so much as a scratch on their bodies? Why else had the past two winters been so cold that double the usual number of sheep had perished, leaving the tribe hungry and isolated in their small valley?

Miryam poured scorn on these suggestions. In her opinion, Lucy was simply a slow-witted foreigner, with a feeble body, ugly face and a nose so small it appeared deformed. Besides, everybody knew that *jinns* never assumed the inferior form of a woman. Why would they, when they had the choice of living as a man?

The argument between the two opposing factions flared up intermittently, depending on how much other activity there was to distract the villagers. Lucy did everything in her power to ensure the debate never got resolved. She knew that if the villagers ever agreed unanimously that she was a *jinn* who should be sealed in a cave high up in the mountains, Hashim Khan would make no attempt to save her. The Khan was willing to exploit her usefulness to him as long as it didn't bring him into direct conflict with the village elders, but he wouldn't raise a finger to save her life if she became an inconvenience. He had ambushed and killed all thirty members of the British trade delegation for the sake of a few horses and some gold trinkets from Amir Sher Ali. She didn't like to consider what value he placed on the life of a mere woman.

Lucy put all such troublesome thoughts aside as she hurried through the gate set in the dilapidated palace wall. One minor blessing of her life as a slave was that she was left with little time for worrying. She skirted the ramshackle west side of the building and entered the enclosure behind the female slaves' quarters.

Her heart sank when she saw Miryam sitting beneath the shade of a shabby tent awning, drinking her favorite beverage of green tea, flavored with hard, salty balls of milk curd. Lucy quickly put down her laundry basket and bowed deeply.

"Peace upon thee, Most Honored Servant of the Great Khan," she murmured in Pashto.

Miryam took several noisy slurps of tea before speaking. "So, you have finally condescended to come back to us."

"I am yours to command, Great One. What is your wish for me?"

"Huh! My wish is that you should go away from here and return to the Eaters of Pig's Lard who are your family. You aren't worth the cost of keeping you in *pilau*."

Miryam hurled the insult with all her usual vigor, but Lucy sensed the tiniest hesitation behind the servant's words. She wished that she dared raise her eyes to examine Miryam's expression, but such a breach of etiquette would have been punished by an immediate whipping. Lucy resisted temptation and bowed even lower. Two years of captivity had taught her that pride was a luxury only free women could afford.

"May Allah show me how to give greater satisfaction, Most Honored Servant of the—"

"Yes, well, enough of that," Miryam interrupted impatiently. She reached inside the sleeve of her *kami* and extracted a precious lump of mutton-fat soap. "Here," she said. "Take this and go inside to give yourself a bath. Karima has heated water for you."

Lucy's stomach lurched with terror. She had been allowed to bathe in soap and hot water only twice before, and both occasions had culminated in death and disaster. "A b-bath, Most Excellent Daughter of Afghanistan? With soap? W-why am I to take a bath?"

"The Khan, blessed be his head and eyes, has commanded that you be brought to him. And that is all you need to know. Go, bathe, and in a few minutes I will bring you clothes to wear."

Lucy drew in a shaking breath. "The Khan, blessings rain upon him, is most generous to his lowly slave."

Miryam muttered something inaudible beneath her breath, then directed a halfhearted clout toward Lucy's ear. "Stop talking and hurry up," she ordered. "Karima's waiting."

Karima had not only provided three copper jugs full of heated water, but she also had laid out a coarse mat for Lucy to stand on, a clean cotton towel for drying and a small vial of scented oil for her body. Lucy viewed all these incredible luxuries with anxiety verging on despair.

"If you give me the soap, I will wash your hair," Karima said, clearly uneasy. Miryam could be as scornful as she wished, but most of the slaves took care never to find themselves alone with Lucy if they could help it. Whether she was an evil *jinn* or merely an ignorant foreigner, her company was better avoided.

Lucy handed over the soap with an absent-minded murmur of

thanks. Why? she thought wildly. Why did Hashim Khan want to see her again? Certainly not to take her into his bed. He had never made any secret of the fact that he found her pale body and curly brown hair repulsive. Besides, she was twenty-three now, an old woman. If he hadn't desired her two years ago, when her skin was still soft and her body plump with good food, he wouldn't desire her now, when her skin was tanned to a dark brown and her body stretched taut with hard, unfeminine muscle.

The fear settled into an ice-cold lump at the pit of her stomach. If not into his bed, then almost certainly into somebody else's. The Khan, like any self-respecting Afghan, would have no other use for a woman. Even the dancing and singing at tribal feasts was performed by young boys dressed up to look like women.

But whose bed was he planning to send her to? He had no more brothers, and his eldest son was still a youth, barely thirteen or fourteen, surely too young even for Hashim Khan to consider a threat.

So who was he planning to kill this time?

Lucy salaamed, prostrating herself on the tiled floor and kissing the toe of Hashim Khan's embroidered right slipper. He wriggled his foot, as if deciding whether or not to kick her, then grunted the command for her to rise. She stood nimbly, taking care never to straighten her back or lift her eyes. The Khan liked his subjects to cringe with appropriate humility when in his august presence.

Hashim Khan belched and scratched his silk-covered belly, reminding Lucy irresistibly of her camel. He then occupied himself for some minutes squashing fleas. When he was comfortable again, he leaned back in his chair. "The *ferangi* woman may sit," he declared loudly.

Lucy thought she must have misunderstood, but seconds later a slave appeared in front of her holding a small stool. Warily, she lowered herself onto the seat, expecting at any moment to hear the roar of the Khan's voice commanding his bodyguard to slit her throat for impudence.

The Khan inspected her huddled figure with undisguised approval, then chuckled. "She is well-behaved for an English-woman, isn't she?" he remarked to a companion outside Lucy's range of vision. "I had a bit of trouble with her in the beginning, but, as you see, she finally understands the true meaning of obedience."

A deep, rather bored masculine voice replied. "Indeed, Excellency, it is difficult to believe she is English. The usual arrogance is entirely lacking. I could wish there were more who behaved like her in my own country. You have accomplished much, Most Excellent One."

Hashim Khan roared his agreement, and while cups of snow-cooled *sharbat* were poured, Lucy risked a lightning-swift glance toward his guest. Other than the fact that he was tall and less than middle-aged, she could deduce little about him. He spoke Pashto fluently, but his accent sounded strange even to Lucy, whose command of the language was not yet perfect.

He's a foreigner, she thought, with a little spurt of excitement. The Khan is entertaining a foreigner! No wonder the villagers had been all atwitter earlier in the day. This event was infinitely more momentous than the birth of twins or a fight with a camel. No foreigner of any nationality had ridden into the valley since her arrival two years earlier.

Her excitement disappeared all too swiftly, replaced by a shudder of foreboding. Oh God, could this unsuspecting man be the Khan's next victim? Would she again be condemned to spend the night watching the nausea and the deadly pains increase, praying the poison would take effect quickly and spare him any further anguish? Please, God, she pleaded silently, don't let Hashim be planning to kill this one, too.

The Khan's voice intruded upon her anguished thoughts. "Well, Man of the Punjab, what do you think of my bargain now you have seen her? I offer her to you with my goodwill in exchange for your guns and your ammunition."

The boredom in the foreigner's voice became more pronounced. "I would like to inspect the merchandise before making a final judgment."

The Khan clicked his fingers. "Please, help yourself to a view. Be my guest."

The foreigner—from what the Khan had said Lucy guessed he must be a Muslim trader from the Punjab province of northern India—strolled across to where she sat. Carelessly, he tossed her veil to one side, then crooked his finger under her chin, tilting her head backward so that her entire face and neck were exposed to his gaze. Lucy looked up into his dark, assessing eyes and felt a curious heat flare in her cheeks. For a moment, he was oddly silent, then he drew the veil back across her face and turned scornfully on his heel.

"Your Excellency undoubtedly sees fit to jest. Of what possible value to me is such an old and withered female? She lacks even the merit of being fair-haired and blue-eyed, like most of her countrywomen. She will fetch no price on the slave market, and she doesn't appeal to me at all."

"I did not offer her to you for your pleasure," the Khan replied irritably. "Take her to the British authorities in Peshawar. They will reward you handsomely for her return."

"If they do not hang me first," the foreigner remarked dryly. "Who is she, anyway, and what is she doing here?"

"She claims to be the daughter of one of their high officials, a man of much importance in the government of your country. Naturally, I have no way of knowing the truth of her claim. My warriors, you understand, found her wandering in the desert, and out of the overflowing goodness of their hearts brought her here to my protection."

"A most understandable decision on their part, Excellency, since the benevolence of your disposition is admired throughout Afghanistan."

Lucy peeked up in time to see the Khan nod a modest acknowledgment. "She has caused me nothing but trouble," he said through a mouthful of sweetmeats. "And yet I have continued to feed her throughout the long months of winter."

"Indeed, Excellency, one sees the extent of your benevolence in the fat padding her bones."

The Khan frowned, but before he could speak the foreigner bared his teeth in a smile. "It is because of your famous benevolence, Most Illustrious Khan of Kuwar, that I take the liberty of pointing out that my rifles and ammunition have a value we can readily agree upon. The woman, on the other hand, has no value at all if the British do not want her. She may be the daughter of an important man, as she claims. Or she may be nothing more than the cast-off whore of a British soldier." The trader paused, the irony of his voice unmistakable. "Since your warriors picked her up in the desert, alas, we have no way of confirming her story. And hence no way of establishing her value to me."

The Khan's eyes flashed with anger. He didn't appreciate having his lies turned so neatly against him. "Indeed, what you say is true, Trader. However, because of *your* great wisdom I take the liberty of pointing out that you are not in a position to strike the best of bargains. Your guards were killed by thieves in the mountains. You yourself barely escaped with your life. Further-more, your weapons—those Enfield rifles whose value we both agree upon—already repose in the hands of my tribesmen. In these painful circumstances, a wise trader would take the woman and be thankful."

The foreigner spoke tersely. "Your words offer enlightenment, Excellency, and of course I bow to your superior understanding of my circumstances. But, it must be admitted, doubts still clutter my mind. If I take the woman and return her to the British authorities in Peshawar, is there not some chance that Your Excellency may find himself the object of a punitive raid by their army? I mention such a possibility only because it is well known how women contrive to twist even the simplest story into a maze of lies and recriminations. She may choose to pretend she was abducted, or something equally outrageous."

"She will tell them nothing. How can she, if she wishes to retain even a shred of her honor? Besides, the British are too busy to launch an expedition against a humble servant of the Amir such as myself. If retribution is called for, it will surely be directed against the Great Amir himself, may he reign forever."

Dear God, Lucy thought. Hashim Khan hopes to provoke the British into attacking Amir Sher Ali! Which must mean that he had switched allegiances, since he had undoubtedly worked hand in glove with the Amir at the time of the trade delegation massacre and her own capture, two years earlier.

Her mind raced feverishly. Who could the Khan have allied himself with now? The Russians, whose spies were everywhere, and whose imperial armies pressed at the northern borders of Afghanistan? Or simply one of the many local contenders for the Amir's throne?

Lucy had no way of knowing if the Indian gun trader understood Hashim Khan's political intentions. Probably not, she thought, since the workings of the Afghani mind were devious even by Eastern standards, and the intrigues surrounding the court in Kabul seemed totally impenetrable to most outsiders.

However obscure the Khan's underlying motives, one part of his message had been easy to understand. The trader must realize by now that he would be killed if he didn't accept Lucy in exchange for his supply of rifles. She looked up, just in time to see him shrug.

"I will take the woman to Peshawar," he said, his voice clipped to the point of harshness.

"I knew you would understand my point of view once I had clearly explained it," the Khan murmured, his chins wobbling with satisfaction. Lucy decided he must be more anxious to get rid of her than she'd realized, or he would never have tolerated the trader's curtness.

Belatedly, the trader seemed to realize his danger. He rose from his chair and salaamed deeply. "May my guns serve you and your men faithfully for many years, Most Excellent Ruler."

"I'm sure they will," the Khan replied. "Allah permitting, you will wish to leave at first light tomorrow morning."

"Yes, I think that would be best."

"You shall have my finest mule as a mount for the woman."

"Your Excellency is all kind consideration. And my own horses?"

The Khan waved his hand in a vague, all-encompassing gesture. "Everything will be taken care of," he said. "Trust me."

Poor trader, Lucy thought wryly. What a rotten deal he's getting. Me and a mule, and maybe the return of his own horses if he's lucky. I hope my stepmother is prepared to pay him a decent reward for bringing me home.

And then the realization finally struck her. *Home!* Hashim Khan was actually planning to let her go! She swallowed hard, closing her eyes and clasping her hands tightly together in her lap. In the whole two years of her captivity, silence had never been so hard to maintain, but she forced herself to sit unmoving on the hard stool, in case the slightest sound from her might cause one of the men to change his mind. God knew, if Hashim Khan understood how willingly she went with the trader, and how determined she was to see that he got paid, he probably would renege on the deal just to spite them both. The Khan of Kuwar was not a believer in making other people happy if he could possibly avoid it.

The gun trader and Hashim Khan engaged in a ritual exchange of elaborate compliments to mark the conclusion of their bargain. The three musicians struck up a triumphant and out-of-tune march, and the Khan rose. He walked over to stand in front of Lucy, who curled at once into a humble ball at his feet.

Incredibly, the Khan stretched out his own hand to pull her upright. "Go in peace, Daughter of a Distant Land, and remember to tell your people of the kindness you have received from the Khan of Kuwar."

Lucy almost laughed, but the Khan wasn't joking, she realized, or even being sarcastic. He genuinely believed she had much to thank him for. She managed to choke back her true feelings and force out a few words of seeming gratitude. She kissed his slipper, resisting the impulse to take a large bite out of his toe. "May Allah reward you in proportion to your years of generosity, Most Noble Ruler."

Hashim Khan was not the man for spotting subtleties. He took her words at face value, patting her on the shoulder and sighing as if genuinely sorry to be losing her. Perhaps he was. He was unlikely ever again to find such a perfect scapegoat for his misdeeds.

"You will spend this night with the Trader," the Khan ordered. "And make sure you do as he bids you. Remember, a disobedient woman is worse than a pool of dog's vomit in the sight of Allah."

On this elegant note, he departed for his sleeping chamber, his dancing boys prancing in his wake. At the threshold of his private quarters, he turned and beckoned to one of his bodyguards. "Show the Trader from the Punjab to the chamber we have prepared," he ordered. "See that the *ferangi* woman goes with him."

The guard salaamed and Hashim Khan waddled into his room. A lissome dancing boy closed the curtains, screening the Khan and his entourage from view. Lucy blocked her ears to the ensuing sounds and looked quickly around. Apart from the bodyguard and a couple of slaves preparing themselves for sleep on the floor of the audience hall, she and the gun trader were alone.

He did not seem to consider this a fortunate circumstance, and certainly not an enticement to lust. As she stood, he inspected her swiftly then turned away, his dark brows drawn in a ferocious frown. Before she could decide whether to risk speaking, the bodyguard gestured, indicating that they both should accompany him down a narrow corridor. The trader strode forward without so much as a backward glance.

She was not in the least offended by his indifference. On the contrary, she was impressed by his forbearance. The Khan had compelled him to accept a terrible bargain, and many men would have shown their annoyance by beating her. Neither the body-guard nor any of the Khan's other servants would have stopped him, so she was grateful for his restraint. As soon as he gave her permission to speak, she would try to convince him that a reward would be forthcoming for her safe return. If he believed in that reward, she was less likely to find herself abandoned somewhere in the mountains between here and the Indian town of Peshawar.

The bodyguard pulled aside a heavy woven curtain and gestured to the trader. "Your room, Honored Trader. May you have a restful night and awake refreshed."

"In the comfort of the Khan's palace, quiet sleep is assured," the trader replied, entering the guest chamber. He totally ignored Lucy as she slipped quietly to a far corner of the room, but this time she couldn't appreciate his good temper. The chamber was hatefully familiar, and her stomach knotted tight with dread. She had been here twice before, and that was twice too often. On both occasions, the men sharing the room with her had died.

Oh God! she thought frantically. Had she been a naive fool, imagining Hashim Khan was willing to set her free? Had she misinterpreted his plan to unleash a British attack on Amir Sher Ali? Was this Indian trader to be added to the list of men killed by her supposed magic powers?

The trader walked across the room, sending a single brief glance in Lucy's direction. Naturally enough, he made no comment on her state of cowering silence. Women never spoke unless spoken to, and slaves were supposed to cower. He seemed pleased with the provisions that had been made for his comfort and was generous with his compliments. If the possibility of treachery on the part of the Khan had entered his head, he gave no sign of it. Lucy couldn't quite make up her mind whether he was unbelievably foolish or amazingly wise.

The bodyguard unrolled the thick sleeping pallet and scattered embroidered cushions at one end. Then, from a roughly carved niche in the wall, he withdrew two heavy woolen blankets, shaking them energetically. Fortunately, they were quite new and therefore reasonably clean, so there was not much dust and no scorpions were unexpectedly set free. Lucy had learned to inspect her bedding very carefully before crawling into it. Finally, the guard pointed to the brass pitcher of cold tea and a tray bearing an assortment of sticky sweetmeats before bowing himself out of the room.

The trader removed his turban and tossed it onto the pallet, then began to unfasten the buttons of his padded cotton jacket. When all sound of the bodyguard's retreating footsteps ceased, he crossed to the entrance of the room and gently drew back the curtain. Satisfied that nobody lurked outside, he turned back into the room and looked directly at Lucy.

"It's quite safe for you to speak," he said quietly in Pashto. "There is no one to hear us. Why are you trembling? What is there about this room that terrifies you so?"

CHAPTER TWO

Lucy was so astonished by his perception that for a second or two she simply stared at him. On the very brink of blurting out the truth, caution returned. She knew almost nothing about this man except that he was Indian, a trader and a Muslim. Such a man was unlikely to harbor tender feelings toward a captive English-woman. Just because he had kept remarkable control of his temper so far didn't mean she could trust him. She didn't know how he would react to the news that Hashim Khan might already have poisoned him, but it was a fair guess that he would blame her.

Lucy took refuge in the pretense of stolid stupidity that had been her defense for most of the past two years. She lowered her head deferentially. "Forgive me, Master. I regret that my woman's brain is feeble. I do not understand your meaning."

"You understand me very well, Englishwoman. In the Great Hall when you prostrated yourself before the Khan, you pretended to fear him, but deep inside your heart I could see that you despised him."

She kept her eyes modestly averted, concealing a fresh flare of surprise. "I regret if my behavior gave the wrong impression, Master. Hashim Khan is the Ruler of all Kuwar, his great wisdom is respected—"

"Spare me your acting, Englishwoman. It isn't very good.

Hashim Khan is a greedy fool, and we both know it. However, fools can be every bit as dangerous as wise men, and that is why I want to know what you fear about this room. You became afraid as soon as the bodyguard showed us in here. Do not deny it. Your face is pale and your hands still tremble. What is there to terrify you in this simple sleeping chamber?"

A little too late, Lucy thrust her betraying hands beneath the thick folds of her veil, disconcerted yet again by the acuteness of the trader's observations. He had scarcely seemed to glance in her direction, and yet he had sensed more of her true feelings than anybody else in the entire period of her captivity.

"I was suddenly afraid I might not please you, Master," she said after a moment's hesitation. "I know you find me old and withered, and I didn't want to be left behind when you set out for Peshawar."

"That last part, at least, is probably true," the trader muttered. He pushed his fingers through his hair, which was thick and dark, and oiled to a high shine. "I suppose the Khan and his men have used your body with roughness," he said brusquely. "But you have nothing to fear from me. Unlike the Great Khan, I value my neck, and I have seen what British gentlemen do to men of my race who violate one of their women. I wish to claim a reward when we return to Peshawar, not a personal visit from the hangman."

"Then you will take me back to India with you?" she breathed. "If you do, I swear that you will be paid well for your troubles."

"Don't worry, Englishwoman, I intend to be paid in full. I hope your family is rich."

When speaking Pashto, as they both were, it was not considered rude to address somebody by the name of their country, but Lucy felt a sudden, inexplicable urge to hear the trader say her name.

"We should introduce ourselves," she said primly. "My name is Miss Lucinda Larkin. My friends and family call me Lucy."

The trader looked at her blankly, then turned his back without answering. Lucy's cheeks grew hot, and she felt unutterably silly. What had she expected, for heaven's sake? English names were always difficult for Indians to pronounce, and no self-respecting Easterner would permit himself to appear at a disadvantage in front of a woman. Of course the trader wouldn't say her name.

She was so busy feeling embarrassed that it was late—dangerously late—before she realized that the trader had crossed to the other side of the room and was pouring a cup of tea. She hurled herself after him, knocking the brass cup out of his hands a split second before he could raise it to his lips.

Silence filled the sleeping chamber. The trader picked up the cup and returned it carefully to the tray. Still silent, he retrieved his turban from the sleeping mat and used the loose flap to mop up the tea soaking into his pantaloons. When he finally looked at Lucy, his eyes were hard with anger. "Is it poisoned?" he asked, his voice cool. "The preserved fruits, too?"

"I don't know. Perhaps." Her mouth twisted in a bitter smile. "I am not in Hashim Khan's confidence."

"Then why did you knock the cup from my hand?"

She twisted the edge of her veil between her fingers. "I can't believe the Khan is prepared to let us go. I keep thinking he must have some scheme to kill us."

"The Afghani code of honor is strict. A host's duty to protect and honor his guest is sacred. Even the Khan wouldn't dare to violate that rule before his people."

"That's true. But the Khan has convinced the villagers I am a *jinn*, so he cannot be held responsible for what happens to any man left alone with me."

The trader's brow quirked upward. "And are you a *jinn*?"

"Of course not," she said, exasperated. "If I had magic powers, do you think I would have spent the last two years as one of Hashim Khan's slaves?"

"Not if you are a sensible *jinn*, certainly. So tell me, English-woman, what happens to the unfortunate visitors who find themselves alone with you?"

She drew in a deep breath. "They die, though so far, none were visitors. There have been no visitors since I arrived here. But the Khan's brothers all died in this room. With me."

The trader steepled his fingers and regarded them contempla-tively. "Ah," he said. "I see."

"I tried to save them," she said tightly. "I tried everything I knew. But it was always . . . too late."

"So you did not actually feed them the poison?"

"No! How could you think such a thing?"

"You could have been forced," he said. "I imagine the Khan is capable of dreaming up many ways to compel a captive woman to do his will."

"I didn't poison them," she repeated. "His brothers were half-delirious by the time the Khan brought me to this room. The first time, I thought his brother was drunk, although I know alcohol is forbidden to Muslims. But from the way he clutched at my robe and heaved himself on top of me . . . I thought . . . I didn't realize . . ."

Her voice tailed away, and the trader touched her lightly on the arm. "Take heart, Englishwoman. I think I shall probably survive the night, so your unhappy experiences won't be repeated. I took care to eat only from dishes already tasted by Hashim Khan."

"Then you suspected him, too!"

"In my travels, I have learned to be cautious."

"Perhaps he truly means to let us both leave," Lucy said, still not quite ready to believe such good fortune. Almost to herself, she added, "I suppose there is no need for him to kill you since he already has all your rifles."

"That is true. But I wonder why he is so anxious for me to take you back to India?"

"He was obligated to offer you something in trade for the guns."

"But why you? I should have thought a *jinn* would be very useful to keep around."

"The villagers blame me for the harsh winter we have just endured. My presence is beginning to cause disagreement among the elders. Maybe the Khan has decided I'm more trouble than I'm worth."

"That could be, I suppose." The trader laid his turban on the table alongside the fruit and tea. "Well, I don't know about you, Englishwoman, but I am exhausted. If the Khan really is going to permit us to set off at dawn tomorrow, I would like to get some sleep. How about you?"

"I am tired," she acknowledged.

"Here." He handed her an embroidered pillow and one of the blankets, then stretched himself out on the pallet without waiting for her thanks.

She had expected to be compelled to share his sleeping mat, since the fact that he found her old and unattractive didn't mean that he would refrain from making use of her body. She reflected wryly that she was no doubt the only person in Kuwar—probably in the whole Afghanistan—who was over sixteen years of age and still a virgin. If the trader had suspected the truth, she wondered if she would be sleeping alone. Deflowering virgins for some odd reason seemed to rank high on the list of favorite masculine pursuits. At least her status as a *jinn* had served one useful purpose: It had prevented her from being forced into the role of town whore.

Lucy folded the blanket in half and tucked the pillow against the corner wall, grateful for the trader's generosity in sharing his covers. Tiptoeing so as not to disturb him, she extinguished the lamp. In the privacy of darkness, she unpinned her red woolen veil, took off her slippers and crept between the welcome warmth of the blanket.

Perhaps it was the strangeness of lying with her head resting on a silken cushion. Perhaps it was the uneasy suspicion that at any moment the trader might wake up, the pain of poison tearing at his vitals. For whatever reason, Lucy found sleep elusive. She lay between the warm layers of her blanket, staring at the unrevealing hump of the trader's body.

He was tall, taller than most men of the Punjab, and broad-shouldered. His skin was dark and his hair raven black, unlike many of the Kuwari tribesmen, whose eyes were sometimes gray and whose hair often had a distinctly reddish glint. When the trader had removed his turban, Lucy had seen a narrow white scar high on his forehead. It looked almost as if he had once suffered a bullet wound. Perhaps he had. The life of a gun runner who plied his trade between India and Afghanistan couldn't be easy. His life must often be at risk.

Lucy stiffened at the trend of her own thoughts. A gun runner! Dear God, what a naive fool she had been! The trader was dealing in *Enfield rifles*. Enfields were Britain's newest and best guns, only recently imported into India. Since the Lucknow Mutiny twenty years earlier, British officials had made sure no guns ended up in the hands of Indian natives. So the most likely way for the trader to have come into possession of such highly prized weapons was to have stolen them. He must have robbed an army barracks somewhere in the Punjab. Which, Lucy concluded, meant that the British government had almost certainly put a price on his head.

She lay in the darkness, listening to the trader's steady breathing. She tried to decide how this new insight affected her personal situation. By the standards she had been brought up with, he was not only a thief, but also a rebel, perhaps even a revolutionary. He might be one of those few, misguided natives who campaigned against all the wonderful improvements of the British government in India. By any standard at all, he was obviously a man to be treated with extreme caution.

On the other hand, rebel or not, he represented the best chance she'd ever had of escaping from Kuwar village, and Lucy considered that a powerful argument in his favor. If only she could be sure he was planning to take her with him tomorrow morning! Would an experienced gun runner risk coming into contact with the British authorities on the off-chance of receiving a reward? Would he slow himself down on the difficult journey back to India by allowing a woman to tag along? Lucy could guess the answers to her questions all too easily, and she didn't like them one bit.

The blur of movement in the doorway caught her unawares, but she had been staring at the outline of the trader's body for so long that her eyes had become accustomed to the darkness. She blinked at the shadow and immediately discerned the shape of a man.

"Trader, watch out!"

Even as she gave the low cry of warning, the trader uncoiled himself from the pallet, lashing out with the speed of a striking cobra to grab the wrist of the intruder. The knife clattered to the floor and the trader sprang forward, the momentum of his leap toppling the would-be assassin backward. The crack of the intruder's skull hitting the tiled floor reverberated through the room.

A beam of light from the corridor refracted from the polished steel blade of the second assassin's knife as he pushed aside the doorway hangings.

"Behind you!" Lucy screamed. "Another one!"

In a single fluid movement, the trader reached into the cummerbund at his waist, pulled out his own knife and whirled around to throw. He acted so swiftly that Lucy didn't see the knife pass through the air; she only heard the dull thud as it landed on target. The second assassin clutched his stomach, swayed on his feet for a second or two then collapsed onto the floor.

The trader picked up the fallen knives of the two assassins, then stood very still in the center of the room, listening.

Lucy swallowed hard. "Is he . . . are they both dead?"

"Yes."

"What are we going to—"

The trader placed his hand flat over her mouth. "Don't talk," he murmured into her ear. "Don't make any sound at all."

Skirting the bodies, he picked up the brass pitcher of tea and made his way to the door. He carefully closed the curtains, then stood there, his body tense with concentration.

After a good five minutes, his vigil was rewarded by the sound of footsteps creeping cautiously along the corridor. The trader silently pressed himself against the left-hand side of the entrance. The footsteps came to a halt, and a head poked hesitantly through the curtains. "Ali? Mohammed?"

The intruder had no time to ask anything more. The trader brought the brass jug crashing down on his head, and he sank to the floor, tea dripping in sticky rivulets over his face.

Lucy gulped.

"He's not dead," the trader said quietly. "I took care not to hit him too hard. He was just the lookout."

"The l-lookout?"

"There had to be one," the trader explained patiently. He put on his turban and readjusted his waist sash to accommodate the three new knives he had acquired. "If the Khan wants to blame you for my murder, he can't very well allow anybody to see his assassins creeping into our chamber. So, there had to be somebody posted as a guard. Probably nobody in the village knows of the Khan's plans except these three men."

"Oh." Lucy turned away and stared determinedly at the corner where she had been sleeping. It was the only place she could look without seeing a body. "You seem awfully good at . . . er . . . um . . ."

"At repelling attacks?"

She supposed that was as good a way as any of describing what he had done. "Yes."

"In this part of the world, people tend to throw knives first and ask questions afterward. I've learned to sleep with one ear open, but thank you for your warnings. They made things easier."

"You're . . . um . . . welcome." The traditional courtesy seemed positively bizarre in the circumstances, and Lucy gave an involuntary hiccup of laughter.

The trader looked at her sharply. "Put on your veil, English-woman, there is no time for hysterics. We must go now."

"Go?" she repeated stupidly. "How can we go?"

The trader smiled. "How can we stay? is surely a better question."

It was the first time she had seen him smile, and her stomach gave an odd little leap of response. "I meant that we can't go because the Khan won't let us."

"If we leave right away, he may not be awake to stop us. At any rate, it is our only chance, so we must take it. Here, let me help you with your veil. We must hurry."

He picked up the large square of finely woven red wool and

placed it over her head. "Do you have pins?" he queried. "I'm afraid this is one article of feminine apparel that always defeats me."

"You need to fold it like this," she said, demonstrating, but her fingers worked clumsily at the familiar task, and as soon as she could, she covered the lower half of her face. For some reason, she felt acutely aware of the trader's close proximity, possibly because after two years among the Kuwari, she was no longer accustomed to appearing unveiled in the presence of a man.

"Very good, Englishwoman." For an instant, the trader's gaze locked with hers, then he turned away, removing one of the dead men's turbans and ripping off pieces of cloth to gag and bind the third, unconscious intruder.

"Fold the blankets," he ordered, as he tested the knots he had tied. "We'll freeze without them even at this time of year. Now, this is our plan. While we are in the palace, we must move without making any sound. Do you know the quickest way out from here into the compound?"

"I think so, although I haven't been inside the palace very often."

"You will have to lead the way because I have seen only the Great Hall and the corridor leading to this sleeping chamber. I'll follow you and carry the blankets." The trader paused, as if to emphasize the tremendous concession he was making. Men in this part of the world didn't carry burdens when a woman was around to do the task for them.

"If anybody sees us, they will think our behavior is very strange."

He smiled wryly. "If anybody sees us, Englishwoman, we shall be dead."

She shivered. "What happens when we reach the outside?" She glanced down at her velvet slippers. "Are we going to walk all the way to India?"

"If need be, but I trust it won't come to that. When we are outside, you are going to the kitchen area to steal provisions."

"You speak of stealing very casually, Trader. Unfortunately, I have little experience in the art."

"And I, unfortunately, have no time to train you," he said softly. "However, Englishwoman, if we wish to avoid starvation on the mountain passes, you will need to steal us some food. I trust your untested skills will prove adequate to the task."

"Why can't you steal the food?"

"Because I shall be in the stables, acquiring our horses."

"You cannot possibly hope to steal horses! Slaves sleep in the stables, and the slightest noise will awaken them!"

"Lower your voice, Englishwoman. I don't plan to *steal* the horses. If you remember, two of them are mine, and a pack mule as well. I shall simply demand from the slaves the return of my own animals."

Lucy doubted very much if the recovery of his horses would be quite as easy as he made it sound. However, she was resigned to the fact that her life was already forfeit, and she might as well die attempting to escape as cowering in the slaves' quarters. She shrugged.

"If we turn right as we leave this room, I believe there is a door that leads straight into the kitchen gardens. Will you follow me, Master?"

Lucy wasn't really surprised or excited when they escaped into the deserted grounds of the palace without seeing a soul. Bludgeoned by the horrible experiences of the past few hours, her emotions had reached the point of exhaustion, and she felt no more than mild apathy when they reached the kitchen gardens in safety. She knew their amazing good luck wouldn't hold. There was no real chance of escape, so there was no point in feeling either fear or hope. The only questions were how soon they would be caught and how much they would be tortured before they were allowed to die.

The trader drew her into the deep shadows of an awning stretched over one of the outdoor ovens. "Dawn is breaking," he said quietly. "We have little time. What's the quickest way to the stables from here?"

"Follow the irrigation ditch," she said, thinking how totally absurd it was even to be offering such information. The ditch ran straight through the center of the village. Admittedly, the trader wouldn't need to walk far, but he would surely be seen or heard by a dozen people before he was halfway to his destination. "The stables are to the east of the palace."

He nodded. "I recall the layout of the village, although I wasn't given much chance to look around." He gave her a little push in the direction of the storage huts. "Go, Englishwoman, and when you have your supplies, walk outside the palace wall and wait for me."

"But of course," she said.

If he heard the heavy irony of her tone, he made no acknowledgment of it. He crept away from her, taking as much care as if he thought they truly had a chance to escape. He glided close to the wall, a silent shadow among the last gray shadows of the night.

Lucy watched him until he disappeared behind the kitchens. She knew she ought to move. He was right, dawn was already breaking and they hadn't much time before the village would begin to stir.

In the end, she walked quite brazenly into the storage hut, so sure she would be discovered that it seemed pointless to attempt any stealth. When several seconds passed and nobody challenged her, she began to feel afraid. Her body shook so violently that her teeth began to chatter. Was there a chance that the trader's plan might work? Was there actually a chance that she wasn't about to die?

Lucy clenched her jaw until her teeth stopped chattering, then wandered aimlessly to one of the shelves. Woven storage bags, empty at this season of the year, lay in a pile in front of her. She picked up two of medium size and waited for some hand to clap down on her shoulder, ready to drag her before the Khan.

Nothing happened. Frantic now with the need to be gone, she began to stuff the bags with provisions: dried apricots and nuts from the distant city of Kandahar, hardened balls of milk curd and strips of smoked goat meat from the village and stale flat loaves of bread from the palace tables, brought here to be ground up and used as a thickening for soups.

Running for the exit, she almost fell headlong over the wooden chest that contained the Khan's favorite tea, so expensive that nobody else in the village had ever tasted it. As she picked herself up, she defiantly scooped out a generous supply. If by any chance the trader did manage to get his horses back, his saddlebags would contain a pot for boiling water. And if the trader failed to acquire any horses, it didn't matter what she stole. She would be beaten and executed anyway.

Her hands were ice cold and shaking as she retied the tops of the loaded sacks with a length of braided goat's hair, then slung them over her shoulder and made for the door. Her luck had held so incredibly long that, try as she might, she couldn't quite quell the wild hope that somehow she and the trader would make good their escape.

She was already outside the palace wall, already allowing the hope to blossom, when Miryam's voice sounded sharply behind her. "Where do you think you're going, Lump of Pig's Lard? And what do you have in those sacks?"

Lucy stopped dead in her tracks, turning around to bow with abject humility. *Please God,* she prayed. *Don't let anybody have heard her voice.* She placed her hand on her heart and groveled. For the last time, she promised herself. Whatever happened, for the last time.

"Most Excellent Mistress, I was sent here by the Khan— blessed be his name forever—in search of supplies."

"Supplies?" Miryam marched aggressively forward. "What supplies, you lying good-for-nothing? Why would the Khan send you to get supplies?"

"He could not sleep, Great One." Lucy held her breath. Two steps nearer, and Miryam would be within range of her head. "He wished me to brew him some tea."

"And for that you needed two sacks?" Miryam demanded. She moved one step closer. Lucy's heart stopped beating. "Show me what you have hidden away in those sacks, Thieving Daughter of a Dog."

She moved the final, fatal step, and Lucy lunged forward, using her head to butt the slave mistress in the stomach with all the force she could command.

Miryam's stomach was well padded, but she was so astonished by the unexpected attack that she staggered, reeling from side to side with the shock. Lucy drew back her fist, then delivered a punch to Miryam's chin that packed all the resentment of two long years behind it. The slave mistress's eyes bulged in disbelief before crossing inwards to stare at her nose. Without a sound, she collapsed into an untidy heap at Lucy's feet.

Lucy sucked her knuckles, which were decidedly sore. "Well done," said a quiet voice behind her. "What an efficient thief you turned out to be."

"You should know," Lucy responded tartly.

"I would like to stay here and exchange compliments with you," the trader said. "Unfortunately, I estimate we have about fifteen minutes before somebody decides he is brave enough to wake up the Khan. I hope you can ride using a man's saddle."

Lucy had never ridden anything but sidesaddle in her life. "Of course I can," she lied.

The trader cupped his hands for her foot, then tossed her up into the saddle. The horse pranced nervously, but she managed to bring it back under control. The trader grunted but made no comment.

"I'll give us each half the supplies," he said, hurriedly buckling one of the sacks onto the rear of Lucy's saddle, then fastening the other to his. He sprang onto his horse with the ease of somebody accustomed to spending half his life in the saddle. His gaze when he turned to her was oddly quizzical.

"Ready, Englishwoman?"

She was so unready it was almost laughable. She drew in a deep breath. "Ready," she said firmly.

A great noise of shouting and screaming arose from somewhere deep inside the palace. Simultaneously, Miryam began to moan and groan and show general signs of returning to consciousness.

"Dear God! The bodies must have been discovered. What shall we do?"

"Ride as you have never ridden before, Englishwoman." He handed her a whip, then dug his spurs deep into his horse's flanks.

"Gallop, Englishwoman!" he called, as his horse sprang forward. "Ride as if we have the devil at our heels, or we shall very soon find ourselves in hell!"

CHAPTER THREE

The trader set such a bruising pace that for the first few minutes all Lucy's attention was concentrated on staying in the saddle. The position of the sun told her they were traveling toward the southeast, but she had only a vague idea where Kuwar village lay and was unable to tell if they were heading directly toward India.

The rough path they had taken out of the village quickly gave way to scree and desert scrub, forcing the trader to rein in his horse from an all-out gallop to a fast canter. With profound relief, Lucy did likewise. She quickly realized, however, that although the danger of her falling out of the saddle was considerably reduced, the chance of her horse stumbling and breaking a leg was greatly increased.

Her riding skills were tested to the utmost during the next few miles. They had ridden less than an hour, but the terrain was such hard going that both horses were showing signs of strain when they encountered a fast-flowing mountain stream crossing their path diagonally. A rough track followed the right-hand bank of the stream, curving away into the horizon.

Thank heaven, Lucy thought, and turned gratefully toward the path.

"Not that way," the trader said tersely. "Through the water."

"But, Master, the path will be faster— "

31

"The water will obliterate our tracks," he said, urging his horse into the stream. "Hashim Khan's men have been gaining on us ever since we left the village. We can't outrun them."

Lucy strained her ears. Faintly, far in the distance, she could hear the thud of horses' hooves, and her heart pounded faster in response to the ominous sound. Dear God, what in the world was wrong with the trader's wits? Why was he worrying about tracks when his pursuers would be upon them at any minute?

"The Khan's men won't need to follow our trail once they can see us," she pointed out, trying not to let her impatience show. "They can't be more than seven or eight minutes behind us. We must get onto dry land and gallop again! Hurry, Master. Please, hurry!"

She should have known better than to offer advice to a man, especially a Muslim from the Punjab. The trader totally ignored her, concentrating instead on urging his horse to move faster through the ice-cold, swirling water.

Lucy scowled at his back. She hadn't really expected him to bring her to safety, so there was no logical reason to feel disappointed by his slow-wittedness. The important question was whether she should resign herself to death at this pig-headed man's side or put her gelding to the gallop in a last desperate bid for freedom.

The trader spoke without turning around. "The Khan's men will catch you before you have gone five miles, Englishwoman. You had better stay with me."

"Listen to their horses, you obstinate oaf!" Lucy was too frightened to waste time wondering how he'd once again managed to read her thoughts. "They're gaining on us! Five minutes more and they'll *see* us!"

"And if you shout much louder, they won't have any need to see us," he retorted grimly. "They will be able to hear with great precision which direction we have taken. Follow me, Englishwoman, and endeavor to keep your suggestions to yourself. Fortunately, the wind is at our backs and they are riding hard. With luck, and Allah's mercy, they won't have heard you."

A couple of minutes later, he guided his horse out of the water onto the far bank of the stream, then quickly dismounted. "Come," he said to Lucy. "This is the place. Pray they do not know of it."

The place was a patch of ground that could not have been more than fifty feet square, since in this area the rocky base of the mountain reached within a few yards of the water. Lucy glanced around her, a task that required only a few seconds. With great luck, she decided, a mouse might be able to find sufficient cover to hide unobserved. Two horses and two humans would be visible for a mile in either direction.

Their pursuers were coming closer by the second. The pounding of horses' hooves had already swollen to a threatening crescendo. Four minutes, she thought frantically. Four minutes, and they'll see us.

The trader, his face impassive, tugged a knife from his waistband and hacked off a branch from the solitary, half-dead bush growing between two large boulders. Dear God, Lucy thought, watching him swirl the branch in the dust. What shall I do? The man has obviously gone completely crazy.

He looked up, and she could have sworn she detected a gleam of amusement in his dark eyes. "Dismount and lead the horse straight ahead," he said. "Quickly! You will find a cave behind that outcropping of rock. I will follow and erase with this branch any footprints we leave."

Her legs were shaking when she slid off the horse, as much from fear and hope as from fatigue. By now, she could hear the jingle of harness on the pursuing horses, and she walked with desperate urgency toward the rocky outcroppings that marked the base of the mountain. A cave? How could the trader have known about a cave? He had supposedly been robbed and then had ridden headlong into Kuwar seeking protection. When had he found time to explore the area around the village?

She walked around the needle-nosed outcroppings of rock and discovered that the cave actually existed! True, it wasn't much of a cave, more a damp, curving hollow in the base of the mountain, but at this moment Lucy thought it looked more beautiful than Buckingham Palace.

With the trader close at her heels, she forced her gelding's head down so that they could pass through the low, narrow entrance to the cave. The space inside was no bigger than a large horse stall, but the ceiling rose to at least ten feet so that the humans and the horses could all stand upright.

She leaned against the gelding, resting her cheek against his sweating neck. The familiar smell gave her comfort. If she closed her eyes, she could almost imagine she was a child again, back in the stables of Hallerton, her home in the English countryside. At any minute, one of the servants would come running out of the kitchen, summoning her to the drawing room. It was the tea bell she could hear . . .

The sounds of pursuit became louder, crushing her daydream in the thunder of galloping hooves. Six or seven horses at least, Lucy calculated, all traveling at breakneck speed. The men of Kuwar village, like most Afghanis, were outstanding riders, and the sandy path alongside the stream would present no obstacles capable of slowing them down.

The trader spoke soothingly beneath his breath to the horses, mumbling nonsense words that gradually calmed them. Their snorting and prancing gave way to stillness and the occasional soft whinny. Taking no chances, Lucy clung grimly to the bridle of her gelding. The closer the Khan's men came, the more difficult it would be to restrain her mount, and she had no intention of allowing a runaway horse to betray their hiding place.

She held her breath as the Khan's men raced past the cave, the noise of their horses' hooves deafening, despite the muffling effect of the rock in front of the cave. Their pace, thank God, didn't slacken. They must have realized their quarry had stepped off the path to ride in the water, but they weren't wasting time searching for tracks. They obviously expected to overtake the runaways at any moment, and given the speed of their pursuit, that was a logical conclusion. Lucy hoped they would keep galloping and avoid thinking for a very long time.

When every last echo of sound had died away, she closed her eyes and leaned back against the wall of the cave to relish the silence. Eventually, she opened her eyes. "Are we going to ride downstream?" she asked. "We'd better hurry, Master, in case they decide to turn back."

"No, we will stay here until our pursuers return. The path they have taken is the route we ourselves must follow."

She understood at once what he intended. He planned to wait until Hashim Khan's men headed back toward Kuwar village, then she and the trader would emerge from their cave and ride serenely on to India, free of pursuit. The scheme, so elegant in its simplicity, was so likely to succeed that she found herself smiling.

"You are amused, Englishwoman?"

She shook her head. "Admiring," she said. "How did you know of this cave, Trader?"

"It is a long story, and a boring one as well."

"But we have time to spare, if you would care to recount it."

"Tell me, rather, how you came to be a captive of the Khan of

Kuwar. You must be one of the very few Englishwomen ever to have set foot on the soil of Afghanistan."

"I am the daughter of Sir Peter Larkin," she said, then stopped. She hadn't spoken her father's name in two years, and her throat suddenly felt tight. Her voice was thick with unshed tears when she continued speaking. "He was murdered here in Afghanistan two years ago, along with all his colleagues."

"I have heard of this man," the trader said softly. "His loss occasioned much grief to the people of the Punjab. It is rumored in the bazaars that the British authorities still have no idea what caused the massacre of this man and his delegation."

"There is no mystery," she said bitterly. "Their deaths were caused by the treachery of Amir Sher Ali. The Amir received my father and the other officials with great courtesy, but he never intended to honor the agreements he signed. We had traveled less than five hours on our return journey to India when we were attacked. Everybody was killed except me—and the Amir's camel drivers."

The trader was silent for some time. "You believe Amir Sher Ali ordered the massacre, even though you were taken captive by the Khan of Kuwar?" he asked finally.

"I'm *certain* Sher Ali ordered the massacre. He planned things very carefully. The day before our delegation left Kabul, he apologized to my father, saying that our horses had become sick and that they wouldn't be strong enough to survive the journey home. So that we wouldn't be delayed, he graciously provided our entire delegation with camels." She smiled, a smile lacking all trace of humor. "We would have done infinitely better without such graciousness. When the Khan's men attacked our caravan, several of the tribesmen were riding horses I recognized as belonging to our delegation. Hashim Khan's brother, who led the attack, was riding my father's stallion."

"And you concluded, naturally, that your horses had never been sick."

"They had rarely looked in more splendid form. Amir Sher Ali simply needed them to use as a bribe. He knew the Khan of Kuwar would not provide his murderous services free of charge."

The trader scratched his forefinger up and down the white blaze above his horse's nose, and the animal rolled its eyes in silent ecstasy.

"The Enfield rifles the Khan stole from me have some very interesting properties," he said meditatively.

"They are British army rifles," Lucy said stiffly. She didn't understand the trader's abrupt change of subject, nor did she like this reminder that he had probably come by his stock illegally.

The trader seemed unperturbed. "Yes, that is true," he said. "Unfortunately, these particular rifles do not live up to the usual British standard of excellence. It is most regrettable, but after a few rounds have been fired, the hammer will jam on the percussion cap and the rifle will never work again."

"You mean they're *defective*?"

The trader winced. "Let us not use such ugly words, English-woman. A trader never likes to hear his merchandise described in such terms. Let us say, rather, that the rifles need a modified firing mechanism in order to work properly. And that mechanism, I fear, can be obtained only in England."

After a moment of stunned silence, Lucy burst out laughing. "Are you telling me, Trader, that the Khan has acquired two dozen absolutely useless weapons in exchange for me?"

The trader's gaze lingered for a split second on her mouth before he glanced away. He shrugged apologetically. "Alas, Englishwoman, I fear it is so."

"Thank you for telling me," Lucy said, her laughter ending. "My heart rejoices in the knowledge that for once Hashim Khan's treachery has not been rewarded."

The trader seemed preoccupied with adjusting the sacks attached to his horse's saddle. He didn't look at Lucy when he spoke. "You converse in Pashto with the elegance of a native-born Easterner, Englishwoman. Do you speak my language, also?"

"Urdu? Much less than I should, given that I spent four years in India. I speak Pashto fluently because it is the language I have used every day for the past two years."

"Then we shall continue to speak to each other in Pashto."

"You do not speak English, Master?"

"I prefer not to," he said shortly. Perhaps realizing his abruptness, his voice was friendlier when he continued.

"Much has happened in India since you were taken captive by Hashim Khan. Last year, Queen Victoria of England was crowned Empress of India, and Lord Lytton has become India's first Viceroy. Your Prime Minister, Mr. Disraeli, is very busy pursuing his dream of a British Empire that spans the entire globe."

Lucy was silent for several minutes, absorbing the news. "It is curious how strongly our minds resist the idea of change," she said at last. "My life after the Khan captured me became utterly different from everything that had gone before, and yet I somehow expected the world outside Kuwar village to stand still, holding its breath as it awaited my return."

The trader responded quietly enough, but his voice was laced with passion. "India has not changed, Englishwoman. Not in the last two years, not in the last two centuries. It would take more than the coronation of a distant queen to alter the way of life among the people of my country."

"Perhaps that is a pity," she replied tartly, irritated by his attitude. Didn't he appreciate the efforts the British government was making to civilize India? To rid the continent of dirt, disease and squalor, and make it more like England?

She lifted her chin. "A country that forces widows to throw themselves on the funeral pyre of their dead husbands is not so perfect that it can safely ignore the need for progress."

"That custom concerns only the Hindus," he said dismissively, reminding her forcibly of the great gulf between the different religious faiths in India. "We Muslims have never required our women to commit *suttee*. We do no need such dramatic demonstrations from our wives in order to be sure of their devotion."

"Well, bully for you," she muttered in English. "I suppose you just keep them locked up in the *zenana*."

He quirked a brow enquiringly, and she gave him one of her best and most insincere salaams.

"My words are not important, Master."

"But please do repeat them, I insist."

"If that is your wish, Master—"

"I believe you said something about the *zenana*."

Two years in Kuwar, Lucy reflected, had transformed her into a skillful liar. She smiled ingratiatingly. "I said merely that the women of your *zenana* must be very happy, Master, because your wisdom as a husband is written on your face for all to see."

"Is that so? How odd, considering that I am not married."

"You're not married?" Lucy was shocked out of her fake humbleness. The trader could not be a day less than thirty years old, and according to the customs of his people he should have been married for at least a decade.

The trader placed his finger to his lips in a warning gesture. "Hush, I hear hoof beats. And this time, the wind is not in our favor. Try to keep your horse and your mouth quiet, Englishwoman."

She fell silent at once, and after a minute or two she heard the

distant clip clop of horses' hooves. This time, the little cavalcade
of searchers was moving at no more than a fast trot, and from the
unevenness of the sound she guessed that one of the horsemen
occasionally broke away from the group to inspect the ground for
hoof prints or other signs of the runaways' trail.

She and the trader were in much greater danger than they had
been before, Lucy realized. If any of the tribesmen chose to cross
over the stream and look more closely at the rocky ledge in front
of the cave, they would be discovered. Not necessarily because of
the blurred tracks they had left, but because the horses would
never remain quiet.

She looked across the small cave toward the trader, seeking
reassurance. She thought how odd it was that his sardonic gaze
somehow brought her comfort.

She said nothing, but he must have sensed her anxiety because
he turned toward her, meeting her eyes for a few brief seconds
before looking away. She watched as he silently drew two knives
from out of his cummerbund. Still in silence, he turned one knife
inward, pointing the tip toward the bottom of his stomach but
leaving an inch of space between the blade and his clothes. With
a swift slash of his hand, he whipped the knife upward over the
middle of his body.

He offered the knife to Lucy. "If the Khan's men stop outside
the cave, you will need to do what I have just shown you,
Englishwoman." His voice was expressionless and so low she
could scarcely hear it.

"I think . . . I could not . . ."

"You must, Englishwoman. Hashim Khan will not grant you so
merciful a death."

She looked down, ashamed of her weakness. "You are right,
Master, but I'm afraid my hand would betray my will."

"Then you must stand here next to me so that I can perform the
task for you if need be." Quickly, silently, he switched places with
his horse. "Hurry, Englishwoman, come here beside me. You do
not want the tribesmen to find you alive."

She copied his maneuver, slipping around her horse to join him
in the center of the cave. Her horse shifted his hindquarters,
jostling her against the trader. She jerked back from the unexpected contact as if she had been scalded. The trader looked at her,
his gaze typically ironic, and for no reason she could think of the
blood crept up into her cheeks, making them flame with heat.

He turned away. "There is grain in my saddlebags," he said.

"Scoop some out so that you have something with which to pacify the horses if they become too restless."

She was about to answer when he shook his head sharply. "Be still. The Khan's men will soon be upon us."

The search party rode inexorably nearer until Lucy could actually hear the voices of the tribesmen and the labored snorts of their horses. Dear God, how she wished sound traveled in only one direction! If either her horse or the trader's chose to neigh loudly, their hiding place would be discovered. She divided her grain into two hands, held one serving out to each horse and prayed as she had never prayed before.

The cavalcade of disgruntled searchers was almost opposite the mouth of the cave.

"Of course we won't find them," she head somebody say. "Why are we wasting our time scrabbling about in the dust looking for tracks that don't exist? She is a *jinn*. She probably gave the horses wings and they have flown away into the sky."

"Hah! You try telling that tale to Hashim Khan and see where it gets you," a voice disagreed. "You'll wish *you'd* flown away into the sky by the time he's finished with you."

Lucy's gelding, scenting the other animals, backed into the wall of the cave, pawing his agitation. The iron of his shoe struck with a metallic thud against a piece of stone.

"What was that noise?" somebody demanded.

"It was a *jinn*, trying to get out of her bottle," another voice answered sarcastically. "Come on, fellows, let's ride a bit faster. This search is a waste of time and I want some food. Those two must have doubled around and left the village from the west. The other search party will have found them by now."

To Lucy's profound relief, there was a general murmur of agreement. The horsemen broke into a slow canter, and the sound of their voices faded rapidly into the distance. At last, even the echo of their hoofbeats was swallowed up in silence.

The trader tucked his knives back into his cummerbund. "Another hour to wait, and then I estimate it will be safe for us to start on our way." A tiny smile lightened the habitual severity of his expression.

"What do you say, Englishwoman? Shall we eat some breakfast while we wait?"

Once the trader deemed it safe to emerge from the cave, they

rode for eight hours without stopping, and darkness fell long
before they finally tethered the horses for the night.

When the exhausted animals had been fed and watered, the
trader built a small fire, while Lucy searched along the riverbank
for a flat stone she could heat up and use to bake a loaf of
unleavened bread.

Returning from her search flushed with success, she kneaded
flour and water together, then smeared the heated stone with a
lump of hardened mutton fat. The sizzle and delicious aroma made
her stomach rumble with anticipation. Wrapping raisins and strips
of dried goat meat in the heated dough, she bowed as she handed
the food to the trader.

He ate in silence, as was proper, accepting everything she
offered with a brief nod.

"You may eat that yourself," he said, when she offered him the
third envelope of dough.

Lucy was surprised. "You have finished, Master?"

"No, but you must be hungry. I can wait until you have eaten
something."

She bowed low. "Thank you, Master," she said, taking a huge,
luxurious bite of the food. She chewed slowly on the stringy meat,
letting the raisins burst with sweetness on her tongue. What a
strange man he was, to be sure. She had never heard of any Indian
or Afghani man allowing a woman to eat before his own hunger
was completely satisfied. She licked her fingers and decided to
stop worrying about his motives. At the moment, she was simply
grateful for his consideration.

As she had hoped, the trader's saddlebags contained a small pot
for boiling water, and so they were able to top off their sumptuous
meal with a bowl each of the Khan's favorite imported China tea.
The delicate, floral scent of the tea drifted pleasantly beneath their
nostrils before floating away on the chill of the night air.

Replete with warmth and good food, Lucy drew her knees up to
her chin and stared into the embers of the fire. In two years, she
couldn't remember eating and drinking so well.

"How did you know of the cave, Master?" She was so relaxed
that she didn't realize she had spoken the question aloud until she
answered her.

"My trading partner was a Ghilzai, a nomad from near
Jalalabad. His family used to travel this route every spring with
their flocks of sheep. He showed me the cave only a few hours
before he was killed."

She yawned. "We were lucky he knew of it, Master."

"Yes, we were." He got to his feet. "Wash the bowls in the stream, Englishwoman, and I will unroll our blankets. It is late, and we should leave at first light tomorrow. We cannot be sure that Hashim Khan won't send a more efficient search party after us."

When she returned from washing herself and the bowls, the fire was banked with stones, and the trader was already curled up in one of the blankets, asleep. The other blanket, neatly folded in half, lay about five feet away from him.

Lucy checked the blanket for snakes and spiders, then crawled between the warm folds. Unpinning her veil, she shook out the trail dust and fashioned a small pillow. She lay down with a small sigh of contentment.

The trader's voice startled her. "Sleep well, Englishwoman."

"Thank you, Master. May Allah grant you peaceful repose."

"I live in hope, Englishwoman."

There was something distinctly odd about the way in which the trader addressed her, Lucy decided. Something about his tone of voice, or perhaps the words he used . . . Something that wasn't quite right. She really ought to decide what it was . . .

Lucy slept.

The next three days passed uneventfully, apart from such minor mishaps as an encounter with a nest of warrior ants and one gloomy night when it was impossible to find firewood or any other fuel for the fire. Fortunately, fire or no fire, they had plenty of dried fruit and nuts to eat, and their water supply presented no problems. Their route to the pass had led them away from the stream by the second day, but at these higher elevations it was easy to find deep patches of snow which melted quickly when brought out of the shadows and into the sun.

The trader maintained a relentless pace, driving the horses to the limit of their endurance each day. However, since he had stolen a plentiful supply of grain, and Lucy had stolen a plentiful supply of food, the journey didn't seem particularly arduous to her. The horses recuperated each night, and her energy actually seemed to increase with each day that passed. In fact, for the first time in two years, she was eating three full meals a day, and her body responded eagerly to the extra nourishment.

"I'm glad you brought the tea," the trader commented on the fourth day of their journey, as she brewed a pot to accompany their noon meal of dried fruit and stale bread toasted over the fire. "It makes mealtime a little more bearable."

She was obscurely disappointed by the implication that he hadn't enjoyed their peaceful moments sitting by the fire. They rarely spoke as they rode, but once seated by the fire they usually chatted in a friendly way about nothing in particular. She had told him about England, describing all the harmless pleasures of a carefree childhood on a prosperous country estate, and he had seemed to listen with interest. True, he had imparted very little personal information in return, but he had always seemed willing to talk about the latest political developments in India.

He was surprisingly well informed about international politics—surprising, because Lucy knew from her father and from other British officials how difficult it was to interest the natives in affairs outside their village, let alone in the alien world beyond India. She supposed that it was the trader's precarious life as a gun runner that sparked his interest in world affairs. After all, he would need to know who was getting ready to fight if he wanted to find the best markets for his merchandise.

"You are amazingly silent, Englishwoman. What have I said or done to offend you now?"

She glared at him. She had almost stopped worrying about his uncanny ability to sense her moods and read her thoughts, but occasionally she found it disconcerting.

"You have done nothing, Master. I am only sorry that my humble efforts to prepare your meals to your satisfaction have not met with your approval."

He poured himself another cup of tea, his eyes gleaming with definite amusement. "Have you noticed, Englishwoman, that you only call me *Master* when you are angry with me?"

"Master, how can you believe such a thing when I am all gratitude for your kind—"

"Do be quiet, Lucy," he said casually.

She stared at him open-mouthed. He pronounced her name Loo-sie, with a slight break in the middle, but his accent gave the ordinary name a curious appeal.

She wrapped her arms around her knees and stared at him over the top of her veil. "You remembered my name."

"Of course."

"But you never used it before."

"It is the English way to leap into intimacy, jumping into

situations without weighing the consequences. Here in the East we realize that time will take care of many things."

"And now you have decided it is time for us to be . . . intimate?

"I have decided only that it is time, with your permission, to use your given name."

"You know you have my permission," she said haltingly, although somewhere deep inside she acknowledged that she had grown almost fond of the sardonic way in which he called her "Englishwoman."

He poured boiling water onto the tea leaves in her bowl and handed it to her.

"Thank you, Trader."

"My name," he said, "is Rashid."

CHAPTER FOUR

They had been traveling for almost a week when the rough, beaten-earth tracks that crisscrossed the mountains began to converge in a single southerly direction. Lucy, for the first time in days, felt the sharp bite of fear. Below them, in the valley, the Kabul River flowed peacefully toward India's northern frontier, but Lucy was ill at ease, drawing little comfort from the knowledge that she was nearly home. The sun shone as brightly as ever, but its warmth failed to relieve her inner chill.

She scowled at the trader's back, which appeared annoyingly unconcerned, just as it had done all morning. The tilt of his head seemed positively merry, and Lucy wouldn't have been surprised if he had burst into song. His heedlessness infuriated her. Didn't he realize that the closer they came to the Khyber Pass, the more vulnerable they were to attack? Up until now, he had chosen a route that avoided the scattered settlements of Afridi tribesmen, who controlled access to the pass. But soon they would have to ride into the open, where they would be at the mercy of any tribesmen whose gun finger itched on the trigger.

So far, Lucy hadn't spotted a single warrior anywhere within shooting distance, but her fear remained. She and Rashid had encountered so little danger over the past few days that she expected each bend in the road to bring them face to face with disaster. As her unreasoning panic increased, the trader's stolid, unhesitating ride forward became more and more provoking.

The distant sound of approaching horses honed Lucy's fear into immediate, razor-sharp terror. They were being pursued, she was sure of it, and by a troop of horsemen riding at a fast canter. Who could it be, if not Hashim Kahn's men? Now that she had tasted freedom, it would be impossible to return to slavery. The chill inside her froze into an icy block of desperation. She urged her mount forward.

"Do you hear them?" she asked Rashid, drawing alongside him on the narrow path. "I knew Hashim Khan wouldn't let us escape so easily! He has sent an army to catch us! Dear God, where shall we hide?"

"There is no need to hide. The sounds you hear are not from Hashim Khan's men."

Strangely enough, she didn't doubt his judgment, and the relief was overwhelming until she realized the ease with which he had calmed her fears. Then relief was replaced by anger.

"How do you know it isn't the Khan's men?" she demanded. "Are you gifted with magic ears that recognize one set of hoofbeats over another?"

"Not hoofbeats," he answered absently. "Harness. These riders have no bells on their harness."

"And the lack of a few bells is sufficient to convince you the riders aren't part of Hashim Khan's army?" If she had stopped to think about it, she would have been amazed at the aggressive way she was speaking to a man who had the power of life and death over her.

"You should know better than I that the men of Kuwar pride themselves on the decorative silver bells embedded in their reins. Besides, these horses approach from the west, and Kuwar village lies to the north northeast." With no change of tone, he added, "I think this ledge looks like a good place to stop. The sand and those boulders make a natural resting place."

"Resting place? Here—where the horsemen are certain to come upon us? Are you run mad, Trader?"

He was silent for a moment, then he said, "I gave you the gift of my name, Englishwoman. Do you find it so difficult to use?"

She didn't answer. A week ago the habits of slavery had still been deeply engrained, and she wouldn't have dreamed of openly defying him, even by silence. But adequate food—and perhaps something in the trader's own attitude—had restored her sense of personal dignity. Her defiance no longer needed to be cloaked beneath the words of slavery. She watched him dismount, frowning her disapproval and refusing to join him.

"Do you plan to sit on your horse and scowl all afternoon?" he inquired mildly.

"Unless you tell me why we're stopping here." She paused for a moment. "Please, Rashid."

He acknowledged her use of his name with the faintest of smiles. "Because the horsemen will catch up with us sooner or later. Better here, where we can control the situation."

"How can we control it?"

"We shall pretend to be nomads. We are on our way to rejoin our tribe, having been separated from them by mischance last winter. Whoever these horsemen may be, I think our best defense is to pretend abject poverty and total ignorance."

"But which tribe shall we claim as our own? I speak only the language of Kuwar valley, none of the other Afghani dialects."

"You are a woman. There will be no reason for you to speak."

"And you? How can you avoid speech? Will you pretend to be dumb?"

He ignored her sarcasm. "No. I shall simply claim brotherhood with whichever tribe the horsemen are least likely to know."

Lucy supposed there was a slight chance that his plan might work. She made a move toward dismounting, but he forestalled her, reaching up and lifting her from the saddle.

"Praise Allah that you look much like any other woman from this part of the world," he said, setting her on the ground and tilting her face up in a cursory inspection. "Although you are definitely too clean."

He dug up a handful of dust and rubbed it into her forehead, sprinkling the residue over her headshawl and grinding it into the weave of the fabric. He stepped back to admire his handiwork, then gave a grunt of approval. "Fortune smiles on us. At least you are brown-eyed and dark-skinned, unlike most of your country-women. There is nothing in your appearance to arouse suspicion."

Lucy repressed a sudden, irrational longing for blue eyes, golden curls and a pink English complexion—an appearance so stunningly beautiful that Rashid would find it impossible to disguise her. Pinning her veil tightly across the lower half of her face, she pushed the foolish longing away. She ought to be following Rashid's example and thanking God that she was so brown and wizened.

She watched meekly as he removed their depleted supplies from the back of his saddle. Unfastening the sack, he scooped up a handful of raisins and tied them in a grubby piece of cloth, along with a bag of flour and a lump of mutton fat. The remainder of the food, including the precious tea, he stuffed back into the sack.

"Here, tie these beneath your *kami*," he said, holding the provisions out to Lucy.

She stared at him blankly.

"There is no other way to safeguard our supplies," he explained, hacking at one of the blankets with his knife. "We must pretend you are with child. It is because of your condition that I am forced to waste time resting in the middle of the day. Like any self-respecting husband, I am not pleased with the weakness you are displaying."

"And whose fault is it that wives become pregnant?" she demanded, quite forgetting that no unmarried English lady was supposed to mention the act that precipitated pregnancy.

Rashid grinned. "A husband proves his virility. A wife takes care of the consequences. That is the way of the East. If you wish to discuss the ethics of it, perhaps you could choose some other time. Make haste, wife of mine, the horsemen are almost upon us. Use this strip of blanket to tie the sack and the blanket over your stomach. Endeavor to keep the mound smooth."

She turned her back as she pulled up her overdress and tried to comply with his instructions. The task was not easy, for her fingers seemed to have turned themselves into a set of wooden thumbs. She shifted the coarse burlap over her abdomen, seeking the precise spot to tie the sack. Incongruously, she found herself wondering how it would feel to carry the child of a man she loved within the warmth of her body. Her cheeks flamed with sudden heat as an ache, unlike anything she had ever felt before, began to throb deep in her womb.

Rashid, naturally, was not afflicted with such out-of-place thoughts, and he spoke from behind her, his voice impatient. "The men are almost upon us. I can smell their horses. Why are you taking so long, Englishwoman? Do you need me to help you?"

Before she could reply, she felt the coolness of his fingers at her back. Oddly enough, his coolness merely increased her sensation of heat. He crossed the makeshift cord around her waist, then turned her around so that he could knot the ends over the sack and the folded pad of blanket. In a couple of seconds, he was finished.

He pulled her straining *kami* down over the resulting bulge and looked at her with a faint gleam of amusement.

"At least seven months along, I would think. From the wealth of your feminine experience, does that seem right to you, Englishwoman?"

"A little more," she replied evenly. She looked up, meeting his gaze with a hint of challenge. "I gave you the gift of my name, Trader. Will you not use it?"

For a moment she thought he would not answer her, then he smiled wryly. "There can sometimes be much danger in a name, Loo-sie, have you not discovered that?"

"How can my name be dangerous? I don't—understand."

"No, I suspect you do not. Perhaps it is better so."

The strange silence between them was broken by a crescendo of sound as a dozen or more horses and riders cantered into view. With much shouting from the men and snorting from the horses, the miniature cavalcade plunged to a halt.

"Remember, say nothing at all," Rashid murmured in her ear, making a great show of pulling her veil lower down on her forehead. "No Afghani woman would speak to strangers when her husband is present."

Lucy nodded, huddling within the dirty folds of her veil as Rashid moved forward to greet their pursuers. They were soldiers, Lucy realized, but not Afghanis or British soldiers, as might have been expected this close to the Indian border. They were Cossacks in full uniform, with two officers leading a dozen men.

The senior officer, recognizable from his myriad rows of gold braid, withdrew his sabre from its sheath, rattled it menacingly, then hurled some remark in Rashid's direction. Lucy had no idea what he said, but she could hear the contempt in his voice even through the barrier of an unknown language.

Rashid bowed very low, looking both worried and humble. "I am honored to be of service," he said in Pashto, the language he and Lucy spoke together and the most commonly used dialect of the region. "But unfortunately this feeble brain of mine is not clever enough to understand the wisdom of your discourse, Most Excellent Horseman."

The officer frowned, gestured irritably to his junior, then barked out some command. The junior officer edged forward and, inclining his head to his superior, addressed Rashid in mangled, thickly accented Pashto.

"My good fellow, we are important peoples from the Great

Motherland of Russia, and we are wishing to become knowing of where we have been lost."

"Most Excellent and Honored Visitor, this is the Safed Koh Mountain range," Rashid replied.

"We have been knowing that," the Russian declared curtly, making no effort to indicate that Rashid should rise from his obsequious bow. "We have journeyed from Qandahar, and we have been lost. We wish to find our path forward."

"The servants of the Great White Queen live just over the Khyber Pass," Rashid offered with an air of supreme innocence. "Most Honored and Noble Russian, Son of the Motherland, do you seek to journey into the lands of the Great British Queen? She is, perhaps, also the Queen of Russia?"

"Of course she isn't, you fool! And of course we don't want to go to India!" The officer drew in a deep breath and lowered his voice. "We wish to be finding the Valley of Kuwar and the palace of Hashim Khan, ruler of the Valley."

Lucy only just managed to conceal a start of surprise. Rashid, still staring meekly at his toes, gave not the slightest indication that the Russian's words shocked him.

"The Palace of Hashim Khan is not easy to find, Most Honored Stranger to Afghanistan."

"You do not tell us something new, old fellow. We have been seeking this Valley of Kuwar for many days. We have urgent messages from our great Emperor to be giving to your Khan."

"Most Illustrious Traveler, I fear that Hashim Khan is not my Khan. He is not even known to me. To my regret, I confess that my ignorant eyes have never feasted upon the beauty of his palace. But my cousin's cousin—blessed be his wandering feet—has told me of the wonders of Kuwar."

"And did he tell you how to get there?" The young lieutenant's supply of patience was clearly becoming exhausted. He looked longingly at the whip coiled on his saddle, and Lucy found herself almost sympathizing with his frustration. She had, on many occasions, wondered how she would endure the flowery ritual that embroidered even the simplest of Afghani conversations.

Visibly gritting his teeth, the officer continued. "We are having messages from Prince Mohammed Ayub, which must be delivered to Hashim Khan immediately."

Lucy gave a startled exclamation before she could stop herself. Without any warning, Rashid's arm lashed out, landing a sharp blow across her shoulders. "Silence, wife!" he thundered.

She covered her face with her hands and bowed low. "I beg your pardon, husband," she said, controlling her seething fury. "Your unborn son caused me a moment of pain."

Rashid did not deign to acknowledge her apology. Bending abjectly toward his knees, he addressed the Russian officer. "Forgive the unseemly behavior of my wife, Most Excellent Leader of Men. She did not mean to intrude her presence upon your eyes, but she is old and for many years was barren. In her pregnant condition, she sometimes forgets her manners. Now what was it that you told my ignorant ears?"

The lieutenant glanced at Lucy with a mixture of disdain and pity, then shrugged. "I said that we are having messages from Prince Mohammed Ayub that must be carried to Hashim Khan immediately."

This time, Lucy managed to control her reaction, although the Russian's statement was astonishing, even at second hearing. Prince Mohammed Ayub was the son of Amir Sher Ali. Ayub had tried to seize power from his father and had been exiled to Persia on charges of treason. Why were these Russian soldiers consorting with a declared enemy of the Amir of All Afghanistan? Extraordinary as it was for Russians to venture so close to British territory, it was surely even more extraordinary for them to carry messages to Hashim Khan from a rebellious son of the Amir. Hashim Khan had always declared himself a friend and close ally of the Amir. Moreover, the Russians had never given any indication that they wished to topple Sher Ali from his throne.

Lucy wondered if the Russians had decided to invade Afghanistan and were hoping to provoke internal rebellions as an excuse for crossing the border. She stole a glance at Rashid, but the trader gave no indication that he recognized the importance of the information he had just gleaned. It was possible that he didn't realize its significance, Lucy reflected. A gun runner presumably didn't care who was fighting whom as long as the battles continued to rage and his profits to soar. She had seen much evidence of Rashid's cunning and his ability to survive, but perhaps she had been wrong in assuming that his quick thinking was based on an overall understanding of the complex politics of Afghanistan.

Lucy quelled a momentary bleakness as she confronted the reality of who and what Rashid really was: a gun runner and a thief. He had shown no qualms about hitting her. Was she naive to assume that his blow had been part of the role he played, and not a genuine expression of anger? With an effort, she turned her attention back to what Rashid was saying to the Cossack lieutenant.

"Prince Mohammed Ayub is undoubtedly a man of great importance, Most Excellent Son of Russia. Unfortunately, my ignorance has such a wide extent that the prince's name is unknown to me. I trust you left him in good health, Excellency?"

The officer rolled his eyes heavenward, obviously muttering some Russian imprecation for patience. "The prince's health has never been better. Now can we return to the subject we were discussing? The route to Kuwar, old fellow. How do we find the palace of Hashim Khan?"

"I will tell you, Most Noble Foreigner. Unfortunately, Allah's command that his servants should always be truthful forces me to inform you, Excellency, that you and your honored companions ride in the wrong direction. Your noble steeds carry you directly away from the Valley of Kuwar. The palace of Hashim Khan lies in the direction of the setting sun. You must go down from these mountains along the path that curves to your left. When you are in the valley, you must follow the River Kabul to the west."

Rashid's directions would take the Russians directly to the city of Jalalabad, where they were likely to find themselves the recipients of a great deal of interested attention. Once again, Lucy found herself wondering what Rashid's motives might be. Was he simply directing the Russians along the quickest route to Kuwar, not even realizing that he was sending them into danger? Or did he know that Amir Sher Ali's deputies in Jalalabad would very likely arrest the soldiers as they approached the city? The Russians and the British had been snarling at each other across Afghanistan for the past thirty years. From the British point of view, Lucy knew it would be better for this troop of Russian soldiers to be penned up in Jalalabad than out creating mayhem with Hashim Khan. But would a Moslem trader from the Punjab realize that? Would he care about the outcome of a quarrel between Britain and Russia? As an Indian native, might Rashid actually hope that the Russians would win in any dispute with the British rulers of India?

Even as she pondered, Lucy acknowledged that she would probably never know the answer to her questions. Rashid could read her innermost thoughts with embarrassing ease, but she could read his thoughts and feelings only when he chose to reveal them.

The lieutenant finished translating Rashid's directions for his superior officer. Scowling ferociously, the captain sheathed his sabre and wheeled his mount around, obviously giving the command for his men to fall in behind.

"My captain is thanking you for your help," the young officer said, tossing a couple of silver coins onto the ground at Rashid's feet. "We go now."

Rashid slid forward to cover the coins with his feet, giving every appearance of being thrilled to receive them. Removing the dirty cloth pouch from his belt, he made haste to open the package. The lump of fat, the bag of flour and the pile of raisins lay exposed to the Russian lieutenant's view.

"Most Excellent Visitor, as a parting gift please help yourself to your choice of my humble provisions."

The young officer eyed the dusty pile of supplies with something akin to horror, but he had obviously been in Afghanistan long enough to know that it was a mortal offense to refuse food when it was offered. Gingerly, he reached out to select three or four raisins. He chewed them slowly, as etiquette demanded, keeping his eyes carefully averted from the gray lump of mutton fat. His ordeal over, he thanked them curtly and rode up to join his captain at the front of the troop. Within a minute, the soldiers had retreated around the bend along the path Rashid had indicated.

Once the soldiers were out of sight, Lucy would have spoken, but Rashid put out his hand, gesturing her to silence. When the last hoofbeat had faded into oblivion, he turned to face her, his expression grim.

"Show me your shoulder. I tried to restrain the force of my blow, but it was necessary for my anger to look convincing. I trust I didn't hurt you too much?"

"I have survived much worse, Trader."

"But not at my hands."

She heard regret in his voice, and for some reason it disturbed her. She turned abruptly away, lifting her *kami* and tugging at the knotted blanket so that she could remove the bulge of her false pregnancy. She needed to reestablish a sense of distance between herself and Rashid. Playing the role of his pregnant wife had been an unsettling experience. She pulled irritably at the makeshift rope, not wanting to acknowledge that her mind still lingered over the highly improper idea of how it would feel to carry Rashid's child within her womb.

The knots finally opened, and the sack and blanket fell to her feet. She turned around, shaking the veil back from her shoulders. "You did not hurt me, Trader. Your blow merely reminded me how glad I am to be an English lady. Thank God I shall never have to endure the humiliations suffered by an Eastern wife."

"True. But you will also never know the pleasures." His voice became arrogant. "Unlike the men of my country, the English are not known for their skill as lovers."

She blushed hotly. "English ladies seek companionship and loyalty from their husbands. They do not wish for skillful . . . for . . . what you said."

"How boring," he murmured, his voice soft and somewhat amused.

"We would say 'sensible' rather than 'boring,'" she returned loftily. "An English lady sees no pleasure in becoming her husband's slave."

"You have, I think, much to learn about the subtleties of my country," Rashid said. "A man in love is as deeply enslaved as the woman who partners him. But we don't have time to discuss the rival merits of Eastern- and Western-style marriage. Come, we have a long way to go if we are to cross the summit of the pass during daylight tomorrow. Let me help you remount."

They rode in silence as they had done every other day, the trader in front, Lucy behind, their weary horses plodding steadily forward, cantering for a few yards when the path became relatively smooth.

For the first few miles after their encounter with the Russians, Lucy waited impatiently for an opportunity to broach the subject of the rebellious Prince Mohammed Ayub and his possible alliance with the Russians. By the time the afternoon shadows had lengthened into evening, wiser thoughts prevailed. What would she gain by voicing her suspicions to Rashid? She had no knowledge of where the trader's loyalties might lie, but from tiny hints in his conversation, she suspected he disliked the increasing power of British rule in India. As she prepared their evening meal, she reminded herself that Peshawar was no more than three days' ride away. Her discoveries—and her worries—would much better be discussed with the officials of the British Raj, than with a merchant whose first loyalties must lie with his guns.

Lucy's stomach gurgled in expectation of its nightly feast. She dropped the flat sheets of unleavened dough into the sizzling fat, sniffed the wonderful aroma and wisely kept her own counsel.

CHAPTER FIVE

The night after they had successfully crossed into British India, Rashid told her that armed Afridi tribesmen had tracked them across the entire thirty-mile length of the Khyber Pass. When Lucy wanted to know why the pair of them had been left unmolested, Rashid replied laconically, "The Afridi know me. I have brought them gifts from time to time."

He meant guns, of course. "I suppose I should be grateful your gifts to them worked properly," she muttered. "Otherwise, no doubt, I would have been slaughtered in payment for your past misdeeds."

He laughed. "Never fear, Englishwoman. Even I am not so foolhardy as to give malfunctioning weapons to the Afridi. The warriors guarding this pass have always received the very best I have to offer."

"You have given them Enfield rifles? Is that what you mean by *the best you have to offer*?"

Rashid looked at her through a drift of smoke from the campfire. "It is illegal for a native of the Punjab to have such advanced weapons in his possession. Did you not know this, Englishwoman?"

She looked away. "Yes, I knew. I realized long ago that you must have stolen the rifles you sold to Hashim Kahn."

"Do you not think it rather dangerous to reveal such insights to me, Englishwoman?"

A bubble of fat exploded on the hot stone with a little hiss. Lucy busied herself with sliding the cooked dough off the stone and onto a tin plate. "I trust you'll not harm me, Rashid. Am I wrong?"

He took the food without answering her. "Everything is not always as it seems on the surface," he said finally. "But you are right to believe I will not harm you. I shall return you safely to Peshawar."

"Is it dangerous for you to enter the city, Rashid?"

"I am not at risk from officials of the Raj. I do not steal my merchandise and I do not work against your country, English-woman, even though I despise much of British policy in India."

"Why do you despise my government, Rashid? What's wrong with our policies? Most Punjabis welcomed the arrival of the British authorities. Your ruler invited us in. Nobody from my country fought to conquer your lands."

"A mouse may sometimes choose to live under the rule of an elephant rather than a tiger. At least with an elephant in control he can see when danger approaches. The fact remains that it will take my people generations to undo the harm well-meaning Britishers have done to them."

"How can you talk of harm when we have achieved so much in the last hundred years?" Lucy asked passionately. "My country has given your people a legal system that is the envy of the world. The courts here are no longer susceptible to bribes, and peasants have the hope of true justice for the first time in their history. We have brought schools to villages, water to barren land and doctors to care for your sick. The roads we have built unite your cities. The telegraph lines we have laid link India to the rest of the world. In every province where the British have ruled, progress has followed."

"All this is true. And in exchange, you have demanded nothing from us save our souls."

"Indian natives are permitted freedom of religious expression," Lucy retorted angrily. "We are amazingly tolerant of your superstitions, except where they are dangerous or wicked."

His smile seemed almost sad. "And who is to decide what is wicked, Englishwoman? What to you are superstitions, to my countrymen are profound expressions of belief. Is it so hard for you to accept that your Christian churches do not encompass all that is good in humanity's religious experience?"

"Have some tea," Lucy said, gritting her teeth. "The water has boiled at last."

The trader threw back his head and laughed. "Ah, I had forgotten! English ladies do not discuss religion or politics, is that not right? Such discussions are reserved exclusively to the gentlemen, even though you British pretend that men and women in your country are equal partners."

"Certain topics are better suited to the masculine mind," Lucy said primly, wondering why in the world she didn't admit the truth of the trader's comments. "The feminine mind, by contrast, is naturally inclined to domestic matters. A well-brought-up lady doesn't enjoy political or religious arguments. Her most intense pleasure and interest is always aroused by matters concerning her family and her home."

"If you believe that, Englishwoman, then you are as much a slave to your heritage as any Indian child bride. You must also be blind to the reality of your own self. You are living proof that a woman's interests can be as wide-ranging as any man's."

Lucy ignored the odd little quiver of pleasure Rashid's remarks generated. The closer they got to Peshawar, the more vividly she began to recall the strictures of her old life. In Lucy's experience, British gentlemen didn't want their ladies to have wide-ranging interests, or indeed any interests outside the home. She suppressed a sigh. As her stepmother often reminded her, Lucy had never fitted well into conventional society. And after two years as Hashim Khan's slave, she wondered if she would ever again manage to adapt to the rigid proprieties of life in colonial India.

"Surely, I have not shocked you into silence, Englishwoman? Do you have no angry response, no stinging rebuttal to prove to me the error of my thinking?"

"Of course not, Rashid. It's not appropriate for me to try to prove you wrong. I realize it's difficult for us to understand each other. We come from very different backgrounds, and you have never been to England. And naturally, in your profession, you cannot have met many English ladies or gentlemen . . ."

Her words trailed away as she heard the note of condescension in her voice. She hadn't intended to sound so patronizing. Not only did she owe her life to Rashid, but she realized that she had no reason for condescension. Rashid possessed more than enough intelligence to grasp any concept she was capable of explaining.

For some reason, though, she felt acutely uncomfortable when she tried to discuss her life and values with him. It was almost as if his presence altered the landscape of her thoughts. That realization was threatening enough when applied to the subject of India. It became even more threatening when applied to the subject of England and English society. If she listened to Rashid for very much longer, she might find her whole view of life changing in order to accommodate the perspectives he had revealed to her.

Lucy didn't feel ready to explore such changes, and she hurried into speech, her voice determinedly cheerful, her smile artificially bright. "Shall we be in Peshawar tomorrow? If so, we have more than enough of the Khan's special tea to brew ourselves a second pot."

The glance he threw at her was disconcertingly sympathetic, but all he said was, "With Allah's blessing, we shall be in Peshawar tomorrow. Another pot of tea would make a welcome celebration to mark the end of our journey."

She felt an emotion akin to sadness as she carried a fresh supply of water from the stream and set it on the hot stone. She crouched beside the fire, blowing at the embers and feeding tiny sticks into the flames, coaxing a fierce burst of heat beneath the cooking stone. The water was icy cold and would take several minutes to boil. Lucy stared into the red heart of the fire and allowed her thoughts to drift.

"What do you think of, Englishwoman?"

"The end of our journey."

"You are happy to return to your people."

"Yes. Yes, of course I am."

"But your face holds sadness, Englishwoman, and many doubts."

Once again, Rashid had divined her mood correctly: Lucy's feelings were oddly ambivalent. The days spent traveling with the trader had been some of the most enjoyable she had ever experienced. Their escape had been dangerous and their path rugged, but Rashid's presence had provided a sense of security and many moments of quiet, mutual content. His conversation—infuriating at times—had stimulated new ideas and fresh perspectives. Their meals had seemed tastier and more satisfying than a gourmet dinner prepared by a master chef. In Rashid's company she had felt more alive than at any time in her life before.

Lucy had no idea why this might be so, but whatever the reason, she knew that she would never be able to express such

feelings once she returned to Peshawar. Tonight was the last night
for honesty, the last night for an admission of how much she had
enjoyed the trader's company. Perhaps, even now, it was too late.
Civilization already loomed too close. British inhibitions, British
propriety, reached out their tentacles, reasserting their claim upon
her.

"The journey from Kuwar has not been unpleasant," she said
carefully. "And I am grateful to you, Rashid, for the protection
you have given me since we escaped from Kuwar. I know you
would have journeyed more swiftly if you had abandoned me
along the way."

In the darkness she could see his grin. "Ah, but then I would
have had nobody to cook my supper, Englishwoman."

"I believe you are quite capable of cooking your own meals,
Trader."

"Perhaps. But I'm sure my culinary efforts would lack your
elegant touch."

She looked down at their final ball of hardened mutton fat,
sitting on a battered tin plate surrounded by some withered strips
of smoked goat's meat. Their eyes met across the fire and she
burst out laughing.

The trader watched her, his gaze lingering on her mouth. "The
kettle boils, Loo-sie," he said at last, his voice husky. "Shall we
have our second bowl of tea?"

Normally, Lucy fell asleep the moment she crawled between the
folds of her blanket. Tonight, sleep remained elusive, hovering
tantalizingly beyond her grasp. Her body ached with the pleasant
fatigue of the day's ride, but her mind refused to relax long
enough for her to sink into the comfort of sleep. She stared at the
stars, brilliant points of silver light in the surrounding blackness,
and listened to the quiet, steady rhythm of Rashid's breathing. The
problems of his dangerous lifestyle certainly didn't seem to
interfere with his rest. Perhaps the profits—and she supposed gun
smuggling would be very profitable—outweighed the worries and
the fear of capture.

He seemed to have no responsibilities, no burden of family to
support, which was unusual in this part of the world. Even if he
had never married, what of the rest of his family, Lucy wondered.
Was his mother alive? Did he care if she worried when he
disappeared on his trading expeditions? Did he have brothers
working in traditional jobs? Sisters who were married and locked

away in the *zenanas* of his friends? Lucy had told the trader endless stories about her own childhood. He, she now realized, had told her only that his father didn't approve of his politics or his profession and that they were barely on speaking terms.

The distant howl of a hungry jackal jolted her into a sitting position. Even though she didn't cry out, Rashid had thrown off his blanket and was crouched at her side almost before the sound of the jackal's howl died away. The moonlight reflected off the steel blade of the knife he held ready in his hand.

"What is it?" he asked quietly. "What troubles you, English-woman?"

"I suppose it was the jackal. Did you not hear it?"

"Yes, I heard it. The jackal has never awoken you in the past."

"I know."

"Your rest is usually deep and untroubled. What causes your wakefulness tonight, Englishwoman?"

"Nothing," she said, looking down at the knife and at his long, brown fingers curled over the handle. "Nothing at all."

"Or perhaps you should more truly say *everything*." Lucy didn't reply and the trader continued, "Tomorrow you will return to your friends and family. After two years living among the people of Kuwar, you will take time to feel comfortable again in British society. It is only natural that you should feel nervous, Englishwoman."

By now, she was almost used to his uncanny skill at reaching right to the heart of her problems. She looked up at him, smiling uncertainly, wanting to make light of her worries. "You call me *Englishwoman*, Rashid, almost every time you speak to me. But I'm not sure how English I feel anymore. Sometimes . . . sometimes . . . I think that the woman who was Hashim Khan's slave will always be at the forefront of my thoughts, crowding out the memories of my earlier life. I am not Lucinda Larkin anymore. How can I be? I have lost her innocence."

Slowly, he slipped the knife back among the folds of his cummerbund. He cupped his hand under her chin, gently tilting her face upward. She had folded her veil to use as a pillow, so her head was uncovered. She made no protest when he reached out with his other hand and slowly pushed back a lock of hair that had fallen across her cheek. They stared at each other in silence. Lucy could read little of what Rashid was thinking, but she sensed that he was troubled, and wondered why. Their silence became so intense it seemed as if the entire world waited for something to happen.

Finally, he touched her lightly on her cheek. "There is no shame in anything you did while you were held as Hashim Khan's prisoner. You know that, don't you, Lucy? You did what you needed to do in order to survive. Be proud that you possessed the courage and the strength of will to keep yourself alive."

She smiled ruefully. "At this moment I don't feel very courageous. There will be so many questions to answer once I am home again. The men will want to know every detail of the massacre that killed my father. The ladies won't want to hear a word about anything so brutal, but they'll be twice as anxious to assure themselves that I haven't adopted any indelicate native customs like eating with my fingers or—" She stopped abruptly.

Rashid squeezed her hand in a fleeting gesture of reassurance. "However prying they are, the good ladies of Peshawar surely cannot be more intimidating than Hashim Khan and his band of cutthroats."

"Huh! That shows how little you know about it," she muttered. "On most occasions the ladies of Peshawar are more intimidating than an entire army riding into battle."

The trace of amusement faded from his expression and his eyes darkened. He leaned toward her until they were almost touching. "Take heart, Englishwoman," he murmured. "You will find that you have more strength than you know. I am predicting you will outwit the ladies of Peshawar as successfully as you outwitted Hashim Khan's soldiers."

"You outwitted the Khan's men, Rashid, not I. You saved my life."

"Did I?" He laughed somewhat oddly. "Then certainly I must claim my reward before it is too late. It seems I have earned it."

She was obscurely disappointed by his remarks, even though she had always acknowledged that he deserved compensation. "I have promised that you will be well paid for your services, Rashid."

He gave another odd laugh. "Well paid? Perhaps. But tonight I do not speak of money. Tonight, I find myself in need of other rewards." His words were no more than a breath of sound against her mouth. He brushed his thumbs across her eyelids, closing them, and a moment later she felt his lips cover hers in a gentle kiss.

The mating and marriage rituals of Kuwar village were considerably more frank then their English equivalent, but Lucy, outcast as a *jinn*, had not shared personally in any of these rituals. She had, in fact, managed to reach the ripe old age of three-and-twenty without ever being kissed. She discovered, to her amazement, that maturity did not help in the slightest in controlling her reaction to this novel experience. Her mouth began to tremble beneath Rashid's, although she wasn't frightened, and she felt the strangest urge to press herself closer to his chest. Her addled brain seemed to be conveying the message that the closer she clung to Rashid, the better she would feel. The falsity of this instruction became apparent when she placed her hands on Rashid's shoulders and leaned against him. The tremble in her mouth immediately extended to her entire body, as if she had developed an acute attack of ague. Inexplicably, she still didn't have the sense to move away.

Rashid did not seem to be behaving any more sensibly than Lucy. As soon as she leaned against him, he made an odd, groaning sound deep in his throat and wrapped her inside the circle of his arms, crushing her thin body against his chest. His lips became hard against hers, and with a little sigh of astonishment, Lucy opened her mouth.

She had no idea what she expected to happen next, but at the touch of Rashid's tongue against hers, a wave of excitement swept through her body. His day's growth of beard rasped against her skin, but the prickles of pain seemed almost pleasurable. Lucy reached up to twist her hands in the thickness of his ebony-dark hair, wanting to feel the strands twined around her fingers. She had been taught that only the sanctity of marriage could make the embrace of a man enjoyable to a lady. Her years in Kuwar Valley must have had a disastrous effect on her ability to behave like a lady, because Rashid's kiss was supremely enjoyable. A delicious languor stole through her limbs, and she lay back on her blanket, instinctively seeking the support of hard ground for her boneless body.

Rashid followed her down onto the blanket. His lips moved urgently over her mouth, sliding down the slender column of her throat, parting the strings of her *kami* so that he could taste the soft, delicate skin above her breasts. Lucy almost stopped breathing. The night stood still and hushed as he pushed the threadbare cloth from her shoulders and eased it down toward her waist.

Her nipples sprang erect in the cold night air, but she scarcely felt the cold. His fingers caressed and stroked until her entire body was throbbing and warm beneath his skillful touch. When his mouth finally replaced his fingers at her breast, she shuddered in uncontrollable response, yearning for some unknown but more intense form of the pleasure he was arousing.

His lips burned their way back to her mouth, a scorching flame against her skin. He kissed her again and again, until even her innocence could not protect her from the knowledge of how deeply the passion had begun to blaze within him—and within her.

Suddenly, she felt fear: fear of the unknown, fear because her body's response had raced so far out of her control. Her mind tensed, and her body stiffened in an automatic effort to regain control over the unfamiliar sensations that threatened to consume her.

Immediately, Rashid became very still. They lay together, unmoving on the blanket, his face wiped clean of all expression. Then he sat up, pulling her *kami* back onto her shoulders, and drew away from her. "I am sorry," he said, his voice hard and somewhat cool. "I did not intend to bring back evil memories."

"You didn't. There are no memories—"

"One day you will find a husband who deserves you, Englishwoman. A man who can give you the home in the country that you long for. A man who will be at your side when your children are born. It will be for him to overcome the darkness of what lies behind you in Kuwar. It will be for him to show you how much joy there can be between a man and a woman. Do you understand what I am trying to say, Englishwoman?"

"I feel—cold."

He didn't take her in his arms in order to warm her. He got up and dragged his blanket a few inches closer to hers. If she had reached out her hand only a little way, she could have touched him. But she didn't. She lay absolutely still.

"I will put some more wood on the fire, Englishwoman."

"Thank you."

"Sleep, now. Trust me, Lucy. You need not fear the jackals tonight nor the ladies of Peshawar tomorrow."

No, Lucy thought, she had nobody to fear save herself. Defiantly, she stretched out her hand until she could touch him.

After a long, silent moment, he turned his hand palm upward, entwining his fingers with hers.

Lucy felt two tears trickle out from beneath her eyelids and roll down her cheeks. Rashid's fingers closed a fraction more tightly around hers.

"The time with you has been good, Lucy."

Warmed by his words, she slept.

CHAPTER SIX

For some obscure reason, the trader chose to approach the city of Peshawar through the chaotic streets of the local market. With great difficulty, Lucy followed him through the narrow, dung-splattered passage he forged between rows of gourd sellers, rice cake vendors and fried fish peddlers.

"Why are we taking this ridiculous route?" she demanded, as a young boy darted almost under the horses' hooves in pursuit of his spinning top.

Rashid avoided a group of children chasing a pet monkey that had slipped its chain. "It is the shortest way to the British compound. Watch out for the camel!"

The beast in question, almost invisible beneath a load of copper pots, had emerged from an alley and was marching with unyielding strides toward Lucy. Both the camel and its master appeared to have every intention of walking straight through her rather than deviating from their chosen path.

Muttering slanderous comments on the mental capacity of the camel and its driver—not to mention the trader—Lucy urged her horse forward. Of necessity, she and Rashid found themselves riding side by side, knees barely an inch apart, toes almost touching. He half-turned and smiled at her, seemingly indifferent to the curses of the irate merchants, forced to press themselves against the wall to allow the horses passage. "I think that camels are not your favorite animal, Englishwoman."

"They have less intelligence than the average sheep and are twenty times as large. Why would anybody like them?"

"Why indeed? Although they have their uses on long journeys."

His reply sounded abstracted, and Lucy looked at him questioningly. He returned her gaze, his eyes dark and without any trace of their usual mockery.

She drew in a quick breath. "What is it, Rashid?"

"We have reached the end of our journey, Englishwoman. It is time for us to part company."

"But we haven't reached my stepmother's house—"

The trader didn't answer. In a single swift movement, he jumped from his horse and tossed the reins toward her. "Catch, Englishwoman!"

She instinctively reached out to grab the reins. By the time she had controlled his skittery horse, he had already crossed in front of her mount and begun to walk at her side. For the briefest of moments he laid his hand against hers in a gesture that was almost a caress. "We must say good-bye, Englishwoman. Our paths diverge here."

"Rashid, no! You can't leave me alone in a place like this!"

He stared ahead, his profile expressionless. "You have no further need of me. You know your way home." He bowed his head, touching his hand to his heart in a formal, graceful salute. "Go with God, Lucy Larkin. May your life be long and blessed with many children."

Her stomach plunged as if she were suddenly falling from a great height, and her throat felt strangely constricted. "But why would you leave me when we are so close to my home? What about your reward from my family?"

"The promise of money always interested you much more than me, Lucy Larkin."

"But where shall I find you? For God's sake, where are you going? *Rashid!*"

He ducked behind a passing wagon without answering her frantic shout, dodging back toward the center of the marketplace. She called his name again, but she couldn't even be sure he heard her voice over the cacophony of merchants' cries. It was impossible to turn the horses around on the narrow pathway, and her gaze managed to track him for no more than twenty yards before he was swallowed up in the thick, milling crowds—one dusty, turbaned head among a score of others.

Lucy knew she had no real hope of finding him. Nevertheless, she dismounted and hunted doggedly on foot for more than an hour before she finally acknowledged that her search was pointless: The trader didn't want to be found and wasn't going to be.

Suddenly bone-weary, the task of controlling both horses began to seem insurmountable. She escaped from the crowded market as quickly as she could, a hand on the bridle of each animal. Her arms ached and her eyes smarted from the dust as she lashed the horses together, then climbed back on her own gelding.

Hours of riding over harsh, mountainous terrain had never seemed so exhausting as the few miles of smooth gravel road leading to the British compound. She could feel herself swaying in the saddle by the time she reached the familiar driveway leading up to her father's bungalow. Her weariness lifted at the sight of the neat, white-painted buildings. The scent of jasmine wafted pleasantly over the high garden wall, and she drew in a deep refreshing breath. Home. Dear God, she had come home!

Lucy didn't recognize the gatekeeper, but that was almost a relief. She wanted to get inside the house before she had to cope with the pandemonium her return would naturally inspire. She gave a polite nod to the servant, thinking how difficult it was to find the right words to announce that you weren't dead.

"Good day," she said, after a brief hesitation. "I am Miss Larkin, the daughter of the *sahib*, Sir Peter Larkin, who died in Afghanistan. Please open the gates. I am very tired and would like to rest after my long journey."

The gatekeeper barely glanced at her. "Be off with you, you brazen hussy! We don't let the likes of you into the house of my master."

Brazen hussy? Belatedly, Lucy gave some thought to just what sort of a bizarre appearance she must present. She resisted the impulse, born of fatigue, to snap at the servant. "I know it must be difficult for you to recognize me," she said. "But despite these clothes, I am English. Lady Margaret Larkin, the *memsahib*, is my stepmother. She will be most angry when she hears that you have kept me waiting outside the walls of my own home."

The gatekeeper stole a worried glance at Lucy. For a harlot or a vagabond, she spoke exceptionally good English, and her horses— though trail-weary—looked of prime stock. On the other hand, her clothing marked her as a mountain barbarian of no caste.

He smoothed an imaginary crease from his pristine white uniform. "My master and his *memsahib* are called Rutherspoon, not the name you say. Why do you waste my time with your foolish lies?"

"Rutherspoon? The people who live here are called Rutherspoon?"

"Of course. Everybody knows it." The gatekeeper gained confidence from the woman's dismay. "The *sahib* is District Officer and a most important man. Now be off with you."

Lucy stared at the servant, torn between wry amusement and a terrible feeling of anticlimax. Good heavens, how foolish she'd been to expect to find her stepmother and stepsister still living in their old bungalow! Lady Margaret and Penelope had loathed India from the day they first arrived, and Lady Margaret had been nagging to leave even before her husband died. She would never dream of staying in Peshawar, not when she had the exciting option of returning to London as a grieving—and wealthy— widow. She had undoubtedly taken the first ship home after hearing of Sir Peter's death.

Lucy felt the urge to cry, but instead a choked gurgle of laughter emerged from her dust-cracked lips. One part of her mind recognized the hysteria that lurked far too close to the surface. Another part no longer cared.

The servant frowned, deeply offended by her unseemly mirth. "There's nothing to giggle about, young woman. Mr. Rutherspoon is a most excellent *sahib*, of great consequence in this region."

"I'm sure he is. I'm sorry." Lucy regained her composure with a struggle. "Well, gatekeeper, if Mr. Rutherspoon lives here instead of Lady Margaret Larkin, then it is Mr. Rutherspoon I must see. Please open the gates. We have business to attend to, your master and I."

The gatekeeper hesitated before deciding that discretion was the better part of valor. In his experience, British *sahibs* and *memsahibs* were all crazy, and this girl might be no crazier than the rest. Washed of her travel dirt and draped in stiff English clothes, she would no doubt fit right in with the other odd specimens who now ruled India. He lifted the heavy bar that locked the gate, then turned his back, symbolically denying responsibility for her penetration of the bungalow's spacious grounds.

Lucy cantered through the gates and rode swiftly to the white marble entrance steps, not giving any of the outdoor servants a chance to stop her. Taking a leaf from the trader's book, she tossed the reins of the horses toward a startled gardener, who had been enjoying a snooze in the shade of a palm tree. "Catch!" she called.

She slid from the saddle and dashed for the front door, making it halfway down the hall before the startled doorkeeper gathered his wits sufficiently to chase after her. She sprinted toward the drawing room, a gaggle of shouting, gesticulating servants snapping at her heels.

Lucy burst into the crowded drawing room. Peshawar's British ladies, assembled for afternoon tea and the polite exchange of slander, returned their teacups to their saucers in perfect unison, their mouths gaping in identical lines of outrage. Seeing herself with their eyes, Lucy became embarrassingly aware of the fact that her clothes were in tatters and that she hadn't bathed in two weeks. Too late, she realized that she smelled more rancid than an overripe pheasant.

A large-bosomed lady, tightly encased in salmon-pink satin, rose to her feet. "What is the meaning of this?" she inquired heatedly, her nose wrinkling as the pungent odor of Lucy's presence drifted across the drawing room. "Mahbub, remove this . . . this *person* at once."

"Mrs. Rutherspoon?" Lucy shook off the servant's restraining hand, guessing that the large-bosomed lady must be the District Officer's wife, and therefore the person Lucy needed to see. "Mrs. Rutherspoon, forgive me for intruding upon your tea party like this, but I am Lucinda Larkin. I've just escaped from two years of captivity in Afghanistan. This used to be my home. I thought to find my stepmother and stepsister here."

Mrs. Rutherspoon sank back onto her chair, her color alarmingly high. "Lucinda Larkin? *Sir Peter's daughter?*" She peered at the dirty, brown-skinned woman in front of her, vainly trying to detect some trace of noble British womanhood beneath the ragged clothing and greasy hair. "But you were reported dead! I attended memorial services in the cathedral myself! Mr. Rutherspoon was there with me, and even the Governor-General came!"

"I'm honored to have been the recipient of such a splendid funeral, Mrs. Rutherspoon, but as you can see, the services were somewhat premature. Happily, I am not dead."

Mrs. Rutherspoon closed her eyes. At this moment, the only thing she could think of that might be worse than having her party interrupted by a beserk native would be to discover that this ragamuffin—this dark-skinned, bold-faced ragamuffin—was indeed Miss Lucinda Larkin. Mrs. Rutherspoon fanned herself, stealing a surreptitious glance at the intruder. The horrid truth was that although the girl looked nothing like any Englishwoman Mrs. Rutherspoon had ever met, she *did* sound undeniably British. And upper class British at that. Mrs. Rutherspoon clasped her hands to her ample bosom, then decided that rather than fainting, which might crumple her new dress, she would summon her husband.

Inwardly congratulating herself on this brilliant solution to a difficult problem, Mrs. Rutherspoon opened her eyes. "Mahbub, send a boy to fetch the *sahib* home. Tell him he is to come at once."

Mahbub bowed and departed, and the assembled ladies released their breath in a collective sigh of approval. Their social leader had not failed them. This was definitely a situation that called for the intervention of masculine authority.

Gathering strength from the silent approval of her audience, Mrs. Rutherspoon braved another direct glance at the intruder.

The woman stared back insolently, her mouth curved in a scornful smile, although what in the world she had to be scornful about was hard to imagine.

Mrs. Rutherspoon shuddered, doubts once again assailing her. Dear God, could any English lady's skin possibly turn such an unbecoming shade of mahogany brown? (Could one become a colored person merely by close association? Or by eating too much native food? She had never trusted the idea of mango chutney, even if the vicar's wife did put up the jars herself.) And surely those were *muscles* visible through the torn sleeves of the intruder's overdress?

Mrs. Rutherspoon surveyed her own plump curves, seeking reassurance. Thank heaven, not a hint of a muscle lurked anywhere in sight. English ladies never developed such things, she was quite sure of it. Their bodies were constitutionally incapable of growing such indelicate appendages.

A discreet cough interrupted her meditations, and she realized that her circle of guests waited for her to initiate some further dialogue with the intruder. Never one to shirk her duty, Mrs. Rutherspoon drew in a deep, calming breath.

"Miss . . . er . . . Larkin, if indeed you should by any chance happen to be Miss Larkin, although that is most difficult to conceive of since Miss Larkin is dead and even if she had been captured would surely never have survived the horrors of her captivity—"

"I am Miss Larkin."

Mrs. Rutherspoon was not accustomed to being interrupted. She bridled angrily. "So you have told us, Miss Larkin, if you are indeed Miss Larkin. In any case, whoever you . . . that is to say, I am sure you must realize that your extraordinary claim raises many difficult matters, which will all need to be sorted out before we can—"

"Offer me a bath?"

Mrs. Rutherspoon rose to her feet and glared at Lucy from her commanding new height. "I have sent for Mr. Rutherspoon. Mr. Rutherspoon is the District Officer."

"And therefore able to resolve everything," Lucy said.

Mrs. Rutherspoon was not a lady to be troubled by subtle undertones of sarcasm. "Of course," she said, relieved to feel the conversation moving onto firmer ground. "The District Officer is the Queen's representative. He is able to resolve everything that does not need to be referred to higher authority."

"In matters of a return from the dead, one wonders who the higher authority might actually be. Although if the District Officer is considered an adequate substitute for Queen Victoria, I daresay God has no cause to quibble."

The assembled ladies gave a gasp of horror, and Mrs. Rutherspoon found herself once again rendered speechless. This wretched, *rude* intruder couldn't possibly be English, she decided, let alone a member of the distinguished Larkin family. Sir Peter had certainly spent far too much time consorting with the natives, but Lady Margaret and dear little Penelope had possessed impeccable taste and exquisite manners. Lady Margaret's comments on the vulgar excesses of Indian culture had often made Mrs. Rutherspoon smile. The real Lucinda Larkin, even after two years in captivity, could never have turned into the sort of odious, sarcastic creature now polluting the most elegant drawing room in Peshawar. Mrs. Rutherspoon snapped her lips together and retreated into a huffy silence.

The vicar's wife, number two in the social pecking order, hurled herself into the conversational breach. "Young woman, we do not take the Lord's name in vain in the District Officer's drawing room. Moreover, we do not presume to judge either God or Queen Victoria."

The intruder, far from appearing properly rebuked, merely looked mutinous. By good fortune, Mr. Rutherspoon himself arrived before she could utter any further blasphemies—either against God or His earthly representatives.

"Good afternoon, ladies. Delightful to see you all." With consummate skill—not for nothing had he been promoted to District Officer—Mr. Rutherspoon made himself heard over a babble of agitated feminine voices. "Harriet, there are two horses eating the roses outside the front door, and Mahbub has been telling me the most ridicul—"

Mrs. Rutherspoon regained her voice. "This woman claims she is Lucinda Larkin."

"What?" Goggle-eyed, the District Officer swung around to face Lucy. "Have you run mad, young woman? Lucinda Larkin is dead!"

"No," Lucy said quietly. "I am not dead. I have been held captive for two years in Kuwar Valley, in central Afghanistan."

Mr. Rutherspoon glared at her. It was a glare he used on recalcitrant natives to great effect. "Young woman, you are offending the memory of a noble British family. Miss Larkin and her father were massacred two years ago. The bodies . . . the remains of the bodies . . . were brought back to India by soldiers of the 59th Light Infantry."

"No," Lucy said again. "My father was massacred, together with all twenty of the men who formed part of Britain's trade delegation to the Amir of Afghanistan. But I was not killed. I was taken prisoner by the Khan of Kuwar. And now I have escaped."

Something about the woman's calm, flat manner of speech carried conviction. The awful realization that this smelly creature might indeed be Miss Lucinda Larkin took hold in the minds of all those present. The drawing room fell ominously silent. Dead, Miss Larkin had been a martyr killed in service to the Empire. Alive, she seemed destined to become an embarrassing blot on the purity of English womanhood. Mr. Rutherspoon mopped his brow.

"I think we should discuss this . . . er . . . this return in my office. M'wife's drawing room is not the place, you know."

"I agree we have much to discuss, but before I go to your office, Mr. Rutherspoon, I would appreciate a hot bath and the loan of some good English soap. Soap is a luxury I have long been denied."

In that, at least, she was obviously telling the truth, Mr. Rutherspoon reflected. Her hair, what could be seen of it, looked matted with grease and dirt. He'd tell the servants to take up some carbolic along with the bathwater, because she was sure to have headlice. His gaze dropped swiftly to her belly. Not pregnant, thank God, or at least not visibly. One less problem to worry about. But, devil take it, he didn't like the obstinate thrust of her chin. If she was Lucinda Larkin, he'd get her shipped out of here on the next available boat, before she could start causing trouble. Let the authorities in England sort out the legalities of the situation, whatever they might be.

Mr. Rutherspoon, like many officials in the British Raj, possessed considerable organizational skills, and he used them now to excellent effect. His wife was summoned to action with a single brisk nod. "Harriet, you will no doubt wish to escort our . . . er . . . visitor to a guest room so that she can refresh herself. I will join you in your sitting room in just a moment." He smiled at the assembled ladies. "I know your charming guests will understand why we must cut short your tea party."

The vicar's wife concealed her disappointment at this abrupt curtailment of the afternoon's excitement. "Dear Mr. Rutherspoon, you always cope so splendidly with even the most *extraordinary* situations." She handed her teacup to a waiting servant and gathered up her fan and gloves. "Come, ladies. We shall call tomorrow and inquire how Mrs. Rutherspoon and her family are faring. Especially dearest Rosamund. Goodness me, Harriet, your daughter will be so thrilled to know that the sister of her friend Penelope is safely returned to civilization!"

"Yes, indeed." Mrs. Rutherspoon managed a weak smile. Her daughter! Dear heaven, how could she have forgotten about her daughter? On no account must Rosamund be allowed to converse with this horrid visitor. Even if the woman did turn out to be Lucinda Larkin, after two years as the captive of wild Afghani tribesmen there was no knowing what terrible native customs she might reveal to Rosamund's virginal ears.

Lucy, escorted by a phalanx of servants, was led toward the rear of the bungalow. Mr. Rutherspoon, whose thoughts had been running in close harmony with his wife's, took the opportunity to draw her aside. He wanted to make sure that she had understood the full implications of the situation.

"Take care that our daughter doesn't come anywhere near her, Harriet. Can't be too careful with a young girl's sensibilities, you know. An innocent flower like Rosamund mustn't be allowed to blossom too soon."

"You may rely upon me, Cecil. Our daughter will be kept out of harm's way. Do you think this woman is an imposter?"

"Hard to say, but there are only two choices, m'dear. Either this woman's an imposter, or she really is Lucinda Larkin. Don't know which case is worse. If she's been a prisoner of the Khan of Kuwar for the past two years, might be better if she had died. Wild Eastern men. A white woman in their power. There have been unspeakable violations of her person, you may be sure of it."

"Unspeakable violations!" Mrs. Rutherspoon breathed. "Oh, Cecil dearest, I cannot bear to think of what crudities this woman may reveal. I must not leave her alone for an instant!" She rushed off in pursuit of their visitor, wondering how many explicit details of Oriental defilement she would be able to extract from Miss Larkin under the guise of offering sympathy.

By nightfall, every servant in the British compound, right down to the boys hired to twirl the ceiling fans in the various drawing rooms, had heard the dramatic story of the woman's arrival at the District Officer's gates and her subsequent claim to be the long-lost Miss Lucinda Larkin. Most found the story unbelievable but were willing to hold off final judgment until seeing the intruder dressed in English clothes. English clothes were notorious for their powers of transformation.

In this decision, the servants were joined by their masters, and by the District Officer himself. "Let's see how she cleans up," Mr. Rutherspoon commented to his wife over an evening glass of sherry. "She might look quite different once she's wearing some decent garments. Dash it all, when you get right down to it, she *sounds* English. None of the natives ever get the intonation quite right, you know. Always a bit of singsong in their voices to give them away."

"I've offered her one of Rosamund's good dresses," Mrs. Rutherspoon said, sounding astonished by her own generosity. "And all the necessary . . . er . . . accoutrements. She is so thin that she can wear garments our dear little girl outgrew when she was fifteen."

"Can't hold that against the woman, you know. If she's been held prisoner, she's probably been kept short of food."

"But she is so dark and *wiry*!"

"Well, not all girls can expect to be as blond and pretty as our Rosamund. Met Sir Peter on a couple of occasions, and he was quite dark himself, you know. Daresay his daughter couldn't hope for fair hair and blue eyes."

"She didn't say a single word to me except please and thank you," Mrs. Rutherspoon burst out, overcome anew by the injustice of it all. "I tried to offer my sympathy, to let her confide some of the horrors of her enslavement to me. After all, I am a married woman and I was determined to be brave, however shocking her revelations. But all she did was thank me for the lavender soap and tell me that she was quite capable of taking a bath alone. She is an imposter, she must be. No English lady would be so curt with the first white woman she has seen in two years."

"She may feel a very proper reserve, m'dear. Even though you are married, with me as your husband you have naturally been shielded from the full demands of man's lower nature."

Mrs. Rutherspoon did not look as grateful as might have been expected for this husbandly protection. She was frowning when Mahbub appeared at the entrance to the drawing room. "Miss Larkin would like permission to join you and the *memsahib*, *sahib*."

"Send her in," Mr. Rutherspoon said heartily. "We are waiting to see her."

Quick, soft footsteps sounded in the hallway. Mr. Rutherspoon rose to his feet, unconsciously holding his breath. He let the breath out in a sigh of disappointment when the young woman appeared in the doorway. There had been no miraculous transformation from plain, thin native into plump, pink-complexioned English-woman. Their visitor, though infinitely cleaner, was still skinny and unattractive, and the borrowed white dress merely emphasized the brown of her skin and the lankness of her dark hair.

Damn it, she knew how to make an entrance, though! Mr. Rutherspoon watched in admiration as the woman walked gracefully into the drawing room, head high, shoulders straight, one hand controlling the movement of her draped skirts, the other lightly clasped around her fan. She halted in front of Mrs. Rutherspoon, dipping into the slightest of curtsies.

"Ma'am, I must apologize for interrupting your tea party this afternoon. When I rode up to the bungalow I had not considered the many months that have passed since my father's death. I assumed that my stepmother and stepsister would still be living here. When the gatekeeper informed me that the new District Officer was in residence, I could think of nothing to do other than bring my plight to his attention."

Mrs. Rutherspoon fanned herself. "That you have certainly done."

"Yes, I'm afraid I have." The woman's huge eyes softened with rueful laughter, and Mr. Rutherspoon recognized suddenly that she was not entirely without beauty. He felt a quickening of purely masculine interest as she turned toward him.

"Sir, I realize that my arrival on your doorstep has caused a great deal of trouble for your family. I also realize that my years in captivity have altered my appearance greatly. However, there must be several people still living in Peshawar who would recognize me. Perhaps Mr. Chester, the vicar, or Mr. Smythe, from the local school?"

Was it just coincidence that she had chosen two people who no longer resided in Peshawar? Mr. Rutherspoon scrutinized her intently. "I'm sorry to say that Mr. Smythe is no longer with us. He passed away at Christmas."

"Oh, I'm sorry. That is sad news. He was a good man and an excellent teacher. Is Mrs. Smythe still here?"

"Unfortunately not. She was advised to take the children back to England, to live with her late husband's brother."

"The climate never agreed with her," Lucy commented. "She probably made a wise decision. Well, if Mrs. Smythe is not here, how about the vicar?"

"Mr. Chester has been summoned to a higher calling."

"He's dead, too?"

"No, of course not. He is now archdeacon of the cathedral, and so neither he nor his wife now live in Peshawar."

"Oh bother!"

"Bother, indeed. However, take heart, Miss Larkin. I daresay, in these special circumstances, Mr. Chester would be prepared to journey here to Peshawar and make a positive identification." Mr. Rutherspoon tugged at his mustache. "Yes, that is what I shall do. I shall send a telegraph message to the cathedral tomorrow. I daresay Mr. Chester might be here with us in as little as three days."

He watched the young woman closely, but Mr. Rutherspoon could detect no sign of alarm at these words, and he decided to abandon all hope of resolving the issue of her true identity that evening. A practical man, he suggested his wife should order dinner served. Dinner still had to be eaten, whoever this woman might be.

Rosamund was summoned to join the party at the last possible moment. A placid, pretty girl with a warm smile and no particular talents, she was clearly destined to make some man a wonderful wife. Frothing out the pink ruffles on her dress with artless satisfaction, she confided to Lucy that Penelope had been her very best friend during the two months they were in Peshawar together.

Lucy, feeling a hundred years old, replied that Penelope had always longed for a friend of her own age.

"You do not look in the least like Penelope," Rosamund commented.

"Penelope is my stepsister. There is no reason for us to look alike."

"Oh." Mindful of her manners, Rosamund then asked with great politeness if Miss Larkin was glad to be back in India. With equal politeness, Lucy replied that she was.

Mrs. Rutherspoon hurried her guest into the dining room before the conversation could take a more intimate and dangerous turn. Lucy, worn out by the events of the day, was more than content to remain on her best behavior throughout the meal. She confined her comments to remarks about the weather in Afghanistan (cold and dry) and the cloth-weaving skills of the Kuwari women (moderate). Even this topic became too risque for Mrs. Rutherspoon's taste when Lucy mentioned the special bright red wool that was used to weave bridal pantaloons. No doubt fearing some dreadful revelation about primitive Afghani marriage customs, she hurriedly changed the subject.

After that, Lucy kept silent, except to praise the excellence of the rice pudding. With complete honesty, she pleaded exhaustion as soon as dessert was cleared from the table, and gratefully received permission to retire to the privacy of the guest bedroom.

Summoned by an urgent telegram, the Very Reverend Archdeacon Otis Chester arrived in Peshawar only three days after Lucy. Ushered into the District Officer's study, the Reverend Chester could not contain his emotional turmoil.

"Good of you to notify me so promptly, Rutherspoon. I knew Sir Peter and his eldest gal very well. This is a bad business, a very bad business."

"You suspect my guest is not the real Lucinda Larkin?"

The Reverend Chester gave a short bark of laughter. "On the contrary, my dear sir. The Lucy Larkin I knew was just the sort of woman to survive two years of captivity in darkest Afghanistan.

When I said this was a bad business, I was thinking of the difficulties ahead of the poor gal."

"She will have a hard time adjusting to civilized society again."

"Yes. And she's not going to be welcomed by her stepmother nor by her stepsister. Lady Margaret inherited a great deal of money from Sir Peter, and she's used it to establish herself in the heart of fashionable London. Now all that money reverts to Lucy, and Lady Margaret's income depends upon Lucy's goodwill. That wouldn't be a happy situation at the best of times."

Mr. Rutherspoon raised an eyebrow. "Not surprising if Lady Margaret resents the change."

"Not surprising at all. Well, I suppose it's all going to be grist for the lawyers' mills. But it's an awkward business, this coming back from the dead. Very awkward."

Mr. Rutherspoon got up and stared out the window at the gardeners watering his rose bushes. "First, we have to be sure that Miss Larkin has indeed made a miraculous return. I won't conceal the truth from you, my dear sir. At first glance, the woman who presented herself in m'wife's drawing room last week doesn't look anything like an English lady. She's brown as a native and thinner than half the beggars you may see on the streets. Mrs. Rutherspoon insists she is an imposter, but I don't agree. Quite apart from the fact that she speaks such perfect English, there's something about her . . . Her attitude . . . her manner. . . . Perfectly polite, but not a streak of humbleness or submission—"

Mr. Rutherspoon shook his head, turning abruptly to face the archdeacon. "Anyway, enough of this useless talking. I'll send one of the boys to fetch her. You may judge for yourself who and what she is."

Lucy followed the servant downstairs, outwardly composed, inwardly trembling. When making her escape from Kuwar, she had never considered there might be doubts about her identity once she returned to India. But doubts there were, assailing her from every side. It was being borne in upon her with increasing force that she had not paid nearly enough attention to how the outside world would view her years of slavery. During those endless months in Kuwar, her rational thoughts had all been centered on the problem of survival. Her daydreams had centered on the possibility of escape. The pattern her life would take once she was back in the outside world had never held a place in either her dreams or her calculations.

It would be ironic—more than ironic—if the Reverend Chester

failed to identify her as Lucinda Larkin. He had once been a good friend, but she needed only to glance into the mirror to know that even good friends might have difficulty in recognizing her. The weight she had lost had affected the contours of her face, so that whereas her cheeks had once been round and rosy, now her cheekbones stood out high and stark, making her eyes seem enormous and draining every vestige of pink color from her darkly tanned skin.

"Missy is here, *sahib.*"

Her years of slavery had made her sensitive to concealed emotions, and Lucy could feel the waves of curiosity emanating from the outwardly bland servant. From his point of view, Lucy realized, it would probably be more entertaining if she were declared an impostor. Certainly, none of the servants felt any sympathy for her plight.

Lucy squared her shoulders and held her head extra high as she walked into the study. She barely had time to register the presence of an elderly, white-haired gentleman standing next to Mr. Rutherspoon before the Reverend Chester strode across the room and clasped her in his arms.

"My dear girl, my very dear Lucy." He kept hold of her hand, shaking it repeatedly. "What a pleasure this is! What a most unexpected pleasure! Only the sight of your father standing at your side could make the occasion more perfect."

Lucy's smile was more than a little tremulous. "He died as bravely as you would have expected, with no word of reproach for his murderers."

"And now enjoys the heavenly reward to which he is so justly entitled. Sir Peter was one of God's most loving servants. Take comfort from that knowledge, my dear."

"I do. But sometimes I am selfish enough to wish that he was still here with me."

"You were close and loyal companions as well as father and daughter. Such feelings are natural, Lucy. It would be odd indeed if you did not miss him. The good Lord does not require you to be odd."

"Ah, dear Mr. Chester! You always make me feel that I am less unworthy than I had feared."

"That is one of the requirements for keeping my job. My Employer has strict rules about it. It is written into my employment contract. I am to make His congregation feel worthy."

Lucy astonished herself by giving a little laugh. "And to think I was afraid you wouldn't recognize me!"

"There could be no danger of that, my dear. Your eyes have not changed, nor the stubborn tilt of your chin. You are a little thinner to be sure, but remember my hobby!"

"Your hobby? Oh, of course, sketching! You are a talented artist."

"Well, that is being too kind, perhaps, but I do pride myself on my artist's eye." He patted her hand, his smile becoming teasing. "I always knew there was a classic oval face hiding behind those plump schoolgirl cheeks of yours."

Lucy laughed again, surprising herself with the sound. *"Classic oval?* Come, dear sir. I'm afraid you have acquired a flatterer's tongue to go with your artist's eye."

"I hope not," the Reverend Chester said quietly. "Flattery is false coin that does not enrich the giver or the receiver. But you must tell us what has been happening to you, my dear, while we all imagined you dead. Why do you not make yourself comfortable on the sofa beside Mr. Rutherspoon and tell us how you managed to make the journey across Afghanistan without losing your life? That is surely the greatest miracle in a whole series of miracles."

"I had an escort," Lucy said. "A Muslim trader by the name of Rashid. He claimed to be from Lahore, and he seemed very familiar with the safe routes out of Afghanistan." She held her breath, waiting for the District Officer to jump in with the information that just such a man was wanted for the crime of stealing Enfield rifles from a British garrison.

However, the name Rashid seemed to conjure up no immediate images of a villain. Mr. Rutherspoon said merely, "These native merchants are the only people who really know the safe passages into Afghanistan, and into Tibet, too. I am forever telling our military fellows that they need merchants, not scouts, to get them safely across the mountains.

The Reverend Chester looked puzzled. "But why did the Khan of Kuwar suddenly allow you to leave, Lucy, when he had been holding you prisoner for two whole years?"

"He didn't exactly allow us to leave," Lucy said dryly. "On the contrary, he seemed quite determined to kill both me and the merchant."

"So you managed to escape?"

"Yes, because the trader had horses and I was able to steal a supply of food. Otherwise, we would never have survived the journey."

The archdeacon and Mr. Rutherspoon were both full of questions, which she answered willingly, giving the two men an account of her trek with Rashid across the mountains to the Khyber Pass. If she edited out all references that might have helped them to identify Rashid's stock-in-trade—well, he had saved her life, and she couldn't quite see why it was her duty to ensure that his activities came under scrutiny by the British authorities. After all, Lucy soothed her conscience, she wasn't *entirely* certain that Rashid had committed any crimes against the British Raj. It was just possible he had come by his rifles honestly.

"You are lucky the Afridi tribesmen didn't attack you," Mr. Rutherspoon commented, as she finally drew her tale to a close. "Our soldiers have been having a lot of trouble with them over these past few months. There's trouble brewing in Afghanistan, and all of us living in this part of India know it."

"Do you think the Russians are stirring the pot?" Lucy asked.

"I think Disraeli's stirring the pot," the archdeacon interjected testily. "The man's obsessed with his vision of the British Empire. He won't be satisfied until the entire map of the world is colored red."

"There are plenty of worse things to be than British," Mr. Rutherspoon commented. "Ask any native in this town if they'd rather have us ruling them, or the Russians. We all know what their answer would be."

"But perhaps they would like to govern themselves best of all." The comment tumbled out before Lucy could stop it.

Mr. Rutherspoon stared at her, his expression pained. "They are children, Miss Larkin, corrupt children, and children cannot govern themselves. That is quite clear to anybody who understands the situation."

Mr. Chester coughed. "Why did you ask about the Russians, Lucy? Do you have any special reason for supposing that the tsar is sticking his fingers into the Afghani pie?"

"Yes. The trader and I encountered a troop of Russian soldiers quite close to the Khyber Pass. They told us they were traveling from Qandahar to Kuwar and had lost their way. They mentioned they had messages to carry from Mohammed Ayub to the Khan of Kuwar."

"Mohammed Ayub?" Mr. Rutherspoon wrinkled his brow.

"Mohammed Ayub? Now why does that name strike me as familiar?"

"He is an exiled son of the present Amir of Afghanistan," Mr. Chester explained. "He organized a rebellion against his father, but the rebellion failed and he was sent into Persia. Are you telling us, Lucy, that the Amir's son has ventured back into western Afghanistan?"

"From the tale the Russians told us, it would certainly seem so."

"I'm sure the Viceroy's office would be most interested in that piece of news," the archdeacon murmured. "Could I ask you, my dear, to write an account of any political information you may have gleaned during your time in Afghanistan? I will take it back with me to Lahore and see that it is carried personally to the Viceroy."

"I am very willing to help in any way I can, but other than this one incident, and my firsthand knowledge that the Khan of Kuwar is totally untrustworthy, I really had no opportunity to learn anything of significance during my period of captivity. Neither the Khan nor the elders of the village trusted me with their political opinions." Unable to stop the bitterness from creeping into her voice, Lucy added, "Women in Kuwar are not considered thinking human beings, and I was a foreigner, which made matters worse."

Mr. Rutherspoon winced. "I'm sure the archdeacon doesn't wish you to recount any . . . um . . . horror of a personal nature," he said hurriedly. "We realize there will be many—events—that occurred during your captivity that you will wish to banish from your memories entirely."

"That is certainly true." Lucy rose to her feet. "For what it's worth, Mr. Chester, you shall have your account of my imprisonment and of our meeting with the Russian soldiers."

"Thank you, my dear."

Lucy stared down at her hands. "Now that we have established who I am, what do you suggest I do, Mr. Chester?"

He smiled gently. "Why that is quite simple to decide, my dear. I recommend that you go home as quickly as we can book you comfortable passage on a fast ship. You must go home to England, and to your family. The past is finished. The rest of your life awaits your homecoming."

CHAPTER SEVEN

Abdullah jumped from the top of the high wall surrounding Rutherspoon *sahib*'s garden and landed safely on agile, mud-encrusted feet. Dodging behind shrubs and bushes, he evaded detection until he could finally squeeze himself in between the rose bush and the crouched marble lion that marked the entrance to the *sahib*'s house. The space was tiny, but fortunately Abdullah wasn't very large. He smiled, pulling a thorn out of his thumb and flicking it carelessly away. Rashid would have been pleased with his pupil's skill at evading detection.

Abdullah saw that he had timed his arrival well. The traveling carriage was already waiting, hood down, silk-fringed parasols raised in protection against the sun. The doors of the bungalow stood open. Rutherspoon *sahib* emerged onto the veranda, together with two women.

Was either of them the one? Abdullah craned forward, parting the leaves of the bush for a better view. No, neither of them could be the woman Rashid had spoken of. One was too old, and even the young one was fat and pasty white. Rashid's woman had creamy skin and lips the color of hibiscus blossoms in early morning when they are touched with dew.

Another voice sounded in the doorway. A soft murmur of laughter drifted into the garden. Abdullah peered through the roses. A slender, dark-haired woman was descending the steps, speaking quietly to the assembled servants.

This is the one, he thought immediately. This is the Englishwoman who has stolen the heart of my master and carries it away with her across the ocean.

The Englishwoman turned to speak to the *sahib*, holding out her hand in a gesture of farewell. Her body swayed with the graceful rhythm of an Easterner, although she was clothed in a European dress of tucked and flounced muslin. The absurd hump that the foreigners called a "bustle" thrust out her pale blue skirts, making an obscene lump in the rear of her body. Her hat was tiny, so Abdullah could see that her brown hair gleamed with auburn highlights in the morning sun, and her huge eyes were fringed with lashes longer and thicker than any he had ever seen on a woman from the cold, dreary lands of the north.

Abdullah was pleased with the Englishwoman's appearance. If his master was to toss and turn at night for the sake of a foreign woman, it was good that she should be beautiful.

Rashid had left Peshawar two weeks ago, but he had been explicit with his instructions, and Abdullah chose the moment to carry out those instructions carefully. He waited until the groom and outriders were mounted on the carriage box and *sahib* Rutherspoon had escorted the other two women back to the shade of the veranda. Then he jumped over the marble lion and took three swift strides to kneel at the feet of the Englishwoman. He was rather pleased with the drama of his appearance and relished the cries of astonishment from the servants.

"A present for you from Rashid, my Master," he murmured in Pashto, and pressed the little drawstring package into her gloved hands.

He waited only to be sure that she had clasped the gift, and then he was off, running across the garden on winged feet. The wall loomed ahead, but the rough plaster offered plenty of finger- and toe-holds to a boy of Abdullah's skill. Safely at the top, he straddled the wall for a split second, looking back toward the carriage.

The Englishwoman had opened the tiny leather bag and had seen what lay inside. She held the bag pressed close to her heart as she looked up at Abdullah. He saw tears sparkle at the corner of her eyes and spill over onto her cheeks. He watched in grim silence as her lips slowly formed the Pashto words for "thank you."

Abdullah frowned and jumped hastily off the wall before one of the *sahib's* servants should catch him and decide to administer a beating. He did not approve of the unseemly lovesickness that had gripped his master. It was a sickness that held out no hope of a cure, and he was not pleased to observe that the Englishwoman seemed to be afflicted by symptoms of the same ailment.

When Rashid came back, he would not tell him that the woman had cried, Abdullah decided. He would say only that she had accepted the gift with a polite smile, which was true, if not the whole truth. Praise Allah that she was about to return to England. Rashid would soon forget her. He had more important things to worry about than a woman.

The comfort and convenience of travel between India and England had been greatly increased since Lucy's outward journey nine years earlier. On their outward journey, the Larkin family had been compelled to undertake the horrendous donkey-and-camel ride from Port Said, where they left their European steamship, to the Gulf of Suez, where they transferred to a wooden sailing vessel for the remainder of their passage to India. Lucy had often thought it was the hardship of their journey that had given Lady Margaret and Penelope such a distaste for India. Her poor stepsister had been so ill from the combination of bad water and constant seasickness that it was a miracle she lived to see her eleventh birthday.

The recent completion of the Suez Canal, linking the Mediterranean Ocean with the Red Sea, meant that ocean liners of virtually any tonnage could now pass from Asia to Europe unhindered by stretches of land. Lucy blessed the achievements of modern science, and the miracles of modern engineering, as the gleaming new Pacific-and-Orient steamship traversed the hundred miles of man-made waterway.

The endless, tranquil days at sea gave her ample time to rest and recuperate from the rigors of the past two years. Mrs. Trimble, a colonel's widow of kindly disposition, had agreed to act as Lucy's chaperone, and the two ladies dealt very well together despite the fact that they had little in common. Gripped by a rather odd lethargy that she didn't attempt to analyze, Lucy would have been content to stay drifting at sea forever.

Her detachment suffered a blow when Mr. Upton, the ship's captain, announced that they were crossing the Bay of Biscay and would soon be entering the English Channel. Within twelve hours, the ship would dock in the port of Southampton. Lucy realized that she was dreading her arrival in England and the forthcoming meetings with her stepmother and stepsister. Wryly, she reflected that she was probably the only person on board who wished that the journey home from India still took several months, as it had done in the bad old days of sails, mutinous crews and precarious provisions.

Mrs. Trimble shared none of Lucy's reluctance to disembark. She became steadily more excited as the sea became choppier, the skies grayer and the wind more chill.

"Fifteen years, my dear Lucinda! Can you imagine it is fifteen years since I last saw our native land! And eight years since poor little George and Freddie were sent home to school. I swear, I shall not recognize them. They will be young men, no longer my little boys. George is already taller than I am and Freddie almost so."

This conversation had already occurred a hundred times in various forms. Lucy, who secretly found the custom of ripping young boys from the bosom of their families and sending them off thousands of miles to English boarding schools totally barbarous, offered her usual reassurance.

"I'm sure you will recognize them instantly, Mrs. Trimble. The bond between mothers and children is so strong you will soon feel as if you had never been separated. Your sons understand why they had to be sent away."

"Do you think so, indeed? Freddie was only seven when we put him on the ship for England, but there was a cholera epidemic that year, and we were terrified we might lose him and his brother. Now he is almost fifteen and George is already seventeen."

"But you have seen photographs, and you have written long letters every month. You are not strangers to each others' thoughts and hopes."

"That is true. The regular mails are such a blessing to us mothers, not to mention the ease and convenience of modern photography. I have received pictures of my dear boys every year. I cannot imagine what it must have been like in the days when even a miniature portrait painted by some itinerant hack was almost more than a mother could hope for. We lead such easy, comfortable lives these days." Mrs. Trimble stopped short and turned to smile at Lucy.

"Ah, my dear, you have been more than good to me on this voyage. I realize how foolish I must sound, and I know we have had this same conversation many times. It is merely that my heart is so full of anticipation that there is no room within me for other topics."

"How else could you feel when you are about to be reunited with your family, Lucinda?"

"You, too, are about to be reunited with your family, Lucinda."

"Yes. But . . . but I am much older than your sons, and the separation from Penelope and my stepmother has not been of such long duration. My anticipation is naturally less intense."

Mrs. Trimble was well aware of her traveling companion's story. Moreover, she had met Lady Margaret in Lahore on one or two uncomfortable occasions, and she understood exactly why Lucinda wasn't excited at the prospect of being reunited with her stepmother. The poor girl was going to have a hard time ahead of her as she struggled for readmittance into English society. Thank God, she has money, Mrs. Trimble thought. However much the high sticklers might wish to pretend otherwise, money could buy a great deal of acceptance. For Lucinda's sake, Mrs. Trimble hoped fervently that it could buy enough to wipe out the stain of two years of slavery in a heathen land.

Mrs. Trimble was too kind and far too tactful to voice any of her thoughts out loud. She bent down to look into the mirror, fastening the clasp of her pearl necklace.

"My dear, we've gossiped so long it's nine o'clock already. Are you not going to the dance tonight? It will be your last chance to say good-bye to many of the people who have become our friends over the past few weeks."

"I shall see them at breakfast tomorrow."

"You should not count on it. There is always such confusion at the moment of disembarkation. Tonight is really the proper moment for good-byes."

"Would it be very rude of me to plead a headache?"

"Not rude, perhaps, but—cowardly?"

Lucy clasped her hands tightly together in her lap. "Mrs. Trimble, may I please have your blessing to remain a coward for one more night?"

"Of course. How could I deny you such a small favor when you have been so tolerant of my incessant chatter about my sons? I will make your excuses to our friends if that is what you wish."

Mrs. Trimble paused for a moment, then rested her hand very lightly on Lucy's shoulders. "Take my word for it, Lucinda, as one who has learned wisdom the hard way. Whatever regrets you have about the years you spent in India, put them behind you. You must live in the present, not in the past."

Lucy laughed awkwardly. "It is the present that I dread, Mrs. Trimble. I'm not sure I shall ever again fit into English society. There was a man who helped me escape from the Khan of Kuwar, a Muslim trader from the Punjab . . . He was a native, probably not even educated, and yet he caused me to question so many things—"

"My dear, I have yet another piece of advice for you, one that you may consider hypocritical but will save you a great deal of frustration. Do not attempt to correct the misconceptions about India which you will be forced to listen to when you reenter British society. Most people resent having their prejudices contradicted by facts, and the more bizarre the prejudice, the more deeply rooted it usually is."

This time, Lucy's laughter was unshadowed. "Mrs. Trimble, I detect the sentiments of a dangerous rebel lurking beneath the guise of a most proper colonel's widow."

"Rebels usually fare better and achieve more if they wear the garb of total respectability. That's a lesson I learned several years too late. I hope you may benefit from it earlier. Play the blushing virgin if you wish to be accepted in the circles where you have most chance of affecting a change in society's beliefs."

Mrs. Trimble picked up her fan and reticule, and walked briskly to the cabin door. "There, now I have shocked you by using the word 'virgin,' which every unmarried woman must be, and no unmarried woman must ever say. A splendid example of just the sort of hypocrisy we've been talking about. Goodnight, my dear. Sleep well. I shall try not to disturb you when I return."

Alone in the cabin, Lucy walked over to the dressing table and sat down in front of the mirror. The candlelight flattered her brown skin, making it appear soft and tinted with pink. But even in candlelight, she looked nothing like a blushing virgin, which was a mite unfair since she was precisely that—at least virginal, if not blushing.

In the harsh light of day, Lucy knew that she looked even less maidenly and innocent. In daylight, her eyes were shadowed with the knowledge of cruelty inflicted and hardship suffered. Her body was taut with unfeminine muscle, and her skin still looked so darkly tanned that most strangers would have a hard time believing she was English. Scowling, Lucy poked at her collarbone and felt a faint cushioning of flesh. At least that was a slight improvement, she decided. After several weeks of sturdy British cooking, her bones no longer stood out in visible relief against her skin. With the colder English climate—if the current weather was anything to go by she should say the *freezing* English climate— she could wear high necks and long sleeves that would disguise her skinniness even further.

Lucy sprang to her feet, suddenly impatient with the narcissistic trend of her thoughts. What did her appearance matter? She didn't intend to reestablish herself in England for the sake of entering the marriage market. On the contrary, she was determined to make a useful life for herself continuing some of her father's charitable projects. Recruiting teachers for a school in Lahore was one of her first priorities. Later on, she might even go back to India . . . Many activities forbidden to a twenty-three-year-old were permissible for a spinster of thirty.

A spinster. The word stuck in her throat, echoing with loneliness. Despite the unconventional life she had led with her father, she had somehow never expected to end up a spinster. She had always assumed that someday she would be a wife and a loving mother. Indeed, her chubby, rosy-cheeked sons and daughters had always been much clearer in her imagination than her shadowy future husband.

May your life be long and blessed with many children. Unbidden, her hands moved to the tray on the dressing table where a soft leather pouch rested next to her hairbrush. Lucy picked up the little bag, pulled open the neck cords and allowed the object contained inside to drop into her hand.

The diamond eyes of the exquisitely wrought gold camel stared up at her arrogantly, but there was no cruelty or malevolence in the beast's expression. The craftsman who created this camel had worked with love and good humor, so that the animal appeared comic in its bad-tempered, cross-gaited dignity. Lucy had only to glance at it to hear Rashid's voice echoing in her ears. *I think camels are not your favorite animal, Englishwoman.*

She stood abruptly, stuffing the costly trinket back inside its pouch. She took her cloak from the hook inside the small closet and wrapped it hurriedly around her shoulders. She would go up on deck and take a walk. It was the way most of her insomnia-plagued nights had ended during this voyage, and it seemed fitting that for these last few miles at sea her thoughts should once again be filled with Rashid. Heaven knew, his image had been with her on every other stage of the journey. She might as well accept the inevitable and carry him with her for these final hours. Tomorrow, she would land in England, and she would bury the memory of Rashid deep in her heart where it could no longer pain her. Tomorrow, her love affair with a Muslim trader from the Punjab would finally be over.

CHAPTER EIGHT

The boat train arrived in London's Victoria Station from Southampton shortly after luncheon. Lucy, more excited than she had expected to be, allowed a porter to take her cases, then scanned the station for a glimpse of Lady Margaret and Penelope. Now that the moment of greeting was finally here, she realized how much she was looking forward to seeing her family again. It will be fun, she thought, to live in the most modern country in the world.

She spotted her father's old housekeeper waiting on the platform, and a wave of happiness surged through her. Lucy had been less than three when her mother died in childbirth. Mrs. Burt, far more than any of Lucy's nursemaids, had filled the role of mother. Buxom, homely Mrs. Burt meant stories at bedtime, scolds and hugs when Lucy fell over and grazed her knee and hot crumpets, toasted on a long silver fork in front of the nursery fire and served dripping with butter. Lucy felt a huge smile curve her mouth upward.

"Mrs. Burt!" She covered the twenty yards of platform that separated them at a run. "Mrs. Burt! You haven't changed a bit! How wonderful to see you."

The housekeeper dipped into a curtsy, then gathered her former charge into her arms. "And it's wonderful to see you, too, Miss Lucy."

Lucy emerged breathless from the hug. "Have you been waiting long?"

"Only a few minutes. The train arrived right on time. Wonderful how punctual these trains are, isn't it? Thousands of miles of traveling and you arrived almost to the minute. It hardly seems natural, does it? And you look a fair treat, Miss Lucy. The image of your mama, if I may say so."

"You certainly may, especially since papa always told me my mother was the most beautiful woman he'd ever met!"

Mrs. Burt smiled, her eyes moist. "We've been waiting for this day ever since the telegram arrived from the archdeacon saying you was alive. Welcome home, Miss Lucy. It's fair marvelous to have you back."

"It's good to be here. I don't even mind the rain!" Lucy smiled. "But where are my stepmother and stepsister? They are brave to sit in the carriage on such a cold day."

Mrs. Burt avoided Lucy's eye. "I hope you're not feeling chilled, Miss Lucy. 'Tis miserable, wet weather for June."

Lucy was too excited to notice the housekeeper's evasion. "And to think this is supposed to be midsummer! I had forgotten how damp England always feels. But we mustn't keep my family waiting, I am so much looking forward to seeing them again. Is Penelope as beautiful as ever?"

"Miss Penelope looks very pretty when she's dressed up," the housekeeper said without enthusiasm. "This way, Miss Lucy. I'll see the porter brings your luggage."

They had reached the main exit to the station before Mrs. Burt could bring herself to tell the truth. "There's the carriage, Miss Lucy. Unfortunately, Lady Margaret and Miss Penelope had luncheon engagements and they couldn't be here to meet you. I daresay they'll be back at the house by the time we get there."

The excitement in Lucy's face died. "Oh, yes. Of course. It was foolish of me not to realize they would be busy."

The housekeeper silently cursed all scheming, avaricious stepmothers and jealous, ill-mannered stepsisters. "Look, there's Tom waving at us, quite forgetting his dignity. You remember Tom, don't you, Miss Lucy? He's been promoted to head coachman. And Jack Fletcher is butler now. Very full of his own importance is Mr. Fletcher, but I remember him when he was no more than underfootman, and a cheeky young man at that. If you live long enough, Miss Lucy, you see it all, and that's a fact."

"Yes, I remember Fletcher, and Tom, of course." Lucy forced a smile, putting aside the hurt of her stepmother's absence. "I remember other things, too, like your boiled suet puddings served with hot golden syrup and vanilla custard. I used to dream about them when I was in Afghanistan and there was no foo—" She cut off the recollection quickly. "Anyway, I hope you haven't lost your expert touch while I've been away."

"That I haven't. You shall have one this very night," Mrs. Burt promised, silently resolving to do battle with Lady Margaret's French chef, whose concept of dessert definitely did not include such inferior British dishes as suet pudding.

Lucy was accustomed to the noise and chaotic activity of Indian cities, but she still found herself overwhelmed by the size and busyness of London. She would not have believed there were so many carriages in the world as she now saw jostling for position on the crowded streets. And the people! Even more than their numbers, she was impressed by their discipline, by the ordered rows in which they walked, and waited for the omnibuses, and crossed the roads. In India crowds of this size would surely have resulted in half a dozen children being trampled to death. Here it looked as if a child walking alone might be quite safe from harm.

Through the gray mist of rain, she peered out of the window at the huge shops, listening to Mrs. Burt give a running commentary on the merits and failings of the various establishments. Farmer and Roger's Great Cloak and Shawl Emporium on Regent Street seemed to extract the housekeeper's highest measure of praise, and Lucy resolved to pay a visit there soon.

A little thrill of feminine pleasure lightened Lucy's mood. Shopping for a new wardrobe in this city would undoubtedly be fun. And when she stopped to think about it, it was several years since she had had the chance to do anything just for fun.

"We've arrived, Miss Lucy. We're home."

Even as the housekeeper spoke, one of the grooms opened the door of the carriage and let down the steps. Lucy scarcely had time for more than a quick glance around the quiet, tree-lined square before a footman with an open umbrella rushed to escort her into the house.

She stepped into the entrance hall.

"Good afternoon, Miss Lucy." The butler, very much on his high horse, greeted her with his most regal bow, snapping his fingers to indicate that the footman should take off her damp cloak and relieve her of her gloves. "On behalf of all the staff, Miss Lucy, may I say how delighted we are to have you back in England."

"Thank you, Fletcher. It's good to be back."

"If there is any way I can be of service, Miss Lucy, you have only to ask."

Nine years had added at least seven inches to his waistline, and she smiled mischievously. "Well, I distinctly remember the last occasion on which you offered me your services, Fletcher. But I'm afraid that next time I get stuck halfway up the apple tree I won't be able to call on you to rescue me. Your *embonpoint* would prove disastrous to us both."

Fletcher stared straight ahead. "On the contrary, Miss, I could be of great assistance. Now that I am such an important personage, I could send one of my underlings to fetch a ladder."

Lucy saw the twinkle in his eye and laughed. "So you could! Ah, Fletcher, I have missed all my friends from the servants' hall these past few years."

"The feeling is reciprocated, Miss Lucy." The butler cleared his throat. "Lady Margaret and Miss Penelope are waiting for you in the drawing room, Miss Lucy."

She drew in a deep, fortifying breath. "Thank you, Fletcher. I shall join them now."

Lady Margaret, ravishing in a day gown of dove-gray challis, and Penelope, equally ravishing in pale blue, rose to their feet as soon as Lucy entered the drawing room. Penelope, looking sulky, stayed by the sofa, but Lady Margaret held out her hands and drifted across the room, every movement delicate and graceful. At forty-four, she was still a stunningly attractive woman.

"My dearest, dear Lucy!" Lady Margaret bent her cheek in the direction of her stepdaughter's face, trailing a waft of ladylike violet perfume.

"My dear, let me look at you!" She stepped back, her china-blue eyes gloating as she summed up Lucy's damp and travel-stained appearance and contrasted it with her own daughter's pink-and-white prettiness. Well satisfied with what she saw, Lady Margaret smiled as she turned back to face Lucy.

"Well, perhaps you are not quite in *bloom*, but you are here, and that is the main thing. We must not be greedy, must we, Penelope?"

"No, Mama," Penelope replied dutifully, although she hadn't the faintest idea what her mother was talking about. Understanding subtleties had never been one of Penelope's skills.

Lady Margaret stretched her smile a little wider. "Dearest Lucy, I'm sure it is miracle enough to have you home with us. We could not hope you would return looking as fresh and unspoiled as you did on the day you left for that ill-fated mission to Afghanistan. After such dreadful experiences as you have endured, it is only to be expected that you would appear so thin and wretched."

"I take heart, stepmama, from the fact that I am nowhere near as thin and wretched as I was a month ago."

Lady Margaret's smile hardened. "Such bravery! Such determined cheerfulness in the face of disaster! I am all admiration, and so is your sister, isn't that so, Penelope?"

"Yes, mama."

"And you, Lucy, you absolutely must not worry about *anything*. My dearest child, take my word for it, we will soon have you restored to perfect health."

"My health is excellent, thank you. The weeks on board ship—"

"Your courage is a lesson for us all, but I beg you, Lucy, do not lie awake at night worrying about your bizarre appearance. Don't fear that I shall force you to go about in society until you are completely recovered. I would not *dream* of asking you to expose yourself to public view at this point in time. Above all, you mustn't despair about your complexion, whatever other people may have said to you. Even though you are so dreadfully brown that one might mistake you for a nativ . . . That is to say, Dr. Burberry's Patented Cucumber Lotion has been known to improve *far* worse cases than your own."

"That is certainly an enormous relief," Lucy said, producing a smile as broad and insincere as Lady Margaret's own. She decided there was something almost reassuring in the fact that her stepmother had changed so little. Lady Margaret still possessed the same biting, poisonous tongue, except perhaps that the sugarcoating was now a little thicker. The difference was that Lucy no longer found her stepmother's barbs wounding. *My skin must be tougher as well as browner*, she thought with a ripple of silent laughter.

A tiny frown marred the otherwise unwrinkled perfection of Lady Margaret's brow as she observed her stepdaughter's amusement. She hastily wiped it away. Frowns were a luxury she couldn't afford at her age.

"Dear Lucy, you must be wondering why your sister and I did not manage to come to the station to meet you."

"Not at all, stepmama. Upon reflection, it was clear to me that you were bound to be too busy."

The answer was not precisely what Lady Margaret had been anticipating. The frown came back and this time could not be banished.

"Much has happened in your absence, Lucy. Your sister is on the verge of forming a most eligible connection."

"Penelope, I'm so pleased for you!" Lucy crossed the room and kissed her stepsister with genuine warmth. "Whoever the man is, he is lucky to have found somebody so pretty to be his wife."

"He says I am a perfect English rose," Penelope reported proudly, fluffing her curls.

"A gentleman of acute perceptions, I can see," Lucy teased gently.

Penelope merely looked blank, so Lucy tried again. "Goodness, it's hard to believe you were in the schoolroom when I last saw you, and now you are old enough to fall in love!"

"He is a baron," Penelope said, as if this explained everything. "His uncle is Under-Secretary of State for Eastern Affairs. He is going to be an important man in the government, and I shall be a Society Hostess." There was no doubt that the words were capitalized in her mind.

Lucy struggled to contain her amusement. "I hope I may be invited to one of your dinner parties. And who is this soon-to-be-important man in the government?"

"Lord Edward de Beaumont, Third Baron Ridgeholm." Lady Margaret breathed the words in an ecstatic sigh. The daughter of an earl herself, she had never quite forgiven a world which required her to marry first an elderly baronet and then Sir Peter Larkin—a mere knight whose title had been awarded as a result of his unaristocratic talent for making money. Her daughter's success in snaring the attentions of a peer of the realm had kept Lady Margaret in a state of tingling excitement for days.

"Is the engagement already announced?" Lucy asked.

"Not precisely, but we expect Lord Edward to make his declaration at any moment," Lady Margaret said. "Lord Edward has been overseas for the past six months on an assignment from the Foreign Office. He returned only three weeks ago and sent a message to us *immediately*. We understood the significance of his prompt attentions, of course—"

"It means he is interested in me," Penelope interjected, anxious for her sister to share this understanding.

Lady Margaret directed a withering glance toward her daughter. "As I explained to Penelope, we must honor Lord Edward's scruples in not seeking to pay his addresses before he went overseas. Naturally, it would not have been proper to seek a promise from her when he was going so far away."

"He went to India," Penelope remarked. "I would not have liked to go there with him, even though he is a baron. I *hate* India. It smells."

"Was it Lord Edward's first visit to that country?"

"Not at all. He was there shortly after your father died and was assigned to discover the truth about precisely what had caused the massacre of the British trade mission to Amir Sher Ali."

"He apparently had little success."

"That cannot be wondered at," Lady Margaret said. "Everybody knows there is no understanding the Afghanis. I'm sure Lord Edward did his best. He dealt with all the people who move in the *highest* circles of the Raj. He was invited to spend a weekend in Lahore with the Viceroy himself."

"Very impressive, but perhaps not the most useful way to occupy his time if he was trying to uncover what had occurred in central Afghanistan?"

Lady Margaret dismissed the complaint with an airy wave of her hand. "He was *most* attentive to me and to your poor sister, helping to arrange our passage back to England and taking care of a hundred annoying details for us. We saw him several times upon his return to England, but then he was sent abroad again and has only just returned. In view of our hopes for Penelope, we could not consider refusing when he invited us to join him and his uncle for luncheon today."

"Naturally not." If there was irony in Lucy's voice, neither her stepmother nor Penelope heard it. "But am I understanding you correctly? Lord Edward hasn't actually proposed marriage to my sister or even declared that his affections are engaged?"

"Mama is confident we'll be able to bring him up to scratch any day now," Penelope confided.

Lady Margaret winced. "Darling, I have explained before that we don't refer to Lord Edward's intentions in those vulgar terms. A lady does not anticipate a gentleman's declaration. She simply behaves toward him with her usual innocent charm."

Penelope didn't blink an eye at this outrageous denial of what they had all been doing for the past several minutes. "Yes, mama. I understand, mama."

"Do you love him?" Lucy asked quietly. "You are still only nineteen, Penelope. There is plenty of time for you to make a love match, you know."

Penelope stared at her stepsister in astonishment. "Of course I love him," she said. "He is a *baron*, with estates all over the country."

Lucy sighed. "Of course," she said. "I can see at once what a lovable person he must be. Is he handsome?"

For the first time, Penelope appeared uncertain. "He is . . . he is very distinguished looking," she said. "And he is fun to talk to. I can always understand what he's saying, not like some of the other gentlemen who prose on forever about international relations and parliamentary elections and all those horrid, boring things. He just talks about my clothes, and I tell him where I have been shopping. He knows everything about the latest fashions, and he always notices when I have a new fan or when I have changed my hairstyle."

In view of his employment at the Foreign Office, Lucy hoped that Baron Ridgeholm also knew at least a little about the Indian subcontinent, although from her sister's description she was not optimistic. Traveling with her father, Lucy had met far too many brainless young scions of noble families who had been sent off to India in the fond belief that they might cause less trouble there than they did in England. Often the damage they inflicted on the Raj was enormous, but their families never heard of it, and thus—as far as English society was concerned—the damage hadn't occurred.

If Rashid had met too many of this sort of Englishman, Lucy reflected, it was no wonder he held the British Raj in such low esteem. If only Rashid could have met my father, she thought. Then he would have formed a different opinion of British rule in India. Then he would have understood how many benefits we are bringing to his country.

"Lucy! Lucy! I swear you haven't heard a word I said in the past five minutes. What in the world were you thinking of?"

"My father," she replied, feeling color stain her cheeks at the partial truth.

"Ah, yes, your father." Anger flared briefly in Lady Margaret's eyes. "Perhaps it is time for us to speak of your late father."

"He did not suffer at the end, mama. The bullet struck him in the heart, and his death was almost immediate."

Lady Margaret breathed deeply. "I do not wish to discuss the manner of your father's end. I advised him repeatedly not to go to Afghanistan. He chose not to listen to me, and the consequences were inevitable."

Lucy walked over to the windows and clutched one of the heavy gold tassels tying back the crimson velvet drapes. She was not going to shed tears in the company of people who clearly cared so little about her father's murder. She struggled to keep the hurt and grief out of her voice. "If not his death, then what did you want to discuss in regard to papa?"

"When you go to your bedroom, Lucy, you will find several communications waiting for you from the family's solicitor. I cannot help but remark upon the fact that your late father disposed of his estate in a remarkably odd fashion."

"Oh?"

"Yes, a very odd fashion indeed. For reasons I shall never understand, your father chose to leave all his capital and all of his property to you."

"To me?" Lucy turned around. "But what about you and my sister?"

"He provided an . . . adequate . . . dowry for Penelope and a small, lifetime income for me. However, I am sure you can see that this is yet another occasion where your father's odd quirks and starts have caused a most awkward and unsatisfactory situation."

Lucy didn't doubt that it was extremely unsatisfactory for her stepmother, whose tastes ran from the merely costly to the superluxurious. It would be interesting to see what size lifetime income Lady Margaret chose to designate as "small."

Still, the terms of her father's will shocked Lucy greatly, since it had never occurred to her that she would inherit his entire estate. Perhaps he had not been as enraptured by his second wife as Lucy had always supposed. There seemed no other reason for the unusual provisions in his will.

Lady Margaret was looking at Lucy anxiously, a hectic flush staining her cheeks. No wonder her stepmother's earlier barbs had been sugarcoated, Lucy thought with a flicker of amusement. In effect, Lady Margaret and Penelope were both her pensioners, a reversal of roles she found almost comic.

"There is another matter," Lady Margaret announced, each

word obviously costing her pain. "Since you are not dead, the monies I have expended over the past two years were not actually mine to spend."

"In fact, they were mine?" Lucy suggested mildly.

Lady Margaret looked as if she might choke. "Yes."

Lucy could not dispell an ignoble desire to pay her stepmother back for innumerable moments of previous humiliation. She produced a smile, kinder and sweeter than one of Lady Margaret's own.

"Please, dear stepmama, I beg you not to give the matter another moment's thought. I would not *dream* of prosecuting you for spending *my* money. I shall speak to the solicitor first thing tomorrow morning and arrange matters so that the purchases you and Penelope have made during my absence are not deducted from your next quarter's allowance. Of course, I rely upon you in the future not to exceed the income papa alloted you."

Lady Margaret, for once in her life, was bereft of speech. She simply gobbled, somewhat in the fashion of a beached codfish. Lucy was ashamed to discover that she felt no guilt.

Penelope, however, was not a young lady to be oppressed by something as abstract as a tense atmosphere. "Will the money papa left me be enough to pay for my trousseau?" she demanded, anxious to get priorities taken care of.

Lucy sighed. "I'm sure it will," she said, "although I can't promise, since I haven't yet read the correspondence from the lawyers."

"You won't have time to read their letters before tea," Penelope said. "It's nearly three o'clock, which means you have only an hour to change. Lord Edward is coming especially to meet you."

"I really would like to meet him," Lucy said. "But please make my apologies for today. I need to deal with all the correspondence from the lawyers, and besides I have nothing suitable to wear. I ordered only the most basic wardrobe from the seamstress in Peshawar."

"Oh, you cannot meet Lord Edward in an Indian frock! They are always so hopelessly out of date, and he would notice at once."

"We could not risk that," Lucy agreed, straight-faced. "Especially since my complexion and I haven't yet had a chance to become acquainted with Dr. Burberry's wonder lotion."

Her stepsister nodded seriously. "You could come to dinner," she suggested. "Lord Edward won't be here. He has to attend some silly old reception at the Russian embassy, so we shall be dining alone."

"In that case, I shall look forward to joining you. Is it eight o'clock, as always?"

"Eight o'clock," Lady Margaret agreed faintly. "We shall be dining strictly *en famille* for the next few days."

"You may start inviting guests again quite soon, stepmama," Lucy remarked kindly. "I plan to go shopping tomorrow, and I daresay by the time I have bought some new clothes, you will be able to present me almost anywhere without disgracing yourself. Fortunately, two years as Hashim Kahn's slave didn't destroy my memory of which fork I must use or how to drink soup. It's only my memory of how it feels to be loved and wanted that has been destroyed."

She left the room before either Lady Margaret or Penelope could summon up a reply.

Lucy found the first few days of her return to London crammed full of visits from lawyers, estate managers and bankers, all anxious to convey to her the news that she was a very wealthy woman. A wealthy woman, moreover, who could dispose of her riches in virtually any manner she chose, unhampered by the constraints of a male guardian.

To the relief of her various advisers, this extraordinary state of affairs did not seem to unhinge her. Aside from fulfilling several charitable bequests outlined in her father's will but not yet funded by Lady Margaret, Lucy made only minor changes in the administration of her estates. These, her advisers noted, were all designed to enhance efficiency. Contrary to their expectations, she didn't embark upon an orgy of purchasing, nor did she discover a need to redecorate her two houses, something Lady Margaret had insisted upon doing, despite the fact that she had scarcely set foot in Hallerton since her return from India.

Mr. Dunstead, the senior solicitor, was so impressed by Lucy's calm good sense that he went so far as to comment to his partner—out of hearing of the juniors, naturally—that Miss Larkin was a sensible woman and a chip off the old block, if ever he'd seen one.

Mr. Dunstead's good opinion might have suffered a slight reversal if he could have seen Lucy closeted with Madame Renier, one of London's most fashionable dressmakers. Taking to Madame's *salon* a trunk full of brightly colored Indian silks and

exquisitely embroidered muslins, Lucy pored over pattern books
and spent hours discussing the merit of various trims. Never a
person who had spent much time worrying about her appearance,
Lucy discovered that two years of total deprivation in Afghanistan
had left her with a hunger for soft, lacy undergarments and
flattering, fashionable gowns.

Madame Renier, recognizing in Lucy somebody who could
elevate still further the reputation of her *salon*, poured heart and
soul into the creation of an elegant wardrobe for her new client.

"You are not pretty," she told Lucy seriously. "You are not the
typical *ingenue*. It is good that you are older, and so not obliged
to wear white. In these Eastern silks, with my cut and style, you
will not be pretty, you will be beautiful. Your eyes and your body,
they are of great allure. The men will notice."

Madame Renier was tucking pins into a bodice at the time she
made this pronouncement. Lucy gazed down doubtfully, wishing
she could believe the dressmaker. "I'm still very thin, Madame."

"In the waist, yes, and in the stomach. That is good." Madame
Renier nipped another quarter inch off the bodice to emphasize her
point. "But in other places, like the bosom and the hips, you have
curves, most decidedly curves. In the bosom, I must always allow
extra material, or pouf! You would split my gown."

Lucy hoped she was being offered a compliment.

It was the height of the season, so Lady Margaret and Penelope
were frequently absent from the house. Most of their entertaining
seemed to take place in the afternoon, at ladies' tea parties, none
of which Lucy found time to attend. At night, however, the three
ladies invariably dined together, and without company. After a
week of meals where the conversation centered almost exclusively
on Lord Edward's pronouncements concerning Penelope's various
gowns and Lady Margaret's calculations of how soon he might be
induced to propose, Lucy decided that it was past time for her to
meet the famous baron.

"When can we expect to see Lord Edward at dinner?" she
asked, during a brief pause in Penelope's rhapsodies over what the
baron had said about the bead trim on her new pelisse. "I am so
much looking forward to meeting such a knowledgeable gentleman."

Her stepmother and Penelope exchanged conspiratorial glances.
"I'm delighted that you happened to bring up this subject," Lady
Margaret said, just as if she and her daughter hadn't been

discussing the baron nonstop throughout the meal. "Penelope and I both agree that you should become acquainted with her future betrothed, and we believe we have the perfect occasion in mind. We think you should meet Lord Edward at a ball."

"Do you have any particular ball in mind?"

"Ours," Penelope said promptly.

"Ours?"

Lady Margaret rushed to explain. "The fact of the matter is, Lucy dearest, that before we heard you were still alive, Penelope and I had already spent a great deal of time planning a ball to be given here in the Grand Ballroom of our hou—that is to say, in the ballroom of your house. It has never been used since your father bought the place, and it's really a shocking waste to have all that gilt and crystal waiting upstairs unseen and unused."

"I'm sure papa would want us to have the ball," Penelope explained. "Remember how he was always telling us 'Waste not, want not'? Just think how wasteful we are being with his ballroom."

"I'm not absolutely sure that was the sort of wastage he had in mind," Lucy murmured. Seeing her stepsister's crestfallen face, she relented. "Did you get as far as setting a date for this ball?"

"Oh, yes! We sent out invitations as soon as we knew Lord Edward was back in England. Mama said even you could certainly not be so mean-spirited as to refuse to pay the bills for a function that was so important to my future."

Lady Margaret winced. Lucy choked back a little laugh. "I'm delighted to know you have such faith in my basic good nature," she said. "May I know when I am hosting this ball so that I can take care of one or two trivial details, such as ordering a ballgown for myself?"

"A week on Saturday," Lady Margaret confessed in a rush. "My dear, I'm sure you will enjoy the occasion and find Lord Edward a most delightful prospective brother-in-law."

Lucy felt, of all things, an odd little tremor of excitement. She was, she admitted to herself, somewhat curious about this baron who so completely dominated the conversations of the Larkin household.

She looked at Penelope, who was holding her breath, and found herself smiling with shared anticipation. "A ball sounds wonderful," she said. "How many arrangements do we have left to make?"

CHAPTER NINE

The rain, which had fallen in a light drizzle every day since Lucy's return to England, finally stopped sometime during Friday night. On Saturday morning, the day of the ball, the Larkin household awoke to a brilliant blue sky, a refreshing breeze and a warm burst of golden sunshine.

In the garden at the center of the square, trees shook off raindrops and unfurled their leaves in a rich green canopy. Geraniums and delphiniums, no longer veiled by a gray mist of moisture, glowed scarlet and purple against their beds of dark earth and lush grass. Lucy, staring entranced from her bedroom window, remembered at last how beautiful her native land could be.

As far as Lady Margaret and Penelope were concerned, the glorious weather added a final promise of success to an occasion they were already convinced would be the highlight of the season. So happy were they as florists and caterers and vintners and musicians and temporary cleaners trooped in and out of the house, that they were almost friendly in their dealings with Lucy. After taking tea together in the drawing room, the three ladies parted on surprisingly amicable terms to dress themselves for the preball dinner.

Lucy, in fact, was a great deal more nervous about the ball than either her stepmother or stepsister could have guessed from her calm demeanor. London might be a more sophisticated city than the border town of Peshawar, but Lucy didn't doubt that she would be the object of much behind-the-hands gossip. Her experience with the ladies of Peshawar had forewarned her that from now on she would always be regarded as exotic, but soiled, merchandise.

There was one advantage, at least, to the fact that her reputation was irreversibly sullied: She had no obligation to dress herself in virginal white. Set free to choose the most dazzling of her Indian fabrics, Lucy had indulged herself with a formal gown of peacock green silk, tantalizingly draped around the bustle with seafoam-colored gauze draperies.

Madame Renier, who was shrewd as well as skilled, judged her client well. She avoided the mistake of dipping the neckline obviously low, and Lucy, relieved that her shoulders were not completely naked or her bosom excessively exposed, neglected to notice that the gown contained little of the whalebone stiffening and padding that normally disguised the true shape of the wearer. Peering into the looking glass merely to frown over her tanned complexion, she never noticed that the cut and trim of the bodice not only flattered her tiny waistline but also emphasized the generous curve of her breast. Delighted with the soft rustle of her skirts, she twirled around Madame Renier's salon without the faintest clue that she looked like an exotic bird of paradise among a cluster of sparrows.

Lucy's dresser, an experienced older woman hired two days before the ball, had a far better idea of the sensation her mistress was going to cause in her peacock silk gown. Rose, during a period of her life glossed over in her references, had worked on the stage, and she could recognize a sensually provocative gown when she saw one. She wondered which gentleman Miss Larkin was setting out to snare, and—since Miss Larkin seemed an amazingly agreeable lady—hoped sincerely that the lure would work. Rose wouldn't mind settling down and staying with Miss Larkin when she was married, she wouldn't mind at all.

"You look magnificent, Miss," she murmured, fixing a jeweled aigrette into Lucy's hair. Long emerald and diamond earrings already quivered against Lucy's cheeks, scintillating with white and green fire every time she moved. "What necklace are you going to wear tonight, Miss?"

Lucy picked up a diamond pendant that had been her mother's, then set it down again on its velvet bed. Her gaze turned to the leather pouch that lay, as always, on the dressing table. Before her conscious mind could reject the action, her fingers reached out and pulled the little gold camel from its home. Its diamond eyes winked at her mockingly, as if it had known all along that tonight it would come to the ball.

"I'll wear this instead of a necklace," she told the dresser. "Could you pin it in the center of my dress, here?"

Very clever, Rose thought approvingly, fastening the broach with a gold pin. For a bang-up lady, Miss Larkin had a real sense of how to make the most of herself. With her neck left bare, the earrings would draw attention to the perfect line of her jaw, and the camel would draw attention to the enticing swell of her silk-concealed breasts. Rose couldn't imagine how a lady like Miss Larkin had learned all these tricks for catching a man's attention, but learn them she obviously had. Miss Larkin would have all the men panting for her by the end of the evening, or Rose didn't know as much about men as she thought.

The dresser fastened the final button on Lucy's obligatory kid gloves, then handed over her fan. "Here you are, Miss. I'm sure you'll be the belle of the ball."

Lucy laughed with wistful amusement. "Thank you, Rose, but you can't possibly have seen my sister!"

Rose, who had in fact seen far more of Miss Penelope Deveraux than she cared to, wisely kept silent.

Lady Margaret and Penelope were already waiting in the drawing room when Lucy arrived downstairs. Penelope wore a white tulle gown, scattered with seed pearls and looped with satin rosebuds. Her blond ringlets were crowned with a coronet of pink roses—an artless style that had taken her dresser more than two hours to produce—and her normally sulky expression had been replaced by a smile of happy anticipation.

"Oh, there you are, Lucy! Do you like my dress?" She held out the skirts as she executed an expert waltz-twirl. "Mama says I look like every man's dream of innocence."

"You look wonderful," Lucy said, banishing an unworthy twinge of envy. "You, too, Stepmama. That shade of lilac is most becoming."

Lady Margaret condescended to smile. Secure in the knowledge that she and Penelope represented all that was most desirable in English womanhood, she felt inclined to be generous.

"And you look quite nice, too, Lucy. Your new gown is a

most—er—interesting color." A happy thought struck her.
"Indeed, you will show off Penelope to excellent advantage as we
greet our guests. Perhaps it is as well that you didn't attempt to
gloss over realities by wearing white."

"Yes, that was my own opinion entirely," Lucy said, realizing
that for once Lady Margaret had no intention of being rude. She
was merely expressing her honest opinion.

"What is that broach you are wearing?" Penelope asked. "Do
you see, Mama? It's a camel, isn't it, Lucy?" She shuddered.
"Ugh, I hate camels."

"In that, sister dear, we are in total agreement."

"Then why do you wear the broach?"

*Because it makes me feel that perhaps Rashid has not totally
forgotten me. Because, as he plans his next foray into Afghanistan, I wonder if he will think of those nights we spent in the
mountains . . . and the night when he took me into his arms and
kissed me and made me understand what it means to be a woman.*

Lady Margaret was busy practicing graceful ways of unfurling
her ostrich feather fan. She spoke absently. "Yes, Lucy, why did
you choose to wear something so singular?"

"It is a little hard to explain. The . . . person who gave me
the broach knew how much I loathed the beasts, and it became
something of a joke between us. Do you see how the camel's eyes
twinkle with a mischievous light?"

"They are diamonds," Penelope said, bewildered. "Of course
they twinkle. That is what diamonds do."

Fortunately, Lucy was spared the need to make any further
explanation by the arrival of their first guests for the preball
dinner.

"Sir Robert and Lady Howard," the butler intoned. "The
Honorable Mr. Cedric Ffoulkes. The honorable Miss Amelia
Ffoulkes."

The other guests were all assembled when Fletcher finally
announced the arrival of the Under-Secretary for Eastern Affairs,
Lord Triss, and his nephew, Lord Edward de Beaumont. Lucy's
head jerked up sharply, curious to see the man who had caused
such flutterings of hope and speculation within her family circle.

A tall, lean, aristocratically featured man stood in the doorway,
immaculate in formal evening attire of white tie and tails.
Although he was doing nothing more remarkable than crossing the
room to greet his hostesses, he seemed to command attention by
the sheer power of his physical presence.

Involuntarily, Lucy's hand reached up to clutch the camel nestled at her breast. For a moment, she swayed on her feet as the room spun around her in a dizzying whirl. Gripping the back of a nearby chair for support, she willed herself to remain upright. She looked again at Lord Edward de Beaumont.

The baron was bowing low over Lady Margaret's hand. "Dear lady, what a treat this is for us all to be here in your home on such a jolly evening. You even procured us the perfect sunset to admire as we stepped out of our carriages at your front door."

Lady Margaret tittered. "The sunset required *all* our powers of organization, my lord. Penelope and I are so pleased you were able to accept our invitation."

"Ah, yes, Miss Penelope." Lord Edward screwed a monocle into his left eye and took Penelope's hand. "How charming you look, to be sure, Miss Penelope. An English rose, encircled by rosebuds. Such a jolly sight!"

Lucy didn't bother to listen to any more of Lord Edward's tiresome drivel. Her breathing slowed, her heart ceased pounding and the world slowly righted itself onto a normal axis. Dear God, but she was becoming obsessed! Her memories of Rashid were beginning to dominate her powers of rational observation. For a split second—for one wild, insane instant—she had actually thought Lord Edward de Beaumont was Rashid!

The baron and Penelope were still engaged in conversation, so Lady Margaret introduced Lucy to Lord Triss.

The Under-Secretary, a middle-aged man of average height and keen eye, shook her hand with evident enthusiasm.

"I'm delighted to make your acquaintance at last, Miss Larkin. You are a young lady of outstanding courage, and it is a privilege to meet you. I knew your father, you know, and he was a fine man. Excellent head for business and an appreciation of the art of diplomacy. He is sorely missed by his colleagues and by his country."

"Thank you, my lord. I miss him, too. He was my friend as well as my father."

Lord Triss gave her hand a final, brisk shake. "Sometime very soon we must have a long talk about your experiences in the East. We have too few people in our government who know anything about Afghanistan, and I warn them that it is a country which will likely cause us more trouble than we care to contemplate."

For some reason, Lucy was having a hard time ignoring the low, deep voice of Baron Ridgeholm and the squeals of girlish laughter coming from her sister. With an effort, she focused her attention on Lord Triss.

"I should be happy to share with you any insights that I have, my lord. I agree with you completely about the potential danger our country faces in Afghanistan. As long as the Russian emperor persists in sending troops to annex territory in Central Asia, I fear that the borderlands of India can enjoy no peace."

Lady Margaret's silvery laugh barely concealed the underlying thread of her displeasure. "Now, now, Lucinda, you must not tease Lord Triss with your advice on how to run the government of India. Despite your long exile from civilization, you must know we cannot have political discussions at one of my parties."

"The fault was entirely mine," Lord Triss said. "I apologize, Lady Margaret, for introducing unseemly topics into your drawing room. Miss Larkin, I shall look forward to speaking with you at a later date, but, in the meantime, may I introduce my nephew, Lord Edward de Beaumont?"

Lucy sank into the requisite curtsy, experiencing a ridiculous sense of disappointment when she lifted her gaze and found herself staring straight into the distorted, bulging left eye of the baron. She had never before had any feeling at all about gentlemen who used monocles. Now she discovered that she found them absurd, even more ridiculous than the old-fashioned quizzing glasses of her father's generation.

"I understand we have each returned recently from the same country," Lord Edward remarked. "India. Tedious, hot sort of place, isn't it? Damned flies are enough to drive a fellow demented."

Lucy was determined to be polite. "Not all of India is hot, my lord. In the north, and in the hill country, the climate can be quite pleasant."

Lord Edward lowered his voice confidentially. "Tell you the truth, Miss Larkin. It isn't only the climate that tries a fellow, it's dealing with the damned natives. From the highest to the lowest, they're all the same. You can't trust the traders in the bazaar, and you can't trust those wretched maharajahs. Sign a treaty with an Indian maharajah, and by jove he'll break the terms before the ink on the paper is dry."

"Maybe if we didn't constantly force the maharajahs to sign treaties they would prefer not to sign, we would find their honor longer lasting," Lucy snapped.

"Oh, I say, that's jolly good." Lord Edward removed his

monocle and polished it busily. "But misguided. Natives never want to sign *any* treaties, Miss Larkin, that's the trouble. There's no pleasing them, you know. They're not in favor of progress like we more enlightened people are. Why I met one old fellow who told me that what his village needed wasn't a telegraph office but more buffaloes!"

Lucy had a guilty suspicion that before she met Rashid she, too, might have thought telegraphs more important than buffaloes. She fixed her mouth into a polite smile, grateful for once to retreat into feminine inanity.

"I'm sure you would know better than I how to deal with the Indian natives, Lord Edward. Naturally, I have no experience in negotiating with maharajahs."

"Naturally not." The baron gave a short bray of laughter. "The world would be a sorry place if we had the ladies negotiating our treaties for us, wouldn't it, Miss Larkin?"

"Since I cannot imagine the men ever allowing us such a privilege, Lord Edward, I have not speculated on the outcome."

"Indeed, speculation can sometimes lead to dangerous conclusions, can it not, Miss Larkin?" The inanity of the baron's smile belied the sudden seriousness of his tone. Apparently losing interest in her views of treaty negotiation, he adjusted his monocle and peered intently at her bosom.

"I say, that's a most interesting broach you're wearing, Miss Larkin, if I may make so bold. Saw a lot of camels in India, of course, but never could get accustomed to them, myself. Preferred the elephants. Quite comfortable to ride an elephant once you get used to the sway. Unusual piece, that broach."

"It was a gift from an Indian friend," Lucy said stiffly, hating the reminder of Rashid in the presence of this oaf, who seemed to exemplify precisely the type of Englishman Rashid had so often mocked.

"Quirky creatures, those natives. They make carvings of the oddest things. Inside some of their temples—"

Lord Edward obviously recalled just in time that the statuary inside Indian temples was rarely a fit subject for an English lady's ears. He cleared his throat. "Ahem, I should say, the workmanship on your camel isn't bad at all, despite the odd choice of subject."

He reached out and very delicately lifted the camel for closer inspection. At no point did his finger touch Lucy's dress, let alone brush against the bare skin above the lace-bordered neckline. For some inexplicable reason, however, she found herself holding her breath, and when Lord Edward let the broach fall back against her dress, she was literally shaking.

"A jolly little piece, isn't it?" he said, turning to greet the hovering Penelope with a broad, if vacuous, smile. "It's been delightful chatting with you, Miss Larkin. We must talk some more about India very soon."

Not if she had any choice in the matter, Lucy thought, sighing with relief as she heard the butler announce that dinner was served. Protocol decreed that she should be escorted to the table by the Bishop of Cirencester, who was deaf as a post and much given to falling asleep between courses. At this precise moment, Lucy considered him the perfect companion.

Dinner did not lighten her mood. True to form, the bishop dozed contentedly between bites of lemon sole and saddle of lamb. Her companion on the left, Sir Robert Howard, was a recent conquest of Lady Margaret's, and he spent most of the meal telling Lucy how fortunate she was to have such a wonderful stepmother. Lucy was required only to murmur agreement, which left her far too much time to listen to conversations being held across the table.

In these conversations, Lord Edward was the dominating figure. On his way home from India, he had served as the official British observer at the signing of a treaty between Turkey and Russia. Having spent three whole days in the company of Turkish and Russian diplomats, he now considered himself an expert on the subject of Central Asia. Despite Lady Margaret's edict against political discussion, he seemed determined to expound his conclusions for the benefit of the dinner table at large. Lucy soon realized that his opinions were compounded chiefly of ignorance liberally interspersed with the worst sort of imperialist dogma.

Lucy glanced at Lord Triss after one of the baron's more outrageous comments and, to her regret, detected nothing in the Under-Secretary's gaze save wry humor. She had hoped better of Lord Triss, but such deliberate blindness was, she supposed, the inevitable consequence of nepotism. The unwelcome thought struck her that in some ways the British were no better than their Indian counterparts. People in positions of power in both countries surrounded themselves with cronies and relatives. The Indians were simply more honest about their corruption.

"The sorbet is not to your taste, Miss Larkin? If not, I can recommend the raspberries."

The bishop had woken up just in time to notice her grimace of distaste. "Oh, no, thank you. The sorbet is delicious."

The bishop's gaze was shrewd. "Take heart, Miss Larkin. Not everybody in government circles believes that we British have a divine mission to spread our civilization and our religion to the farthest corners of the earth."

She stared at the bishop in surprise. "You weren't asleep?" she asked, then wished she could have bitten off her tongue. "I'm sorry, my lord. Two years in Afghanistan have taken their toll upon my manners."

"But not, I trust, upon your common sense. You would be well advised to remember that the Foreign Office rarely sends fools upon its errands. There is no need, since they contain within their ranks an abundance of intelligent men."

"But Lord Edward is a consummate fo—that is to say . . ."

The bishop's eyes twinkled. "Are you sure, my dear, that he is anything of the sort? Look closely before you form your final judgment."

Lucy continued her study of the baron with renewed interest after this exchange. Regretfully, she came to the conclusion that the bishop was mistaken. Even if the Foreign Office rarely sent fools upon its missions, Lord Edward de Beaumont must be the exception who proved the rule. Well-meaning he might be, but the third Baron Ridgeholm was indubitably a fool.

By the end of the meal, Penelope, who had barely concealed her yawns during her beloved's discussion of British imperialism, was bubbling and smiling again as Lord Edward devoted his attention exclusively to her. Having delivered himself of fifteen minutes of nonsense about Asia, Lord Edward seemed all set to spend the rest of the evening discussing Penelope's clothes.

They will make ideal marriage partners, Lucy decided. *Good-looking but with scarcely a brain to share between them. Heaven help their children!*

Lucy had no idea why the thought of Penelope's and Lord Edward's children depressed her so profoundly, unless it was because she could detect not the smallest sign that either potential parent was actually in love with the other. She gave herself a mental shake. How ridiculous it was to be worrying about whether or not Penelope and the baron loved each other! Hadn't she always believed that the best marriages were based not on fleeting physical attraction, but on companionship and mutual interests?

Hadn't she told Rashid precisely that during one of their heated arguments?

Her hand crept up to the neckline of her gown, and her fingers closed around Rashid's camel. The gold felt warm, almost vibrant, from contact with her body. Unaccountably, her gaze flew to Lord Edward at the other side of the table. His head was in profile, and he seemed fully engaged in talking with her sister, but Lucy could not shake the odd impression that he had, in fact, been looking at her. Heat—which must have been caused by too much champagne—flamed in her cheeks as Lord Edward leaned closer to Penelope, bending his head to hear some murmured confidence.

She would have to swear off champagne for the rest of the night, Lucy decided. The unaccustomed alcohol was giving her a most irrational desire to weep.

The guests gathered for Lady Margaret's ball agreed it was destined for success even before the musicians struck up the notes of the first waltz. Lady Margaret, a smiling lilac vision, floated onto the dance floor escorted by Lord Triss, to signal the start of the dancing. Joined almost immediately by Penelope and Lord Edward de Beaumont, the room was soon a glittering kaleidoscope of graceful, twirling couples.

Lucy was relieved to discover that she did not lack for partners, and for a few dances she reveled in the harmless, almost forgotten pleasures of light flirtation, blazing chandeliers and lilting, well-played music. The covert glances and snide comments that had followed her everywhere in Peshawar did not seem to be a problem here in cosmopolitan London.

It was Cedric Ffoulkes who enlightened her to reality. A tall man of about thirty, with thinning blond hair and a loose lower lip, Lucy knew him only as the brother of one of Penelope's friends. All too soon, she was forced to view him in a less pleasant light.

They had scarcely taken a single turn around the ballroom when Ffoulkes's hand crept upward from her waist, splaying out against her spine and propelling her so close that the requisite twelve inches between her body and his was precipitously narrowed.

"Mr. Ffoulkes, you are crushing the front of my gown," Lucy said, smiling to soften the impact of her words. She did not want to hurt the man's feelings simply because he was a clumsy dancer.

Ffoulkes's hold became tighter and more overtly lecherous. "No need to pretend with me, m'dear, I'm a man of the world.

Your stepmother explained how you managed to stay alive out there in Afghanistan. Tonight's entertainment must seem pretty tame in comparison to what you've been accustomed to over the past few years."

"If you consider it entertaining to tend a vegetable garden with your bare hands, to wash clothes in an ice-cold mountain stream and weave goat hair into carpets, Mr. Ffoulkes, then indeed the last two years of my life have been one long round of reckless gaiety. I myself never managed to find much that was amusing in such occupations."

Cedric Ffoulkes was no longer smiling. "Cut line, Lucinda. If the tribesmen had wanted gardeners, they would have killed you and saved the menfolk in your father's contingent. We all know how those savages love to get their hands on a white woman. Tell me, m'dear, were they very—rough?"

Lucy was shaking so hard she was afraid her knees would not support her much longer, but she refused to give Ffoulkes the satisfaction of seeing her distress.

"I do not recall that I gave you permission to use my Christian name, Mr. Ffoulkes. I would be grateful if you would escort me back to my stepmother. Let me assure you that you labor under several misapprehensions."

Ffoulkes totally ignored her request to leave the dance floor. "No need to get on your high horse, m'dear. Nobody's blaming you for seeking reentry into society. After all, it wasn't your fault you were captured."

"You're too generous, Mr. Ffoulkes."

He preened. "It's a pleasure to be generous to a woman like you, Lucinda. You just need to understand that if you reenter society, it will be on our terms. You're a beautiful woman, and the gown you're wearing shows you know how to display yourself to advantage. You will not find yourself short of offers, and I want to get mine in first. I will show you the best of good times, m'dear, inside the bedroom and out."

Some miracle of self-preservation prevented Lucy from slapping his face. Even at the height of her anger and despair, she realized that if she precipitated a scandal on the dance floor, she was likely to emerge the loser. Feeling that she danced in the middle of a nightmare, she maintained her poise only by the exertion of dogged, superhuman will. Ffoulkes's hold on her was so strong that without screaming or otherwise causing a terrible scene she had no way of loosening herself from his grasp.

Refusing to respond to any of his conversational gambits, she counted out every second of the remaining bars of music, then tore herself from his arms and marched off the floor without once looking to see if he followed.

Lady Margaret had temporarily disappeared, so Lucy had no choice other than to join her sister, who was talking animatedly to Lord Edward.

"Oh, Lucy, isn't it a lovely ball?" Penelope asked, her cheeks flushed, her smile pretty.

"Delightful."

"Lemonade, Miss Larkin?" the baron asked politely.

She could barely control her trembling sufficiently to speak, much less hold a glass. "Thank you, but not at the moment."

"I think you would find the taste refreshing, Miss Larkin. Pray, allow me."

The ice cold glass was placed firmly in her hand, and her fingers wrapped around it. She took a sip simply because it was easier than arguing and found, to her surprise, that the sharp tang of the lemons did serve to calm her somewhat. She saw Ffoulkes out of the corner of her eye and shuddered, remembering the hot, pawing grip of his hand against her back. She jumped when she realized that Lord Edward had moved much closer to her and was talking again.

"It is very warm in here with so many candles blazing, isn't it, Miss Larkin?"

"Very warm, indeed, my lord."

"When you consider the temperatures we both endured in India, it is hard to believe that we can find an English ballroom hot, isn't it?"

Dear heaven, didn't the man ever talk about anything save clothes and the weather? Lucy sighed, forcing herself to respond politely.

"Yes, it's surprising, but somehow ballrooms always seem to become overly warm."

"That being the case, Miss Larkin, would you care to accompany me out onto the balcony for a breath of fresh air? It's a jolly little balcony, you know."

The musicians were already playing the opening bars of a gavotte, and Penelope was being escorted onto the dance floor by a handsome young sprig whose name Lucy couldn't remember. The prospect of breathing some cool night air was suddenly more than appealing.

"Thank you," she said, with genuine gratitude. "Some fresh air would be welcome."

The baron gestured to indicate that she should precede him into the balmy night. Once outside, he leaned against a stone support pillar and stared down at the moonlit garden.

"When the rain sets in as it has over the past few days, I wonder why everybody in England does not develop rust spots. Then we have a perfect day like today, and I realize all the rain is worth it for the sake of the green it leaves behind."

"It is the grass and trees that are so magnificent," Lucy agreed, gradually allowing herself to relax in the baron's undemanding presence. "I'm sure there are many places in the world where flowers bloom in more color and variety, but our green hills and wooded valleys must be unique."

"Are you pleased to be back in England, Miss Larkin?"

"Well, yes, I had thought so." She sounded so hesitant, even to herself, that she added briskly, "Of course, I am delighted to be home."

Lord Edward did not seem to hear the subtle undertones of doubt in her reply. Turning back from his inspection of the garden, he smiled at her easily.

"Have you had a chance to explore any of the London shops as yet, Miss Larkin? They are such jolly places. I'm sure it's a pleasure for all of us who have spent time in primitive countries like India to discover that within a half-mile walk we may purchase new boots, select the style of a new overcoat and admire the latest fashion in Parisian hats."

To her amazement, Lucy found herself responding to his smile. "I have explored *dozens* of London's shops, my lord. The most delightful thing is that I still have so many more left to visit!"

"If I may say so, Miss Larkin, your purchases have been made to delightful effect. Your gown is exquisite."

Lucy put down her empty lemonade glass, her smile fading as she remembered Cedric Ffoulkes's insulting comments about her dress. Her voice stifled, she admitted, "I fear that the—um—cut and the vivid color may create a . . . a wrong impression."

Lord Edward examined her gravely. "Not to any man of discernment, Miss Larkin. The cut merely reveals the skill of an expert dressmaker. As for the color, it is the perfect complement for the auburn highlights in your hair and the creamy color of your skin. The impression is altogether delightful, I do assure you."

Lucy felt her lacerated pride begin to heal itself under the baron's soothing words. No wonder Penelope liked to listen to him talk about clothes, she thought with wry amusement. She looked up, trying not to fix her gaze on the horn-rimmed monocle and its annoying distortion of Lord Edward's eye. "Thank you," she said. "I am honored to have pleased such a connoisseur of feminine fashions."

"Jolly good show." Lord Edward beamed. "If you are cooler, Miss Larkin, perhaps we might take a toddle around the dance floor? I believe the musicians are getting ready to play another waltz."

Lord Edward might have the vocabulary of a schoolboy and the political understanding of a gnat, Lucy reflected, but his manners were in some ways superb. Somehow, he had sensed she was distressed and had set out to restore her equilibrium with innocuous chatter and small compliments. No wonder Lady Margaret and Penelope were charmed! Her sense of perspective returning, Lucy mentally dismissed Cedric Ffoulkes as an oaf and a scoundrel. Twenty minutes earlier, she would have sworn that the night could hold no further pleasure for her. The dance floor had loomed as a torturous spectre of further humiliation. Now it reverted to nothing more than a polished surface on which two people might partner each other with modest enjoyment.

"I would love to dance," she said, placing her gloved fingertips lightly upon the baron's outstretched arm.

"Jolly good," he replied. "Shall we go in?"

Lucy soon discovered another reason why her sister Penelope so much enjoyed Lord Edward's company: He was, quite simply, the best dancer she had ever partnered. Unlike Ffoulkes, his hand seemed barely to touch her spine, and yet he managed to convey every nuance of his intentions. Asking occasional courteous questions about her journey home and the people she had encountered on board ship, the baron twirled her around the ballroom in an odd, half-dazed state that she could not properly identify. She supposed that it must be the reaction to her horrible experience with Cedric Ffoulkes that caused her to focus so obsessively upon Lord Edward's dark, aristocratic features. It must be that she feared to glimpse Ffoulkes as she whirled around the floor.

Lord Edward did not look in the least like a typical Englishman. More like an Arab or even a man from farther East—

Lucy broke off her wild thoughts. Lord Edward's skin was slightly tanned, as might be expected with somebody who had just returned from six months in India. He was, of course, nowhere near as dark as Rashid, nor did his hair have the same glistening sheen.

A ripple of unease coursed down Lucy's spine as she realized how consistently her thoughts returned to the same bizarre fantasy. Lord Edward must have felt the slight tremble of her body. He looked down at her, and she stumbled, missing the beat of the dance.

Lord Edward eased her back into the simple rhythm. "Are you cold, Miss Larkin? I trust you didn't take a chill while we stood talking out on the verandah."

"No, I'm not cold." And indeed she was not. The surface of her skin had begun to burn with little prickles of heat.

The baron guided her into a final, dazzling spin, and for a split second she felt his gloved hand against the naked skin of her back. She sank into a curtsy. He bowed, as protocol decreed, over her hand. "Jolly good show, Miss Larkin. That was a splendid dance, what?"

"Yes, splendid. Thank you."

When Lucy walked off the dance floor she was shaking again, but this time it wasn't with rage, or even with fright. It was with desire.

Lucy spent the rest of the night wondering who was the fool. Lord Edward de Beaumont, Third Baron Ridgeholm, about to become engaged to Penelope Deveraux. Or Lucinda Larkin, spinster, obsessed by the memory of a vanished Punjabi trader.

CHAPTER TEN

During her two years in Kuwar Valley, Lucy had learned—at least theoretically—many things that were kept hidden from most young, unmarried English ladies. Quite early in her captivity, she realized that men didn't need to feel tender emotions in order to experience physical desire. As time went on, she began to understand that women, too, could experience passionate physical responses to men they didn't like. Since her own relationships in the village never reached the point of sexual completion, she had filed the information in a distant compartment of her brain and more or less forgotten about it.

The half-forgotten knowledge returned to ease her troubled thoughts during the sleepless hours following the ball. Lucy was not adept at self-deception, and she had long since accepted the fact that Rashid attracted her. For some reason, the Punjabi trader aroused emotions and passions within her that no other man had ever evoked. To most English people, such an attraction would seem repellent, even perverted. But her years as a captive had made Lucy realize that skin color and place of birth were inadequate bases on which to form judgment of a person's character.

She supposed it was inevitable that Lord Edward should provoke some of the same passionate feelings as Rashid, given that her mind kept making a bizarre connection between the two men. Lucy gradually convinced herself that the desire she felt for Lord Edward was not caused by the waltz they danced together; it was a straightforward result of transposed feelings that she cherished for Rashid. Besides, as she had learned in Kuwar, it wasn't necessary for a woman to like or admire a man in order to feel desire for him.

Lucy shaped her pillow into a backrest, finally abandoning the idea of sleep. She tried to analyze the similarities between Rashid's appearance and Lord Edward's. They were both tall and strongly built. They both had white, even teeth and a prominent nose. But there—surely?—the similarities ended. Rashid's hair had been long and he wore it oiled to a high shine. His skin was significantly darker than Lord Edward's, and his eyesight was exceptionally keen, with no need for a silly monocle. Rashid's hands had been calloused; they showed the scars of a life lived on the edge of danger. Lord Edward's hands . . . had been gloved for most of the evening.

The comparisons churned around Lucy's head until she eventually dropped into a light, uneasy doze. Her sleep was deep enough for Lord Edward to walk into her dreams, and light enough for Lucy to be furious with herself for allowing him entrance.

As he had in real life, Lord Edward escorted her courteously onto the balcony for a breath of fresh air. Once outside, however, he didn't lean indolently against the pillar. Instead, he removed his monocle, tossing it carelessly into the garden below. He turned to Lucy, his eyes gleaming with secret laughter and his calloused hand—Rashid's hand—reached out to caress her hair.

"I was waiting for you to come home to me, Lucy," he breathed.

"I came as quickly as I could."

"I know, but I was impatient for your arrival. I wanted to do . . . this."

The dream Lord Edward placed his arms around her waist, pulling her gently against him. His head bent inexorably closer. His mouth hovered no more than an inch from her own. Her lips parted in breathless anticipation. Another second, one more, and she would feel his mouth against hers.

The longed-for kiss never came. His hold around her waist slackened, and he touched her lightly on the arm.

"Your tea is getting cold, Miss."

Disappointment was so strong it caused real physical pain.
Lucy dragged open her eyes and glared at her maid. Only years of
training prevented her from snapping at the servant. She sighed.
"What time is it, Rose?"

Oh-oh, Rose thought. *Things last night hadn't gone well. The
man must be a fool.* "Almost noon, Miss, and there is a gentleman
from the Foreign Office waiting in the drawing room to speak with
you."

Lucy's heart gave a little leap. "Lord Edward de Beaumont?"

So that's the way of it, Rose concluded. *Lord Edward was the
gent who inspired the peacock silk dress and brought the glow of
excitement to Miss Lucinda's eyes.* Rose scented problems. She
hadn't needed three days in the Larkin house to know that Lord
Edward de Beaumont was destined for the nincompoop Penelope.
She replied with genuine regret.

"No, Miss. 'Tis a Mr. Percy. He's personal secretary to Lord
Triss, so he says. I've brought hot water up, so's you can wash,
Miss Lucinda."

Half an hour later, Lucy was downstairs. The affable and deeply
apologetic Mr. Percy explained that the new British ambassador to
Russia was about to leave for St. Petersburg, and Lord Triss very
much wanted Miss Larkin to discuss her impressions of Afghanistan before the ambassador left England. This afternoon at two
o'clock was the only time the ambassador could spare from his
hectic round of predeparture engagements. Could Miss Larkin
join the Under-Secretary at the Foreign Office in Downing Street
for a brief discussion?

"I have already explained to Lord Triss that my experience in
Afghanistan was very limited. I was confined to a small valley,
and, like the other women, I was not allowed to be present at any
of the village elders' discussions. However, such impressions as I
have, I will be happy to pass on. Two o'clock this afternoon will
be quite convenient."

"Lord Triss will be most grateful. He realizes you must be tired
after last night's ball."

"Since I escaped from Kuwar Valley, I have scarcely known the
meaning of the word 'tired.' The lives of the Afghanis, particularly of the women, are unimaginably hard by our standards. I find
that after two years of constant labor, I crave activity. I shall be
glad to have something constructive to do this afternoon, rather
than sitting at home and receiving endless courtesy calls."

"Lord Triss will send his carriage for you, Miss Larkin. He insists that you should not be put to the inconvenience of bringing out your horses. It will be here at half-past one."

The room Lucy was escorted into later that day appeared more like a pleasant sitting room than an office. Green velvet draperies framed tall, narrow windows. Books filled two capacious bookshelves, a Persian carpet added color to the floor and portraits—presumably of past Foreign Office dignitaries—gazed down sternly from walls like ancestors in a country home. Only the papers overflowing on the corner desk indicated that business was indeed conducted in this congenial setting.

Lord Triss and three other men rose to their feet as the footman closed the office door behind Lucy. The Under-Secretary came forward and took her hand.

"My dear Miss Larkin, I am most grateful to you for accepting my invitation at such short notice. May I introduce His Excellency, the Viscount Merton, who will shortly become our ambassador in St. Petersburg. And you already know Lord Edward, of course, and Mr. Percy, whom you met this morning. If you don't mind, Percy will take a few notes to remind us all of what we say."

Lucy acknowledged the introductions, while Mr. Percy pulled up a chair for her and saw to it that she was provided with a cup of tea. She wondered what Lord Edward's function was supposed to be, since Mr. Percy was the official note taker. Perhaps the new ambassador was to be regaled with some of Lord Edward's bizarre insights, gleaned as a result of his three-day meeting with the Turks and the Russians in Vienna.

As soon as Lucy was settled and her tea drunken, Lord Triss began to speak. "Forgive me if I seem to lecture you, Miss Larkin, but I want to explain why I am so anxious for our ambassador to hear your story. As you know, Mr. Disraeli, the Prime Minister, is an ardent proponent of what has become known as the 'Forward Policy.'"

"I am familiar with the term," Lucy said quietly. "In contrast to Mr. Gladstone, his predecessor, Mr. Disraeli believes that we should protect our imperial rights in India by vigorously asserting control over all neighboring and buffer states, particularly in the north. He considers Afghanistan a legitimate sphere of British influence, and that was one of the reasons my father was asked to head a trade mission to Amir Sher Ali."

"Very concisely put, Miss Larkin. You may not know that Mr. Disraeli has warned Amir Sher Ali that he may not sign any treaties without first getting approval from the British government. In other words, Great Britain will consider any attempt by Afghanistan to exercise an independent foreign policy as an act of aggression."

"Unfortunately," Viscount Merton interjected dryly, "the Russian emperor believes in the identical policy, except with a Russian twist. He believes that Imperial Russia should protect its southern borders by vigorously asserting control over all neighboring and buffer states. He considers Afghanistan a legitimate sphere of Russian influence. That is why he is attempting to sign 'friendship' treaties with the Amir of Afghanistan. The emperor considers any undue British interest in Afghanistan to be an act of aggression. So far, he has not defined what he means by *undue interest*."

Lucy could not help thinking that the policy of both Britain and Russia had more in common with small boys arguing over who owned which toys than with sensible adults resolving important world issues. As a mere woman, she was wise enough not to express her opinion.

Lord Triss tugged at his mustache. "The problem is, of course, that Afghanistan cannot be both a Russian and a British sphere of influence at one and the same time. And at the moment, we have no idea whether the Amir favors signing a treaty with Great Britain or with the Russian tsar."

Lucy could no longer keep silent. "I would guess, my lord, that his preference would be to sign nothing. I imagine the Amir dreams of an Afghanistan which is free to make its own decisions, unhampered by the power plays of two alien giants."

Lord Edward spoke for the first time. "What would give you such an idea, Miss Larkin? Do you have any reason for supposing the Afghanis don't appreciate our honest offers of trade, industry and the other benefits of modernization?"

"The best of good reasons, Lord Edward. They murdered my father and his entire delegation rather than honor the treaty we had required them to sign."

"Then why did they sign the treaty in the first place?" the Viscount demanded irritably. "Your father didn't ride in with an army of soldiers at his back, demanding compliance."

"The Afghanis don't like to argue with their guests, and they viewed the trade delegation as guests. Just as we neither understand nor trust the Afghanis, so they neither understand nor trust the people of the Western world. The Afghani code of honor is extremely strict. It merely operates on quite different principles from the ones on which we Britishers base our behavior. Agreement between our governments is likely to prove very difficult to achieve simply because quite often we genuinely won't understand each other."

"If the Afghanis have such high regard for their guests, then why was your father's delegation ambushed while still under the Amir's protection?"

"By Afghani standards, the Amir had no part in that ambush," Lucy explained quickly. "We know that the Khan of Kuwar was paid to do the deed by the Amir, but that is no offense as far as the Amir is concerned. We had never been guests of the Khan, so no rules of hospitality were broken."

"A meaningless distinction, surely."

"Not from the Amir's point of view. I have listened to many conversations between Afghanis, and I understand the rules. Few things are ever stated directly. I would be willing to stake my life on the fact that the Amir never openly expressed his wish that our trade delegation should be murdered. The Khan of Kuwar merely read between the lines and drew the correct conclusions."

The ambassador frowned. "If Amir Sher Ali is so anxious to remain independent, why has he recently sent out unmistakable signals indicating that he would be willing to sign some sort of mutual defense agreement with the tsar?"

"Perhaps because he wishes to have some counterweight to the overwhelming and threatening power of the British Raj in India?"

The ambassador stiffened. "The British Raj is no threat to any peaceful nation!"

"But the Amir may not understand that. He is like a mouse, wondering how best to hide from the two elephants fighting over his head. If he cannot dig into the ground and remain invisible, what choice does he have but to climb on the back of whichever elephant seems momentarily less threatening?"

"A very vivid description, Miss Larkin, but what if we do not want the mouse to climb on the back of this particular elephant?"

"Then I daresay we could crush it. But is that really necessary? Our government sees every move made by the Amir as a threat to our position in India, whereas I suspect that much of what the Amir does is related to his position *within* Afghanistan."

Lord Edward spoke again. "Could you clarify for us, Miss

Larkin, why you have this impression? Are you aware of specific incidents that you feel threaten the Amir's control over his own country?"

Lucy was surprised to discover just how many political opinions she had formed during her two years in Afghanistan. Aided by skillful questioning from Lord Triss, she explained about the fierce tribal and personal loyalty which motivated most Afghanis. "The idea of a nation is alien to them," she said finally. "It is a foreign idea, imported less than a hundred years ago. Any ruler in Kabul will have to win the loyalty of local tribal leaders by repeated acts of valor or at least by proving that it is more profitable to be part of an Afghani nation rather than simply a member of, say, the Kuwari tribe."

"And, in your opinion, has Amir Sher Ali won that loyalty?" Lord Triss asked.

"I think not. He has merely succeeded in putting down local rebellions, usually with the help of foreign weapons, and that is not the same thing as earning personal loyalty. Afghani tribesmen can be bribed into fighting for the Amir on a short-term basis, as I believe the Khan of Kuwar was bribed to murder my father. But in the end, the vast mass of Afghani people will require more than threats and bribery to keep them loyal to a central government. They will need pride in the man who leads them."

"In the meantime," Lord Triss muttered, "loyalties can be bought by whoever holds out the promise of the biggest bribe. And at the moment, I fear it is the Russian emperor who is dangling the most enticing carrots. Our government is intent upon offering threats, not promises."

The ambassador sounded worried. "We certainly don't want the Russian emperor taking over control of Afghanistan. He has already seized power in far too many of those Central Asian states. Can you imagine the consequences if there were Russian soldiers garrisoned all along the northern frontier of India? There's no guessing what mischief the tsar would be up to once he had a toehold on the Indian subcontinent."

"And the tsar is certainly stirring the Afghani pot," Lord Triss said. "We have evidence of his meddling in the internal politics of the country. Miss Larkin, please explain to the ambassador about your encounter with Russian soldiers almost at the foot of the Khyber Pass."

"You know about that incident?" Lucy asked in some astonishment.

There was a tiny silence, then Lord Edward rose to his feet. "More tea, Miss Larkin?" He took her cup without waiting for her reply. "The Reverend Chester reported your experience to the appropriate officials in Lahore," he explained. "The report was transmitted to London and came across my uncle's desk."

"But we appreciate a first-hand account," Lord Triss emphasized. "If you could tell us your impressions of exactly what happened, Miss Larkin?"

To the best of her ability, Lucy described the encounter, the roles she and Rashid had played and the Russian lieutenant's revelation that his troop of soldiers had been in contact with one of Amir Sher Ali's exiled and rebellious sons.

"The Amir's hold upon his throne is shaky," Lucy concluded, "and like any other cornered animal he is likely to prove dangerous. He will use any means he can find to protect his position."

"And you think a treaty with the Russian emperor is one method he may use?" the ambassador demanded.

"Either that, or the Russian emperor may decide to dispense with Amir Sher Ali altogether and install one of his own puppets on the throne. The presence of Russian soldiers so far south suggests that the tsar has decided to take an active interest in who sits upon the throne of Afghanistan."

Lord Triss and the ambassador continued to question Lucy closely for another half-hour, at which time the ambassador was forced to leave for another appointment. He shook hands with Lucy, offering generous praise for the insights she had provided.

"I will send for my carriage," Lord Triss said, as soon as the ambassador had left the room. "Miss Larkin, I echo the viscount's compliments. I cannot thank you enough for all the information you have provided. Your first-hand observations will prove invaluable not only to the ambassador, but also to me when I present my recommendations on Afghanistan to the Foreign Secretary."

Lord Edward rose languidly to his feet. "With your permission, Miss Larkin, we won't send for my uncle's carriage. A walk home through St. James's Park would be very jolly, if you would allow me to escort you."

Lucy happened to be looking at Lord Triss, and she thought she detected a hint of laughter in that gentleman's shrewd gray eyes. She turned somewhat uncertainly toward Lord Edward, but could detect no cause for his uncle's amusement. Lord Edward, monocle and vacuous smile both in place, looked exactly as he always did.

Nevertheless, even in Lord Edward's tiresome company, a walk through the park promised to be pleasant. Since returning to London, Lucy had felt her body stiffening from lack of exercise.

"Thank you," she said to the baron. "It's a lovely afternoon, and a walk would be refreshing."

The long, soft twilight of an English summer day had barely begun as they entered the park where a few children were still bowling hoops along the paths. The Serpentine gleamed silver in the setting sun. Ducks squawked as they surfaced from the mud with tasty water snails or other delicious bugs, and a royal keeper threw fish to the waiting pelicans. Lucy felt herself seized by the same odd mixture of contentment and restless expectancy that had gripped her last night when she waltzed with Lord Edward.

"I trust you are quite recovered from the exertions of the ball?" he queried politely.

"Quite recovered, thank you. Enjoying oneself is hardly an exhausting occupation."

"Indeed not. But as hostess you had several irksome situations to take care of. Making sure the good bishop did not doze off into his soup plate must have required a certain amount of ingenuity."

Lucy swallowed a gurgle of laughter. "Actually, I'm not sure the bishop is as sleepy as he pretends. I suspect he has perfected the art of waking only when he feels something interesting is being said."

"Heaven forbid! At most parties, he could safely doze from the soup to the dessert."

"Last night he remained awake to listen to you, my lord. He seemed to find your remarks on Turkish and Russian politics most enlightening."

The baron stopped, apparently to admire the passage of a swan and a retinue of half-grown cygnets. "And you, Miss Larkin? I gather you did not share the bishop's admiration for my views."

"There is no reason for you to suppose that, my lord."

"On the contrary, Miss Larkin, there is every reason." He laughed softly. "Shall I tell you why? Although you always remember to keep your expression fixed into a miracle of polite blandness, you never remember to control your voice. Believe me, it speaks volumes."

Lucy clasped her hands in front of her in an effort to disguise the odd trembling that had begun to overtake her. Only one other man had ever possessed the uncanny ability to read her thoughts.

She stared up at the baron, looking for . . . looking for she knew not what.

"Very well, my lord, if my voice has already betrayed the truth, I will admit it. I am not convinced that three days in the company of a few diplomats qualifies you as an expert on the aspirations and motives of two large and complex empires."

"I have also read several good books on the subject," Lord Edward offered mildly.

Could that possibly be laughter she saw lurking behind his concealing monocle? But surely Lord Edward didn't have sufficient intelligence to mock himself in such a subtle fashion? Lucy shook her head to clear it of a sudden dizziness.

"I saw my sister at luncheon today," she said, feeling an obscure need to remind herself that this man was shortly destined to become her brother-in-law. "Penelope was in raptures over the exciting time she had last night at the ball. She mentioned particularly how much she enjoyed your company and the several dances she shared with you."

"Miss Penelope is still young," Lord Edward replied. "If she marries the right man, I am sure she will become a happy and loving wife. At the moment, she needs constant encouragement about her own good qualities so that she will not feel so desperately inadequate in relation to you."

"*In relation to me?*" Lucy could not have been more astonished if the baron had suggested Penelope felt inferior to the local crossing sweeper. "But she is probably the most beautiful debutante in London this year!"

"And a widgeon whose mama has not allowed her to develop a single independent thought on any important topic. Have you never noticed how intimidating she finds your exceptional intelligence?"

"I never thought . . . She is so pretty . . . " Lucy stumbled to a halt and once again turned to look at her companion. The baron returned her gaze with a flash of his monocle and a typical, meaningless smile. Unbidden, a vivid memory flashed into Lucy's mind, of Rashid dealing with the Russian soldiers. He, too, had disguised his quick-wittedness and his acute perceptions behind a facade of blank stupidity.

"My lord . . . " Her tongue suddenly felt too thick and clumsy to voice the questions that buzzed insistently in her head. How could she ask a respectable English nobleman to remove his monocle and sweep back his hair so that she could check for the

scar that had run high into a Punjabi trader's hairline? She looked
down at his hands. They were gloved, of course. What else had
she expected? It would have been the height of bad form for a
gentleman to walk out in public without his gloves. Why hadn't
she thought to look at his hands when they were in Lord Triss's
office? Now it was too late.

"Is something bothering you, Miss Larkin?"

She drew air into her constricted lungs. "Yes, something
bothers me. I want to know . . . I need to know if you
are . . ."

*If you are the Punjabi trader who rescued me from the Kahn of
Kuwar. If you are the man who kissed me that night under the
stars. I want to know if you are the man I fell in love with, despite
all the barriers that should have kept us apart.*

She sought desperately for some words that might be more
socially acceptable, then seized on them gratefully when they
finally came to her. "I would like to know if we have ever met
before, my lord. In Afghanistan, or in India, or . . . or somewhere like that."

There was an infinitesimal pause before he replied. "If we had
met before, Miss Larkin, I am quite certain I would remember the
occasion."

Lucy was too accustomed to the subtle evasions of Afghani
conversation not to notice that Lord Edward hadn't precisely
answered her question. Her heart began to hammer at suffocating
speed.

"My lord, will you please answer me directly? I must have a
straightforward reply. Have we ever met before?"

They were passing under the spreading arch of two rows of
ancient horse chestnut trees, and Lord Edward's face was in
shadow. He turned slightly, polishing his monocle before swing-
ing around to face her. "By jove, Miss Larkin, that's an odd sort
of question to ask a chap."

"But I do ask it, my lord."

Lord Edward's voice was flat and uncompromising. "No, Miss
Larkin, we have never met. Whatever gave you the idea that we
had?"

His denial could hardly have been more absolute. Lucy tried to
ignore the wave of desolation sweeping over her. "A feminine
fantasy, my lord. It was nothing important."

"I expect the return to England's colder clime has been a bit of
a shock to the old system, what?"

Dear God, they were back to discussing the weather! Lucy shut her eyes in momentary despair. "No doubt, my lord."

They walked in silence for a few hundred yards, until Lord Edward gave a bark of inane laughter. "We've made excellent time, by jove! Look—we're almost back at your house, Miss Larkin."

Lucy smiled grimly. "Jolly good show," she said.

CHAPTER ELEVEN

On Monday morning, while eating her way through a solid British breakfast of steamed haddock and poached eggs, Lucy decided it was time to take a stern grip on her wandering imagination. Rashid, she reminded herself firmly, was a gun runner plying his trade somewhere in the Punjab. Lord Edward was an English baron about to propose marriage to Penelope. Clearly, no connection between the two men existed save in Lucy's overwrought mind.

You have been back in England for two weeks, she lectured herself. It's time to forget about the past and begin mapping out a sensible future for yourself.

"I'm relieved to see that you have such an *enormous* appetite," Lady Margaret remarked, watching Lucy spread butter on a slice of toast. "You looked so haggard when you came downstairs this morning that I felt sure you were sickening for something horrid. I saw the sallow tint of your complexion and the dark circles under your eyes and was *most* alarmed."

Lucy decided she must be looking far better than usual for Lady Margaret to launch such a blatant attack. It was reassuring to know that her sleepless nights were having so little effect on her appearance. "Perhaps I'm coming down with some tropical fever that gives one a craving for fish," she suggested helpfully. "I was thinking how much I would like another portion of the haddock."

Lady Margaret shuddered. "I cannot imagine eating so heartily at this early hour. My own constitution is so delicate that I can never tolerate more than dry toast and weak tea before noon."

"Except for the hot chocolate and sponge cake you have sent to your room every day," Penelope reminded her.

Lady Margaret's eyes shot fire toward her hapless daughter. "A pitiful effort to tempt my appetite, and one that is almost never successful." She changed the subject hurriedly. "Do you accompany us to Amelia Ffoulkes's morning concert of harp music, Lucinda?"

The combination of the Ffoulkes family and harp music was enough to send even Lucy's sturdy constitution into immediate decline. "Thank you, stepmama, but I still have a great deal of legal correspondence to catch up on. I fear I must forego the treat of hearing Miss Ffoulkes play."

"Why do you need to do something so unpleasant as catching up on legal correspondence?" Penelope asked. "Surely, that is what solicitors are for?"

"True, except that I have this odd desire to understand how other people spend my money."

Lady Margaret rose to her feet, clearly abandoning all hope of bringing Lucy to any proper understanding of how a lady should behave. "Then come, Penelope, or we shan't have time to change. Let us leave your sister to her ledgers."

Lucy escaped to the cozy tranquility of the room that had once served as her father's study. She read through several papers, then walked over to the empty fireplace and curled up in the leather armchair that still bore the imprint of her father's body on its worn surface.

She had many advantages, she realized, in planning for her future. Few women ever enjoyed the degree of independence that Lucy had acquired under the terms of her father's will. Wealthy, not subject to any man's guardianship, the choices before her seemed almost limitless in comparison to other women of her station.

However, a few moments of reflection was all she needed to realize that her options were narrower than they appeared at first. Society had no room within its ranks for women who wished to pursue a career. On the other hand, after years of traveling and working with her father, Lucy couldn't tolerate the thought of a

lifetime devoted to the trivial diversions of the London social
round.

She pondered her situation all morning, and by lunchtime she
had reached her decision. Her father had always wanted to bring
the benefits of free schools and skilled doctors to the people of
India. She would dedicate her life to continuing his dream.

Her goals might be idealistic, but Lucy's nature was practical.
She had been ostracized by the Kuwari villagers for the crime of
being a foreigner. She had been ostracized by the ladies of
Peshawar for the crime of surviving a massacre. And she had been
insulted by Cedric Ffoulkes for the crime of surviving two years
of captivity. She had no desire to spend the rest of her days as a
social outcast, even if she was doing something useful and
bringing improvements into the lives of the downtrodden.

Mulling over the problem as she sipped her afternoon tea, Lucy
reached the only logical conclusion. She needed to redeem her
reputation, and the best way for a woman of any social level to
redeem her reputation was to marry. Therefore, she would marry.
Soon.

Fortunately, Lucy saw no particular obstacle to achieving her
goal. She didn't rate her personal charms high, but she placed
great faith in the power of her father's fortune. She felt confident
that a generous enough payment would entice any number of
impoverished aristocrats to overcome their moral scruples about
marrying a fallen woman. If only Lord Edward had been poor—
She quickly blocked out the rest of that thought.

At dinner time, Penelope dropped the news that Lord Edward
was taking her to the Royal Academy Exhibition the next day.

"His attentions become more marked by the moment," Lady
Margaret exclaimed. "Dearest child, I live in *hourly* expectation
of receiving his request to pay you his addresses."

Lucy's resolve to settle her own future hardened. Spurred on by
a curious inner urgency, she visited her lawyers the next morning.
Only with the greatest reluctance was Mr. Dunstead finally
persuaded to arrange interviews with a few suitably impecunious
scions of the aristocracy.

"I shall not consider anyone less than a viscount," Lucy said,
her eyes dark with merriment. "Since I am buying a most
expensive husband, I may as well select him from the top
drawer."

Mr. Dunstead looked pained. "Miss Larkin, this is scarcely a matter for levity. The selection of your lifelong companion necessitates the most grave and careful consideration."

"But that is precisely what I am giving it, dear sir. My viscount and I will probably have far more in common than most young people who imagine themselves in love. After all, we shall be making a most fair exchange: my money for his respectability. What more could I ask of a future husband?"

Three interviews were accordingly arranged, during which a drunken earl and two pompous viscounts made it plain that they considered Lucy's fortune barely adequate payment for the honor of bestowing their names and (bankrupt) titles on the daughter of a man who had earned his fortune in trade.

Lucy rejected them all, well aware that her rejections met with nothing but relief. Her dark beauty and all-too-evident intelligence had not been considered assets by any of the three prospective husbands.

"The chaps would all think I'd married my mistress," one rejected viscount reported to the other. "Woman's too damn sultry-looking by half."

"Couldn't agree more," the other viscount replied. "Dashed woman looked me straight in the eye and said she hoped for a large family and did I know of any reason I wouldn't be able to play my part! Dashed humiliating, and never so much as a blush on her cheek when she said it."

"Of course, she would have been fun for a fellow to take to bed." The first viscount sounded wistful.

"I don't know, old chap. Seemed a bit of a tiger to me. I want a virtuous woman for my wife, somebody who'll lie still and let a fellow get on with it. That Larkin woman looked as if she'd enjoy herself too much for a chap to be comfortable. You'd never be able to leave the house without wondering who was taking your place in her bed. It would ruin the hunting season."

Lucy's unsuccessful foray into the husband market left her depressed but not defeated. She soon decided she had aimed her sights in the wrong direction. What she needed was a husband who shared her goal of service to humanity. Clearly, what she needed was a minister of religion. What better way to restore her respectability?

Penelope's betrothal to Lord Edward still hadn't been announced, but the aura of breathless anticipation throughout the Larkin household had reached oppressive proportions. On Tuesday afternoon, Lucy set off in pursuit of fresh quarry.

Reading in the morning newspaper that the Foreign Missionary Society was holding its quarterly meeting, Lucy dressed herself in sober gray linen and set off for the genteel suburb of Brixton where the society headquarters were located. She passed through rooms crowded with ministers recently returned from darkest Africa and ladies sorting garments intended to clothe naked savages. Eventually, she came upon a small room filled with missionaries dedicated to the task of bringing salvation to the people of India.

They were all good, kind men, Lucy decided two hours later. Unfortunately, their enthusiasm for converting heathens was equalled only by their total ignorance of the culture they planned to supplant. She could only hope none of these well-meaning men would cause mortal offense before they learned to adapt to a society where caste rules were so inflexible that a glance at a man's clothing was sufficient to judge his religion, his income, his occupation and his heritage. And where a sip out of the wrong cup, or a bite of the wrong morsel of food, could lead to a man and his family being exiled—made "out-caste"—for the rest of his life.

Exhausted by her inability to bring any touch of reality to the missionaries' discussions, Lucy abandoned her hopes of finding a soul mate and, leaving a large donation, summoned her carriage for the drive back to town. Reluctantly, she faced the fact that marriage to any one of those naive young men would bring nothing but torment to her and unhappiness to any minister unlucky enough to marry her.

Her mood as she changed for dinner was distinctly gloomy. She would not have believed that finding a husband could prove such a difficult business. She wasn't being picky. She hadn't specified that her prospective mate must be able to guide her through the trackless wastes of a high mountain plateau or that he should be able to keep her entertained by his insights into world politics. She hadn't insisted that he be tall and dark, with white, even teeth and an aquiline nose. She hadn't said that he must have black eyes gleaming with silent laughter or a mouth that could ravage her soul with a single kiss—

Lucy jumped to her feet, furious at the betrayal of her own thoughts. She pressed her fingers hard against her eyes in an effort to shut out the haunting images of Rashid.

Rose looked at her mistress uncertainly. "Will you be wearing the camel broach again tonight, Miss Lucinda? I know it's one of your favorites."

Lucy stared down at the camel on her dressing table. It stared back with eyes that were far too knowing. She picked up the wretched beast and stuffed him at the very back of her handkerchief drawer.

"No," she said, her voice hard. "No. I am tired of the camel. I shall wear my mother's pearls."

Lucy's mood was not improved when she reached the drawing room and discovered that her stepmother was hosting an "intimate" dinner party for at least thirty people. The only guests Lucy recognized were Cedric Ffoulkes and Lord Edward de Beaumont. A charming choice for a predinner chat, she decided acidly. She could either be propositioned or driven crazy by fantasies.

Lord Edward solved the problem of deciding which man represented the lesser evil. Leaving Penelope surrounded by a coterie of admiring young men, he sauntered over and cornered Lucy by the punch bowl.

She made no attempt to hide her displeasure. "Good evening, my lord. I did not expect to find you dining here again tonight."

"And I am delighted to see you, too, Miss Larkin."

His tone of voice was so bland, she wondered if he understood the irony of his own remark. She searched his face for any hint of laughter but could find none. Lord Edward seemed his usual pompous self. With a small inner sigh, Lucy reached for the punch ladle.

"Allow me," Lord Edward said, expertly filling a glass and passing it to her. His hands, she noted, were as smooth and manicured as the hands of any other British aristocrat. She sighed again, angry at her inability to stop searching for nonexistent clues. Hadn't the wretched man told her point-blank that they had never met before?

Lord Edward didn't seem to hear her sigh. He smiled cheerfully. "You look most charming this evening, Miss Larkin."

"Thank you."

"Yellow is a flattering color for you, especially with that attractive beige lace trim. You should choose it often."

"Thank you."

"There has been no sign of rain for the past week. It seems as if we are going to enjoy a dry spell—"

"Do not," she said, her voice low and passionate. "Do not, I beg of you, talk to me about the weather."

Lord Edward adjusted his monocle. "Not even the weather in India?" he asked.

"*Especially* not the weather in India."

Lord Edward appeared nonplussed. "But I am such a poor conversationalist, Miss Larkin."

"Then now will be an ideal opportunity for you to improve your skills."

"But what if I make some grievous error, Miss Larkin? If I may not talk about clothes or the weather, I fear I may stumble onto some subject which a gentlemen should never discuss with a lady. For example, I might find myself telling you that you are particularly beautiful when you are angry and that your eyes sparkle with the richness of warm sherry when you look at me. Worse yet, I might tell you that one small curl has escaped from your carefully arranged chignon and now nestles against your cheek in a way that makes me yearn to see your hair spread out on my pillow. My powers of conversation are so limited I might even find myself telling you that your lips have parted as you listen to me, and when I see them tremble I wonder if you long to kiss me as much as I long to kiss you. Would you care for some more punch, Miss Larkin?"

Lucy's heart was pounding so hard that she felt as if she must suffocate. "Who are you?" she demanded. "Dear God, *who are you*?"

Lord Edward thrust his glass into the hands of a passing footman. "A fool," he said, his voice harsh with self-condemnation. "I am an arrogant, unthinking fool. I beg you will accept my apologies." He dipped his head in a curt nod. "Your servant, Miss Larkin."

Without waiting for her reply, he swung on his heel and pushed his way across the crowded drawing room. Only the butler's stentorian announcement that dinner was served prevented Lucy from running after him.

In normal circumstances, Lucy would have been enchanted to find herself seated at dinner near the famous poet Mr. Robert Browning. But tonight her mind was in such riotous, tumbling confusion that she could barely concentrate sufficiently to make sense of what he was saying.

Mr. Browning was stout around the middle and possessed an

impressive gray beard that flowed over his shirtfront. It was hard to credit that this elderly, dignified gentleman had once been so madly in love that he had snatched the frail Elizabeth Barrett out from under the nose of her oppressive, tyrannical father and rushed her away to a clandestine marriage. Only his eyes, sharp with intelligence, betrayed the genius at work behind the placid facade.

Lucy greatly admired Mr. Browning's most recent work, a murder mystery told in verse, but she contributed almost nothing to the discussion ebbing and flowing around the great poet. Every nerve in her body strained toward the other side of the table, where Lord Edward, seated in his usual position next to Penelope, seemed to be laughing and talking as if nothing extraordinary had happened.

But something extraordinary *had* happened, Lucy assured herself grimly. Either Lord Edward was a womanizer of the most dissolute kind or . . . what? Or he must have some special justification for speaking to her with such teasing, seductive intimacy. If he had known her before, there would be some excuse for the provocative nature of his remarks. If he had rescued her from certain death, for example. Or if he had already slept beside her on a thin blanket and taken her into his arms to comfort her from the howls of a hungry jackal. If he had kissed her and felt the depth of her response . . .

Lucy snapped her mind shut. No more, she decided, taking a tiny spoonful of lemon ice and trying to force it down her tight, burning throat. She would endure this tortured self-doubt no longer. Tonight, as soon as the men returned to the drawing room after smoking their cigars, she would find some way to be alone with Lord Edward.

Tonight, she would find out once and for all if Rashid, Punjabi gun runner, was one and the same person as Lord Edward de Beaumont, Third Baron Ridgeholm.

At ten o'clock, the ladies retired to the drawing room to drink tea and suppress boredom by gossiping about any acquaintances not present to defend themselves. The gentlemen remained at the dinner table to drink port, smoke cigars and regale each other with bawdy stories.

Thanks to the influence of the Prince of Wales, who vastly preferred flirting with the ladies to swapping hunting stories with the gentlemen, the lengthy separations of earlier generations were

no longer fashionable, and Lucy needed to wait scarcely more
than half an hour before the tromping sound of masculine
footsteps was heard in the hallway.

Etiquette decreed that no lady could stand up as the men entered
the drawing room. Theoretically, therefore, all the ladies were
helpless in deciding which man would speak to whom.

Lady Margaret and Penelope were past masters at controlling
the outcome of this supposed lottery, but tonight Lucy was
determined to outwit them at their own game. Murmuring a polite
explanation that she had spent far too much of the day sitting
down, she stood on guard by the door, ready to take any action
necessary to obtain five minutes alone with Lord Edward. Since
her reputation was already in tatters, she felt it scarcely mattered
if the guests at the dinner party were confirmed in their opinion
that Miss Lucinda Larkin was unacceptably "fast."

Lord Edward was the fifth gentlemen through the door. With a
quick *glissade*, Lucy thrust herself in front of her stepmother and
bared her teeth in a predatory smile.

"My dear Lord Edward!" she proclaimed, linking her arm
through his as if they were the best of bosom friends.

"Miss Larkin." There was a certain wry resignation in the
baron's acknowledgment.

"My dear, *dear* Lord Edward." Not to be outdone by a mere
stepdaughter, Lady Margaret pushed herself forward, bearing a
cup of tea triumphantly aloft.

Without the faintest tinge of guilt, Lucy brought the heel of her
dainty satin slipper down on her stepmother's toes, simultaneously tightening her grip on the baron's arm. "My lord, you
simply must come and see the interesting photographic plates my
father produced during his stay in the Punjab. I know you would
find the pictures he took with the Maharajah of Jaipur utterly
fascinating."

"I'm sure I would, Miss Larkin. Is it absolutely necessary to see
them now?"

"Yes." She didn't bother to elaborate, but simply propelled the
baron out of the drawing room into the hallway.

Lady Margaret appeared so chagrined at this unprecedented loss
of her prey that Lucy almost felt sorry for her. Almost. "We shall
see you in a few minutes, stepmama," she called airily. "Why
don't you offer that cup of tea to Mr. Browning? I'm sure he looks
thirsty."

With the determination of a steamroller laying down one of the new macadam road surfaces, Lucy marched Lord Edward along the remainder of the hallway and into her father's study.

She indicated the small sofa. "Please do sit down, my lord."

He complied without comment, and she mentally congratulated herself. Step one of her plan was in place. Long since past the stage of caring about propriety, she reached behind her back and pushed the heavy oak door closed. It latched with a quiet, well-oiled thunk.

"Lady Margaret arranged to have all my father's papers shipped home," she remarked, her voice sounding quite calm, although her pulses were pounding at three times their normal speed. "I came across the photographs just yesterday and knew you would be interested in them."

"Because of my love for India, of course."

"Of course."

Suddenly, she could not trust herself to mask the tremor in her voice, and she crossed hurriedly to the shelf where her father's Indian journals and memorabilia were stored. *Dear God, what if she were wrong? Even worse, what if she were right? Could she bear to see her sister married to Lord Edward? Could she endure knowing that Rashid was her brother-in-law?*

"Here are some pen and ink sketches of Calcutta," she said. "You will see that my father has captured the mood of the bazaar to perfection."

Lucy carried the portfolio over to the sofa. Deliberately clumsy, she managed to trip over a bump in the Turkish carpet. The portfolio of sketches, interspersed with notes and sheets of tissue paper, scattered in a wide arc over Lord Edward and the sofa. Step two of her plan was accomplished.

"Oh my goodness, gracious me!" Fluttering her hands in passable imitation of Lady Margaret at a moment of crisis, Lucy sank onto the sofa alongside the baron. She clutched incompetently at various floating pieces of paper and succeeded in wafting several sketches onto the far side of Lord Edward.

"Allow me," the baron said, moving to get up.

"Oh, no, please don't disturb yourself!"

Lucy plucked up the necessary final ounce of courage and leaned across Lord Edward's lap, pretending to reach for a flimsy tissue tracing. Abandoning the pretense at the last moment, she reached up and pushed back the lock of hair that always seemed to flop forward over the left side of his forehead.

She found the evidence that she had longed for—and dreaded.

Disappearing into Lord Edward's hairline was a narrow white scar that looked as if it had been etched by the path of a bullet. Lucy had seen the scar before. The first time had been in a dirty bedroom in a rundown, mud-brick palace. The last time had been under a black, star-pierced sky when Rashid had taken her into his arms and kissed her.

Time lost all meaning as Lucy sat motionless on the sofa, her hand resting against Lord Edward's forehead, blood coursing like wildfire through her veins. The silence thickened, filling with bittersweet memories.

Slowly, Edward reached up and covered her ice-cold fingers with the warmth of his own hand. "Ah, Loo-sie," he said, his voice soft with rueful laughter. "You did not have to go to such lengths to discover the truth."

She finally managed to speak. "You told me we had never met."

"I lied. For both our sakes." He removed his monocle, tossing it impatiently onto a side table, no longer needing the disguise. Then he turned and cupped her face with his hands. His eyes burned with a fever she had seen in them once before. "God in heaven, Loo-sie, what am I going to do about you?"

"Kiss me?"

She could not believe she had actually said the words out loud.

He stared at her mouth as if mesmerized. "Dear God, I must not. Do not let me commit this folly, Lucy."

Even as he spoke, his head bent closer to hers, his dark gaze betraying the intensity of his desire. Her lips parted in breathless anticipation until finally—finally—he claimed possession of her mouth.

The moment she felt the hard, seeking pressure of his kiss, Lucy was lost. The months of separation vanished in a flash. Her body became flame, her mind a spinning void. Reality began and ended with the sensations that consumed her. Her body remembered the pleasures of his touch, and her breasts grew heavy with need. She reached out, twining her hands in the thickness of his hair, urging him closer. When his fingers reached inside the ruffled neckline of her gown, her pleasure intensified until she moaned softly.

He bent to kiss the swell of her breasts where they crested above the lace of her gown.

"Lucy, help me." He murmured the plea against her skin, his

voice harsh with need. "Lucy, tell me that I must stop. Tell me that I must not use you so."

For answer, she clasped her hands more tightly around him and kissed the top of his head while he nuzzled her breasts.

"Do not stop, my lord," she whispered. "My lord, please do not stop."

The significance of the muffled shriek she heard took several seconds to penetrate Lucy's passion-clouded brain. Even when Lady Margaret tottered into the room, hands clasped to her bosom, Lucy didn't fully comprehend the problem. Only when Edward stood up and walked over to the window did she grasp the fact that they had been discovered—and by her stepmother of all people.

Lady Margaret removed her hands from her bosom just long enough to clutch the edge of the desk for support. Her gaze slid over Edward and fixed upon Lucy with a potent mixture of horror, fury and disbelief. Finally, she managed to speak.

"And what, may I ask, is the meaning of this utterly *shocking* display?"

CHAPTER TWELVE

"I am sorry to have distressed you, stepmama. We didn't think . . . we did not expect to be observed."

"That is hardly an adequate explanation for such *frightful* behavior, Lucy."

A little too late, Lady Margaret was struck by some of the pitfalls inherent in her accusations. She drew in a deep breath and warned herself to reflect a moment upon her best course of action.

She could rarely remember another occasion when she had been faced with such a terrible dilemma. On the one hand, convention required her to condemn Lord Edward as a cad and insist upon restitution. Only an immediate betrothal, followed by a swift marriage, would redeem Lucy's reputation. On the other hand, since Lady Margaret's most fervent wish was to acquire the baron as a husband for Penelope, she could hardly insist that he marry Lucy.

A woman of little passion herself, Lady Margaret had been genuinely shocked to see her stepdaughter and the baron embracing in a fashion she considered utterly degrading. She had stormed into the study in the heat of the moment and spoken without pausing to think. Now she wished she had been sensible enough to retire quietly, without telling anyone what she had observed.

Damnation, but how was she to extricate herself from this miserable coil?

The happy solution occurred to her almost at once. Lord Edward was a man. Men were all victims of their own base, physical natures. Therefore, a man could not be blamed if he was enticed into indiscretion by a designing female.

Lucy, Lady Margaret decided, was the villain of this particular piece. Everyone agreed that she had been subject to all manner of foreign perversions during her captivity in Afghanistan, and as a result she must have acquired an unladylike sexual appetite. Lucy had no doubt been the aggressor in that appalling kiss, the fallen woman who lured Lord Edward on. And since gentlemen were not required to make restitution to fallen women, the baron had no need to offer marriage to Lucy.

Lady Margaret gave a heartfelt sigh of relief when she arrived at this satisfactory solution to her problem. The only remaining hurdle was to bring the other two participants in the drama to a similar understanding of what had occurred.

Lord Edward had remained silently by the window ever since Lady Margaret entered the study. He appeared lost in thought and hadn't once turned around to look at either woman. Lady Margaret was on the very brink of speaking when his voice interrupted the strained silence of the room.

"Lady Margaret, I think it would be helpful if Miss Larkin were permitted to retire."

Lady Margaret couldn't have agreed more. It would be much easier to bring the baron around to a correct realization of the facts without Lucy there to interfere.

"Lord Edward has the right of it, Lucinda. Go to your bed chamber, please. I will make your excuses to our guests and speak with you later."

She was considerably relieved when her stepdaughter, after one anguished glance in the direction of the baron's uncommunicative back, left the room without saying a word. So far, so good. Lady Margaret began to breath a little more easily.

Her optimism suffered a setback when the baron turned from his contemplation of the moonlit garden. For one thing, he didn't quite look like the same Lord Edward she had previously known. The tight line of his mouth and the hard light in his eyes totally changed the cast of his expression. His voice, too, sounded lower and more powerful.

"You will already have deduced, my lady, that I have a high

regard for your stepdaughter. I am aware of the fact that you are not officially Miss Larkin's guardian. However, since you stand in the role of her mentor, I would like to ask your permission to request Miss Larkin's hand in marriage."

Lady Margaret was horrified. She hadn't considered the possibility that the baron would offer marriage to Lucy without being coerced. She rushed to put an end to this undesirable act of gallantry.

"My dear, *dear* Lord Edward. I have always admired your high moral tone, but at this moment my admiration knows no bounds." She peered at him through half-closed lashes, saw that he was not impressed and swiftly adopted a new tack. She lowered her voice confidingly.

"I am sure I understand how it is," she murmured. "You, my lord, are a man of impeccable honor and you wish your actions to be everything that is noble. But in this case, dear sir, you may take my word for it: You have no reason to feel either guilt or responsibility."

"How so, my lady?"

A lesser woman might have been deterred by the ice in Lord Edward's voice. Lady Margaret merely plunged straight ahead.

"My lord, *I understand* how easily the little incident I witnessed came about. My unfortunate stepdaughter cannot help the brazen air she exudes, and, of course, as a woman of the world, I understand how such an air must appeal to your—um—manly senses."

"However appealing Miss Larkin's personal charms may be, that is no excuse for my behavior. A gentleman is required to resist his physical impulses. My offer of marriage stands, Lady Margaret."

Drat the man! Why the devil was he being so awkward? Lady Margaret shaped her mouth into a brave, slightly tremulous smile. It was a smile she had used to devastating effect on both of her husbands.

"My lord, you are too utterly good, but you have my word upon it that nobody need ever know of this regrettable little incident." With a dab of lace handkerchief to her tearless eyes, she pressed home her point.

"*Dear* Lord Edward, please don't consider making yourself the sacrificial lamb upon this worthless altar. I have long ago accepted the fact that after the unspeakable things that happened to my poor sweet Lucy in Afghanistan, she cannot hope to attain a respectable marriage."

A dangerous glint appeared in the baron's eyes. "To what unspeakable things do you refer, Lady Margaret?"

"Oh, well, you understand—unspeakable *masculine* things." She fluttered her handkerchief. "Naturally, I have never inquired into the sordid details. That would be too horridly indelicate. But we all know Lucy must have performed many . . . tasks . . . in order to survive among such a hostile community of savages."

"You mean, perhaps, such indelicate tasks as learning how to turn camel turds into cooking fuel?" Lord Edward inquired with chilly courtesy. "That is certainly a useful skill for people living in a community lacking in firewood."

"N-no, that is not what I meant." Lady Margaret, pale to the gills, made haste to turn the conversation away from the horrifying indelicacy of animal waste and its possible uses. Good God, the man had no sensibility! It was almost enough to make one think he *deserved* to wed Lucy. However, Penelope's interests could not be set aside so lightly. The man was a baron, after all, and Lady Margaret had carefully checked out the rumor that he enjoyed an income in excess of thirty thousand a year. Such an income was not to be sneezed at. Putting away her handkerchief, Lady Margaret decided that the time had come for a full frontal attack. Her voice acquired a brisk, businesslike edge.

"My lord, I appreciate your offer for my stepdaughter's hand, but, as I have said before, it is unnecessary. You have not ruined Lucy's reputation: She has no reputation to ruin. I plan to recommend that she leave for Hallerton tomorrow in order to make a prolonged stay in the country."

Lifting his monocle, Lord Edward surveyed Lady Margaret with a cool scrutiny she found extremely disconcerting. "Let me say, my lady, that I understand you very well," he remarked at last. "Allow me to assure you that none of the slanders you have cast would deter me from offering marriage to Miss Larkin if it were not for the fact that I believe she will be far better off without me." He paused for a moment, then added. "Unfortunately, I am not really in a position to offer marriage to Miss Larkin."

Lady Margaret, with her remarkable capacity for hearing only those parts of a conversation that she wished to hear, honed in on the baron's final sentence. Not in a position to offer marriage? What an ominous phrase! She certainly didn't want to inveigle

Penelope into marriage with a man who had—for example—lost his fortune.

"What do you mean?" she asked worriedly. "Why are you not in a position to offer marriage, my lord?"

For a moment it seemed he would not answer, then he shrugged. "I shall be leaving shortly on another mission for my uncle. I am likely to be overseas for some time in a rather remote part of the world."

"Oh, is that all!" Lady Margaret smiled in relief, the subtle insults of the baron's conversation already forgotten. Penelope would not be thrilled at the prospect of visiting Africa or Baluchistan or any of the other hideous spots where Lord Edward might be sent. A few months away from civilization was, however, a small price for a girl to pay in exchange for a title, an eventual position in London society and a virtually unlimited income.

A brilliant idea struck Lady Margaret. Perhaps the baron might be persuaded to marry Penelope and then leave her behind in England! This would certainly please Penelope far better than a boring six months in Calcutta or Bombay or whatever God-forsaken town the baron was planning to visit. Lady Margaret clasped her hands to her bosom and returned to the attack.

"My dear, *dear* Lord Edward. A trip overseas is no reason to abandon all thoughts of matrimony—provided, of course, that those thoughts are aimed in the proper direction. Knowing that *the right wife* waited loyally for your return would make your months overseas fly by on wings of happiness. If you were married to somebody suitable to your station—a young, innocent, beautiful girl like Penelope, for example—your future would be settled. Think how delightful it would be to know that your faithful helpmeet waited quietly for your return in the coziness of your own dear home."

"Beaumont Hall has twenty-four bedrooms," the baron commented neutrally. "It could more easily be described as an oversized, underheated railway station than a cozy little home."

Lady Margaret gave one of the trills of coquettish laughter that so delighted her middle-aged suitors. "My lord, do you not realize that under the ministrations of the right woman, even a railway station may begin to feel like a home?"

"I realize precisely that," Lord Edward said quietly. "It is one of the reasons I have found it so damnably difficult these past few weeks to prevent myself from begging Lucy to marry me. She not only can make a mountain campsite feel like home, she is also the most beautiful and courageous woman I have ever met. I'm sure you will understand why I am sorely tempted to run up to her bedroom and drag her off to the nearest bishop who will grant us a special license."

Lady Margaret could almost feel herself turn green. "My lord, you would not! You could not!"

"No, I will not. Lucy deserves far more than I am able to give her, and in my calmer moments I accept that fact. But now, if you will excuse me, Lady Margaret, I wish to remove myself from temptation before I take some action we shall both regret. I bid you good evening."

Lady Margaret, for the first time in her life, wondered if she might faint when she had no desire to do so. Lucy *beautiful?* Lucy *courageous?* Lucy *the perfect homemaker?* She pulled feebly on the bellrope. "I will ask Fletcher to show you out, my lord."

"Thank you." The baron inclined his head in a curt nod. "With your permission, Lady Margaret, I will await my carriage in the hall. I think we have little left to say to each other."

Lady Margaret, tottering feebly toward the sofa, could only agree.

By dawn the next morning, Lady Margaret was firmly convinced that the hideous events of the previous night could all be blamed upon a single person: her wicked, scheming, immoral stepdaughter.

The torrid embrace with Lord Edward de Beaumont was merely the beginning of Lucy's misdeeds: Penelope's fading (possibly vanished) hopes of matrimony; Lord Edward's extraordinary rudeness; the curiosity of her guests over the cause of Lady Margaret's disappearance from the drawing room; the resignation of the French chef (who was tired of Mrs. Burt commandeering the stove to cook suet puddings); and last, but not least, Lady Margaret's inability to snatch even a wink of sleep. All of these disasters could be laid directly at Lucy's door. Fueled by a strong sense of injustice—after all, she had merely been trying to do what was best for *everybody*—Lady Margaret marched along the corridor and demanded admittance to her stepdaughter's room.

Lucy, already up and dressed despite the early hour, opened the door at once. Lady Margaret cataloged the lengthy list of Lucy's offenses. Lucy meekly agreed that she was grievously at fault.

Lady Margaret frowned. She was spoiling for a fight and hadn't anticipated such meek submission. "Your poor little sister will be devastated when she discovers how you have betrayed her. Lord Edward would have offered for her last night if you hadn't behaved in such a disgusting fashion."

"I think you are wrong, stepmama. I don't believe the baron would ever have offered for Penelope."

"Nonsense," Lady Margaret declared, delighted to have found something to argue about. "You know nothing of the matter, Lucy. He stood on the very brink of marrying your poor, innocent sister until you came home and disgraced us all by your antics."

Lucy didn't raise her voice. "I have apologized for my conduct, stepmama, it was inexcusable. But what happened last night has nothing to do with Lord Edward's failure to marry my sister."

"No gentleman wishes to marry the sister of a girl who is *fast*."

"Maybe not. But that isn't why Lord Edward failed to offer for Penelope. He is intelligent and experienced enough to know that they would never have been happy together."

Lady Margaret was so incensed she snorted. "Then why was he so marked in his attentions to us?"

"That is the whole point," Lucy said wearily. "His attentions were to both of you. I expect he felt responsible for easing your return into English society."

"Why would he feel any such thing?"

"He knew and admired my father. He was officially responsible for investigating the massacre that took my father's life. It was natural for him to be interested in your well-being."

Lady Margaret preferred not to answer such unassailable logic. "You are a cruel sister, Lucy, but even your stony heart must be troubled by the knowledge that poor little Penelope will spend the remainder of her days a lonely spinster."

Lucy smiled faintly, her first smile of the morning. "On the contrary, stepmama, I expect Penelope will have found a new beau before the summer is out. She is young, pretty, eager to please, and she possesses a handsome dowry. There must be a dozen eligible bachelors already anxious to win her favor."

"What does it matter how many other men seek her hand, when she is confined to her room, heartsick, desolate and weeping for Lord Edward?"

Even Lady Margaret realized that the vision of Penelope weeping for the baron when a host of handsome young men were lined up waiting to take his place lacked a certain degree of reality. Lord Edward's chief attraction to Penelope had been his unfailing willingness to talk exclusively about her. Any young man prepared to do the same could be assured of an equal measure of Penelope's affections.

"It is pointless for us to continue this conversation," Lady Margaret asserted. "Your presence in town is an embarrassment to us all, Lucy. I must request that you remove yourself immediately to Hallerton, where you cannot cause any further trouble."

Her stepdaughter, mercifully, refrained from pointing out that Lady Margaret was a guest in Lucy's town house rather than the other way about. Seeming almost indifferent to her fate, Lucy agreed without protest that she would take the next morning's train to Hallerton.

Lady Margaret would have set off on her shopping expedition with a far less tranquil mind if she could have guessed her stepdaughter's plans for the remainder of the morning.

Summoning Rose, Lucy politely requested the maid to pack for an extended stay in the country, and explained she would be leaving the next morning for Hallerton, her childhood home.

"I would very much like you to accompany me, Rose, but I won't be entertaining a great deal, and I understand if you prefer to seek another, more exciting post in London. I would, of course, pay you this quarter's salary in lieu of longer notice, and I understand Mrs. Hesseltine is looking for a new maid. I will ask my stepmother to recommend you." Lucy's smile became a touch rueful. "I'm afraid my recommendation is not likely to win you many friends."

A quarter's salary! Most mistresses would consider themselves generous if they offered a month. Rose was astonished to discover she wasn't even tempted by the prospect of such riches. "I'll come with you, Miss Lucinda, if you don't mind. I've always had a fancy to spend some time in the country."

Rose's friends would have split their sides laughing if they could've heard the lie. Miss Lucinda merely smiled the smile that always inspired the oddest feeling of warmth in Rose's innards.

"Why thank you, Rose," she said. "I shall enjoy Hallerton so much more in your company. I have a few errands to complete this morning before we leave. Could you choose a cape for me to wear?"

"I can come with you, Miss, easy. Nellie can help with the packing."

Lucy accepted the green linen cape that Rose handed her and fastened the frogs, while the maid selected short white kid gloves and a tiny white straw hat decorated with green silk ribbons.

"Thank you," she said, buttoning the gloves, while Rose skewered the hat in place with an elegant jeweled pin. "But I don't need anyone to accompany me. I'm sure I shall be back before lunch."

Lucy left the house with an absent-minded nod for the footman and a firm refusal of his offer to summon the carriage. Her mind and emotions were in such turmoil that she desperately needed to walk—and to be alone. For a split second, she wondered if she ought to have brought Rose with her, then dismissed the question as absurd. At this stage in her life, her reputation had passed well beyond the point when it could be redeemed by the presence of a maid. Solitude was a luxury she could now permit herself.

Her thoughts tumbled in hopeless, unsettling confusion for the twenty minutes it took her to walk to the bachelor quarters Edward shared in his uncle's house. Beneath all her confusion lay the bitter ache of hurt feelings. She could understand (perhaps) why Edward had chosen not to reveal his true identity during their dangerous escape from Afghanistan. She couldn't begin to understand why he had deliberately lied to her ever since her return to London. Was she afraid that she would make some ridiculous appeal to his sense of honor? Was she afraid that she would insist upon an offer of marriage simply because they had been forced to spend lonely nights together under the stars? Could he possibly have understood her character so little?

Lucy found number 25 St. James Street without difficulty. As she raised the gleaming brass knocker on the front door, it occurred to her that Edward might not be at home. He undoubtedly took his duties at the Foreign Office more seriously than she had once supposed and might even go into his office every day, an almost unheard of practice for a gentleman.

An elderly footman opened the door. On hearing her request to speak with Lord Edward, he glanced uneasily over his shoulder, obviously seeking guidance from some superior servant who lurked deeper in the dark recesses of the hallway.

"Can I help you, Madam?" A stout, dignified butler surged forward, the personification of disapproval. In well-appointed bachelor households, unaccompanied ladies didn't knock upon the front door. The butler obviously considered himself personally affronted.

Lucy was feeling too reckless to be properly intimidated by the butler's uptilted nose. "I would like to speak with Lord Edward de Beaumont," she said politely. "Please give him my card and tell him that I plan to leave town tomorrow. He will understand that the matter is somewhat urgent."

The butler took the corner of Lucy's card between his fingertips, then dropped it onto the footman's waiting salver before he could be contaminated. "I shall see if his lordship is at home, Madam. Please follow George into the drawing room." He turned to his underling. "The *small* drawing room, George."

Lucy followed the footman, amused rather than annoyed by the butler's evident disdain. She was immeasurably relieved to learn that Edward was at home—if he hadn't been in the house, the butler would simply have said so. At this moment, she felt a feverish anxiety, an almost obsessive need to see him and hear his answers to her questions.

"If you will wait here, Madam, the butler will be with you shortly." The footman bowed and withdrew, closing the door behind him. Lucy grimaced wryly. No doubt he was afraid she would make off with the family silver if left to roam freely through the hallways.

She walked over to the window and eased herself behind a high-backed chair, lifting the lace curtain so that she could see out into the garden. In Kuwar most of her life had been spent outdoors, and since her return to England, she had sometimes found the overfurnished rooms of London town houses claustrophobic. Looking out over a lush prospect of green grass and leafy trees helped to lessen her feeling of oppression.

"Uncle Harry, what the devil have you done with— *Lucy!*"

She whirled around at the sound of Edward's voice, and they stared at one another in taut silence.

"I'm sorry," he said at last, gesturing to his clothes. "I had no idea you were in here."

He wore narrow-striped formal morning trousers, but he had not bothered to put in the studs needed to fasten his shirt. It hung open, revealing his white linen undershirt and several inches of darkly tanned skin. Convention demanded that he should leave the room immediately. Since he didn't leave, Lucy ought to have kept her gaze averted from his blatant exposure of masculine flesh. Instead, they continued to gaze at each other, both of them seemingly afflicted with an identical paralysis.

Lucy finally managed to swallow. "How did you darken your skin?" she asked.

His gaze was fixed on her mouth, and he blinked before answering her question. "With a tobacco dye," he said. "It's virtually impossible to wash off, except with a special lye soap that removes almost as much skin as it does brown dye."

Why did you kiss me last night? Why did you leave without coming to see me? What do you feel when you look at me? Lucy stared down at her hands. "Where did you learn to speak Pashto so fluently, my lord?"

"My grandfather took me out to India when I was sixteen, and we discovered that I have a knack of picking up foreign languages." He turned abruptly. "I should not . . . I cannot stay here with you, Miss Larkin. I'm not dressed to receive visitors. I was looking for my uncle and had no idea you had called."

Lucy suddenly regained the use of her legs. She hurried across the room, putting her hand on his arm to stop him leaving. "Edward, please don't go! There is so much I must ask you." She used his name unconsciously, not even aware that she had done so. "Oh, Edward, why didn't you tell me the truth? Why did you deliberately set out to deceive me? In the park, when I asked if we had ever met before, why did you lie?"

Edward swung around, his eyes dark with remorse. "Lucy, I didn't want to lie to you. I did what I thought would be best for *you*. Dear God, can you not see that it would be a thousand times better if you had never discovered the truth?"

"No. Why would it have been better?"

"Oh God, Lucy, because I cannot speak to you as I wish. And because this is torture for us both." He reached for her hand and clasped it between his. Somehow, without either of them taking a step, their bodies swayed closer together. Edward raised her hand to his mouth and kissed the tip of her fingers.

"Lucy, go now, and I will call on you this afternoon. If anybody saw you here with me like this, you would be lost— "

"I'm sorry, Madam, but His Lordship is not in his rooms at the moment." The butler stepped into the drawing room followed by the footman, who dropped his silver salver on witnessing the couple in front of him. Even the butler was so startled that he quite failed to administer George the reprimand he deserved. Silence reigned supreme until the butler recovered himself sufficiently to deliver one of his most repressive coughs.

"I did not expect to find you here, my lord."

"Did you not? Then you have had a happy surprise. You may leave us, Connors. You, too, George." For a man whose shirt tails flapped outside his trousers, Edward managed to sound quite impressive.

The butler sniffed. "Certainly, my lord. I will send in the housekeeper with refreshments." Confident of having made his opinion quite plain, the butler waited for George to pick up his salver and marched from the room. This time, the doors were left ostentatiously open. The servants, Lucy reflected ruefully, had clearly decided that family silver was not the object at risk.

She felt bereft when Edward moved away from her, although she realized that he had no choice in the matter. Respectable servants wouldn't stay in a house where a man entertained fallen women. Could one be a fallen woman, she wondered, while remaining a virgin? It was beginning to seem a terrible waste to endure the shame without enjoying any of the possible pleasure.

"I'm sorry," she said, refastening her cape. "I should never have come here, my lord, but I leave for Hallerton tomorrow morning, and I felt some things needed to be discussed between us. I realize now that you owe me no explanations."

"On the contrary, I think I owe you several. Instead, I am merely going to ask for yet another favor. Would you please never reveal to anyone that I am the man who escorted you out of Kuwar? There are reasons why it will be better if nobody ever finds out that Lord Edward de Beaumont and Rashid, the Trader, are one and the same person."

"You have my promise." She held out her hand. "Good-bye, my lord. I wish you well in your future endeavors and thank you from the bottom of my heart for your role in my escape from the Khan of Kuwar."

He stood stock still in the corner, and for a moment she was afraid that he would not shake her hand. Then he moved and gave her hand one brief, firm shake. "Your thanks are unnecessary, Miss Larkin. If you recall, you saved me from drinking poisoned tea, so I am at least as much in your debt as you are in mine."

"Perhaps, since our debts cancel each other out, we may consider ourselves friends."

"Yes." Edward drew in a deep breath. "Yes, I daresay we could call ourselves friends."

Lucy knew that she ought to leave before she said or did

something disastrous, like throwing herself into Edward's arms and begging him to kiss her. But the strange paralysis gripped her again, and she simply stood there, separated from him by no more than a few inches of space—and a heart overflowing with regret.

She had no idea how long they both stood there before a new disturbance in the doorway marked the sudden arrival of Lord Triss, Edward's uncle.

Lord Triss, accompanied by the smug-looking Connors, marched into the drawing room and eyed the silent couple sternly. "This is a fine how-do-you-do," he asserted gruffly. "I am shocked and disappointed, Edward. And I must say, Miss Larkin, I would have credited you with more . . . discretion."

As if shaking off a heavy mantle of uncertainty, Edward slowly drew himself up to his full height. The power of his presence flowed into the room, dominating the setting. "I think you have misunderstood the situation, uncle. I am sure you will be delighted to know that Miss Larkin recently honored me by agreeing to become my wife."

Lucy paled, Connors gasped and Lord Triss shot one startled, questioning look toward his nephew. Edward's dark brows rose in an expression of faint, unmistakable hauteur. "The wedding will make no difference to my commitments to you," he said.

"Ah, I see." Lord Triss did indeed seem to find the final remark enlightening. Lucy scarcely registered its meaning, let alone its possible significance. Lord Triss bowed over her hand with charming, old-fashioned courtesy.

"Miss Larkin, it will be a pleasure to welcome you into our family, and I congratulate Edward on his excellent choice of a bride. Nevertheless, fiancée or not, you shouldn't be here, my dear. Allow me to offer you my escort home."

Lucy felt her brain reeling. Her glance swept Edward's face, but she could read nothing there of what had prompted him to make his shocking announcement.

"I will call upon you and your stepmother this evening," he said courteously, but without meeting her gaze. "Until then, Miss Larkin, I trust you will think kindly of me."

"She is your fiancée," Lord Triss interjected, a shade too heartily. "My dear boy, I daresay she will think of you a deal more than kindly. Come, Miss Larkin. Your family will be wondering what has kept you so long. Fortunately, my carriage was summoned a quarter of an hour since. It should be waiting for us by now."

"I am coming, my lord." Lucy hesitated, then held out her hand once again to Edward. "Until this evening, Lord Edward."

He bowed, scarcely touching her hand. "Until this evening."

CHAPTER THIRTEEN

When the footman announced Lord Edward's arrival soon after dinner, Penelope had already retired to her bedroom suffering from an attack of strong hysterics; Lady Margaret was delivering her umpteenth lecture on the subject of Lucy's wickedness; and Lucy was wondering longingly if she might not imitate her sister and thus get carried up to the delightful privacy of her bedchamber.

Tension in the Larkin household had mounted inexorably throughout the afternoon. In retrospect, Lucy could see that Penelope's hysteria had been inevitable ever since Lord Triss requested permission for his nephew to call on Lady Margaret and formally request Miss Larkin's hand in marriage.

Confronted with this proof of her sister's perfidy, Penelope burst into tears and declared that her life was ruined and that she would never be able to eat again. She underlined the sincerity of this declaration by refusing the steamed cod at luncheon and by *almost* refusing a chocolate eclair the (reinstated) French chef had prepared for dessert.

By teatime, when Lady Margaret was once again trying to tempt Penelope's appetite, this time with iced fairy cakes, Lucy had spent three and a half hours listening to her stepmother and stepsister bewail the loss of Lord Edward's title, Lord Edward's money, Lord Edward's properties and Lord Edward's dazzling position in London society. Lord Edward himself did not seem to be very much missed.

By dinner time (nobody noticed that Lucy had consumed nothing save a cup of tea all day), the full significance of Lord Edward's defection struck home. Crying into her mock turtle soup, Penelope visualized a life in which the baron would never again sit next to her at dinner. "He will never be able to tell me how much he admires the pink silk chiffon gown Madame Pinochet delivered yesterday. I daresay I shall never have the heart to wear it!"

This shattering realization was the final straw. Even the meringue surprise could not avert disaster. Tears grew into sobs, sobs into great heaving gasps and gasps into full-fledged hysterics. Lucy, Rose and Mrs. Burt carried Penelope to her room, dipped her face into cold water, then spent the best part of half an hour calming her down so that she could sleep.

Lucy was exhausted by the time she finally made her way downstairs to the drawing room. Lady Margaret reclined on the sofa, her hand pressed to her brow, a box of fortifying bonbons conveniently close.

"I vow, Lucy, you must have a heart of steel. My nerves are quite shattered by poor Penelope's distress. I could not have borne to witness any more of her tears."

"She has stopped crying now, stepmama."

"Thank heaven! The poor, brave child! Ah, if only I had known that I nurtured a viper at my bosom when I welcomed you back into my home! A stone-hearted viper, no less."

Lucy, who had already heard the same accusation a dozen or so times, wondered if vipers had hearts; she rather thought not. Her attention wandered and her ears, which had been straining all evening to hear just this sound, suddenly detected the rumble of an arriving carriage. Her stepmother's words became no more than a background mumble as her entire being concentrated on sounds coming from outside the drawing room. The clatter of carriage steps being let down. Footsteps climbing the marble entrance stairs. A crisp rat-tat-tat on the door knocker. Murmurs of greeting from the servants. Feet walking purposefully along the hallway. A footman announcing the arrival of Lord Edward de Beaumont. Edward's voice. Her heart, beating so loudly that it drowned out all other sounds. Dear God, he was here!

"Good evening, Lady Margaret, thank you for agreeing to receive me at this late hour. Good evening, Miss Larkin."

Lucy tried to smile and to hold out her hand, but discovered to her chagrin that she couldn't move a single muscle. Her body seemed to have petrified onto the sofa.

Edward, as so often happened, sensed her problem. He came and stood before her, taking her hands and bowing over them just as if she weren't staring at him like a mesmerized rabbit cornered by a hungry stoat.

"Miss Larkin, you look even lovelier than usual this evening."

She tried to say "Thank you, my lord." Her throat muscles moved just enough to produce an odd croaking sound, like a rusty winch grinding inside a well.

Lady Margaret smothered a sigh and rose to her feet. Good lord, but Penelope would have handled this proposal so much better! However, since they obviously couldn't snare Lord Edward for Penelope, perhaps it would be wise to put the best face possible onto this match between her stepdaughter and London's most eligible—and richest—bachelor. She crossed over to the sofa, concealing her impatience by stretching out her hands and adjusting her mouth into a coy smile.

"Lord Edward, I understand from your uncle that you have something of *particular* importance you wish to discuss with me."

Whatever Lucy's failings, the baron, thank God, knew how to behave. There would be compensations in having him as a son-in-law, Lady Margaret reflected as he turned once again to face her. His bow was courteous, his words precisely right for the occasion.

"Indeed, I have something special to say, my lady. I have called here this evening because I wish to discuss the future of your stepdaughter. As my uncle, Lord Triss, mentioned earlier today, I would deem it a great honor if I might be permitted to pay my addresses to Miss Larkin."

Lady Margaret gestured toward the sofa. "You see her before you, my lord, all shy smiles and eager anticipation."

An impartial observer might have considered that Miss Larkin looked more inclined to burrow her head into a hole between the cushions rather than to hear Lord Edward's proposals. Lord Edward, fortunately, did not seem perturbed by this evidence of Lucy's uncertain state of mind. Taking her hands again, he pulled her gently to her feet and escorted her over to the bay window, where he drew back the draperies, unveiling a view of the dark

London street and the shadows of a distant hackney cab. Lady Margaret remained in the drawing room, but the position of the furniture and a large Chinese screen enabled them to maintain some illusion of privacy.

"Miss Larkin," Edward said softly. "May I have the great honor and privilege of asking you to become my wife?"

Lucy's stomach knotted with a sensation somewhere between excitement, reckless anticipation and fear. Despite hours of worrying about what she would say, now that the moment of decision was actually upon her, she realized that she didn't know what her answer would be.

Did she want to marry a man who was proposing out of a sense of duty? Was Edward, in fact, proposing out of duty? She had recognized days ago that she was fathoms deep in love—not with Rashid, not with the foolish Edward who was on public display here in London—but with the man she had seen tantalizing glimpses of hiding behind both impersonations.

So much for the state of her own feelings, but what of Edward's? He had kissed her with passion on two occasions, which presumably meant that he found her attractive. But he had never given the smallest indication that any of his deeper emotions were involved in their relationship. Lucy knew that men could feel passion for women they actively disliked. Did Edward dislike her? Would he propose marriage to a woman he disliked, even if he felt he had compromised her?

A rueful smile flickered briefly across Edward's mouth. "You keep me in nerve-shattering suspense, Miss Larkin. I had hoped you would not find the decision such a difficult one. Your acceptance of my suit would make me a very happy man."

He looked as if he truly wanted her to say yes. Perhaps, even if he didn't love here, he would continue to lie so gracefully that she would never discover the truth about his feelings. Provided the bubble of her dreams never burst, would it matter if she lived in a fool's paradise? She wanted—desperately—to convince herself that she would be happy if she seized the chance to marry him. But she couldn't. Not without asking him how he really felt. Tightening her grip on his hands, she raised her eyes to his.

"Why do you want to marry me, my lord?"

There was a fatal moment of hesitation before he replied. "Because I love you more than life," he said at last.

His voice was flat, expressionless, and she didn't believe him for an instant. She knew already that he would lie when he felt it necessary, and for both their sakes he no doubt felt it necessary to lie.

If she had a shred of common sense, she would refuse him. She had money, she could lead a useful, independent life. Stiffening her resolve, Lucy sought for a polite way to express her refusal.

"Thank you, my lord," she said, her voice firm although her body trembled. "I am appreciative of the honor you do me, but—"

He lifted her gloved hands and brushed them very gently against his cheeks. Her words of refusal died away, and she gazed into the dark, unfathomable depths of his eyes.

"Don't turn me down, Loo-sie," he murmured. "Please."

She heard herself speak as if the words came from a great distance. "I appreciate the honor you do me, my lord, and I would be . . . delighted to accept your offer."

His breath exhaled in a sudden, sharp sigh, He turned her hands over and pressed a swift, hard kiss into the cup of her palms. Lucy recognized the dark, hot leap of desire in his eyes and felt a quick shudder of answering passion. At that moment she didn't even care whether or not he loved her. To experience the mysteries of the marriage bed in his arms would be enough.

His voice was unexpectedly husky when he spoke. "I will do everything in my power to make you happy, Lucy. You have my word on it."

"I hope we may make each other happy, my lord."

He circled his thumb lightly around her palm, and she felt the movement throughout her body. "This morning you called me Edward. I find the strangest need to hear you say my name again."

She looked up at him, memories of another occasion vivid in her mind. "Given names can be powerful weapons, my lord. I have been told it is rarely wise to plunge headlong into such dangerous intimacy."

He smiled, obviously remembering their months-old conversation, just as she did. He murmured in Pashto, "Ah, but Englishwoman, you Britishers are so free and easy with your use of personal names. Could you not bring yourself to humor me in this small matter?"

Her blood turned hot and thick in her veins at the sound of his teasing voice—Rashid's voice. The desire to feel his arms around her became so intense that it was a physical ache tingling beneath her skin. Looking away from him, she pressed her hands to her burning cheeks.

"Speak my name, Loo-sie," he murmured, still speaking Pashto. "Tell me if you truly wish to marry me."

She responded in the same language. Somehow it was easier to reveal the truth in an alien tongue. "Yes, Edward, I wish to marry you."

"Good," he said, his voice rich with satisfaction. "I think it must be very soon."

The wedding date was set for the fifteenth of July, precisely three weeks and one day after Lucy accepted Edward's proposal. Plans for the wedding ceremony positively flew ahead, thanks in large measure to the combined efforts of Lord Triss and Lady Margaret.

Lady Margaret exhibited her usual ruthless efficiency in organizing the details of the wedding. Her heart, however, was never entirely in her work. Torn between pride in snaffling such an eligible bachelor for such an unpromising stepdaughter and resentment at Penelope's lost chance of early matrimony, she vacillated between plans to make the ceremony the talk of the season and biting comments on Lucy's unworthiness.

"It is positively *inviting* gossip to have the wedding ceremony so soon after the betrothal announcement," she wailed one morning. "For heaven's sake, Lucy, can't you imagine what everyone must *think*? What *can* people think when everything is arranged in this awkward, helter-skelter fashion?"

"Naturally, they will think I am pregnant," Lucy responded with infuriating calm. "Did you decide what we should tell the caterers about the smoked salmon, stepmama?"

"*Enceinte*, Lucy! *Enceinte!* Only the lower orders become pregnant. What about the smoked salmon?"

"Fortunately, stepmama, I am neither *enceinte* nor pregnant. And all of your friends who can count to nine will eventually discover this happy fact for themselves." Scarcely pausing for breath, Lucy added, "The catering manager needs to know if we wish to serve smoked salmon at the wedding breakfast. Personally, I am very fond of smoked salmon."

"The girl is quite lost to all shame," Lady Margaret confided later to an intimate circle of some forty acquaintances assembled to endure another session with Amelia Ffoulkes's harp. The London Season was not without its penances. "She isn't even planning to wear white! Says it doesn't flatter her complexion, which heaven knows is true, but in the circumstances she ought at least try to pretend she goes to her marriage bed *intact*. Poor darling Penelope is doing her best to lend countenance to the affair by acting as bridesmaid. She, of course, will have to wear pink, so as not to make the comparison too utterly odious."

"Surprised that Penelope gal isn't throwing a tantrum about having lost de Beaumont to her sister," remarked the dowager Duchess of Ashford in a penetrating whisper. "The chit cast out enough lures until it was obvious the baron wouldn't have her."

Lady Margaret glared balefully in the direction of the duchess. "My dearest Penelope is *much too refined* to contemplate marrying a man who is forever junketing off to heathen parts of the globe. Penelope's heart will be given only to a man whose delicate sensibilities match her own."

"Harrumph," muttered the dowager. "That should leave her plenty of fools to choose from. The gal has about as much sensitivity as my bedpost."

Sensitive Penelope was, in fact, bearing up remarkably well under the strain of her stepsister's forthcoming marriage. After devoting herself to forty-eight hours of recurring hysterics, she emerged from her bedroom determined to prove that Lord Edward de Beaumont was the last man on earth she would ever have married. Casting around for a suitable specimen to replace the baron as her admirer-in-chief, she settled on the Honorable Peregrine Petersham. Mr. Petersham was the younger son of an earl, very rich and blessed with traditional blond British good looks. He was also an artist.

Lady Margaret regarded Mr. Petersham as a worthy successor to the perfidious Lord Edward. Not only did he possess almost as large a fortune as the baron, but his paintings had been hung at three successive exhibitions of the Royal Academy. Neither Penelope nor Lady Margaret had the least interest in art, which they considered utterly time-wasting now that photography could reproduce any pretty scene quicker and better than the fastest sketch artist. However, Mr. Petersham enjoyed a reputation as a cultural lion in London society and therefore was a highly satisfactory gentlemen to worship at Penelope's shrine. Lady Margaret invited him to every possible prenuptial festivity and filled her idle moments with calculations as to how soon he might be induced to propose. A Christmas wedding would really be amusing to plan . . .

In the meantime, there was Lucy's wedding to be brushed through as well as might be achieved. The morning of the

ceremony dawned overcast, but the rain held off and Lady
Margaret declared this a "good sign." She now considered the
wedding ceremony to be her show, and she was anxious for it to
go off well, despite the dreadful handicap of having Lucy as the
bride.

Ten o'clock approached, and the family members assembled in
the drawing room waited with varying degrees of impatience and
excitement for the bride to descend.

Penelope, ravishing in pink ruffles, flirted with Mr. Petersham,
who was far better at this pastime than Lord Edward. He was,
unfortunately, not quite as good at paying compliments, although
he had said this morning that Penelope looked sweeter than the
sugar plum fairy, which was one of his better efforts.

At ten o'clock precisely, Lucy descended the staircase, escorted
by the Bishop of Cirencester, who had offered to stand in stead of
her father and give her away. Miraculously, he looked wide awake
and rather pleased with himself.

Lucy paused in the doorway for a few seconds, a slender vision
in deep ivory satin. Her delicate lace-embroidered veil was held in
place by a circlet of cream rosebuds entwined with ivy. The gown
had no frills and no ruffles, but the seed pearls stitched along the
seams emphasized the femininity of her figure and the graceful
line of her body. Her hair, and the dark golden glow of her skin,
shone through the concealing lace veils, transforming her into a
vibrant, exotic presence in the gray morning light.

For a moment, there was silence in the drawing room, then
Penelope exclaimed, "Why, Lucy, you look truly lovely!"

"Thank you, Penelope." Lucy accepted her sister's astonishment with a wry inner smile.

"Yes, Lucy dear, you look very nice, even though your dress is
so plain." In a rare burst of honesty, Lady Margaret admitted, "I
must say that color flatters your complexion. Perhaps you were
wise to choose it, after all."

"Lord Edward will think you are very beautiful," Penelope
said. "You have chosen just the sort of gown he admires most."

Lucy hoped—very much—that her sister was right. She wanted
to wipe out Edward's memories of a gaunt Afghani prisoner and
replace them with the image of a desirable, fashionable woman.
She didn't want their relationship to be based on pity.

She took her place in the carriage next to the bishop, feeling so
tightly strung that she scarcely recognized the streets they drove

through on the way to the fashionable church of St. Margaret's, Westminster.

The bishop took her ice-cold hand into his and patted it affectionately. "I knew and admired your father, Lucy, and I am sure he is very happy as he watches the step you are taking today."

"I pray it is the correct one, my lord."

"I've known Edward since he was a young boy, my dear. He was a rapscallion when he was young, but never an ounce of malice in him, and he's grown into a fine man, even if I prefer not to inquire too closely into his affairs for fear of what I may discover. Bishops of the English Church, you know, are not supposed to nod with approval when they suspect one of their flock is living the life of a Musselman half the time he is overseas."

"Has Edward talked to you about his trips to India?"

"Other than the fact that he takes on unspecified assignments for his uncle, he has mentioned nothing and, as I say, I don't probe for fear of what I may hear. He is a lonely man, my dear. Isolated of necessity by the work he has taken upon himself. He is not much in the habit of confiding his thoughts to other people, but I know he must love you a great deal or he would never have asked you to marry him."

Lucy was silent, and the bishop regarded her shrewdly. "He has trained himself not to bare his soul, my dear. He will tell you his feelings eventually, I am confident of it. Be patient. I am sure, like the rest of us, he will not long be able to resist the magic of your smile."

Lucy laughed, only a trifle wistfully. "I hope most sincerely that you are right, my lord."

The carriage drew to a halt in front of the church. For a moment, the sun came out from behind a cloud, lighting the age-darkened stone with a flash of warm color. The bishop spoke quickly as the footmen prepared to open the door and let down the steps.

"My dear, Lord Edward needs a very special woman as his wife, and I am confident you are that woman. I wish you both a lifetime of joy and adventure together."

Joy and adventure. The bishop's words rang in Lucy's ears as she began the slow procession down the church aisle. At the altar steps, Edward waited for her, resplendent in the dark gray trousers and lighter gray tailcoat of his formal morning clothes. The church was crowded, but as she drew closer to Edward, Lucy was aware only of him. When she finally stopped at his side, he took her hand and greeted her with a smile so full of warmth and admiration that her throat constricted with sudden tears. During these past few weeks she had learned to read behind the various facades Edward mounted so skillfully, and his expression no longer seemed unfathomable. His eyes were dark not with secrets, but with intense, controlled emotion. His voice was deep and confident when he spoke his vows, but his hands, normally so strong and competent, shook slightly as he placed his ring on her finger. She was glad to know that this ceremony inspired such intense feelings within him.

The vicar spoke, his voice indulgent. "My lord, you are now husband and wife. You may kiss the bride."

"It will be a great pleasure," Edward said, turning to lift her veil. His smile crinkled his eyes and softened the hard line of his mouth. He bent and dropped a chaste kiss against her cheek. "Later," he whispered, before straightening. "Later, we will do this properly."

Lucy's cheeks burned with embarrassment, but her heart lifted with hope. Perhaps the Bishop of Cirencester had been right. Perhaps Edward truly loved her. Dear God, she hoped so!

Lord Edward de Beaumont and his new bride arrived at Ridgeholm, his country seat in Sussex, on the afternoon train. Ten servants and two carriages waited at the station to escort the newlyweds to Ridgeholm Hall. Thirty more servants lined the marble-pillared entrance, curtsying and bowing as their master and mistress entered the ancestral hall.

The general consensus of opinion among the servants was that the new Lady de Beaumont looked every bit as beautiful as they would have expected. A rich, handsome nobleman like the baron could enjoy the pick of the crop when it came to choosing a bride, and Lord Edward seemed to have chosen well. However, as the housekeeper confided to the butler in strictest confidence, it would have been nice if his lordship could have chosen somebody who looked a bit more English.

"Still, she seems pleasant enough," the housekeeper conceded. "Greeted us all with a smile and a kind word, which is more than what some ladyships bother about."

"We'll see how she carries on after they've settled in for a few weeks." The butler reserved judgment. "It's easy enough to be all smiles on the first day of your honeymoon."

"D'you think they're in love?" the housekeeper asked wistfully.
"They might be, you know."

"Shouldn't think so, Mrs. Dorsey, I shouldn't think so at all. At
dinner time, they sounded as if they couldn't find a thing to talk
about. Went on about their wedding as if they was discussing
somebody else's tea party. *It was good to see Cousin Bertram
again,* she says. *It's years since we have met.* His lordship nods.
The champagne was particularly good, he replies, *and also the
pheasant.* Then it's her turn to nod, and they're back to discussing
the weather again. The pair of 'em must have talked about every
cloud they've set eyes on since breakfast this morning."

"'Tis a funny old way to carry on," the housekeeper agreed.
"But, then, I always say there's no understanding haristocrats."

The butler pulled out his pocket watch. "Time to take in their
evening tea tray. In the small sitting room, the master said. And
then it's bedtime for the newlyweds. I'll tell you the truth, Mrs.
Dorsey, they don't look all that excited about what's ahead, and
that's a fact."

Far from being excited about the night ahead, Lucy had
progressed since the wedding ceremony from a state of eager
curiosity, through resignation, to her present state of stupefied
nervousness. Unless things improved considerably, she reflected
wryly, she and her new husband might yet spend their wedding
night discussing the weather.

Her conversation with Edward in the train had been a little
stilted, but not unmanageably so. Being married was a new
experience for both of them, and Lucy was sure they would
eventually relax with each other and move on to a new level of
intimacy.

They had separated to change for dinner as soon as they finished
greeting the senior servants, and Lucy looked forward to this
separation as a time to rest and recover her composure. All would
eventually be well, she reassured herself, handing the silent Rose
her blue silk hat with the perky ostrich feather trim. Lucy might be
a total novice as regards what lay ahead, but Edward—somehow
she was quite certain of this—was an expert in the field. Surely,
he would soon find a way to put her at ease?

She discovered, unfortunately, that her bedroom was not
conducive to rest or relaxation. Drafty and dank, papered in
flocked green velvet, it had all the coziness of the Crystal Palace
Grand Exhibition Hall. The pelting rain outside the windows

added to the overall impression of gray, miserable gloom. And Rose, normally so cheerful, crept around the echoing chamber, a town mouse lost in country splendor.

But it was the huge, antique bed that finally reduced Lucy to ignominious panic. Brooding over her from its gilded dais, the carved, curtained monstrosity mocked her with its threat of the night ahead.

Unlike most young ladies, Lucy had been curious rather than fearful about her initiation into the physical aspects of marriage. Her response to Edward's kisses had suggested that, contrary to rumor, the intimacies of marriage might be positively enjoyable, at least in certain circumstances.

The looming bed destroyed all such optimistic thoughts, and Lucy began to remember—vividly—that few Afghani brides found their wedding nights happy. She had seen several, in fact, who emerged bloodied and tearful from the first encounter with their new husbands.

What if she had been wrong about Edward? Lucy wondered, accepting the linen bath towel Rose offered. What if he didn't have the skill or the interest to take her virginity without causing pain? What if the rumors she had heard were true, and ladies really did suffer throughout their life as they endured the unpleasant demands of their husbands' masculine appetites? Sitting down to allow Rose to dress her hair, Lucy began to debate the merits of acquiring an immediate, incapacitating headache.

All might still have been well if she and Edward had been able to eat a quiet meal together. Unfortunately, the cook had prepared a banquet of five courses, served by more footmen than Lucy could count and presided over by a butler of such fierce aspect that he made Fletcher seem positively friendly. Every word she and Edward exchanged was overheard by ten other people, and they soon retreated into the stilted conversation of bare acquaintances. Dear heaven, Lucy thought with a rueful grimace, but she was sick of discussing the weather! She had never before appreciated the delight of the Afghani climate, where it was either hot or cold for weeks at a stretch, rendering the weather useless as a topic of conversation.

Thankfully, once the horrible dinner was over, Edward didn't leave her alone. He declined brandy or cigars, and guided Lucy into a small sitting room made cheerful by a blazing fire.

"I've asked Timms to serve tea early this evening," he said, sitting down in a chair across the fire from her. "I'm sure you must be tired after such an eventful day. You will probably want to go to bed early."

If she said yes, would he think she was eager to receive his attentions? Or would he take her reply at face value and leave her to sleep alone? What did she want to have happen? Did she want to postpone her initiation into the mysteries of marriage?

Half-laughing, half on the verge of tears, Lucy thought that it had never been so difficult to answer such a simple question.

Edward saved her from giving a reply. "Oh God, Lucy, this is ridiculous!" he said, springing to his feet. He paced restlessly for a few moments before kneeling beside her chair and running his hand over the back of his neck.

"Lucy, it's time for us to be frank with each other, or we're going to start talking about the weather again, and I think that might be fatal to our health! One or the other of us would probably explode with apoplexy. I swear we have discussed every raindrop that's fallen since we got here—"

Lucy smiled. "Not quite. And we haven't yet made any telling comparisons with the rainfall in India."

"And I beg we do not start!" Edward took her hand and rubbed his thumb rhythmically across her knuckles. "Lucy, we are husband and wife, and I think we can deal more honestly with each other than this. I don't want to bring back harsh memories for you, but I know better than most people what you must have endured during your captivity, and I understand how you must be dreading the night ahead." He raised her hands and kissed them gently.

"Lucy, promise me that you will remember always that I am not one of your captors, and I will never hurt you or require you to perform any—" He broke off, springing to his feet in a single impatient movement.

"Yes, Timms, what is it?"

"Tea, my lord, for you and her ladyship."

"You may leave the tray on the table by the fire. And Timms . . ."

"Yes, my lord?"

"Her ladyship and I will not require anything further tonight."

"Very good, my lord."

"Timms . . ."

"Yes, my lord?"

"Shut the door as you go out."

The butler left the room in less than a minute, but to Lucy's intense frustration, her precarious moment of intimacy with Edward seemed to have vanished. He retreated to the sofa and stared into the leaping flames of the fire.

"Will you pour?" he asked.

"Certainly." A flash of inspiration seized Lucy as she lifted the heavy silver pot. Pouring a cup of fragrant China tea, she added lemon, then crossed the room and knelt in front of Edward. Bowing her head, she murmured in Pashto: "Would my lord care to have sugar in his tea?"

Edward accepted the offering gravely, taking two or three sips before setting the cup on the table. "Thank you, but I need no sugar," he replied, also in Pashto. "The tea is made sweet enough by your presence. Will you share some with me?"

"If it pleases you, my lord."

She did not move from her position in front of him, so he took his cup, raising it slowly to her lips and tilting it for her to drink. When she had finished, he returned the cup to the table and leaned forward to clasp her hands.

"Light of my Life," he said softly. "I care only that you should be happy. Are you happy, Loo-sie?"

"Very happy, my lord."

"May it always be so, woman of my heart."

"To be your wife brings me happiness," Lucy said, thinking how miraculously easy it was to speak the truth when she took refuge in the lilting, flowery rhythms of Pashto. Perhaps Edward felt the same, for he made no effort to switch their conversation back into English.

"My heart beats more swiftly when I see the beauty of my bride," he said, caressing her cheeks. "Most beautiful of women, I drown in the dark promise of your eyes."

The seductive stroking of his fingers burned her skin and set a thousand pulses racing. Trembling with pleasure, Lucy tilted her head backward, lifting her mouth to receive his kiss. She closed her eyes, overwhelmed by sensation when Edward traced the outline of her lips with a gentle fingertip.

"Look at me, most beautiful of women," he commanded, his words a velvet caress. "Keeper of my heart, look at me once more before I kiss you."

Her eyelids felt almost too heavy to obey, but she slowly opened her eyes and stared into the mesmerizing darkness of Edward's gaze. She could not guess what emotions he read in her face, but his expression changed from tenderness to desire, flooding his lean, bronzed features with all the sensuality normally concealed behind the mask of his disguise. She reached out to touch his cheek, and he took her hand, guiding it to his heart.

"Most beautiful of women, feel the power you exercise over me. In your presence, my heart races and my body is feeble with desire."

Shocked by her own daring, Lucy took his hand and placed it beneath the swell of her breast. "Feel the power you exercise over me, my lord. In your presence, my heart races and my body is feeble with longing for your possession."

Edward held her gaze for a long, silent moment. then he gave an odd, harsh sigh, and his hands curved upward, cupping her breasts and brushing her nipples with his thumbs. They peaked to an aching hardness beneath his touch. He gave her no time to think about this strange new experience or about the tension suddenly vibrating in the air between them. Drawing her swiftly onto the sofa, he held her a willing captive in his arms.

He looked down at her, his eyes slumberous. "Light of my life, your lips promise me the joys of paradise. Let me taste them now."

She offered no resistance as he bent his head to claim possession of her mouth. The moment his lips touched hers, she knew this kiss would be nothing like the others they had shared. This time there was no reluctance on his part, no hesitancy, no holding back. He took his time, tasting her mouth with unhurried pleasure, probing and nudging with his tongue until her lips parted to receive him. Slowly, expertly, he explored the warm honey of her mouth until she moved her lips hungrily beneath his, seeking some more intimate form of contact, although she had no idea precisely what. His kiss deepened when he felt her response, increasing its mastery until her body trembled in his arms and her thoughts tumbled in a whirl of chaotic sensuality.

"Loo-sie, we cannot stay here." His voice was a husky murmur against her mouth, an unwanted intrusion into the dark, heedless turmoil of her desire.

"Where must we go?" she asked, dazed by the fever in her blood.

"To my room. To bed." He stood up, lifting her easily into his arms, and carried her across the room. Before he could open the door, it swung open. A footman, staring rigidly into space, spoke woodenly.

"Goodnight, my lord. Gooodnight, my lady."

"Goodnight, James." Edward sounded almost amused, but the cloud of Lucy's passion disappeared the instant she saw the servant. Scarlet with embarrassment, she struggled to free herself from her husband's arms.

"Edward, what will he think?" she whispered, mortified. "Please put me down. I can walk!"

His eyes gleamed with laughter. "Are you sure, my heart? If you can walk, then I cannot have kissed you properly. I must try again as soon as we are upstairs."

He reached the top of the grand staircase and strode easily along the corridor. A smothered gasp indicated the presence of Lucy's maid.

"Goodnight, Rose." Edward spoke smoothly. "Thank you for waiting up, but your mistress won't need you tonight."

"Very good, my lord. Sleep well . . . That is . . . er . . . Good night, my lady."

Lucy wondered if it was possible to die of embarrassment. At this moment, it seemed likely. "Edward, for heaven's sake! Please, *please*, put me down!"

"Certainly, my heart."

He stepped into a bedroom and closed the door with his foot. He laid Lucy on the bed and immediately sat down beside her. Smoothing a loose curl away from her forehead, he leaned over and kissed the spot where the curl had rested.

"Dear God, Lucy," he said, and there was no longer any hint of laughter in his voice, only stark, urgent desire. "I have wanted to make love to you for so long. Kiss me, my heart. For God's sake, kiss me."

CHAPTER FOURTEEN

It looked like this was going to be a very long night indeed, Edward reflected grimly, tearing himself away from his wife's tempting kisses. God in heaven, how was he going to hang onto sufficient willpower to control the urgency of his lovemaking?

He looked down at Lucy. She lay on his bed, her rumpled dress revealing an enticing few inches of slender ankle, and her hair already beginning to tumble from its pins. His body hardened with a hot, fierce rush of desire. His wife! God, how he wanted to make this woman his wife in fact as well as in name.

Edward grimaced ruefully. So much for all those fancy vows he'd taken, swearing to himself that he wouldn't make love to Lucy until after he returned from Afghanistan. In his heart, he'd always known he lied.

The guilt that had been gnawing at him all evening hooked its claws a little deeper into his gut. Lord knew, he had no right to marry Lucy when he was committed to a mission that might well cost him his life. But the temptation to allow himself a few weeks of happiness had proven too strong. Duty to his country had surrendered to desire for an extraordinary woman. And he hadn't even put up much of a fight.

He wondered when he had started on this slippery slope to involvement. Had it been when he saw Lucy bow before the Khan of Kuwar, and knew instinctively that she despised the fat slug from the depths of her being? Or had it been that night he kissed her under the stars? Or later, when he sent Abdullah to give her the diamond-eyed camel? Certainly, when he saw her again in London, it was already too late to pretend he didn't care.

Lord Triss had been furious about his nephew's involvement with Lucy. Edward was valuable to the British government, both in his role as a bumbling British diplomat and in his role as a Punjabi gun runner. Lord Triss wasn't prepared to lose one of his most effective agents.

"You've agreed to undertake a mission that's important to your country," he complained after Lady Margaret's ball. "Stop mooning over Lucinda Larkin, Edward, it's dangerous. I've never seen you come so close to betraying your disguise. The pair of you were practically making love out there on the dance floor. This isn't the moment to let your emotions overrule your common sense. For heaven's sake, you're the man who told me there are a million beautiful women in the world, so no man should settle for just one. Find yourself a pretty opera dancer, and get your mind out of your britches. You have the Russians to worry about, and their plan for Afghanistan. Forget about Lucinda Larkin."

Edward, unwilling to admit even to himself that he needed Lucy, not just any woman, tried to follow his uncle's advice. His lack of success had been spectacular. The talented, experienced women of the demimonde suddenly had no appeal. Lucy, as courageous and witty as he remembered her—and three times as beautiful—haunted his dreams.

His uncle warned him to stop visiting the Larkin household, but Edward disobeyed, swearing that he wouldn't allow Lucy to penetrate his disguise. Even in that, he'd deceived himself. Surely, he had always known Lucy was far too perceptive to be tricked by a change of clothing, a drawling accent and an oversized monocle? Hadn't he secretly hoped she would recognize the man behind the mask? Why else had he played his role of bumbling diplomat so poorly? For a man whose life had often been saved by skillful acting, Edward realized he had been remarkably inept at maintaining his disguise when Lucy was near.

So now, for good or ill, he and Lucy were married. Tonight, however, he wanted to forget about the long-term problems of their relationship. Right at this moment, a more immediate problem confronted him: He wanted to make love to his wife.

Edward never doubted that Lucy had been raped by her Kuwari

captors. He guessed that the rapes had occurred frequently and over a long period of time. Her attitude the first night they met suggested that she expected him to demand sexual services. Edward didn't need to be a paragon of sensitivity to realize that sex for his wife was almost certainly associated with pain and humiliation.

He had been surprised and delighted by Lucy's eager response on the few occasions he had kissed her, but Edward didn't delude himself. He had detected the immediate stiffening of her body whenever he pushed the boundaries of their embrace beyond a simple kiss, and he anticipated that it would take weeks of nerve-wracking patience before he managed to bring Lucy to the point where he could finally seek consummation. And then their time together would be measured in days, not weeks.

Edward grimaced wryly. God in heaven, what a prospect! Not only to be celibate, but to be celibate in the face of such temptation! But the last thing he wanted was to add to Lucy's fears, and at the moment she looked very frightened.

Moving slowly so as not to startle her, Edward reached out and pulled two or three pins from her hair. Then he smiled casually, determined to lower the level of sexual tension between the pair of them.

"Shall I get your hairbrush while you take out the rest of these pins? Since I was the one to send Rose to bed, I will do my best to prove what a good lady's maid I can be."

Lucy seemed preoccupied with pleating a series of folds into her silk skirt. "Usually I get undressed before Rose does my hair for the night."

She couldn't be offering to have him undress her—could she? Gritting his teeth, Edward pushed the tempting thought aside. He smiled again.

"Tonight, let's reverse the order, shall we? Hair plaited first, and then we can see what further help you need."

He got up and crossed to the door connecting Lucy's bedroom with his. He found her brush without difficulty on the dressing table and returned to his room, feigning a composure he definitely didn't feel.

Lucy sat propped against the headboard of his bed. During his absence, she had removed all the pins from her hair, and it now cascaded over her shoulders in a rich fall of dark, gleaming chestnut brown. Her eyes sparkled, a faint blush stained her cheeks, and she looked altogether good enough to eat.

Edward muttered a trenchant curse beneath his breath. Resisting the impulse to stride across the room, rip off Lucy's clothes and fling himself on top of her, he held out the hairbrush. He hoped his smile didn't look as strained as it felt.

"Success! Your maid has everything very well organized. Er . . . why don't you sit at my dressing table?"

"You could sit here." She patted the bed. "It's more comfortable here."

From Edward's point of view, that was debatable, but there seemed no gracious way to refuse. He sat beside her, breathing in her lavender perfume and trying to ignore the increasing ache in his loins. He ran the brush through her thick tresses, watching the candlelight ripple over her curls, and wondering how he was going to keep his hands off the rest of her body. He slipped the brush underneath the weight of her hair, pulling it through his fingers and lifting it away from the nape of her neck. When he felt as though he might explode from frustration if he didn't touch her, he bent his head and pressed a swift, open-mouthed kiss against the back of her neck.

She didn't jump away as he had feared. She turned slowly in his arms, reaching up to touch his face and finally to push his hair away from the bullet scar high on his forehead.

"How did you get it?" she asked softly.

He tried to focus his thoughts on the old wound, as opposed to the wandering caress of her fingers. "By carelessness. By assuming my opponent was disarmed because I had taken away his rifle. Thank God, he was a terrible shot, and I was still young enough to jump fast, or I would never have lived to benefit from my lesson: Never assume you've disarmed your opponent until he's dead and you've searched his body."

Lucy grazed her fingers lightly over the ridge of scar tissue. "I'm glad you survived," she whispered.

Her husky words served as a final spark to the glowing ember of his desire. For a few blazing moments, Edward didn't care if he was doing the right or the honorable thing. He swept Lucy into his arms and kissed her—hard. His lips moved urgently over her mouth and slender throat, then trailed, moist and seeking, to the upthrusting swell of her breasts above her satin evening gown.

Lost in the pleasure of his own passion, his kiss became more masterful with every second. His tongue thrust purposefully into Lucy's mouth, at the same time as his hand sought the fastening

of her gown. Holding her tight with one arm, he undid the tiny
concealed hooks with an impatient skill born of long practice.

Her bodice was hanging half off her shoulders before he
registered the unpleasant fact that Lucy's yielding softness had
changed to a rigid, dolllike stiffness and that she was no longer
returning his kisses, merely enduring them. With a shudder of
self-disgust, Edward released her.

"I'm sorry," Lucy said at once, dipping her head so that a
curtain of hair fell forward concealing her face. "Edward, I'm so
sorry." She tugged at her gown in a pathetic attempt to restore
some modesty and dignity to her appearance.

Edward cursed himself roundly. "You have nothing to apologize for," he said, his voice curt. "It is I who should apologize.
Would you like to return to your own room?"

Lucy glanced up, her cheeks scarlet behind the veil of her hair.
"It's not that I don't want to be a good wife, Edward. It's just that
I'm not sure what to do." She looked away again, twisting her
hands tightly together. "Everybody assumes that I
am . . . People think that during my captivity in Kuwar
village . . ." She drew in a deep breath, obviously seeking the
courage to continue. "The fact is, Edward—"

"The fact is, my dear, that you have nothing to explain," he
interrupted gently. "What happened in Kuwar is past, and you
must strive to put those experiences out of your mind." He
crooked his finger under her chin and urged her to look up. "Lucy,
can you believe me when I say that the physical union of a woman
with a man is not always painful? That a man need not be cruel
and thoughtless, and a woman need not be debased?"

Lucy gave her husband a wry smile. "Certainly, I will believe
you, Edward. You see, I think you may have misunderstood my
problem."

Edward went cold. "Are you—injured?" he asked.

Lucy swallowed a gasp of laughter. "No, Edward, I'm not
injured. The truth is, I am a virgin. Probably the oldest virgin ever
to emerge from Afghanistan." Speaking in a rush, before she
could lose courage, she confessed the whole. "Not only am I
virgin, but I'm rather an ignorant virgin. You see, Edward, I'm
not terribly certain what I'm supposed to do when you—um—
make advances to me. That is probably why you find my reactions
so unsatisfactory."

Edward regarded her in stunned silence. "You are a *virgin*?" he
said at last.

She laughed ruefully, aware of the total absurdity of the situation. A bride was not usually called upon to apologize for her innocence. "I'm very sorry, Edward, but actually I am. I saw one or two babies being born in Kuwar when I was first taken prisoner, but that didn't help me to understand how the babies were conceived in the first place. My mother died when I was a child. My father naturally was entirely silent on the subject—"

"But what of the Kuwari tribesmen? They couldn't have ignored such a beautiful woman in their midst, particularly the daughter of one of their enemies. Lucy, my dear, *please* accept that there is no need to pretend with me. There is no shame in anything that may have happened while you were in Afghanistan. I met the Khan of Kuwar. I, of all people, understand that you had no choice—"

"Nothing happened to me when I was a prisoner in Kuwar," Lucy said. "At least nothing of the sort everybody is so convinced must have happened. The Khan kept me locked up in his palace for the first two months of my captivity, and by the time I emerged the other Kuwari warriors all believed I was a *jinn*."

"Because of the way Hashim Khan's brothers died?"

"Exactly. By the time you arrived, some of the villagers were beginning to wonder if they could have been mistaken about my magic powers, but the men were all sufficiently frightened to prevent them attempting any sexual advances. They believed I would rob them of their potency if they slept with me, and the women believed I would make them barren." Her smile was only a little tremulous as she looked at Edward. "So you see, everybody assumes I am a woman of vast experience, when the reality is that I'm almost as ignorant as the most naive English schoolgirl."

For a second, Edward stared at her in blank astonishment, then he burst out laughing. Taking her into his arms, he rested his cheek against her hair, nuzzling gently. "Oh, Lucy, my poor sweet, what a tale of woe!"

"It is rather, isn't it?"

Edward grinned. "What a relief to know that I have only to explain the mechanics of the procedure! Some might consider that a daunting task, but in comparison to wiping out two years of bitter memories, it seems a mere nothing, I assure you."

Lucy twisted the button on his jacket. "And will you explain the . . . mechanics of the procedure?"

"It will be my pleasure," Edward said huskily. He took her

hands and held them against his face. "Most beautiful of women, I believe this is a lesson best taught by practical demonstration. Are you ready for the first assignment, my heart?"

She nodded, a little frightened at what might lie ahead, even though her body already ached with the need for some fulfillment she couldn't quite visualize.

Edward was too experienced a lover to give her fear time to develop. He took her into his arms, his mouth seeking hers, his tongue trailing lightly into her mouth, teasing and enticing her into what had already become a familiar pleasure.

Encouraged by the new honesty between them, Lucy allowed herself to relax, to sink into the feelings aroused by Edward's kisses. Gradually, beneath his expert ministrations, the reality of her surroundings faded away. With every touch of his mouth, with every caress, something deep within her struggled to be free. Her body ached. Her skin burned. Her breasts tingled. The touch of his hands brought her the illusion of relief, but her inner yearning increased step by inevitable step.

She progressed so far and so swiftly along the path of arousal that she scarcely noticed when Edward drew off her bodice and camisole, tossing the offending garments to the floor along with his jacket and shirt.

"Lesson number two, my heart," he whispered, propelling her back against the pillows, his knowing hands already tracing the curve of her naked breasts.

Heat arrowed from her chest into the lower part of her body. Instinctively, she arched herself up to his mouth, giving a soft moan of incoherent pleasure. Passion vanquished her inhibitions even as it destroyed the remnants of her self-control. Through the haze of her desire she recalled the fact that ladies were not supposed to enjoy the bothersome masculine attentions of their husbands. The worry that she might be undesirably wanton vanished as soon as Edward cupped his hands around her breasts and closed his mouth over her quivering nipples. If these strange, glorious sensations were the reward for becoming a woman of easy virtue, then Lucy had no wish to remain respectable.

Time and space lost all meaning. Lucy was aware of nothing save the masterful caress of her husband's fingers and the enticing pressure of his mouth against hers. His lips slid down her warm skin toward her waist, feeding her hunger yet leaving her starved for something more.

The coolness of air struck her skin as he unhooked the

waistband of her skirt and petticoats. Skillfully, he slid the heavy clothes over her hips, baring her lower body to his view. Lucy's breath caught in her throat as the flick of his tongue around her navel changed the nighttime coolness into a sudden raging heat.

"You are truly the most beautiful of women," he whispered, moving away from her for a moment to strip off the remainder of his clothes. His nakedness shocked Lucy, but the shock was exciting rather than frightening. A stab of longing pierced the depths of her being as he returned to the bed. His lips moved quickly up her body, trailing kisses, and when his mouth once again settled over hers, Lucy arched her hips, unconsciously inviting him to take more intimate possession of her body.

"Not yet, most beautiful of women, not quite yet."

Her husband's words broke Lucy's intense self-absorption. His body was hot and hard and urgent against hers, but for the first time she became aware of the fact that when she moved, he trembled in her arms. Not fully understanding the connection between her movements and his reaction, she twisted beneath him, wanting to see his face more clearly.

Edward made a sound deep in his throat and caught her hips, forcing her to lie still. A rueful smile crossed his lips.

"My heart, if you wish me to remain sane during this course of instruction, I must beg you not to jump ahead to the final lesson."

"I would like to be a . . . good pupil."

"Light of my life, you are the best pupil any man could ever hope for. Much too good for my self-control."

She didn't entirely understand what he meant, but thankfully he didn't seem perturbed by her wanton behavior, so she reached out to stroke the dark hair that angled down from his chest toward his flat stomach. When her hand hesitated in the region of his waist, Edward's eyes clouded with an emotion somewhere between despair and laughter.

"Dear heaven, Lucy, but you are a most talented student! Ah no, my heart, don't stop."

"Should I not?" Greatly daring, she allowed her hand to dip toward his groin. He groaned. Breathless, provocative, she peeped at him through half-closed lashes. "I hope I am progressing in the right direction, master?"

He reached for her hand and dragged it against his arousal. "Now you are," he murmured, pulling her into his arms, trapping her hand between their two bodies. Against her breasts, she could feel the strong steady beat of his heart. Against her thighs, she could feel the thrusting pressure of his hips. His hands moved over her body, impatient, ardent, arousing.

"I dreamed of holding you like this during those long nights under the stars." Edward's voice was rough. "Do you remember the last night of our journey when the jackal woke you?"

"Of course I remember. I remember also that you kissed me."

"I wished our kiss might never end. When I went back to my own blanket, you reached out and took my hand. Our fingers barely touched, but in my dreams I tasted your kisses in my mouth and felt your thighs parting to receive me. Dear God, I have wanted you for so long, Lucy."

Knowledge of her ability to arouse him became the ultimate aphrodisiac for Lucy. Blood raced through her veins and a sweet weakness seized her. The instinctive demands of her body had long since drowned out fear of Edward's possession. She watched his face, drawn taut with desire, and gloried in her power to overcome his awesome self-control. She guessed that few people ever succeeded as she had in stripping away the layers of his disguise, and she wanted to carry her discoveries to the ultimate limit.

"Love me, Edward," she whispered.

He brought her to a state of white-hot readiness. Drowning in a sea of a new sensations, she made no protest when his hand slid over her stomach, seeking admission to the dark, throbbing place between her thighs.

But when his fingers finally touched the core of her, Lucy gave a startled cry and pushed herself upright in the bed, startled out of her passion-induced stupor. Edward ceased his intimate probing, but he didn't move his hand, despite her confused efforts to free herself.

"Edward, no!" she protested.

"The final lesson, keeper of my heart," he said softly. "Don't close yourself against me, Lucy. There will be only one moment of pain, and then I swear I will bring you pleasure."

Edward's words were tender, but his voice was harsh with the strain of controlling his desire. Lucy heard only the harshness. The horror stories of the Kuwari village women and the strictures of her Victorian upbringing finally caught up with her. Fearful, bewildered, shamed by her own tumultuous response, she tensed in shocked resistance.

Edward's body pulsed with a need that surpassed anything he had ever known. Somehow he managed to remain still, to wait for his wife to regain some measure of calm. Holding her captive beneath his straining body, he claimed her mouth again, waiting patiently until her little sigh and the parting of her lips told him what he wanted to know.

Ignoring his own aching need for release, he teased her sensitive nipples with his mouth until gradually her panic-stricken tension dissipated. Slowly, tenderly, he resumed his stroking.

Lucy didn't want to respond. Twenty-three years of social conditioning convinced her that she ought not to be feeling— could not be feeling—what she actually felt. In the end, though, Edward's masterful lovemaking conquered her most deeply rooted inhibitions. Her pulses throbbed to the erotic rhythm of his touch. Her hip arched against his hand, quickening to the pace he set. Her nails dug into the firm, tanned skin of his shoulders, and her teeth clenched together in an effort to contain her cries. And then, when she wondered how she could bear the painful pleasure for another second, her body convulsed in a spasm of unimaginable release.

Dazed by what had happened, she lay on the bed, staring up into Edward's dark, aristocratic features. Her body quivered with the aftermath of climax, and yet she felt frustrated, as if some deep, inner need remained unfulfilled.

Edward brushed a damp curl away from her forehead. "My heart," he whispered. "Let me show you how much more there can be."

"There . . . is . . . more?" Lucy could barely speak.

"Much, much more." Edward thought he had never seen anyone as beautiful as Lucy. She lay beneath him, panting slightly, her hair a wild tangle of brown velvet, her skin still warm with the flush of desire. He had never before felt such an intense need to give a woman satisfaction. Ironically, he had also never known such fear of causing pain.

When her fingers twined in his hair, pulling him down to her, the final vestige of Edward's control snapped. He parted her thighs and thrust into her, his penetration swift, deep and immediate. Lucy's sharp cry gave him pause, but only for a moment. As their bodies locked together, he drove deep into her silken softness, slipping his hands beneath her hips to press her body high and tight against his.

Lucy was astonished when the seering moment of pain disappeared in a wave of pleasure. As Edward's movements quickened,. she responded, automatically lifting her hips to welcome his thrusts. Her mouth sought his, her hands dug into his skin and she realized that her body was once again hot and feverish to his touch.

Edward sensed her desire rising to meet his. Surrendering to the demands of his body, he claimed possession of his wife with an urgent, climactic passion that demanded and received the reward of her ultimate response. Together, they soared to the heights, lost in the febrile, glittering dance of ecstasy. Together, they drifted down from the peak. Together, they fell asleep, weary survivors of an experience whose devastating intensity neither of them was quite ready to acknowledge.

The chill of a predawn breeze woke Edward from his sleep. He clasped his hands behind his neck and leaned back against the pillows. For a moment, he stared straight ahead, deliberately not turning to look at the woman who lay curled innocently at the opposite side of the bed.

He was, Edward acknowledged, in a terrible quandary. How was he going to face Lucy over the breakfast table and inform her that he would be leaving for India by the end of the month? And how the devil was he going to face months of separation from Lucy? The morning after the night before was bringing its inevitable wagonload of problems and regrets.

But whatever reason and honor might dictate, Edward couldn't be sorry for what had happened. During the past few years, he had slept with women in three different continents. Last night, for the first time in his life, he had made love.

Lucy. His wife. God in heaven, how loving and responsive she was! The memories crowded in, and Edward succumbed to temptation. He rolled onto his side, propping himself on one elbow so that he could look at Lucy.

She slept the deep, exhausted sleep of fulfillment, her waist-length hair tumbled over the pillow, her mouth swollen with the imprint of his kisses. The curve of her arm, the slope of her shoulder, the tiny mole at the nape of her neck—every part of her body brought back some vivid memory of pleasure. Desire, unwelcome but insistent, stirred within Edward as his gaze traced the mound of her breast and the slender, supple length of her legs hidden beneath the linen sheet. In comparison to other women, her entire body was taut with muscle. Edward couldn't understand how he had once found the typical plump, soft female body attractive.

She stirred, and the sheet slipped a little, to reveal one firm breast and a pink nipple, erect and enticing in the pale light of dawn. Edward resisted the urge to lean over and take the tempting nipple into his mouth. Lucy needed her sleep.

He lifted a strand of her rich, chestnut hair, winding it around his forefinger. When he had first met Lucy in Kuwar, her hair had been so oiled and impregnated with dirt he had thought it was black. He lifted the lock of hair and rubbed it softly against his cheek. What would happen if he never came back from Afghanistan?

You know damn well what would happen. Your wife would marry again, probably as soon as her obligatory year of mourning was over. Lucy was young, beautiful, and at his death she would become rich beyond most men's dreams. Of course she would marry again.

The primitive intensity of his jealousy surprised him. In other circumstances, it would certainly have amused him. He realized that he didn't want any other man to experience the wonderful, sensuous richness of Lucy's lovemaking. He was the man who had shown her what passion between a man and a woman could be like, and, by God, he didn't want anyone else to benefit from his lessons.

Edward cut off his maudlin train of thought, offended by his dog-in-the-manger attitude. Heaven knew, it was selfish enough to have married Lucy. He had absolutely no right to wish that she would turn herself into an imitation Queen Victoria, permanently chained to the rituals of death and widowhood. Besides, he thought, managing a wry smile, there was always the remote possibility that he might not die. After all, he'd survived pretty handily for the past dozen years. The trouble was that until now he'd never cared very much whether he lived or died. When playing games with fate, it helped if you didn't care overmuch about the outcome. Like a tightrope walker who ignored the abyss gaping beneath his feet, Edward had crossed precipices and chasms, shaking his fist in the face of danger. The desire to return to Lucy had taken away his crucial advantage. Now he cared.

Time to get up. It would probably be easier for both of them if he was dressed and out of the way before she woke. Just one kiss wouldn't hurt, though. A light one. Something she couldn't possibly feel since she was sleeping so deeply.

He leaned over, breathing in the warm, drowsy smell of her skin. He touched his mouth to her cheek in a caress so delicate it was scarcely a kiss. She woke at once.

"I'm sorry," he said. "I didn't mean to disturb you." *Didn't he?*

Her brown eyes were huge, dark with awareness of all that had passed between them. "Since my time in Kuwar, I've slept very lightly."

He dropped a chaste kiss on her forehead, wondering why with this woman, unlike all others, the desire to possess her increased the more he was near her. He sat on the edge of the bed, telling himself that—soon—he would get dressed. A brisk gallop might take the edge off his restlessness.

"Go back to sleep, Lucy. I'll take my clothes into the dressing room so as not to disturb you."

"Actually, I'm not very sleepy. Just—lonely."

Edward's mind went blank. He stared at Lucy, aware only of the thick, pounding beat of his heart and the shy, husky appeal of his wife's words.

"Is this better?" he asked, lying back against the pillows and stretching out his arm for her to rest on. "Less lonely?"

"Much better." She snuggled against him, then hesitantly rested her hand against his chest. "This is very comfortable, Edward."

He was glad one of them felt comfortable, because he surely didn't. In her innocent search for a more comfortable position, she had insinuated her legs between his, with predictable consequences. Edward contemplated hauling his wife on top of him and demonstrating just what effect her little wriggles were having. Clenching his fists, he resisted the impulse. Her initiation was still too recent for him to risk embarrassing her. Besides, she was probably sore, and he damn well ought to control his sexual urges for at least the next twenty-four hours. Control was good for the soul. The Bishop of Cirencester had reminded him of that only the other day.

"Edward?"

"Yes."

"The oddest thing."

"What?"

"I think I may expire if you don't kiss me."

His heart stopped. He turned to look at her, his throat tight with emotion. She smiled at him, a tiny teasing smile that tore at his gut.

"I love you," he whispered, gathering her into his arms. "Wife of my heart, I love you more than life."

CHAPTER FIFTEEN

For a week, Lucy lived cocooned in the private paradise she and Edward had created for themselves. Each day, after a leisurely breakfast, they spent the long, summer hours riding across the local hills, exploring the fertile valleys, talking about anything and everything that caught their attention. They shared memories of Afghanistan and discussed local politics, international affairs, the future of India, their childhoods, their families, their favorite foods and a hundred more subjects on which it suddenly seemed vital to hear the other's opinion.

At night, as early as they could, they closed themselves into the privacy of their bedroom, where they explored the seemingly limitless boundaries of their passion.

Lucy's first warning of trouble came as she and Edward settled down after dinner on Saturday.

"The vicar will expect us to attend morning service tomorrow," she said, smiling up at Edward as she poured their nightly cup of tea. "And I daresay by Monday we shall have to brace ourselves for a round of visits from the neighbors."

"We are lucky they have kept away for an entire week." Edward made the appropriate response, but he didn't really seem to be paying attention. A rain squall, the first in several days, had chilled the air, and a sudden gust of blustery wind unhinged the latch on a casement window.

"Are you cold?" he asked, getting up to close the window. "It's miserably wet and windy out there. Shall I ask one of the servants to light a fire?"

"Thank you, but I'm not cold. Besides, isn't it almost bedtime?" Lucy busied herself with rearranging the sugar tongs and the cream jug, still feeling a little shy of acknowledging, however obliquely, the truth of what passed between them each night in the seclusion of their bedrooms.

She was surprised when Edward glanced at his watch instead of coming to sit beside her on the sofa. "It's only nine o'clock," he said.

Surely, he knew that she had no interest in the time? "Bedtime" had nothing to do with the clock. It arrived when neither of them could tolerate another minute in each other's company without making love.

Edward poured himself a second cup of tea and stirred it with excessive concentration. "A message from my uncle was delivered today," he said abruptly.

"From Lord Triss?" A warning danced with icy fingers along Lucy's spine. Trying to sound unconcerned, she asked, "Does he need you to return to London?"

Edward set down his still-full cup. "Not to London," he said. "To India. He wants me to leave at the end of next week on the *Empress of India*, the new P and O steamer. I should not be away for more than . . . for too long."

To India! Dear heaven, he was going back to India! "This is very sudden, isn't it?" Lucy asked.

"Not entirely. I promised my uncle some time ago that I would return to the East. The *Empress* is so much faster than other ships, it seemed sensible to take advantage of her imminent departure."

Lucy's thoughts raced as she sipped her tea. Could this trip be the real reason Edward had been so anxious to push forward the date of their wedding? The question immediately arose as to why he had wanted to marry her before he left England. Out of love? Or out of duty, because he had so thoroughly compromised her reputation? She feared the latter, although with time she had hoped to change his mind.

And now it seemed as if time might not be on her side. Lucy was not a fool. She understood at once that she was not included in Edward's travel plans, but she feigned incomprehension. The prospect of being separated from her husband was so terrible that she could not—would not—face it. She forced a smile, hoping Edward wouldn't divine the grim determination hiding behind her cheerful expression.

"My dear, why do you sound so unhappy? A trip to India is no reason for us to be wretched. True, Lord Triss has given us rather short notice, but we have a house full of excellent servants. I daresay they will not find it impossible to pack our trunks in five days. We can travel via London and say good-bye to my stepmother and Penelope on our way to Southampton."

Edward was not deceived. He knew she had understood. He turned away, unable to bear the hurt in her eyes. "Lucy, you know I can't take you with me."

"Why not? I am healthy and accustomed to travel. I know India, and the climate doesn't exhaust me as it does many people. Why should I not accompany you?" She placed her hand on his unyielding arm, her throat aching with unshed tears. "Edward, I am your wife and my place is at your side. Do you not wish me to accompany you?"

If only she knew, Edward thought. *God, if only she knew how badly he wanted to take her with him.*

Unfortunately, there were a dozen compelling reasons why he could not. Once he made contact with Abdul Rahman Khan's supporters, his life might well depend on his powers of concentration and observation. One slip, one misread signal, and he would never live to enjoy a second chance. With Lucy sharing his days and pleasuring his nights, Edward knew he could all too easily become distracted. And in his profession, men who allowed themselves to be distracted usually ended up impaled on the end of somebody's dagger.

There were other problems. In order to cross into Afghanistan unobserved, he would have to shed the trappings of an English nobleman and once again become Rashid, the Punjabi gun runner. It was Edward's uncanny ability to immerse himself in the role of an illicit gun trader that had prevented his unmasking by the dozens of French and Russian spies working along the Indian-Afghan frontier.

For Lucy's own sake, he could not tell her the truth about his mission. She had suffered enough at the Khan of Kuwar's hands and knew too well how Afghani warriors treated spies and traitors. He could not condemn her to months of worry about his safety. In addition, she was one of the few people in the world who knew

Lord Edward de Beaumont and Rashid, the Trader, were one and the same person. If she came with him to India, the difficulties of carrying off his dual role would be vastly increased. Lucy was a perceptive woman. It would be all too easy for her to stumble onto the truth of his plans, and thus be thrust into the midst of his danger. For this reason alone, if for no other, he had to resist her pleas to come with him.

"Lord Triss doesn't expect me to be away for very long," he said. "Perhaps as little as five months. My uncle is sorry to interrupt our honeymoon, but he needs my special knowledge of Afghanistan." That much at least was the truth. Ignorance of Afghanistan within the Foreign Office ranks reached unbelievable proportions.

"Why does he need you at this precise moment? What is happening in Afghanistan that requires immediate attention?"

He gave her his approved cover story, which was true, as far as it went. "Amir Sher Ali has agreed to send a delegation from Kabul to confer with a high-level British delegation in Peshawar. Lord Lytton himself will be conducting some of the negotiations."

"The Viceroy? Then these negotiations must be very important."

Edward nodded. "The Amir claims that he seeks a lasting settlement of all border disputes, and he wishes to accommodate our government's insistence on sending a British representative to Kabul. Lord Triss wants me on hand to offer advice to the British negotiators. Most of them, unfortunately, have little first-hand knowledge of conditions within Afghanistan."

"Obviously, your work will be crucial to the success of the talks, and I wouldn't dream of intruding upon it. Although, personally, I would be highly suspicious of the Amir's intentions. If he is proclaiming peace so loudly, it probably means he needs a breathing space to improve his preparations for war."

Edward laughed. "I agree completely. Either that, or some faction within Afghanistan is about to launch a successful *coup d'etat* and Sher Ali wants to preempt their attack." He sobered, realizing how easily he had allowed himself to be sidetracked.

"But that isn't the point, Lucy. This trip of mine is designed for speed rather than comfort. My days will be filled with difficult negotiations, and my nights will be filled with endless diplomatic dinners and receptions. You will be much happier and more at ease if you remain in England."

Lucy looked up at him, her eyes bright with tears. "You may, if you wish, order me to stay in England. You are my husband and you have that right. But do not, I beg of you, tell me that I shall be *happier* if I remain here. That is insulting to us both. I thought I deserved more honesty from you, Edward."

Without waiting for him to reply, Lucy pivoted on her heel and walked blindly toward the door. She had taken no more than half a dozen steps when Edward caught up with her. He gripped her arms and swung her around to face him.

"All right," he said harshly. "You win this particular battle, Lucy. I am no match for your tears. Come to India with me if that is what you wish, but I pray we don't both regret this."

She didn't like the feeling that she had torn the concession from him against his better judgment, but the relief of knowing they wouldn't be separated overcame all other emotions.

"It is very much what I wish," she said softly. "Oh, Edward, thank you for allowing me to come. You will not regret it, I promise you."

She stared up at him, her eyes dark with love, her mouth full and soft, waiting for his kiss. Looking down at her, Edward realized he didn't even care if his decision was wise. He cared only that it had made her happy.

He took her into his arms, holding her tight against his chest. Alarms set off by twelve years of hard-won experience sounded loudly inside his head, but he silenced them with a lingering, intoxicating kiss.

The rumblings of his conscience were harder to ignore, but he drowned the irritating noise by carrying Lucy up to his bed and playing love games with her until laughter and passion chased all reasonable thoughts into the darkness of oblivion.

Only later, as he lay spent and exhausted on the tangled sheets, did the worries crowd in again, denying Edward any chance of sleep. He stared into the shadowed corners of the room, feeling the warmth of Lucy's arm across his ribs and the icy chill of fear within his heart.

He would keep her safe, Edward swore silently. As long as she never found out he was returning to Afghanistan, there would be no danger for either of them. To put it simply, as long as he lied through his teeth, all would be well. One thing, above all else, was certain: Lucy must never again see Rashid.

The sea voyage back to India was vastly different from Lucy's homeward journey two months earlier. Lost in love for her new husband, she laughed away the days and made love all night. If she sometimes sensed a frightening urgency to Edward's love-making, she refused to acknowledge it. Their marriage was perfect, and she would permit no cloud—however distant—to hover on the horizon of their happiness. Each day, she allowed herself to become a tiny bit more confident that Edward had married her because he loved her. Each day, she blossomed a little more under the reassurance of that love.

After a month of travel and several days in Calcutta so that Edward could confer with the Viceroy, Edward and Lucy set out on their long journey east to Peshawar. Another woman might have been nervous at the prospect of returning to a town where she had been so thoroughly scorned, but Lucy knew Anglo-Indian society too well to worry. Lord Edward de Beaumont, Third Baron Ridgeholm, would be a glittering star on Peshawar's limited social scene. Lady de Beaumont would be welcomed accordingly.

Lucy's assessment proved entirely correct. From the moment of her arrival, when she and Edward were greeted by a brass band and two little girls carrying posies of flowers, it was obvious that the local dignitaries had suffered a convenient attack of collective amnesia. Lord Edward was fawned over as the personal envoy of the British Foreign Secretary. And nobody was crass enough to remind anybody that the beautiful Lady de Beaumont had once appeared in Mrs. Rutherspoon's drawing room dressed in ragged native clothes and smelling distinctly rancid.

Mr. and Mrs. Rutherspoon hosted the official dinner party to welcome the new arrivals. Mrs. Rutherspoon, whose imagination was not of a high order, seemed to have no difficulty at all in disconnecting her memories of the disreputable Miss Larkin from the present splendor of Lady de Beaumont.

While the men lingered over brandy, she took her seat next to Lucy in the drawing room. "And how are you enjoying your visit to Peshawar, my lady? I trust you have not found the overland journey to our little town too ennervating?"

"The new railway lines make the journey quite easy, although very long, of course."

"Ah, yes, so very long, indeed! One always hopes that the natives will learn to be more efficient. Train journeys in our own dear England never seem to take such a tediously long time."

"That is possibly because England is scarce four hundred miles from north to south, whereas India is close to three thousand miles long and almost as wide from east to west."

Mrs. Rutherspoon merely looked blank, and Lucy decided not to attempt any more lessons in advanced geography. "And how is your daughter Rosamund, Mrs. Rutherspoon? I hoped I might see her again tonight."

Her hostess perked up. "So sweet of you to remember little Rosamund!" she purred, apparently finding nothing odd about Lucy remembering Rosamund while Mrs. Rutherspoon vigorously maintained the fiction that Lucy had never before set foot in India. "My dear little girl is in England, preparing to make her debut. My mama, the dowager Lady Thorne, the widow of Sir Albert Thorne, has agreed to present her next year. Rosamund's papa and I are most hopeful that she will marry while she is in England and thus be spared the necessity of returning here to India. We shall miss her most dreadfully, of course, but fortunately it is only another five years until Mr. Rutherspoon is entitled to home leave."

Five years sounded a very long time to Lucy. She was reminded of Mrs. Trimble, her companion on the voyage back to England, who had been separated from her two sons for most of their childhood. Now Mrs. Rutherspoon, who obviously loved her daughter, was condemning herself to a similar fate.

What a bizarre, uncomfortable life imperialism imposed on its civil servants, Lucy thought. Governing India required Great Britain to send thousands of highly trained individuals into permanent exile, without ever allowing those individuals the luxury of growing new roots in the country where they were destined to spend most of their lives. Rosamund had been born in India. How would she feel living with a grandmother she had never met, in a country she had never seen and yet was obligated to consider "home"?

Lucy's somewhat gloomy train of thought was interrupted by the arrival of the gentlemen. Mrs. Rutherspoon fluttered off to capture Lord Edward. Lucy remained seated and was joined by her host, who greeted her with what seemed genuine pleasure.

Unlike the ladies of Peshawar, his amnesia was not all-encompassing. "Thank you for your letter, Lady de Beaumont. It arrived about a month ago, and I was delighted to hear that you had enjoyed a safe and comfortable journey home. The account of your ship's passage through the Suez Canal was most interesting."

"The speed of the mail is one of the Canal's greatest blessings,"

Lucy remarked. "Only four weeks for a letter to travel from London to Calcutta! It's almost unimaginable."

"And at a cost of pennies," Mr. Rutherspoon agreed. "Although sometimes I wonder if all this speed of communication is such a marvelous thing. In some instances, we would be better served if the messages coming out of London could all get lost at sea like they used to in the old days."

"You are not an admirer of Mr. Disraeli's policy in regard to India?"

Mr. Rutherspoon cleared his throat. "I'll be honest with you, my lady. I believe Mr. Disraeli's Forward Policy will prove disastrous for the British Raj. We don't need to be aggressively seeking new boundaries for our empire. Half the world is already under our direct control. How can we govern more?"

"There seems to be no shortage of willing administrators."

"Willing is not the same as competent. Here in India, for example, we should be concentrating on improving the efficiency of our civil service and the native soldiers, not chasing off in pursuit of some mythical Russian army that may or may not be threatening our northern frontier."

He lowered his voice. "My theory is that the Russian emperor would forget about Afghanistan if we didn't keep declaring that the country lies exclusively within our sphere of interest. He never had any interest in marching in until we ordered him to keep out."

"You believe the Russian emperor is childish enough to go to war simply because our government has asked him not to?"

Mr. Rutherspoon grunted. "Why would Tsar Alexander or anyone else want to acquire a country that consists of impenetrable mountains and squabbling goat herds? The tsar is using British interest in Afghanistan as a diversion. He has to find some way to keep his serfs too busy to notice that they're starving. What better way to occupy them than to conscript them into the army and send them off to fight the wicked British in Afghanistan?"

"Has he considered recruiting them to plant food so that they would no longer be starving?"

"Hah! That is not the way of emperors, my lady. I'll admit, it's a relief to know that Lord Edward de Beaumont is here to advise our team of negotiators. This may be Great Britain's last chance to avoid a terrible mistake in Afghanistan. We need a few voices of cool reason to hold back Lord Lytton's crew of imperialist hotheads."

"My husband has made no public statement concerning his instructions from the Foreign Secretary," Lucy said.

"True, but I have known Lord Edward for some years. He doesn't say much of consequence when he's at a social gathering, but I've noticed that whenever he is involved in a treaty negotiation, or in some discussion with the natives, we end up with a sensible agreement that can actually be implemented. The trouble with the Viceroy is that he's playing to the political gallery back home instead of considering the situation under his nose."

Back home. Mr. Rutherspoon had lived in India for over twenty years. He condemned the lack of understanding shown by British politicians legislating for India across thousands of miles of ocean and a universe of misunderstanding. And yet, like his wife, and like every other Anglo-Indian Lucy had ever met, he still referred to England as *home.* For the first time, Lucy found herself questioning whether Great Britain could ever govern India satisfactorily when the governors all considered themselves aliens in a strange land.

"You are looking amazingly pensive, my love." Mr. Rutherspoon had been called away by a guest, and Edward came to take his place at Lucy's side.

"Mr. Rutherspoon gave me a great deal to think about."

"I am alarmed. Experience has warned me to be wary of that particular expression of yours. I fear I am to be subjected to another of your lectures on the inalienable right of educated women to cast votes in public elections."

She smiled. "Not tonight."

"I am amazingly relieved."

"Prematurely, perhaps. Tonight, you are to receive a special treat. I plan to lecture you on the need for Great Britain to avoid going to war over Afghanistan."

"What a horrible prospect! Worse even that the rights of women. If I listen with due humbleness, what is my reward?"

"You become better informed."

"Somehow, such a reward quite fails to tempt me. Could you not stretch your imagination a little?"

She pretended to give the matter serious consideration. "Well, let me see. What sort of reward would you have in mind?"

He bent his head and murmured in her ear. "Anything that involves your naked body in my bed would be acceptable."

"My lord, I'm shocked by your lewdness!" She flipped open her fan. "But since this is a *very* important subject, you shall have

your wish. One naked wife in exchange for your earnest attention
to the subject of British war policy in Afghanistan."

"One *willing* naked wife," he amended, his eyes gleaming with
laughter—and something more.

Lucy yawned, concealing the little coil of excitement already
tightening inside her. "La, my lord, you drive a monstrous hard
bargain."

He reached out solicitously to raise her to her feet. "Others have
commented on the same thing. If you are ready to leave, my dear,
I believe we should be on our way. Let us find our host and
hostess. Oh, look, how fortunate, they are coming in this
direction."

"Leaving already?" Mr. Rutherspoon said.

"I'm afraid we must." Lucy might be blushing, but Edward's
voice was as smooth as cream. "My wife has something she
wishes to discuss with me, and I feel a most urgent need to
become better informed."

"Actually," Lucy interjected, "I am a little tired. The strains of
the train journey must be catching up with me."

Mrs. Rutherspoon found this quite understandable, if disap-
pointing, and she said her good-byes, pressing "dear Lord and
Lady de Beaumont" to regard the Rutherspoon house as their
own. Edward promised that they would certainly do so, and the
Rutherspoons and de Beaumonts parted on the best of terms.

As soon as Edward and Lucy had returned to their own rented
accommodation—a modest bungalow, which was all Peshawar
had to offer under the stress of so many visiting diplomats—
Edward dismissed the servants and propelled Lucy into their
shared bedroom. He seated himself on a straight-backed chair of
carved Indian mahogany and folded his arms.

"You see me before you, all dutiful attention," he said, his eyes
dancing. "First, sweet wife, I listen to your lecture and then you
give me my reward. I am all eager anticipation."

"Edward," she protested, "you cannot possibly have taken our
silly exchange seriously."

"Oh, yes, my heart. Very seriously, indeed. Pray do not delay
any further with your fascinating lecture on the subject of British
foreign policy. I can hardly wait to be—better informed."

Lucy decided to ignore the dangerous, enticing gleam in her
husband's eyes. "It seems to me," she said, clasping her hands
primly in her lap, "that Mr. Disraeli errs in thinking he can find

the perfect, safe boundary for our empire. If we extend the boundary of northern India up into Afghanistan, where will the Prime Minister declare the borders of our next safety zone? Uzbek? Khiva? Edward, do not look at me so."

"How so, my love?"

"As if . . . as if you will pounce upon me at any moment and tear off my clothes."

"Why should I do that, my heart, when you have promised faithfully to perform the task yourself?"

"I promised no such thing!"

"How do you propose to end up naked and willing in my bed if you never undress?"

Lucy decided to ignore this question. "I have not yet finished my lecture," she said with considerable dignity. "I have *lots* more to say."

Edward inclined his head politely. "You were, I believe, discussing where Mr. Disraeli might draw the final boundaries of the empire, bearing in mind the strictures of his Forward Policy. Have I mentioned to you that your lips are quite the most kissable lips I have ever seen on a woman anywhere in the world?"

"Yes. I mean no. Edward, will you please stop staring at me!"

"I don't wish to miss a single one of your wise words, my love. Do, pray, continue."

Lucy drew in a labored breath. "In my opinion, Afghanistan should be established as a strong, independent nation under an honest, efficient ruler who will dominate the warring tribes and factions. Its borders would then be guaranteed by a world—"

"A most admirable goal," Edward said. "My love, I am so grateful for your lecture. I cannot begin to tell you how much better informed I now feel upon this important subject. Please take off your gown."

"Edward!"

"My love?"

"You are not keeping to the terms of our agreement. You said you would listen dutifully until I had finished. I have barely begun."

"My heart, you have now learned the first and most important rule of diplomatic negotiation. Assume that your opponent will change the agreed terms of the treaty at his earliest opportunity. Please take off your gown."

She could have refused, of course, but she had no real desire to postpone their lovemaking. Tonight, before she told him her incredible, wonderful news, she wanted to tantalize him just a little, to dazzle the worldly, jaded Lord Edward de Beaumont with the seductive powers of his wife.

Her gaze locked with his for a moment, then she slipped off her evening slippers and bent to pull her gown up to her knees. Untying the embroidered satin garters that held her stockings in place, she slowly pushed the filmy silk down her legs and over her ankles. She could feel Edward's gaze burning against her skin as she tossed the stockings onto a chair.

The pins in her hair came out next. Shaking the heavy curls so that they drifted around her shoulders, she watched the highly satisfactory effect of her actions upon her husband.

"I can't take off my dress until somebody unfastens the buttons," she murmured. "Shall I summon a maid?"

"I think you know better," Edward said huskily, rising to his feet.

He made short work of the tiny pearl buttons, and soon slipped the dress from her shoulders, along with her chemise. The dress fell in a pool at her feet, and she stepped out of it, pivoting slowly beneath his ardent gaze.

"You become more beautiful each day, I swear it," he said. "Ah, Lucy, how did I survive before I loved you?"

"By loving many other women?" she suggested teasingly.

"No. By walking through life only half-alive." Abandoning their game, he kissed her deeply, his tongue filling her mouth with the promise of ecstasy to come. Not halting their kiss, he guided her to the bed. Her knees connected with the cool, linen-covered mattress and she fell back onto it, unashamedly pulling him with her.

His hands stroked over her breasts, cupping each in turn, until her nipples sprang into revealing hardness beneath his touch. Trailing kisses along her collarbone and between her breasts, he finally took one of her swollen nipples into his mouth.

Instantly, he went still.

"What is it?" Lucy pushed herself up in the bed, struggling to free herself from the pleasant haze of rising passion. "Edward, what is it?"

"I think you must know. Even I can feel the changes in your body." Slowly, sensuously, Edward's hand traced an inquiring path over her stomach. Then his hands once again cupped the new, heavier fullness of her breasts. His voice thick, almost unrecognizable, he framed her face with his hands.

"Lucy, my heart, can it be . . . are you with child?"

She laughed with the delight of confirming his guess. "Yes, how did you know? I have been almost certain for nearly two weeks. I think our baby will be born in seven months, at the end of March or the beginning of April."

"You must have conceived while we were still in England." His normally austere expression softened with wonder. "So soon! I never dreamed it would be so soon." His hands circled her tiny waist. "There doesn't seem to be much room inside here for a baby."

A rueful smile curved her mouth. "That problem will soon be taken care of. Unfortunately, I am likely to expand in several inelegant directions."

"And then you will be more beautiful than ever." He kissed her deeply, one hand tangling in the mass of curls spread out over the pillow, the other stroking her flat stomach with an odd mixture of desire and reverence. "I want to see your body swell as my son grows inside you. I wish I could already feel his legs and arms kicking against my hands."

"You have played the role of a Punjabi trader for too long," she said, stirring drowsily. "You begin to think like a Moslem. How do you know I carry your son and not your daughter?"

For a split second, his whole body stiffened, and Lucy wondered if he desired a son so much that he was offended by the mere thought that she might be pregnant with a girl. But his tension disappeared as quickly as it had come, and she began to think she must have imagined it.

He tickled her stomach with tender, teasing fingers. "In my family we have a history of twins. Perhaps you are carrying both a son and a daughter."

Speechless, her eyes wide with alarm, Lucy stared up at him. Laughing, Edward dropped a loving kiss on her nose. "Never fear, my heart, I doubt if you need to worry. We don't have *that* many twins sprouting from my family tree!"

Once again, his hand traveled down her body, no longer searching for signs of her pregnancy, but simply seeking to bring her pleasure. When his fingers explored the silken softness between her thighs, she writhed with sensuous satisfaction.

"I love you," he whispered.

Despite the passionate intensity of their lovemaking, he rarely expressed his feelings in words, and Lucy's heart soared high with happiness. She sighed his name, arching her hips to invite his penetration, her lips clinging to his in willing surrender.

He entered her, accompanying his possession with gentle, skilled stroking. She thrilled to the warmth of him, a warmth not only of physical closeness. The warmth was there in every caress, in the dark intimacy of his eyes, in the husky tones of his voice, in the tender urgency with which he claimed her body.

"I love you," she murmured, as she felt control slipping away. "I can't wait to see the child we have made together."

With a low, harsh groan, Edward allowed the rhythm of his thrusts to build to a shattering crescendo. The taste of him was in her mouth, the scent of him in her nostrils. She was no longer sure where her body began and his ended. And at last, in perfect harmony, they found the wild, triumphant release they sought.

They lay together for a long time, bodies entwined, throbbing with the aftermath of completion. Edward was the first to speak. "Was I too rough? Does the baby make it feel different for you?"

"No . . . It was wonderful." Lucy reached up and touched him lightly on the cheek, already half-asleep. These past few days, it had seemed as if she could sleep forever.

Edward smoothed the tangle of curls out of her face, but sleep claimed her totally before he could say anything more. Gently, he drew the thin linen sheet over her shoulders. Her body seemed so slender beneath the covers. Too fragile to give birth easily. And yet her appearance of fragility must be deceptive. She had survived months of semistarvation in Kuwar.

Against his will, Edward felt his hand drawn once again to her stomach.

His child. Lucy was going to bear his child. He hadn't considered—hadn't allowed himself to consider—the possibility that she would conceive so swiftly. Although what else had he expected when they often made love two and three times in a single night?

What, in the name of heaven, was he going to do about Lucy? Today, the message had arrived from Abdul Rahmen Khan, summoning him to the top-secret, all-important meeting in the heart of the Afridi stronghold. Next week, Edward would have to leave for Afghanistan. The future of an entire nation might depend on what happened at that meeting, and there were a lot of people trying to make sure that Edward and Abdul Rahmen never met.

He hoped to God he could outwit them.

He hoped to God he would live to see the birth of his child.

CHAPTER SIXTEEN

Gossip in Peshawar maintained that the talks between the Amir's emissaries and the British delegation were not going well. The approach of winter meant that the pass over the Hindu Kush into Afghanistan would soon be closed, and the pressure of lack of time was added to all the other pressures affecting the negotiators.

Lucy had good reason to believe the pessimistic rumors. Edward had been working twelve-hour days ever since his arrival in India, but recently his workload seemed never-ending. After sixteen hours at the negotiating table, he would return to their rented bungalow, apologize for his late return, then immediately closet himself in his study. Conversation between the two of them became limited to the exchange of brief, everyday courtesies.

Lucy, made sleepy by her pregnancy, was never awake when he finally came to their bed, but despite her fascination with the changes occurring in her body, she was too much in love and too perceptive not to notice the gray tinge of fatigue developing beneath Edward's tanned complexion.

"My dear, you need rest," she said one night, entering his study with a cup of tea. "I'm sure you didn't come to bed last night at all."

"I have work to finish." Edward accepted the tea with a quick nod of thanks. "Don't wait up for me, Lucy. I shall probably be late again. Very late."

"Edward, those papers won't run away in the night." She laughed softly. "I wish they would, but sadly every one of them will still be waiting for you tomorrow morning. My dear, I doubt if you've had twelve hours sleep in the past week. Please come to bed with me."

"I can't." He rose without looking at her and walked over to the window. "I told you before we left England that I would be busy, too busy to dance attendance on you. Please don't interrupt me any more, Lucy. I simply don't have time for playing husband at the moment."

Lucy couldn't control the hurt that shadowed her eyes at his curt words. "I'm sorry," she said coolly. "I didn't mean to intrude on your work. It won't happen again." Back rigidly erect, she walked from the room.

Edward gripped the arm of the chair to stop himself running after her. *It's for your own sake, Lucy my heart,* he whispered. *I don't want you to question me when I leave, and I shall be leaving very soon.*

His silent apology didn't relieve his feelings at all. When the sounds of her footsteps had completely faded, he picked up the inkstand on his desk and hurled it at the wall. It crashed in a splatter of blue ink and shattered china.

He scowled at the dark stain spreading slowly over the whitewashed wall.

Unfortunately, his pointless act of vandalism didn't make him feel one bit better.

Mr. Carradin, senior aide to Lord Lytton and leader of the British team of negotiators, was a seasoned diplomat. As such, he had long since learned the value of interspersing hard-hitting bargaining sessions with pleasanter diversions. On Saturday evening, a week after Edward's rebuff to Lucy, Mr. Carradin decided the weather was cool enough to permit ending his dinner party with some informal dancing. Receiving this message early on Saturday morning, diplomats and long-term residents of Peshawar alike perked up and found themselves looking forward to a break in their routines.

Lucy did not share in the general anticipation of pleasure. Edward seemed positively buried in work, and he had already announced that he would be unable to accompany his wife to Mr. Carradin's party.

"But you should go, my dear," he said. As was his habit over the past few days, he didn't look at her as he spoke. "You certainly deserve a break from this tedious round of solitary meals and early bedtimes."

Lucy wanted to remind him that she wasn't a child who needed entertaining every minute of every day. She had endured two years in Afghanistan when sometimes days might pass without a single person speaking to her other than to hurl abuse. Here in Peshawar, she had a household to control, neighbors to visit, baby clothes to sew and books to read. Boredom was the least of her problems.

But she said nothing, or at least nothing that honestly indicated what she was feeling. Conversation with the remote, silent man her husband had become was difficult, and she dreaded overstepping the invisible boundary he seemed to have set between the two of them. She hoped Edward's withdrawal from her was caused by nothing more than pressure of work, but she feared that somehow it was caused by her pregnancy. The night she had told him he was to be a father, he had seemed thrilled. Ever since then, however, their relationship had become steadily more strained, until now on the rare occasions they found themselves alone they conversed with the wary courtesy of strangers.

Without her husband at her side, Lucy didn't expect to find the dinner party particularly enjoyable. But dressing up for the occasion gave her something slightly more useful to do than worry about her marriage, so she made her toilette with care and set off for Mr. Carradin's house under the escort of a groom, an outrider and the *ayah* who served as her maid. Edward appeared in the hallway, complimented her on her gown and bade her farewell with his now habitual formality. Too hurt to be as perceptive as usual, Lucy quite failed to notice the agony of indecision in his gaze as he watched the pony trap pull away from the doorway.

Mr. Carradin was an excellent, sophisticated host. Food served at British households in Peshawar tended to be less than palatable. He had improved the standard by the simple device of allowing his cooks to use some of the native spices and by not attempting to serve such British treats as roast beef and Yorkshire pudding— delicacies that basically defied the imagination and churned the stomach of any Indian chef.

The tasty food added to the lustre of a party that was a success from the outset. The prospect of after-dinner dancing lifted the spirits of the guests. The promise of cooler weather ahead after the ennervating drought of the past season made even the dreariest soul cheerful, and the permanent residents of Peshawar put forth their best efforts to entertain the visiting dignitaries. Peshawar was so far north that it attracted few visitors in the normal course of events, and this sudden inundation of diplomats and foreign princes was highly exciting. The diplomats, for their part, were glad of the prospect of a few hours away from the bargaining table. Chatter between courses was lively and sprinkled with polite chortles.

Since the gentlemen outnumbered the ladies by a considerable margin, Lucy found herself seated among a group of high-ranking diplomats, including a dour Russian nobleman who had been sent to Peshawar as an emissary from the tsar and a young Tuscan count from the newly united country of Italy.

Discreet questioning on Lucy's part soon revealed that nobody, least of all the Tuscan count himself, had any idea why he was in an obscure Indian border town observing treaty negotiations that were entirely without interest to his country. Count Guido was, however, a charming flirt, and Lucy enjoyed listening to him compliment her in seductively accented English. Dinner, on the whole, was rather enjoyable. It was certainly a vast improvement over the alternative, which would have been to sit at home and moon over Edward.

The dancing afterward was less agreeable. Because of the shortage of female partners, Lucy felt obligated to dance as much as she could, although her usual sleepiness was already overtaking her. She wasn't suffering from the dreadful nausea that she had heard some pregnant Kuwari women complain of, but she soon discovered that her stamina was sadly lacking. Instead of dancing light-footed until the early hours, by eleven she was forced to retreat to a cool corner of the makeshift ballroom. She wanted nothing so much as to be left alone to catch her breath and doze quietly till the dancing was over.

Her solitude lasted less than two minutes. Monsieur Armand, a French gentleman she had met briefly before dinner, came and stood beside her.

"If you do not dance, my lady, I shall take zis opportunity to converse wiz Mr. Carradin's most beautiful guest." He gestured to the chair. "If I may be permitted?"

She fanned herself, smothering a sigh of regret for her lost isolation. The Italian count had flirted all through dinner, and she had rather enjoyed his company, so it was not that she objected to hearing silly compliments. But something about Monsieur Armand struck a false note, and she would have preferred to sit alone. Good manners, unfortunately, prevented her from replying honestly.

"Of course, *monsieur*, I should be delighted to have your company. Are you here to attend the treaty negotiations, also?"

"Not at all, my lady. Alas, I am not ze diplomat. I am a merchant of furs."

"Of fur?" she asked, wondering why in the world a fur trader would visit a hot country like India. "Then you are in Peshawar on holiday, *monsieur*?"

He laughed heartily. "Not at all, my lady. Peshawar is not ze ideal spa for a vacation, no? I seek a supply for sheepskins. For ze famous sheep from Afghanistan. It is called *garakul* by ze natives, but in France we say Persian lamb."

"Oh, yes, of course." Lucy immediately understood. "I had heard that this particular wool is becoming fashionable in Paris, particularly for winter hats and as a trim for berlin capes."

He laughed again. "You are right, my lady. We 'ave given zis wool a new name. We call it Persian lamb instead of *garakul,* and now fashionable ladies 'ave decided zey cannot live wizout it. Was it not your Mr. Shakespeare who said 'What's in a name?' We merchants could tell him zere is very much in a name. Ladies of fashion will never wear *garakul*. But Persian lamb? Ah! zat is a different pot of fish."

"So, do you plan a trip into Afghanistan, Monsieur Armand? That's rather a risky venture this late in the year. You must take care the passes are not closed by the time you and your guides are ready to come out."

"Ah, no! I do not go into Afghanistan. I 'ave been told it is of all places most dangerous. Your so-good 'usband 'ave give me zis warning 'imself. Ze tribesmen, you know, zey are always at war. I wait 'ere in Peshawar for my contact to arrive. He 'as promised me a mule train loaded wiz sheepskins. I am in expectation of a most 'andsome profit when 'e finally arrives."

Lucy hoped that Monsieur Armand would not wait in vain. Her experience had shown her that Afghans and Europeans had quite different perceptions of time. *September 1877* meant something very specific to Monsieur Armand, and to most other Europeans. To an Afghani sheepherder, it could mean anything or nothing at all. Monsieur Armand's contact was just as likely to turn up in

September of next year as September of this. What's more, he would probably be offended if the Frenchman wasn't waiting for him, and would go back to his tribe complaining of the unreliability of *ferangi* traders.

A flourish from the two violinists—who, together with the vicar's wife at the piano, constituted the orchestra for the night—announced the start of the final waltz, although it was still early. The young Tuscan count promptly appeared at Lucy's side, claiming that she had promised him this final dance.

Lucy wasn't at all sure she had done any such thing, but she allowed herself to be led out onto the dance floor anyway. The Tuscan, despite his outrageous compliments, was much more enjoyable company than the French merchant.

She didn't regret her decision. The count not only proved to be an expert dancer, he made her laugh with wry witticisms and harmless jokes. After they had said farewell to Mr. Carradin, Count Guido requested permission to escort her home. "So beautiful a *baronessa* should not ride through the streets alone."

"Hardly alone, *signor conte*. I am surrounded by servants, and the streets of Peshawar contain few dangers at this hour."

"For so beautiful a woman, is always danger," the count murmured, his eyes soulful. "I will keep you entertained with amusing stories from my past life of wickedness. That is better than traveling alone, no?"

Lucy laughed and moved over in the pony trap to accommodate him. She signaled the driver to begin the short drive home.

"Tell me, *signor conte*, before you regale me with your wickedness, do you already have a wife back home in Tuscany? Or are you merely betrothed? I am somehow quite certain that a gentleman as eloquent and eligible as you cannot have entirely escaped the matrimonial nets of Tuscany's ladies."

"Alas, the lady I love has spurned me, *signora baronessa*. She married a man of age to be her grandfather but with a fortune large enough to satisfy even my love's so enormous hunger for jewels and fine clothes."

Some underlying note of pain broke through the deliberate overdramatization of his words. "I'm sorry," Lucy said, resting her hand on his arm for an instant. "But, you know, *signor conte*, I cannot help thinking that marriage to a lady who is hungry only for jewels would not make for much happiness. You deserve better."

He smiled. "You are doubtless entirely correct, *baronessa*. It is a pity, is it not, that we foolish human beings so rarely manage to love with good sense? From the sadness in your eyes, I am sure you understand what I say."

"I'm not sad," she said quickly. Too quickly. She tried to recover by producing a lighthearted laugh. "I assure you that Lord Edward is a most wonderful husband, *signor conte*."

"And you are a most loyal wife, *baronessa*." His eyes twinkling, he raised her hand to his lips, bestowing an elegant, lingering kiss. She did not pull her hand away, but neither did she feel even a quiver of response. How odd, she thought, that if Edward touched me, my skin would turn to flame, whereas this handsome, charming count arouses no more feeling in me than a lost puppy.

The carriage had drawn up outside the entrance to her bungalow. The count restored her hand to her lap with a rueful laugh, then sprang from the pony trap and quickly walked around to open the door. "Alas, *baronessa*, I regret to perceive you are as virtuous as you are desirable. An affaire with you, *baronessa*, would have been delightful."

She allowed her hand to tighten momentarily on his supporting arm. "*Signor conte*, no affaire could ever be as delightful as marriage to someone you love. Perhaps you should stop protecting your emotions by flirting only with ineligible ladies like me. Risk your heart, *signor conte*. You have nothing to lose save the terrible burden of emptiness you now carry."

He escorted her to the shaded portico of the bungalow, then once again carried her fingers to his lips. This time the action wasn't flirtatious, but brief and respectful. "Someday, perhaps, I will find the courage. It requires much courage, I think." His former, flirtatious manner returned almost at once, and he swept her a deep, exaggerated bow. "If you ever tire of trying to melt the reserve of your so-cold English baron, remember that I am the expert in frivolous affaires."

She laughed, wondering why she wasn't offended by his boldness. Perhaps it was because she recognized that beneath the light banter, he felt as lost and bewildered as she did. She had the odd feeling that if she actually agreed to become the count's mistress, he would find excuses not to accept her offer. "Thank you for an enjoyable evening, *signor conte*. I regret that your time and finesse have been so sadly wasted tonight."

"Not wasted, *baronessa*. Invested with hope for the future."

His grin was cheeky—and contagious. Laughing, she stepped

into the hall. "Well, *signor conte*, you may live in hope if you wish. Let's say that if I ever decide to have an affaire, I will remember your unique skills."

"An interesting promise but one, I regret, you will have no occasion to act upon." The voice that spoke from the darkened hallway was soft, cold and deadly. His face a mask of controlled fury, Edward strode toward the doorway and nodded to the count. "My wife appreciates your escort service, *signor conte*. My driver will be pleased to take you to your destination." He slammed the door without waiting for the count's reply.

Lucy was appalled, almost as much by Edward's rudeness to the count as by the obvious misinterpretation he had placed on her silly, teasing remarks. "Edward, he is a mere boy," she murmured.

"A mere boy who is three or four years older than you," he said. "And known as a reckless womanizer throughout the diplomatic community. What are you trying to do, Lucy? Punish me for neglecting you? Does it take so little to make you restless? A mere two weeks of hard work on my part, and already you are looking for a new man to warm your bed?"

If she had stopped for a split second, she would have realized how out of character Edward's accusation sounded. If she had listened to the pain behind his words, she would have realized that something must be troubling him greatly for him to speak with such harshness. But Lucy didn't stop to think and she wasn't listening. Her emotions had been on a six months' merry-go-round, and she was in no condition to make subtle judgments about her husband's state of mind. To top off everything else, she felt guilty because Edward was partly correct: She *had* flirted with the count to ease the pain of her husband's rejection. And that guilt made her feel angry. By what right did Edward condemn her for flirting when he hadn't attempted to apologize for his own weeks of coldness and neglect?

"Why shouldn't I seek another man to entertain me?" she demanded hotly. "You are certainly never available!"

Say that you will be there in the future, she pleaded silently. *Say that you love me and that you don't regret marrying me.*

Edward's brows drew together in a black frown. "You are my wife, and you carry my child. Is that not reason enough to expect absolute propriety in your behavior?"

"I behaved with perfect propriety! You are deliberately misunderstanding a harmless remark."

"To promise an affaire strikes you as harmless?" Edward grabbed her hand and propelled her into the drawing room, where an oil lamp had been left burning by the houseboy. Goaded by some demon he couldn't control, he banged the door shut, turning to her with eyes blazing and mouth sneering. "Or have I been a fool, sweet wife? Have I hit upon the problem? Do you carry some other man's child that you wish to foist off onto me?"

Lucy felt the blow of his words as if he had punched her in the stomach. She sank onto the sofa because her legs would no longer support her. Instinctively, she cradled her arms about her waist, protecting her child from the bitterness of its father's accusations. "My God, Edward, how can you ask me such a question? How *dare* you ask me such a question? You, of all people, should know the child I carry is yours. I was a virgin when we married!"

"I know of a dozen ways for an experienced woman to fake the appearance of virginity. The Kuwari tribeswomen probably taught you a dozen more. A few cries, a modest blush, a little feigned ignorance and the trick is done."

Edward had no idea where his angry taunts sprang from. In reality, he didn't question Lucy's chastity for an instant, nor was there any doubt in his mind that he was the father of her child. But the desperate need to prevent her questioning his departure had tormented him all week. The need to build a wall between them, at the same time as his heart and soul yearned to spend every moment locked in her arms, resulted in a total disconnection between the words his mouth spoke and the emotions his heart felt.

"Your accusations are despicable, Edward." Lucy swallowed hard, choking back tears. Pregnancy had already reduced her to a state where she could sob for twenty minutes over a burned muffin. If she allowed herself to start crying now, she doubted if her tears would ever stop.

She wanted very badly to escape from this nightmare confrontation while she still retained some shred of dignity. She lifted her chin defiantly.

"I think we should continue this conversation some other time, Edward." Her words sounded harsh as they squeezed out over the lump in her throat. "I'm very tired and I would like to go to bed." She started to rise, but Edward pushed her back onto the sofa.

"Not yet," he said. "If you are so hungry for a man's attentions, let me remind you that I am the man to answer your hunger."

"I don't want . . . a man's attentions." *I want you. Oh God,
I want you*.

He smiled without mirth. "You lie, sweet wife. Your eyes tell
me that you lie. You want to make love." He took her into his
arms, holding her with passion but without tenderness. His body
was heavy over hers, his weight enforcing his will. His head bent
purposefully toward hers.

It was degrading to respond when he had barely spoken to her
for the past week, Lucy told herself fiercely. How could she kiss
a man who had just hurled such grotesque accusations at her? She
wrenched her head sideways to avoid his kiss, but he captured a
lock of her hair and held her head immobile.

"Don't!" she spat out. "Edward, no!"

He ignored her protests, covering her mouth and kissing her
with hard, hungry aggression. A shudder shook her frame at the
first touch of his lips, but with all her might she resisted the
insidious flame of desire licking at her willpower. She would not
tolerate his advances. She must not. She . . . would . . . not.

"Open your mouth to me, Lucy." His words were low and
deep, a command that contained the faintest hint of a plea. "Don't
lock yourself away from me."

"I don't want—"

His tongue slid into her mouth as soon as she opened it to speak.
As his kiss intensified, her skin began to tingle with little
firebursts of pleasure, and her lips parted wider to accept the deep
thrusts of his tongue.

Soon there was no need for him to hold her captive. She lay
quiescent beneath his mouth as he trailed his hands over her body,
seeking her breasts and brushing his thumbs over her nipples until
they sprang into aching hardness beneath his touch.

Lucy despised the helpless response of her own body. Why was
she allowing herself to melt into his arms? She and Edward ought
to be talking, reasoning out their problems, not lying on the sofa
coupling like mindless animals.

The comparison was so humiliating and so apt that she renewed
her struggles to escape. She strained and twisted, fighting her own
body's weakness far more than her husband's strength.

Edward stopped kissing her long enough to frame her face
between his hands. "Lucy, don't fight what we both long for," he
murmured.

"I don't long for anything," she panted.

"Do you not, my heart?" He manacled her wrists together in

one strong hand and let the other hand roam slowly over her stomach and down to her thighs. "You don't desire that I touch you—here?"

Despairingly, she closed her eyes as she felt the wild, hot leap of passion burn in her veins. She bit her lip to prevent herself crying out, but she knew her cries would have been of satisfaction, not of protest.

"You choose not to answer in words, Lucy, but your body can't conceal the truth from me. Kiss me, my heart."

With a soft moan, half of regret, half of yearning, she ceased her struggles and returned Edward's kiss. At the touch of her tongue, his kiss gentled magically, and the aggressive probing of his hands changed to a slow, delicate caress.

Lucy's body began to writhe with pleasure. Tonight, as on every other night, Edward's touch was like a match to the dry tinder of her passion. When he held her in his arms, when she felt his body tremble in her clasp, she wanted nothing more than to bring their lovemaking to its inevitable, burning conclusion.

His hands still held her prisoner as he drove into the heated softness of her body, but she welcomed the captivity. She felt the convulsive surge of Edward's pent-up desire, and she arched to meet him, taking him between her thighs with willing abandon. The coil of ecstasy spiraled inside her, mounting toward the familiar, exquisite sunburst of release.

She thought she heard him whisper her name, a murmur of regret and longing, as he buried his face in her neck and spent himself within her. Throat tight with unshed tears, body trembling, she held him against her heart and followed him into the blind, soaring rapture of her climax.

As soon as their heartbeats slowed and their breathing resumed its normal pace, Edward picked her up and carried her into the bedroom. Without speaking, he laid her on the bed and took her into his arms, cradling her against his chest. He drew the muslin curtains, closing them into a world bounded by the gauzy limits of the draperies.

Inside their tiny universe, silence reigned as he led her again and again to ecstasy. Each time, she thought her body must have passed beyond the point where response was possible, but each time he proved her wrong. He made love to her with a passionate, desperate urgency, as if seeking some means of imprinting the shape and texture of her body permanently on his mind. And all the while, no word was exchanged between them.

It was nearly dawn when she finally fell into an exhausted sleep on the rumpled, sweat-soaked sheets.

It was high noon when she awoke and discovered Edward had left the bungalow.

CHAPTER SEVENTEEN

"What do you mean the *sahib* left early this morning?" Lucy demanded, barely able to keep still while the maid fastened the buttons on her morning gown. "Did he pack a suitcase? Where did he go?"

The *ayah* looked at her pityingly. Variations of this question had already been asked a dozen times. "Your lord told his servant that he leaves for Delhi this afternoon. I was instructed to give you your lord's letter when you awoke. That is all I know, *memsahib*. Does the *sahib*'s letter tell you nothing more?"

Lucy had no need to look at her husband's note to recall exactly what it said, but she read it again anyway.

My dearest,

I am summoned to consult with Lord Lytton on our current deadlock in negotiations with Amir Sher Ali's representatives. Events within Afghanistan are escalating out of control, and the Amir must accept a Resident British Agent in his capital if he wishes to avoid war. Lord Lytton suspects, with some justification, that the Russian emperor is using his armies massed at the northern border of Afghanistan to influence political decisions pending in Europe. I fear it may be some weeks before I am able to return to you. Take care of your health for the sake of our child, whom I long to see, but most especially take care of yourself. I love you.

Edward.

As a source of political information, the note could be considered interesting. As a source of details about Edward's personal plans, it was severely lacking. Lucy closed her eyes, trying not to let frustration overwhelm her. She pulled a chair up to the dressing table and allowed the *ayah* to start brushing her hair.

"If my husband doesn't leave for Delhi until this afternoon, did he tell you where he planned to spend this morning?" she asked, not really expecting the maid to give her an answer.

"Of course he told me where he was going this morning," the *ayah* replied, as if she had made this perfectly plain several times already. "He sees first the barbarians from across the mountains, then he meets with His Excellency the Prince Carradin for lunch." No Indian native could ever be convinced that the personal envoy of the Queen-Empress Victoria could be plain Mr. Carradin. To the *ayah*, he was always "Prince" Carradin.

Lucy's heart gave a little jump of relief. *Edward was still in Peshawar! She still had a chance to see him.* She glanced at the clock on her bedside table. Almost one o'clock. She didn't waste time wondering why it had taken so much questioning to elicit such simple information from her maid. She had accepted years ago that Britishers often failed to phrase their questions in a way that produced the desired answers from their Indian servants.

"My hair looks wonderful," she said, sweeping up a few straggling ends and skewering them haphazardly in place with a tortoiseshell comb. "Could you hand me my blue hat and parasol, please?"

"But, *memsahib*, you haven't eaten."

Lucy pulled on her gloves. "I'll eat when I return. Send one of the boys to fetch the pony trap, would you?"

Less than twenty minutes later she was at Mr. Carradin's lodgings, being shown into his private sitting room, which obviously served more as a study than a place of repose.

"My dear Lady Ridgeholm." The diplomat rose from his seat behind the desk, greeting her with a friendly smile. "You look perturbed, my lady, and a little hot. Allow me to offer you some refreshment."

"Thank you, but I have no time. I understood that I might find my husband here with you, Mr. Carradin. Am I too late? Could you tell me where he has gone?"

"Lord Edward? Alas, no, dear lady, I fear you have been misled. I'm sure your husband left some time ago for Delhi—he was anxious to catch the earliest possible train from Lahore. But I will be happy to see that a message is forwarded to him if that is of any help to you. I trust nothing is amiss at home?"

"No, nothing. We are . . . I am very well." Her supply of energy seemed to drain away in a single, despondent gush. Lucy tightened her hold on her parasol, forcing herself to face Mr. Carradin with a polite smile.

"I had hoped to see Edward once more before he left, but my messages can just as easily be contained in a letter."

"Good, good. I shall be delighted to include your letters in the diplomatic pouch traveling to Delhi each week. That way, you'll be sure your news gets through swiftly and safely."

"How very kind," Lucy murmured. "I must not keep you any longer, Mr. Carradin."

He walked with her to the front door. "My dear Lady Ridgeholm, you have not delayed anything important. At my age a gentleman considers himself privileged when a beautiful young woman takes up his time. I'm sorry you missed Lord Edward, but I'm sure you will be hearing from him before the end of the week. I expect a courier from Delhi next Friday."

"How kind," she said again mechanically, allowing Mr. Carradin to hand her up into the carriage.

"Shall I have the pleasure of seeing you at the Rutherspoons' soirée next Saturday, Lady Ridgeholm?"

"I believe so. Good-bye, Mr. Carradin. Driver! You may take me home."

Lucy had no idea what impulse caused her to turn around at the last moment before leaving the grounds, and even less idea what caused her to lean back, shielding her movement behind the polished cotton sun canopy affixed to the open pony trap. The brilliant light of the early afternoon sun was dimmed by the fringe of the canopy and the decorative tassels of her parasol, so that when she stared into the dark windows of Mr. Carradin's lodgings the contrast was less intense than might have been expected. She could see the inside of Mr. Carradin's study quite clearly. There were two men inside the study. Two men. Mr. Carradin and her husband.

Lucy knew then why she had been so fearful ever since she

awoke and found herself alone in the bed. She was not a clinging
wife who disintegrated at the mere thought of her husband taking
a necessary business trip. But at some primitive, intuitive level,
she had never quite believed Edward's note, never quite believed
he was going to Delhi, or she wouldn't have chased him so
frantically. At some subconscious level she had known that if
Edward really planned to travel to Delhi on a routine mission for
Lord Lytton, he wouldn't leave her with only a note to inform her
of his whereabouts. Her instincts had all warned her that there
could be only one reason for his secretive departure—he was
planning to return to Afghanistan. ‑

When she became aware of her surroundings again, she saw
that the carriage was just passing the Rutherspoons' bungalow.
Quite calmly, she leaned forward, tapped the driver on the
shoulder with her parasol and ordered him to stop. "I have to visit
Mrs. Rutherspoon," she informed the driver. "I will return in her
carriage, so you may go home now."

The driver did not question his mistress's order, which seemed
no more peculiar than many others he had been given. He bowed
respectfully, opened the door of the pony trap and waited just long
enough to see the *memsahib* safely inside the Rutherspoon gate.
He then set off at a brisk trot for the bliss of an afternoon doze
under his favorite banyan tree.

As soon as her carriage turned the corner, Lucy spoke to the
Rutherspoons' gatekeeper. "I have just remembered. I have
forgotten something. Please open the gate; I must leave at once."

The gatekeeper inspected his visitor with unabashed interest.
The servants in Peshawar had not suffered from the same
collective amnesia as their employers, and the gatekeeper knew
precisely who this lady was. Apparently, whether wearing native
rags or elegant English clothes, the poor woman remained equally
strange. Fortunately, it was not his job to stop his British masters
from doing crazy things. If it had been, he would never stop
working. His job was simply to protect the Rutherspoon property
from undesirables. Thus, if this demented English lady wished to
dismiss her carriage and walk unattended in the heat of the
afternoon sun, it was not the gatekeeper's business to stop her.

He smiled kindly and swung open the gate. "Certainly, *memsahib*. May Vishnu bless your footsteps." He offered the blessing
with sincere goodwill. The mad needed all the protection they
could get.

"Thank you. Er . . . there is no need to mention to anybody that I have called."

"But you haven't called, *memsahib*. You are leaving."

"How true!" She smiled, and for a moment the gatekeeper wondered if anybody who looked so beautiful when she smiled could actually be mad.

"Thank you again," she said, pressing a coin into his hand. "I appreciate your help."

The gatekeeper accepted the tip, stuck a peeled twig between his teeth and watched thoughtfully as the Englishwoman walked off down the road. To his considerable interest, she dodged behind a hollow in the wall and tried to make herself inconspicuous when she heard the rumble of approaching carriage wheels.

The gatekeeper glanced down at the silver *rupee* she had given him. He shrugged. For a silver *rupee*, the mad Englishwoman could hide behind as many walls as she desired. He sat down on his stool and chewed his twig. At this time of the day, there wouldn't be many callers. He closed his eyes for a snooze.

Mr. Carradin had his lodgings in a large house built in the Indian style, with a separate, unoccupied *zenana* and a rambling collection of service buildings closed within the encompassing compound wall. As Lucy expected, the doors to the servants' quarters stood open at this hour of the day. She encountered many surprised glances but no opposition when she entered the rear courtyard and walked across the well-swept, beaten earth to the main house. There were some advantages to being an English lady.

"Good afternoon," she said, walking into the kitchen. She gave her words the sort of ringing intonation Mrs. Rutherspoon used when communicating with her most difficult housemaids. "I have remembered something important I must discuss with Mr. Carradin. Please don't let me keep you from your duties."

As she had anticipated, the servants exchanged nervous glances, but none of them attempted to stop her as she swept out of the kitchen and walked briskly toward Mr. Carradin's office. The murmur of low voices drifted out into the hallway. Lifting her hand to knock, she hesitated then opened the door without knocking.

The two men in the office froze to their chairs.

"How nice to see you again, Mr. Carradin," Lucy said breezily.

"And Edward, too. What a surprise!" She smiled sweetly. "What brought you back from Delhi so soon?"

The men exchanged swift glances, and Mr. Carradin turned a most undiplomatic shade of embarrassed red. Edward finally unfroze himself from the chair and came forward to take her hand. She clasped her parasol and pretended not to notice.

She knew he was aware of her rejection, but he took her elbow without comment and guided her toward the room's only arm-chair. "Lucy," he said quietly. "You look hot and tired. Please sit down and let me send the boy to fetch something cool for you to drink."

She sank into the chair, but stared up at him defiantly. "No wonder I appear hot and tired. I've been chasing about town all day trying to find you."

"I explained in my note that I have been summoned to Delhi."

"And the *ayah* told me that you planned to lunch with Mr. Carradin. Why wouldn't you speak with me when I called here an hour ago?"

Mr. Carradin's brick-red complexion turned puce. He cleared his throat and sidled toward the door. "I will go and rassle up the servants, Edward. I'm sure Lady Ridgeholm would enjoy a glass of fruit juice. Ah-hem! I will be back directly, my lady. Yes, indeed."

Lucy gazed into her husband's eyes. "You are going to Afghanistan," she said flatly, scarcely waiting until the elderly diplomat had left the room.

Edward's gaze slid sideways. "Afghanistan? Why in the world would you think such a thing?" He walked over to the desk and picked up a steel nib pen, playing with it. "Lucy, where is your carriage? We didn't hear it draw up. Did you send it home?"

"Yes."

"You shouldn't be walking around in this heat, my dear. It isn't good for you in your condition."

"I am much stronger and healthier than I was when we escaped from Kuwar. A fifteen-minute walk isn't likely to overset me, Edward."

"No, but at this time of day the sun could give you heatstroke. My dear, let me escort you home in one of John Carradin's carriages as soon as you have taken some refreshment."

"You haven't answered my question, Edward. Why are you going to Afghanistan?"

He flung the pen onto the desk. "Lucy, I'm not going to

Afghanistan. I've no idea where you would have acquired such a strange idea—"

"You left without saying good-bye."

Edward turned slowly, and his voice was grim when he spoke. "I thought, after what happened last night, that you might prefer to receive my apologies by letter."

"I would never prefer our communication to be by letter. I have thought for the past week that we are in great need of honest conversation. Last night . . . last night made no difference to my opinion."

He drew in a deep breath. "Then I will apologize to you now, in person, for my conduct. Will you accept that my barbaric treatment of you sprang in part from the knowledge that I was about to leave Peshawar?"

"How long have you known you would have to go to—Delhi?"

"For some days. As I told you in my note, Lucy, Lord Lytton wishes to consult with me about the Amir's real intentions, which are certainly not easy to discern at the bargaining table. I speak Pashto, a fact which nobody in the Afghani delegation realizes. Nobody in our own delegation knows it either, save for John Carradin. Because of my knowledge of Pashto, I have valuable insights to give the Viceroy. For instance, we know all too well that the Amir has formed an alliance with the Russians, but we have never understood his reasons for signing the treaty. I have learned that the Amir dislikes and mistrusts the Russians, and only maintains his alliance with them in order to protect himself from the rivalries of other tribal leaders within Afghanistan."

"Could you not inform the Viceroy of this in a written report?"

"Possibly. But Lord Lytton needs somebody close at hand to lead him through the maze of tribes and princelings all competing for British support. I am personally acquainted with many of the rival khans now seeking our assistance, or threatening to do battle with us. Naturally, Lord Lytton would like to hear my opinions at firsthand."

It all sounded wonderfully plausible. Too plausible, perhaps? Lucy knew from past experience that her husband was a master at inventing believable stories. She stood up and approached the desk where he was standing. Her legs suddenly trembled, but not with fatigue. "Why did Mr. Carradin lie to me earlier on this afternoon?"

"He didn't lie, my dear. He told you I had left town, and at the time he believed he was telling the truth."

"But you were here for lunch, and you were in his study only a few minutes after I had left the house. Isn't it strange that I called during the only period you were *not* with Mr. Carradin?"

"My dear, John and I ate lunch at the negotiating table, not here in his house. You find me here now simply because I unexpectedly obtained some important information which I decided should be shared with John at once. I therefore delayed my departure for a couple of hours. You must have been driving out of one gate as I entered by another."

Did she believe him? Lucy wasn't sure. "Edward, swear to me that you are not returning to Afghanistan."

His hands closed over hers, enfolding them in his firm, reassuring clasp. "I swear it," he said softly. "Lucy, I swear I am not returning to Afghanistan." He raised her hands to his lips and brushed loving, tender kisses over her knuckles. "Lucy, my heart, I love you so much."

A cough and the rattle of glasses on a brass tray alerted them to the fact that they were no longer alone.

"Freshly squeezed guava juice for you, Lady Ridgeholm." Mr. Carradin bustled into his office followed by a young, turbaned servant. "The cook has mixed it with well water, so you will find it pleasantly cool."

"Thank you." Lucy accepted the pale pink juice with gratitude, although it was not one of her usual favorites. She couldn't understand why she was so thirsty until it dawned on her that she had not eaten or drunk a thing since Mr. Carradin's party the night before.

Edward refused the offer of a drink. "If you will excuse me, sir, I am going to drive my wife home as soon as she's finished her juice. Could I beg the use of one of your carriages, do you suppose?"

"Certainly, my boy, certainly. Chander, see that the carriage is sent round from the stables right away." He dismissed the young servant and turned back to his visitors. "Well, Edward, do we have anything further to discuss before you leave for Lahore?"

"I believe not, sir. I plan to set out this afternoon, as we arranged. As soon as I have seen Lucy safely tucked up in bed, that is. She must be exhausted after all this activity."

"Indeed, she must." Mr. Carradin shook Edward firmly by the hand. "Never fear, my boy. We shall keep an eye on her whilst you are gone."

Edward laughed a touch ruefully. "I fear you will have your work cut out, sir."

"Nonsense. I am an old hand at keeping the ladies under control. Well, the best of luck in your endeavors, my boy. I shall eagerly await news of your success. In the courier's bag from Delhi, of course."

Lucy's throat closed up and, despite the heat of the room, the blood in her veins turned to ice. During the months of her captivity, she had learned to listen for the tiny nuances that might mean the difference between life and death. She could not fail to hear the subtle undercurrent to Mr. Carradin's words. In that moment she knew beyond a shadow of a doubt that wherever Edward might be going, it was not to Delhi.

She made no comment to indicate her suspicions, however. She was obviously never going to discover the truth by asking, therefore she would uncover it by guile. She smiled politely to Mr. Carradin, and allowed Edward to escort her into the carriage. Once they were home, she didn't utter a word of protest when he insisted on taking her to their bedroom and summoning the *ayah*.

"Rest, my heart," he murmured, sitting on the edge of her bed and taking her hand lightly in his own. He had already taken off her shoes and skirt and unfastened her bodice. Fortunately, he hadn't insisted on undressing her any further. Which was useful, seeing that she planned to follow him right out of the house.

"I have to leave soon, so when you wake up I shall probably be gone. But I promise to write faithfully from Delhi every day."

She smiled, inwardly seething. *Rest, my heart.* What did he take her for? A complete moron? How dare he lie to her at the same time as he used his special endearment!

"Thank you, Edward," she whispered tremulously. "I shall look forward to hearing from you." *The devil she would.* Mr. Carradin probably had a stack of letters already sitting on his desk waiting to be delivered at appropriate intervals. How were they planning to handle her specific questions? With postscripts written in haste by Edward's "secretary"? She barely stopped herself from screaming.

"Make sure your mistress sleeps," Edward instructed the *ayah*. "She has had an arduous day."

That was certainly true. And she had an even more arduous time ahead of her. Lucy fluttered her eyelashes and faked a yawn. "I am almost asleep," she said drowsily. "Have a good journey, Edward, dearest."

He looked at her quickly, and for a second her heart stopped beating. Had she given herself away? She mustn't forget that Edward was as perceptive as she was. She opened her eyes and smiled sleepily. "You are lucky I feel so tired, Edward, or I shouldn't allow you to leave without nagging to come with you. It must be the baby making me feel unusually compliant."

He laughed and rumpled her hair. "That sounds more like my Lucy." He kissed her forehead. "Take care, my heart." He strode quietly from the room.

As soon as the door closed, Lucy shot bolt upright in the bed. "I'm hungry," she said to the startled *ayah*. "You were quite right, I should have had something to eat before I went out this morning. Could you bring me some fruit? And perhaps some rice pudding?"

Nothing in the lord's instructions prohibited her from bringing the *memsahib* food, and the *ayah* departed willingly. When she returned bearing a platter of sliced mango, dates and sweetened rice cooked in buffalo milk, she thought at first her mistress had fallen asleep wearing her hat. When she looked more closely, she saw that the bed was empty save for a bolster stuffed under a sheet and a discarded bonnet arranged on the remaining pillow.

Unable to think what else she might do, the *ayah* screamed, dropping the tray of food for good measure.

CHAPTER EIGHTEEN

Lucy timed her disappearance well. Edward had already left for wherever he was going, and the servants ran around giving each other mutually conflicting orders about what to do and where to search for their missing mistress. Everybody, of course, was so busy discussing where to look that nobody actually set about the bothersome task of looking.

From her not-very-efficient hiding place behind a sack of rice in the pantry, Lucy listened with considerable relief as the *ayah* decreed that an urgent message must be sent to the lord *sahib*. This was exactly what Lucy had hoped for. And, as she had expected, one of the servants knew precisely where Edward had gone. The lord *sahib* was, according to the groom, "at his other house with the servant Abdullah."

Edward's other house? Lucy's worries coalesced into a hard lump of fear, and irritation over the partronizing way she had been treated changed into ice-cold determination to discover exactly what was being concealed from her. Emerging from the pantry into the kitchen, she told the goggle-eyed cook that he needed to set better traps for the cockroaches and informed the groom that she would go with him to the *sahib's* other house.

The groom was clearly distressed. "*Memsahib*, your lord does not wish you to go there. I cannot take you."

Lucy drew in a deep breath. "If you do not take me at once, you will no longer have a job in this household. You and your family will leave my service before sundown."

A gasp of subdued outrage rose from the servants, and the groom blanched at the injustice of her threat. Lucy steeled herself not to apologize. "Go now, at once, and fetch my carriage."

With the greatest difficulty, she held her tongue while the chastened groom scurried to hitch a fresh horse to the pony trap. The other servants watched in various degrees of disbelief and horror as their sweet, gentle *memsahib* turned before their eyes into a hatchet-faced, implacable mistress.

"Hurry," was all she said to the groom when he indicated he was ready to leave. "I shall hold you responsible if the master has left his other house before I reach him."

The groom whipped up the horse, and Lucy reflected how sad it was that any of her servants could believe her capable of such harsh and unjust treatment. The groom's behavior was a shocking indictment of the conduct of his former British masters. She would have to apologize handsomely to him as soon as she had achieved her more pressing purpose of finding Edward.

The servant drove fast and silently, halting the carriage in a Moslem quarter of the city on the fringes of the market. Lucy recognized the general area. They weren't more than a few hundred yards from the point where "Rashid" had abandoned her after their escape from Kuwar.

"Here is the lord *sahib*'s house guarded by the servant Abdullah," the groom said, bowing with an obsequiousness that had previously been entirely lacking in his demeanor.

"Thank you," Lucy replied. "Please wait with the carriage. I'm grateful to you for driving me here so quickly."

The groom bowed, head nearly touching his knees, and Lucy sighed, reaching out her hand to pull him gently upright. "Your job is quite safe," she said. "I have no intention of dismissing you. Have no fear."

She walked up to the barred and bolted door, with the groom's profuse thanks echoing in her ears and a blush of remorse staining her cheeks. She didn't like achieving her purpose by intimidation, however necessary it might have been.

The door of this small, dilapidated "other house" fronted directly onto the street, with the women's and servants' quarters presumably located at the rear, in traditional Indian style. She was in the midst of reaching up to pull the bellrope when the door opened. Rashid stood framed in the darkened hallway.

Lucy could find no words of greeting. She and her husband stared at each other in tense, edgy silence. Eventually, she blinked, trying to overcome her shock. After all these weeks of living with Edward, it was startling to find she still hadn't quite succeeded in melding together the separate images she carried of the English aristocrat and the Moslem gun runner. Seeing her husband brown-skinned, turbaned and clothed in the garb of a Punjabi trader, the reality of his English heritage faded and he once again became Rashid: a man who exerted a powerful attraction over her but whom she scarcely knew.

Telling herself that this was Edward, her husband, the man who only one night earlier had taken her into his arms and made love to her until they both were nearly faint with exhaustion, she forced herself to speak. "I w-was looking for . . . I n-needed to talk to you."

Edward's gaze flew from her to the groom, who was occupying himself by flicking away flies with the thong of his whip. The groom realized he was being observed and looked up, returning his master's gaze without any hint of recognition.

Silently, Edward reached out and pulled Lucy into the garlic-and-clove scented hallway. He pushed the door shut behind her before speaking in grim, angry Pashto. "Why are you here, Englishwoman? You put many lives at risk by following me."

She gritted her teeth at the coldness of his words but instinctively replied in the same language. "I am not *an Englishwoman*. I am Lucy, your wife. You lied to me, Rash—Edward. You swore to me you were not going to Afghanistan."

"Perhaps because I wished to avoid precisely this sort of dangerous encounter. My safety lies in two things, Englishwoman: secrecy and total immersion in my role. I cannot allow myself to remember the weaknesses of Lord Edward de Beaumont when I conduct the business of Rashid."

Weaknesses? Was that how he considered his feelings for her? Lucy swallowed hard, uncertainty replacing anger. "I have betrayed no secrets of yours, ever. I have never told a single soul that you are Rashid. Besides, to whom would I betray your secrets? It seems to me that all the important people already know."

"You alone have knowingly seen me both as Rashid and as Lord Edward."

"How can that be? Your identity as Rashid is obviously no secret to your uncle—"

"Lord Triss knows that I assume a disguise in entering Afghanistan. That is the full extent of his knowledge."

"What about Mr. Carradin? He knows you are planning to return to Afghanistan, that much was clear to me this afternoon. All that nonsense about messages from the Delhi courier—he was encouraging you to go and risk your life!"

"Mr. Carradin knows that I plan to make contact with certain vital people at a meeting place within Afghanistan. He also knows that Peshawar is rife with spies determined to prevent any member of the British delegation making contact with the men I seek. Mr. Carradin has no idea what role I will play in order to reach the agreed rendezvous in safety. I repeat, nobody in the world except you has actually seen me in both my role as Rashid and as my true self. Even Abdullah, the young boy who takes care of this house, knows me only as a Punjabi trader. I send him away whenever I plan to make the change of roles, for the sake of his safety as much as for mine. What he doesn't know, he cannot reveal. But you, Englishwoman, can unfortunately reveal a very great deal."

"Than take me with you," she pleaded. "Edward, you know I would be of help to you. Think how it was when we encountered those Russian soldiers! A man and his pregnant wife are much less likely to become objects of suspicion than a man traveling alone."

For a moment his voice softened. "Lucy, you cannot possibly journey with me. My meeting has been endlessly delayed, and winter already spreads its icy fingers into the mountains of the Hindu Kush. The travel would be too difficult for you."

"It wasn't before, when we escaped from Kuwar."

"Before you did not carry a child," he said, his voice hardening once again. "When we escaped from Kuwar, your body had been toughened by two years of forced labor. Now it is soft after months of pampered living. No words of yours will sway me, Lucy. I tell you again that you endanger my life and the lives of all I am hoping to meet if you linger here. It is past time for me to be gone. Abdullah already waits with my horse at our agreed meeting place."

She turned away, knowing he was unlikely to answer her but compelled to ask the questions anyway. "Where are you going, Edward? How long will your meetings in Afghanistan take? Is there any hope that you can return before the passes are closed by winter snow?"

He hesitated, and for an endless moment she was convinced he would not answer. "I travel only as far as Qur'um," he said finally. "It is a small nomad winter settlement that lies less than two days northeast of the Khyber pass. It lies within fifteen miles of the point where you and I encountered the Russian soldiers when we made our escape from Kuwar."

"Then there is hope you will be back in Peshawar before winter closes the pass?"

"There is always hope."

"Edward . . ." She turned back to face him, wanting to touch him, to kiss him farewell, but somehow afraid to initiate any intimacy with this man who was her husband—and yet was not. She tried to superimpose the image of Rashid over her images of Edward, but her eyes were blinded by tears, and perhaps for that reason, she could not get the picture straight in her mind.

"Edward," she repeated helplessly. "I am stronger than you think. Let me come with you." She didn't add her unspoken fear: *Or I am afraid I will never see you again.*

"You cannot come with me, Lucy. Please don't ask again. Go home now. You are the wife of Lord Edward de Beaumont, and you carry his child. As such you owe him absolute obedience, should he demand it. And he does, Lucy. On this occasion, he demands that you return home and ask no more questions. He also asks that you reveal nothing to anybody of what you have learned here today."

Lucy realized in that moment why she was having such difficulty in collapsing the two separate images of her husband into one: It was because Edward himself kept the identities separate. When he donned the clothes of Rashid, he did not so much play a role as enter into a totally different life. His ability to stop thinking and behaving like a British aristocrat was probably the chief reason he had managed to survive so long in such a dangerous profession. With regret, Lucy recognized that by pulling him out of character and forcing him to acknowledge her as his wife she achieved nothing save to put his life at risk. The greatest service she could do him would be to leave—and quickly.

The tears she had been holding back spilled onto her cheeks as she reached for the latch of the front door, pulling it open with stiff, jerky movements. She couldn't bear to look at him, and she spoke more to the roadway than to him. "Good-bye, Edward. Have a safe journey and come back as soon as you may. I will be waiting anxiously for your return."

He didn't reply, and she stepped out into the dirt-packed path, fumbling in her reticule for a handkerchief. The door closed behind her with a soft click. Blinded by the sun and her tears, she didn't at first recognize Count Guido, who stood talking to her groom.

"*Signora baronessa!*" The count's exclamation finally alerted her to his presence. "I saw your carriage and I have awaited with great impatience your arrival. But what can be the cause of such sad tears in such a beautiful lady?"

Lucy pushed her wet handkerchief back into her reticule and forced a smile. "Good afternoon, *signor conte*. How are you today?"

"Less well for seeing you so troubled."

"I am concerned over a sick servant who has delivered a stillborn child," she said. "In this part of the world, childbed fever is so often fatal." *Dear God, had the count seen Rashid? Had he overheard her farewells?* She racked her brains trying to remember exactly what she had said. A sinking feeling in the pit of her stomach warned her that she had called Edward by name after the street door was opened. But even if the count had heard, would it matter? He didn't seem the sort of young man likely to be very swift at putting two and two together.

"You are good to express such concern over a servant you can scarcely know, *signora baronessa*." The count politely handed her into the pony trap.

"I have known her for several years. She once served my father. May I offer you a ride, *signor conte?* Or do you still have business in the market?"

"Not at all. I was searching for a trinket for my young sister, but without success. Peshawar is not a city with much that is beautiful or original for sale." The count climbed into the carriage, and Lucy instructed the driver to return home.

"I learned only recently, *signora baronessa*, that you had lived in India before. Your husband also has spent much time in India, I believe?"

"His family has commercial interests in Bombay. He went there as a very young man to assist his grandfather."

"Then he probably speaks the native languages fluently, which must be a great advantage in his work for the British government."

"There are so many dialects spoken in India," Lucy replied evasively. "And, unfortunately, we Britishers seem to lack the skill of other Europeans in learning foreign languages. My husband would be the first to admit that he is no linguist."

"I sympathize. Learning the foreign tongues was not easy for me either, as my poor tutors would inform you."

"Your excellent English repays your hard work, *signor conte*."

"Thank you. To change the subject, I have a small matter of business to discuss with Lord de Beaumont. In connection with the treaty negotiations, you understand. Would it be convenient for me to call upon him now, do you suppose?"

"I'm afraid that my husband has left for Delhi, *signor conte*. But I'm sure Mr. Carradin would be able to answer any questions you may have or direct you to the appropriate member of the British delegation."

"Of course. It is of no matter." The count pulled out a large gold pocket watch. "But it is four o'clock, *signora baronessa*. What a happy coincidence! The hour of the English tea. If your husband is not at home awaiting you, why do you not join me on my verandah? I have the new tin of English digestive biscuits which I will be delighted to open in your honor. They are not yet soaked by the humidity and remain—do you say 'crunchy'?—as the day they left Birmingham."

Whether it was the appeal of the biscuits, the lack of desire to return to a bungalow without Edward or sheer inertia, Lucy found herself accepting the count's invitation. She leaned back against the hot leather seat cushions, conducting a polite but desultory conversation with less than one tenth of her attention.

To her great relief, it seemed obvious that the count had heard nothing of her final exchange with Edward. Which meant, thank goodness, that she wouldn't need to make any difficult explanations either to the count or to Mr. Carradin. No doubt Mr. Carradin would have found some effective method to swear the young diplomat to secrecy, but he was a flirt and a chatterbox, hardly the ideal person to guard an important secret. As Edward had pointed out, Peshawar was thick with spies and infiltrators of every stripe and description. It would be all too easy for the count to let drop some careless remark in the wrong circles that would identify Rashid as Lord Edward, an agent of the British government.

And how the Russians and their informers would love to get hold of that little tidbit! Thinking about it, Lucy decided she wouldn't be in the least surprised to discover that several of the people she had met at recent social events were actually spies.

Monsieur Armand, for example. She would be willing to bet that the French sheep skin merchant traded as frequently in information as he did in *garakul* wool. She could only thank her lucky stars it hadn't been Monsieur Armand waiting outside the door when she said good-bye to Edward.

Her lucky stars were obviously in the mood to be capricious. Lucy's suspicions about Monsieur Armand had scarcely formed when her groom drove into the small grounds attached to the count's bungalow. And there, seated on the verandah sipping tea, was Monsieur Armand, together with another man whose name Lucy couldn't remember.

"Alas, it seems I have unexpected visitors." The count turned to Lucy and pulled one of his endearing, comical faces. "I am desolate, *signora baronessa*. I thought, at last, we would be alone, you and I. Sometimes I fear that our great love affaire is destined never to start."

"Then perhaps we should simply resign ourselves to becoming friends," Lucy replied with a laugh, allowing the count to assist her from the pony trap. "Have I not made that suggestion before, *signor conte*?"

"But, naturally, I cannot take such suggestions seriously. For me, a woman so beautiful as you is a challenge not to be resisted. Please, *signora baronessa*, be seated." The count bowed to indicate that Lucy should proceed to the verandah, and directed the groom to the stables, advising the servant to tend to the horse who was drooping from the heat.

Lucy herself was hungry and thirsty enough to be quite relieved that tea was already served. Her chief emotion about Monsieur Armand at this moment was not suspicion, but a wish that he and his good-looking companion should not have eaten all the digestive biscuits.

A blessed late afternoon breeze stirred the hot air as Lucy acknowledged Monsieur Armand's greeting and sank into a comfortably cushioned, basket weave chair. Monsieur Armand made haste to introduce his friend, Monsieur Bruno, a partner in the sheep skin trade who had only just arrived in Peshawar.

Lucy scrutinized Monsieur Bruno as he apologized in French for the fact that he spoke almost no English. Odd that she should have thought she recognized him, particularly since his features seemed unfamiliar now that she saw them more closely. She shrugged off a persistent feeling of unease. Really, she would have an intolerable few months if she allowed her worries about

Edward's safety to taint every chance acquaintance with the suspicion that he was less (or more) than he seemed.

Her suspicions of Monsieur Armand were based on nothing more than a faint discomfort in his presence—the sort of discomfort that had been life-saving in Kuwar Valley but was out of place in Peshawar drawing rooms. If her doubts about Monsieur Armand were baseless, she certainly shouldn't extend them to a man who merely happened to be Monsieur Armand's partner.

Lucy did her best to contribute her share of both English and French platitudes to the ensuing conversation, in between sipping excellent tea, eating sandwiches and munching on tasty, crisp biscuits. She was quite glad of the need to concentrate on the ebb and flow of French, because she found that if she allowed her attention to wander even for a moment, her mind immediately blazed with frightening images of the danger that lay ahead of her husband. She knew all too well that in a country like Afghanistan, teetering on the edge of chaos, not even the most consummate survival skills could guarantee Edward's safe return.

A serving boy brought out fresh boiling water and a decanter of red wine for the count, who grinned his apologies. "The Italian soul is not designed for the consumption of tea," he admitted. "Would you care to join me in some wine, Monsieur Armand? Monsieur Bruno?"

"No, I zank you. We must not detain you, my colleague and I. We come again anozzer day. Our business wiz you, zey are not important."

"Please don't let me send you away, *messieurs*." Lucy finished her tea and rose gracefully. "In truth, I have been absent from my home long enough to cause concern, and I should never have stopped for tea. The count tempted me with his offer of biscuits newly arrived from England, which were as delicious as he promised."

The count sprang to his feet. "But of a certainty, *signora baronessa*, I must escort you home."

"Of a certainty, *signor conte*, there is no need whatsoever for you to leave your other guests. My bungalow is no more than a few minutes' drive from here."

After another ten minutes of polite argument, the count agreed to summon the carriage and to allow Lucy to depart without any accompaniment other than her driver. She felt as if she had won a major battle. All three men insisted upon assisting her into the pony trap. All three men insisted upon standing guard and waving as the little carriage pulled out of the driveway. Monsieur Bruno cast one longing look over his shoulder toward the shaded verandah, but then resumed his gallant waving.

Lucy returned the waves measure for measure, but her hand was suddenly shaking. She didn't know whether to jump from the carriage and insist upon speaking privately to the count or to continue home as if nothing had happened.

She swallowed, trying in vain to moisten her throat, which was suddenly parchment dry. Dear God, she finally remembered where she had seen "Monsieur Bruno" before! His glance toward the verandah had been all she needed in order to trigger the key to her memory. The last time she had seen "Monsieur Bruno" look over his shoulder in that precise fashion she had been wearing a sack of food strapped to her abdomen to imitate pregnancy, and he had been wearing the uniform of a Russian Cossack soldier. "Monsieur Bruno" was no more a French sheep skin merchant than she was. He was, in fact, the captain of a troop of Cossack soldiers who had lost their way in the maze of barely discernible tracks on the Afghani side of the Khyber Pass.

Hard on the heels of this realization came one that was far more frightening. If the count ever mentioned to Monsieur Bruno that he had seen Lady de Beaumont bidding a tearful farewell to a Moslem trader, Edward's life would be in twice as much danger as before. And—worst of all—she was the person responsible for Edward's increased danger.

The short journey back to the bungalow seemed interminable. In an agony of impatience, Lucy jumped from the carriage and ran to her room, calling for her *ayah*. Tossing her hat and parasol onto the bed, she splashed her face in the bowl of tepid water on her dressing table. Clearly, this was no longer a situation she could handle alone. Should she call on Mr. Carradin personally, or send a note explaining the situation? Was she overreacting in thinking something needed to be done right away? After all, there was no reason to suppose that the count had any intention of telling his visitors that he'd seen Lucy in the marketplace. Such a trivial incident surely couldn't have been of much interest to him.

Like a red-hot poker blazing a path through the thicket of her mind, Lucy suddenly recognized a dreadful truth: She had no reason whatever to suppose that the count could be trusted; no reason whatever to suppose that his presence in the marketplace this afternoon had been accidental. Just because he was charming and made her laugh didn't preclude the possibility that he was a spy. On the contrary, charming spies were probably far more successful.

With the all-too-clear vision of hindsight, Lucy realized that the count's behavior had been a touch off-key. Given that he must have seen Rashid quite plainly, had he not accepted her tale of a sick maidservant a little too easily? If he had been a genuinely innocent passerby, would he not have asked more questions about the supposed maidservant and what she was doing living in a house owned by a Punjabi merchant? Add these doubts to the fact that the count had been talking to the groom while waiting for Lucy to put in an appearance, and his behavior became even more strange. Surely, he must have asked the groom why Lady de Beaumont's carriage was standing in this shabby, unfrequented part of town? And the groom must surely have replied that the *memsahib* was visiting her husband.

Lucy shivered despite the heat. If the count was a spy, then it followed as certainly as night after day that the presence of Monsieur Armand and the Cossack captain on his verandah was not mere coincidence. The three men must be working together, and the count would already have passed on the news that Edward had left town in the guise of a Punjabi trader. She had to warn Mr. Carradin, so that the three spies could be arrested before their information about Edward could be spread any further. What's more, she couldn't risk being spotted by any of the men going to Mr. Carradin's home.

The *ayah* entered the bedroom and salaamed. Lucy looked at her thoughtfully. They were much of a size, and two Indian women could move around the streets of Peshawar far less conspicuously than Lady Edward de Beaumont and her maid.

"Please bring me a spare set of your clothes," she said to the *ayah*. "I will replace them later with new ones. And send somebody to find the groom. He's to be brought here to my room immediately."

The *ayah* scurried away, returning less than five minutes later carrying a bundle of freshly laundered clothes. She sidled into the room, salaamed again and waited in obviously tense silence.

"What in the world's the matter with you?" Lucy asked, taking the bundle with a brief word of thanks. "You're acting as though you expect me to chop off your head at any moment."

Greatly daring, the *ayah* spoke up. "The groom is the father of many children," she whispered.

"And I hope he will live long enough to be the father of many more," Lucy said, realizing at last what was wrong. Her threats earlier that afternoon had produced a more devastating effect than she'd anticipated. "Look, the groom is not in any danger of losing his job, Dira, and neither are you nor any of the other servants. So, please hurry up and help me into these clothes. I assure you I haven't any intention of dismissing you."

The *ayah* was too relieved to learn that her livelihood was safe to question why the *memsahib* wanted to clothe herself in native garments. "Why, honored lady, you look like one of us!" she exclaimed when her mistress was dressed, then clapped her hand over her mouth in horror at what she had said. British masters rarely appreciated being told they looked like their servants.

A timid knock at the door announced the arrival of the groom. it took Lucy several valuable minutes to convince him that he was not in trouble, and another few minutes before he was willing to admit that he had spoken to the count. With quiet, persistent questioning, Lucy extracted an account of what had been said. As she feared, the groom had told the simple truth: that the *memsahib* wanted to see the lord *sahib* before he left town and therefore had come here to his "other house."

"I did not mean to do anything wrong, gracious lady."

"You did nothing wrong," Lucy assured him, her heart hammering so fast she could scarcely breath. She searched in her purse for a silver *rupee* and pressed it into his hand. "You have served me well, and I am grateful."

The delighted servant exited the room heaping blessings on the *memsahib*'s head. Lucy scarcely heard them. A note to Mr. Carradin wouldn't suffice, that much was certain. She needed to see Mr. Carradin right away, in person, so that she could explain the situation to him and seek his aid. Surely, the British government would have the power to arrest a Russian officer masquerading as a French merchant? Dear God, Edward didn't need to fight off Russians at his back as well as confront all the normal hazards of dealing with warring factions within Afghanistan!

The *ayah* was fast regaining her confidence, and she protested loudly when Lucy announced that they were going out on foot. Lucy ignored all the protests.

"It's still light," she told the wailing *ayah*. "We shall be perfectly safe."

"But why will you not take the carriage, honored lady? It is not fitting for you to walk."

She could hardly say that two Indian maidservants hurrying through the streets would be unlikely to attract a second glance from anybody, whereas Lady de Beaumont's carriage would be instantly recognized by the entire diplomatic community—including Monsieur Bruno and his fellow-conspirators.

"I wish to walk," she said in her haughtiest manner, reflecting ruefully that it would no doubt take her months to overcome the harsh reputation she had acquired with her servants in just this one day.

Still grumbling under her breath, the *ayah* followed Lucy out of the bungalow and onto the main dirt road, which connected virtually all of the diplomats' various lodgings and bungalows. In fact, the distance on foot to Mr. Carradin's house was scarcely more than the fifteen minutes it took by carriage, since the road was so rutted that any speed faster than a brisk walk risked a broken ankle for the horse.

Lucy had been correct about one thing, at least. In their simple *saris*, their faces veiled, she and Dira blended in with the other pedestrians to the point where nobody cast a second glance in their direction. It was an hour when the streets were busy with people taking advantage of the remaining light, while the evening breezes blew away the worst of the day's heat and made walking tolerable. Like any other Indian street, this one was alive with noise and color.

Lucy's spirits gradually lightened as she and the maid walked toward Mr. Carradin's lodgings, jostling good naturedly with the crowds on the sidewalk. Goodness, but she had blown a small molehill into a very large mountain. What, after all, could the Russian captain, alias Monsieur Bruno, do even if he discovered Edward was entering Afghanistan in the guise of a Punjabi merchant? There were no telegraph offices in Afghanistan, no border police, no efficient systems of communication. Edward would be over the pass and lost in the trackless wastes of the arid high country long before the Russians could mount an effective pursuit. This, after all, was the same captain who hadn't been able to find his way from Qandahar to Kuwar without getting lost.

Lucy quickened her pace, eager now to reach Mr. Carradin. She had learned her lesson. After today's experiences, she was going to become the most virtuous, stay-at-home wife Edward could possibly want. She would ask Mr. Carradin to place all three conspirators under arrest, and that would be the end of the matter as far as she was concerned.

This was certainly the day for fate to play games with her, Lucy reflected. As she passed by Count Guido's driveway, Monsieur Armand and the Russian captain walked out of the gate and entered the flow of pedestrians. Like Lucy and her maid, the two men seemed to be progressing in the direction of Mr. Carradin's lodgings.

For one heart-stopping moment, panic overwhelmed her, then courage returned in full measure. This was an opportunity not to be missed. She drew her veil higher over her face and grabbed her maid's hand, indicating by gesture that the maid was to remain silent and follow Lucy. Cautiously, feet making no sound in the dirt, the two women edged closer to the two men.

Their conversation did not seem to be the stuff of high drama. "I am looking forward to my dinner," Monsieur Armand said in French. "This heat takes away my appetite at lunchtime."

"Wretched country," the supposed Monsieur Bruno agreed. "But they say the heat down south makes this part of the country seem pleasant. And if you'd ever felt the cold in Afghanistan in the middle of the winter, I tell you, you'd prefer this heat. That mountain chill is a cold to cut through a man's bones."

"Thankfully, my friend, I am not required to venture into Afghanistan. That is your part of the deal."

They were only a few hundred yards from the entrance to Mr. Carradin's lodgings, and so far the men had said nothing that could not have applied equally well to sheep skin merchants as to spies. Frustrated, Lucy wished she could have gleaned some idea as to whether or not the count had revealed anything about Edward. However, she recognized that any serious investigation should be left to Mr. Carradin, and she allowed the distance between herself and the two men to increase slightly.

It was a street urchin who betrayed Lucy's presence to the spies. A small boy, still inexpert in his thievery, jostled against Monsieur Armand, presumably hoping to snatch a pocket watch or some other valuable trinket.

"Oh, no you don't, my lad!" Bruno exclaimed in French. Then he lunged after the terrified boy, who somehow managed to squirm between the two men and leap into the roadway, almost knocking Lucy off her feet in the process.

"Let him go," Armand said, as the boy dodged bullock carts and donkeys and disappeared into a narrow alley. "He didn't get anything, after all."

He turned to walk on, when his attention was suddenly attracted by the *ayah* who was muttering reassurances in English and trying to reaffix Lucy's veil which the street urchin had ripped almost entirely off. Lucy turned away, indicating with frantic hand gestures that the maid should be silent, but the maid couldn't see what threat was posed by two harmless European gentlemen. She was much more worried about the pearl pin that had somehow become lost in the dirt.

Unfortunately, Monsieur Armand didn't seem to share the general European perception that all natives were indistinguishable. His eyes narrowed, and he gave a small exclamation before reaching out to grip Lucy's arm, thrusting her hard against the wall and clamping his hand over her mouth before she could scream. When the *ayah* emitted a shriek of outrage, Armand simply ordered Bruno to take care of her.

Bruno obeyed, screening the maid from any passersby with his body and knocking her unconscious. He then swung her up into his arms, presenting a perfect picture of a considerate master carrying home his fainting servant.

Monsieur Armand looked at Lucy, his expression openly mocking. "My dear Lady de Beaumont, zis is a most big surprise. My colleague and I, we are most 'appy to be of service to you at zis moment."

"I need no services, Monsieur Armand."

"Oh, but, Lady de Beaumont, I zink you do. You have ze choice. I will remove my hand and you will accompany me quietly. Or you may try to scream just once, and your fate will be as your servant's. Shall I remove my hand, *madame*?"

Lucy nodded, then tried to smile, hoping against hope that a bluff might work. "Monsieur Armand, I would be very grateful if you would let me and my maid return home at once. It would be most embarrassing if word got out in British community that I had ventured forth into the streets dressed in native costume. I hope I can rely on your instincts as a gentleman to forget this little incident."

"Indeed, Lady de Beaumont, I am all concern for your problems. But, alas, for me zere is also embarrassment. Imagine if word got out in ze British community zat perhaps Monsieur

Armand is not a merchant of furs, but a seeker of informations. I zink, all in all, my embarrassment is greater than yours."

"I don't understand."

"Do you not, my lady? Oh, I zink you do. Walk, please. My lodgings are very discreet and very private and quite close to here. We will discuss zis most interesting situation where we are alone."

"I can't come to your lodgings, *monsieur*. It would not be proper."

He laughed. "*Madame*, please. Do not insult your intelligence and mine wiz zis feeble pretense. I am curious only for one zing. Why do you follow me and my colleague? What do you hope to learn?"

"I wasn't following you. I wanted to see Mr. Carradin."

"And for zis you dress up in native costume and roam ze streets?"

Her laughter had a bitter tinge. "At the time, it seemed like a good idea. A way to remain inconspicuous."

"Forgive me, Lady de Beaumont, if I tell you zat I find your story difficult to believe."

"Eventually, Monsieur Armand, you will have to let us go."

"My dear Lady de Beaumont, I can zink of no reason at all why zat should be so. It is one of ze advantages of India zat it is so easy to dispose of an unwanted body. Ze police here, zey have not ze skills of your English policemen. The so sad end of the so beautiful Lady de Beaumont will be mourned by all."

It was clear that she had absolutely nothing to lose by running. And Mr. Carradin's house was fairly near. Monsieur Armand was so confident of his superiority that he had loosened his grip on her arm to the point where it offered almost no restraint. Lucy would have liked to dash straight forward, toward Mr. Carradin's house. Unfortunately, Bruno blocked her way. To dodge backward around Monsieur Armand was almost impossible, so she had no choice other than to wait for a side alley, where she could break away and run all in one movement. A narrow alley came up soon enough, and she jerked her arm free, tearing down the alleyway and screaming for help.

The element of surprise worked in her favor, and she might even have succeeded in her ploy if luck had been on her side. The alley ended in a high, barred gate, and she had no time to reach up and tug at the bell rope before Armand caught up with her.

He seized her shoulders in a vicious grip. "You should not have run," he said, his voice cold with fury. "You definitely shouldn't have run."

His fist landed squarely beneath her chin, and a scarlet starburst of pain ended abruptly in cool blackness.

CHAPTER NINETEEN

When Lucy regained consciousness, she was lying on a comfortable sofa in somebody's study, presumably Monsieur Armand's. Her jaw felt as if it had been pulverized, and her head ached abominably. Otherwise, she seemed in amazingly good shape.

Her momentary surge of relief vanished as soon as she became alert enough to take better stock of her surroundings. She wasn't alone. Messieurs Armand and Bruno were seated in the same room, discussing—in calm, polite French—where and by what method to kill her.

Bruno, she soon learned, favored a quick, simple slash of the knife. Armand, on the other hand, favored devising some convincing form of accidental death. His personal favorites for the "accident" were either death-by-bullock-cart-wheels or death-by-drowning.

Lucy wasn't prepared to die in any fashion and considered both these methods particularly horrid. Bruno merely considered them inconvenient.

"Why do we need such elaborate preparations?" he asked impatiently. "I slit the woman's throat, or her belly, or wherever Indians are most in the habit of knifing their victims, and then we toss her body into a ditch and the maid along with her. If the authorities find them before the dogs and the jackals, they will

238

assume they were robbed. Her servants will confirm that the woman insisted on walking out with only her *ayah* for protection. If we are lucky and the dogs get there first . . ." He paused, before continuing lightly, "Then, my friend, there will be no need for explanations, because there will be no identifiable body."

"Hmm, perhaps you are right. Although the Indians don't go much for knifing, you know. Strangling is more their style. The legacy of the *thuggees*, and all that."

"So we strangle her." Bruno shrugged, clearly indifferent to the precise method of dispatch. "Let's have done with talking, my friend, and get on with the action. I must leave for Afghanistan at dawn if I am to have any hope of staying reasonably close to Lord Edward. There's little enough chance of picking up his trail, as it is. I daren't ask too many questions because the tribesmen are as likely to slit my throat as to answer. I'm grateful for the count's information, of course. Knowing that Lord Edward has left already and in what disguise makes things easier for me. At least we know that the meeting must be scheduled to take place soon! But God damn it! Still nobody can say more than that Abdur Rahman will meet the British representative somewhere close to Tor Kham!"

"That is one of the reasons the Kahn of Kuwar is sending a band of his men to meet up with you," Armand reminded him. "The Khan swears that an informer will bring him the information soon, and then his men will lead you to the place of meeting. Holy Mother of God, Abdur Rahman is living on Russian territory! How is it possible that none of your spies and none of the Amir's spies and none of the Khan's spies can tell us where this meeting will take place?"

"If only we dared risk killing Abdur Rahman while he is still on Russian soil!"

"We would face an outcry from every nation looking for an excuse to complain about Russian intervention in Asia. The tsar deserves better service from us in his goal to expand the Russian Empire to its natural limits."

"Perhaps the woman knows something about the meeting," Bruno said, not sounding too hopeful. "The count insists her husband is crazy about her. He may have been indiscreet."

"If the British have chosen Lord Edward for this mission, you can be sure he is too professional to be indiscreet," Armand said.

Bruno shrugged. "What have we got to lose by asking?"

"Before we kill her."

"Before we kill her. Whatever she says can make no difference to that decision."

The conversation was taking a distinctly downward spiral, and Lucy decided it was time to make her wakefulness known. Stirring noisily on the sofa, she groaned as if just regaining consciousness. In fact, groaning wasn't difficult since the act of moving her head caused a grinding sensation of pain, similar to little men with hammers pounding nails into her teeth and jawbone.

The men eyed her with disfavor as she struggled to sit up. "Water," she murmured. "Please give me water."

"Zere is no water," Monsieur Armand said. "Here, drink zis."

This was brandy, and Bruno's expression suggested that it was an appalling waste of good liquor to bestow it on a woman destined to die so soon. Lucy sipped the strong spirit cautiously, wanting to swallow enough to ease her throat and conquer her nausea without taking enough to blur her mental faculties.

"Where is Dira?" she asked, setting the glass aside.

"Dira?"

"My maid."

"She is in ze kitchen," Armand said smoothly. Too smoothly. "Never fear, *madame*, she is quite well."

Which probably meant that Dira was dead, or would be shortly. Despair and guilt threatened to overwhelm Lucy, but she fought it back. Despair could all too easily overcome the will to survive, and Lucy had no intention of dying. The child she carried was reason enough to fight for life, even if it hadn't been imperative to reach Edward and warn him.

"Why have you brought me here?" Her voice contained an annoying tremble, despite the fortifying effect of the brandy.

Monsieur Armand's reply was brisk. "Come, *madame*, you know quite well why you are here. You have ze power and ze knowledge to unmask me as well as my colleague, Monsieur Bruno, and our ally, ze count."

Bruno spoke to Lucy for the first time, switching the conversation to French. Perhaps he really didn't speak or understand much English. "The count tells us your husband has left town, *madame*. Where is he going?"

Lucy picked up the brandy glass and took another slow sip. "I could tell you that he has gone to Delhi for consultations with the Viceroy," she said.

Bruno scowled. "But you will not waste our time with such answers, *madame*. We know that Lord Edward goes to Afghanistan for a meeting with Abdur Rahman. If their meeting is satisfactory, your government will abandon Amir Sher Ali to the wolves already eager for his blood and throw their support behind Abdur Rahman, who is the only person strong enough to unite the warring tribes of Afghanistan. There is a faction within the British government that wishes to see Afghanistan established as a strong, independent nation, and your husband is a leader of that faction. A very inconvenient leader, whom we Russians intend to see does not succeed. Afghanistan is a natural part of our great motherland, and we don't wish to see it become independent." His eyes lit with an inner fire. "You Britishers will be forced to acknowledge the truth before this century reaches its end. India may be the playground of your Queen Victoria, but Afghanistan is part of the imperial destiny of Mother Russia. In generations to come, the tsar and his people will make Afghanistan great."

Lucy decided she could safely ignore the rhetoric and concentrate on the meat of Bruno's oration. "If you know all this, *monsieur*, why do you ask me where my husband has gone?"

Bruno hesitated. "Because we would like confirmation of the exact meeting place."

Lucy drew in a deep breath. This was it, she told herself. Her one and only hope for escape, and she must grab it with both hands, despite the risk. "No, *monsieur*," she said steadily. "You do not ask me this question because you would like confirmation. You ask because you and your fellow-spies have no idea where the meeting between my husband and Abdur Rahman Khan is to take place."

"But you know?" Monsieur Armand interjected, unable to conceal his excitement. "Your husband has told you?"

"If I did know, *monsieur*, I would be a fool to share my knowledge with you. To speak would be to sign my death warrant."

"Nonsense. We promise you safe passage back—"

"*Monsieur*, you have asked me not to be foolish. Now I ask you the same. Why should you allow me to live once you know where the meeting is to take place?"

"I don't believe you know anything about the meeting place," Bruno said. "This is nothing more than a play for time, and as far as I'm concerned, it isn't working."

Lucy forced herself to look at him without fear. "I know a great deal more than you imagine, *captain*, both about you and about this important meeting place."

Monsieur Armand gasped at Lucy's use of the title "captain," but Bruno refused to appear impressed. "One of your husband's informers told you of my rank," he said aggressively.

"Not at all." Lucy allowed herself to smile. "We have met before, you and I, although I don't believe I shall tell you where. I know that you are the commander of a troop of Cossack soldiers recently operating within the borders of Afghanistan. I know that you were sent on an urgent mission from Qandahar to Kuwar and lost your way, causing great danger to your men when you passed first near the Khyber Pass and then near the town of Jalalabad."

"*Sacré Dieu!*" Bruno and Armand exchanged worried glances, obviously wondering how many other people shared this incriminating information. Lucy could almost see them thinking that perhaps it would not be wise to kill this interfering Englishwoman until they discovered exactly how much she knew—and how much various other people might know, also. It was Monsieur Armand, all propitiating smiles, who spoke.

"*Chère madame*, your information is most enlightening. I suspect that you have some proposition you wish to make to us?"

"Yes. A very simple proposition. I myself will lead the captain to the meeting place between my husband and Abdur Rahman, but on condition that my husband and I are allowed to go free as soon as I have led the captain there."

Once again, Bruno and Armand exchanged glances. This time they were lightning swift and full of satisfaction. Monsieur Armand stroked his mustache. "That seems a very fair bargain," he said. "Quite satisfactory."

Of course it seemed satisfactory, Lucy reflected. In fact, it probably seemed outstanding from Monsieur Armand's point of view since he had not the slightest intention of keeping it.

"We will need to travel fast and hard," Bruno commented hastily. Perhaps he realized that his colleague's acquiescence had been suspiciously easy. "I doubt if you will you be able to keep up with the pace I set, *madame*."

"I have probably traveled harder and faster within Afghanistan than you, captain. Have no fear. I shall meet whatever pace you set."

The Russian captain still wasn't quite satisfied, although from his perspective he had little to lose. If Lucy was lying and didn't know the meeting place, he would be no worse off. In fact, in some ways he would be better off, since Lucy would be much easier to murder on a mountain in Afghanistan than in the

British-controlled town of Peshawar. Nevertheless, he tried to probe the precise extent of her knowledge.

"Who else knows about my past activities in Afghanistan?" he asked.

"Captain," she chided gently. "We have already agreed that I am not a fool. If I respond *nobody*, will you believe me? And if I tell you that Mr. Carradin knows everything that I know, do I sign his death warrant? You may not trust me, captain, and I certainly don't trust you, but at this moment we are more or less equals. You need me. And as long as you need me, I have some hope of living. Don't expect me to impart information that is going to change the balance of power between us."

"Since we are being so frank, you will understand when I say that you must at least give us some indication of where the meeting place is to be. We cannot afford to set out on a wild-goose chase. Time is too short."

"The meeting place is not more than thirty miles northeast of the Khyber Pass, captain, and that is all I plan to reveal to you. Budget your supplies accordingly."

She could tell from the expressions of the two men that she had given them information that coincided with whatever knowledge they already possessed. She drank the final swallow of brandy, more to disguise her shaking hands than because her throat was still dry. Dear heaven, but she had committed herself to a dangerous course of action! She would have to lead Bruno close enough to Edward's appointed place of rendezvous that she could slip away from camp and complete the journey on foot. Not only was her own life at stake, but the lives of people crucial to the future peace of Afghanistan and northern India. From what she had heard, it seemed obvious that Bruno had orders to kill Abdur Rahman Kahn before he could rally the dissident tribesmen and unify Afghanistan. And Edward had undoubtedly been included in Bruno's assassination orders.

"We leave from the other side of town at dawn tomorrow morning," Bruno said. "You will come with me now to the house where I plan to spend the night. Armand, you will see about the carriage?"

"At once." Monsieur Armand rose and bowed over Lucy's hand, just as if they were saying good-bye at the end of a delightful dinner party. "Alas, *madame*, we must part company now."

She reminded herself that an hour earlier this man had been

arguing over the most effective method for disposing of her dead body. She retrieved her hand. "Good-bye, *monsieur.*"

"Let us say rather *au revoir, chère madame.*" He flashed an encouraging smile. "I wish you and the captain every success in your mission to find Lord de Beaumont. *Bon chance et bon voyage.*"

Only champagne and chocolates were missing to complete the sensation of unreality. "Thank you," Lucy said, and left her response at that. It probably wouldn't be wise to point out that she was well aware she and the Russian captain pursued Edward with diametrically opposite purposes in mind. Choosing the way to behave toward her captors was like walking a thin wire over a high mountain gorge. If she seemed too stupid, she ran the risk that Bruno would simply cut his losses and slit her throat. If she seemed too clever, she ran the same risk but for the opposite reason.

Monsieur Armand then turned to say farewell to Bruno. Unfortunately, he spoke rapidly in a language Lucy couldn't understand. She guessed it must be Russian, which confirmed her suspicion that Monsieur Armand was no more French than she was. The fact that both men spoke the French language so fluently meant almost nothing since all Russian aristocrats learned French in their cradles and often spoke it better than their native Russian.

Monsieur Armand departed to summon the carriage, which arrived promptly. A shabby, hooded affair, drawn by a mule, it was unlikely to attract any attention on the Peshawar streets even at this late hour. Unlike his partner, Bruno made no attempt to put any gloss of social nicety upon the reality of the situation. He filled the few spare minutes of waiting for the carriage by binding Lucy's wrists in front of her with a length of narrow cotton cloth and tying an efficient gag over her mouth. He then rearranged her veil so that his handiwork was invisible at first, swift glance.

He took out a small dagger concealed beneath his jacket and showed it to Lucy, not threateningly, but with businesslike efficiency. "I have taken the necessary precautions, *madame*, to prevent you doing something foolish. However, to discourage you from any dramatic action such as attempting to throw yourself from the carriage as we pass Mr. Carradin's lodgings, you should know that I shall hold the knife against your side, and that I shall not hesitate to use it."

Lucy shuddered, the gag inducing a sudden feeling of nausea. She remembered that she had scarcely eaten all day, but there was nothing she could do about it in her present state except pray she wouldn't vomit.

True to Bruno's word, the journey across town was completed with the tip of the knife pressed against Lucy's side. The pressure he exerted was sufficient that when the carriage jolted over a couple of extra-deep ruts, Lucy actually felt the nick of the knife point in her flesh. What with one thing and another, she was remarkably pleased when they arrived in a poor, but not squalid, section of town far removed from the area of the British bungalows.

Bruno conducted her to a small, windowless room in what was clearly the *zenana* section of the tiny house. "I will bring you the supplies you need for the journey," he said, untying the gag and the binding on her wrists. "A guard will be posted at your door. He is one of my men and utterly loyal. For the ride out of town you will wear the clothes you have on now."

"I have eaten almost nothing all day, and I am very thirsty. May I have some food and drink?" She asked the question as much to gauge Bruno's character as to assuage her hunger. Somewhat to her surprise, he agreed without hesitation. "We have bread and cheese and goat's milk, or water if you prefer."

"Water, please."

He saw her considering look and smiled coldly. "You wonder why I am so considerate of my prisoner, *madame*? The explanation is simple. At this moment you offer me the best chance of reaching my goal. I need you alert and healthy. It does not suit me that you should faint with hunger on the first stretch of the journey."

Lucy was grateful that she wouldn't be forced to spend the next few days riding captive to a sadist, but she wasn't entirely pleased to discover that Bruno was a man moved more by stolid common sense than by momentary passion. Somehow, she was going to have to make her escape from him, and to achieve that escape she would need to exploit his weaknesses. Down-to-earth common sense wouldn't be an easy character trait to turn to her advantage.

In the meantime, however, it was wonderful to know that she could fall asleep without disciplining herself to ignore the pangs of gnawing hunger. She had spent too many months of semistarvation in Kuwar not to appreciate the simple pleasure of a full stomach.

Only a few minutes passed before a silent European man brought in a tin plate bearing two varieties of cheese and a

generous serving of flat, Indian-style bread. Lucy tucked in with
a hearty appetite. For a woman who two hours ago had teetered on
the brink of being murdered, she decided she wasn't faring too
badly.

The first day of travel passed more in boredom and minor
discomfort than in actual hardship. Bruno had provided Lucy with
adequate supplies, including a donkey to ride on, blankets to sleep
in, thick felt boots with leather soles and a heavily padded cotton
jacket. At this early stage of the journey, most of this equipment
was rolled and stored at the back of her saddle, since until they
started the climb to the pass, heat and flies were far more of a
problem than cold and biting, blizzard-producing winds.

Bruno, for obvious reasons, was not attempting to approach the
pass with a full troop of uniformed soldiers as an escort. However,
Lucy had no trouble identifying the half-dozen men in his
entourage as out-of-uniform military volunteers. She thought she
half-recognized some of their faces as members of the Cossack
troop she- and Edward had encountered months before in the
mountains.

She didn't understand their Russian conversation, but on a
couple of occasions she could deduce that Bruno impatiently
reminded the men not to salute him. That was merely the most
obvious of the mistakes the soldiers made. They hadn't traveled
very far before she concluded that the men must have been chosen
for their fighting and survival skills rather than their acting
abilities. It would have been hard to imagine a group of men in
civilian clothes who looked more like Cossack soldiers.

Lucy wasn't sure whether to be amused or worried sick by their
inadequacy as actors. The Afridi tribesmen guarding the pass were
capricious in their activities, and such an obvious troop of soldiers
ran a grave risk of being wiped out by Afridi warriors before they
had ventured five miles into Afghani territory.

Bruno had made some effort to equip himself like a merchant
anxious to trade European luxuries for Afghani sheep skins. He
had brought along four pack mules loaded with hunting rifles, tea
and tins of English biscuits. These latter, strangely enough, were
known to be enormously popular among Afghani warriors of
every stripe and description. They would munch chocolate cookies with gusto while waiting in ambush for unsuspecting enemies
to pass within gun sight. Ironically, Lucy reflected that the
digestive wholemeal biscuits she consumed with such pleasure on

the count's verandah had no doubt been filched from this supply
of camouflage trading goods.

Fortunately, they hadn't left British-controlled territory by the
time Bruno gave the order to set up camp for the night, so her fears
about the Afridi weren't immediately put to the test. Lucy offered
to help prepare the evening meal, partly because she wanted to
appear cooperative, but mainly so that she might have a better
opportunity of stealing some extra food. Her gamble paid off. The
soldiers assigned to cooking duty were only too delighted to share
the burden of turning uninspiring supplies into edible meals.

Lucy found the military rations almost luxurious. Remembering
how she had considered herself to be living high on the hog during
her last journey simply because she had raisins *and* flour *and* dried
goat's meat, she had no difficulty at all in turning the ample
rations into a tasty meal.

Stealing food from her captors was almost too easy to be a
challenge. Smacking their lips over her cooking, nobody paid
much attention to how she accounted for the supplies. Without any
fear of discovery, she secreted raisins in a cotton pouch at her
waist. Sticks of hardened goat's cheese, together with muslin-
wrapped balls of cooked rice, were hidden in her saddle pack. She
was careful to stash away only the amount she would need to
survive for two days in cold, high country, but, nevertheless, she
was surprised at the captain's carelessness in failing to keep a
closer watch on her.

The captain did not strike her as a man who was normally
careless, nor was he slow-witted; but by the third day of their
journey Lucy had concluded that his vision was so limited as to
severely impair his abilities as an undercover commander. Every
step of their journey made a confrontation with Afridi tribesmen
more likely, but Bruno showed no concern. Infuriatingly, his lack
of concern paid off when a small band of marauding warriors
swooped down on the Russians just before dusk.

Lucy shuddered with anticipation of the worst. Stolidly, without a hint of subtlety or finesse, Bruno fell into his role as a
merchant. One of the soldiers who spoke a smattering of Pashto
was summoned to act as interpreter.

"We are merchants," the soldier said to the fierce-looking
Afghani fighters. "We look for *garakul* sheep skins that have been
promised us by the Ghilzai."

The Afghani warrior seemed to sense nothing strange in the
soldier's manner or in the timing of this supposed trading venture.

Perhaps he, along with his countrymen, considered all Europeans so crazy that traveling at the start of winter seemed no crazier than anything else the *ferangi* might do.

"We tax all voyagers on this pass," the Afridi spokesman replied. "You must pay the agreed toll." *Tax* and *tolls* were a new concept for the Afghan warriors, and they rather enjoyed the legal overtones it added to their age-old practice of extortion.

"We are willing to pay the tax," the soldier replied.

The bargaining continued only briefly. The Afridi departed, six rifles and four tins of biscuits the richer, and Bruno simply gestured for his men to continue riding. The thought that the Afridi were quite likely to shoot him in the back didn't seem to cross his mind, and—perversely—not another sign was seen of the supposedly fiercesome tribesmen. Perhaps they were all too busy eating chocolate cookies, Lucy reflected wryly.

That night, as she prepared the meal, Lucy observed Bruno more closely than ever. He was a Russian military officer to the core of his being, she concluded, with all the faults and all the virtues of that calling. She couldn't understand what had prompted him to volunteer for an undercover mission for which he was so patently unsuited. He shared a reasonable rapport with his men, but it was the rapport of an unsentimental, by-the-book officer for a troop of seasoned combat soldiers. His instruction that the men should not salute before they spoke seemed his only concession to the secret nature of their assignment, and his conduct toward his men scarcely deviated in any other respect from what might have been expected of an officer in uniform leading a troop of soldiers into battle.

And that, Lucy felt sure, was exactly how Bruno viewed his current assignment. As far as he was concerned, his mission to murder Edward and Abdur Rahman Kahn was a battlefield operation. She concluded that Bruno must view her own role as something like that of a field scout recruited from the native population to lead the army over rough or dangerous territory: tolerated and necessary, but not altogether trusted. And eminently expendable once the operation was complete.

The mildness of her treatment never deluded Lucy into thinking she was safe. She never doubted that Bruno would kill her as soon as she had served her purpose of leading him to Edward and Abdur Rahman Kahn. In the meantime, he had obviously decided there was no reason to worry about trouble from a mere woman surrounded by a troop of veteran Russian soldiers. She was miles from Mr. Carradin and the other British authorities, and moving farther away every day. The prospect of her running to seek sanctuary among the Afghanis was clearly unimaginable to him, and he seemed to assume that no European woman would even contemplate roaming alone in the terrifying mountains. She hoped this feeling of calm superiority on Bruno's part would be sufficient to get her out of the camp once she was close enough to Edward to make her escape.

Lucy's feeling of relative security was abruptly shattered at dawn on the fourth day of their journey when Bruno demanded concise directions to their destination.

"We must continue to proceed in a northeasterly direction," Lucy said, anxious to keep her revelations to a minimum—not least the revelation that she herself was relying heavily on memories of her previous journey in order to determine which trail the men should follow.

"I want the name of our destination," Bruno said grimly. "And an estimate of how many days' march it will take to reach it."

"Less than five days, unless we encounter real opposition from the Afridi."

"I need a name, *madame*. It is time for you to give me the name of the meeting place."

"Why should I give you such information?" she parried. "We agreed to a bargain: my safety, and my husband's safety, in exchange for my services as a guide."

"You will give me the information," he said softly, "because if you do not, I shall beat you. A bargain, *madame*, requires the power to enforce it. You have no power."

"And you," she said, trembling, "have no information."

For answer, he reached out and grabbed her, calling two of his men to hold her immobilized as he ripped off her padded jacket. Then he unfurled his horsewhip and brought the lash stinging down on her back in a single economical movement. The men didn't attempt to hold her up, and she fell to the ground with the force of the blow.

Bruno looked at her dispassionately, a man executing his duty, without joy but equally without sorrow. "Resistance is not possible, *madame*. Do not prolong this unpleasantness. The name of the meeting place, if you please."

Would he kill her if she gave him a name? Surely, not without checking first to see if the name was accurate? Besides, his experiences in the past must have convinced him that in this

desolate countryside a name would be of little value without a
guide to follow up the name with directions. And he certainly
couldn't hope to recruit an Afghani tribesman as a substitute
guide. Surely, she could safely give him a name?

The whip descended again, this time from the opposite direction. The cuts crossed with artistic accuracy in the middle of her
back, and she felt a sudden searing pain in her womb.

Fear for her unborn child eliminated all thought of further
defiance. "All right," she gasped. "All right, I will give you a
name." She gagged with the effort of speaking, and he handed her
his flask of brandy. She sipped gratefully, hating herself for her
gratitude. How swiftly a prisoner descends to the point of being
thankful to her captors for any spark of humanity, she thought
bitterly.

"Abdur Rahman Khan will meet my husband in a village called
Qim Koh." She named a village that she guessed was about fifteen
miles northwest of Qur'um, the place where Edward had said he
actually planned to meet Abdur Rahman. That fifteen miles of
error would, she hoped, be a sufficient margin of safety for her to
make her escape and reach Edward unobserved.

"Qim Koh. I know of this village." Bruno narrowed his eyes
reflectively. "It is possible, I suppose. And now, *madame*, I
would like an accurate estimate of how far we are from this village
of Qim Koh."

"Not more than three days, if we ride swiftly." She estimated
that Qur'um was about two days' hard march to the east, but she
didn't want the captain to know their destination was quite that
near. He might guard her more closely as they neared their destination.

"Three days," he said meditatively. "I think the timing should
be about right."

"But you cannot expect just to ride openly up to the village,
captain!" Lucy was genuinely horrified. "This meeting takes
place under the protection of the Afridi tribesmen who control this
part of Afghanistan. Your men . . . our whole party . . .
would be slaughtered before we could come within half a day's
ride of the village boundaries. In fact, our progress is probably
already being watched."

"I shall take care of that situation," he said. "You may ask the
sergeant for a dressing for your wounds."

"Thank you," she said.

Her irony totally escaped him. "You are welcome, *madame*."

* * *

Acting on Bruno's orders, two men broke off from the main troop that afternoon and rode away in a westerly direction toward Koh-i-Baba. Lucy guessed that they had been sent to make contact with the Khan of Kuwar's band of warriors. If she was correct, it probably meant that the Russian captain planned to set up ambushes at all the access routes into the village where Abdur Rahman and Edward intended to meet. Even Bruno, she thought, could not be hoping to launch a full-scale, frontal attack on the village itself. He must realize that his men would be slaughtered.

It was clear that the time had come to make good her escape. Quite apart from the fact that Bruno would likely beat her to death when he discovered that she had lied about Qim Koh, she estimated that after today's travel, Qur'um now lay less then two days' walk to the north. She certainly wanted to be well away from Bruno before any of her old enemies from Kuwar joined the Russian officer's band of merry men.

With five men left, including Bruno, there were unfortunately plenty of nightwatchmen available to guard the camp, and she had long ago discarded any hope of sneaking away while her captors slept. Within the first day of leaving Peshawar, she had realized that the hour immediately following the evening meal provided her only realistic chance of escape.

Once the men had eaten, they settled down for a smoke and a cup of tea, which they poured strong and boiling into their tin cups and laced with cheap brandy until it was cool enough to drink. Bruno didn't allow even mild drunkenness in his men, but they were more relaxed at this point of the day than at any other.

Lucy had taken advantage of this nightly period of relaxation to heat water for washing, and then to walk out of sight of the men to bathe and take care of her other personal needs. Each night, she had gradually extended the period of her absence, noting with relief that her absence never raised any alarm from Bruno or his troops. The previous night, she had been gone for twenty minutes, and her return had scarcely caused so much as a turned head from the men still gathered warm and comfortable around the campfire.

Despite this seeming laxity, she didn't hope for a very big head start. She guessed that Bruno had a seasoned military man's sense of impending danger, and that while he might be unconcerned for twenty minutes, when twenty-five minutes passed without a glimpse of her, some inner alarm signal would automatically trigger. It might, if she was lucky, take another five minutes to organize a quick search of the campsite surrounds. Thirty minutes in total before Bruno would realize that she had run away.

Thirty minutes. All her finagling added up to, at best, thirty minutes' head start. Her only other protection would come from the darkness and the fact that mules or horses at night were more unwieldly than humans, so the men would have to pursue her on foot.

When she handed out the bowls of onion-flavored rice that night, she wished she had some magic potion to sprinkle over the food that would send all the men deep into slumber. Barring such magic, she could do no more than make the portions a little more generous than usual, her garnish of dried peas and pepper a little tastier. Fortunately, the chill mountain air added zest to the men's appetites, and they ate with relish.

"How is your back?" Bruno asked as she gathered up his dish for cleaning.

"The sergeant gave me some salve," she said neutrally. "He cleansed the wounds with alcohol, and he believes there will be no infection."

"Good, good." Bruno seemed genuinely pleased that the prognosis was favorable. Perhaps he preferred his victims healthy when he killed them. "The food was well prepared, *madame*. Armand was correct in saying that you are not in the least like other English women."

This was definitely not the night for him to begin thinking along such lines. "I have been taught how to cook over an open fire, that's all, captain, but I'm glad you enjoyed the meal." She balanced his dish on the top of her pile and hastily departed to the spot where a bucket of hot water had been left for her alongside a portable oil lamp.

She made short work of the dishes, then had to slow down her pace. Tonight, she mustn't suddenly be quicker than she had been every other night. She stacked up the clean dishes, ready to return them to the soldiers, then detoured via the animals.

Again, this detour was the one she had taken care to make every night, and her actions aroused no interest at all on the part of the men. She removed the pilfered strips of goat's cheese and balls of rice from their hiding place and secreted them in the capacious inner pockets of her jacket. The donkey brayed softly when he scented the food, and Lucy held her breath as she heard the momentary silence from around the campfire. Seeing the familiar sight of her petting the donkey, the men's usual chatter soon resumed.

Heart pounding, knees knocking, Lucy walked over the rough sage grass to return the clean bowls and cutlery to the soldiers. It seemed incredibly difficult to do something she had done easily on each one of the preceding five nights. Everyone seated around the fire must surely hear the throbing drumbeat of her heart. How could they avoid scenting her fear? How could they avoid realizing that tonight was different, that tonight she planned to run away?

But nobody, thank heaven, seemed to sense her nervousness. The men murmured drowsy thanks as she handed back their utensils, and one jumped up to unhitch the pot containing her water from over the fire. Thank God, she was only required to murmur her thanks in French. At this moment it was a blessing that she shared no common language with the soldiers and none of the men expected her to speak.

She feared Bruno far more than his troops. Bruno, who might have tunnel vision, but who presumably was blessed with the fighting instincts of any other experienced military commander. Surely, any reasonably competent battlefield veteran learned to smell fear and rebellion? She kept out of his line of sight as she walked slowly toward the dark perimeter of the camp. Thirty minutes' head start. Was she going to get her thirty minutes?

She had chosen her escape route as efficiently as she could. Perforce, she had decided to run back over the terrain she and the Russians had covered earlier in the day, otherwise she would be running blind into unknown countryside. Late that afternoon she had spotted a narrow trail, too rugged for horses, that stretched east and then seemed to circle back north. If she could manage to find it again in the darkness, she hoped it would eventually connect her with the main trail to Qur'um. Visually, the odds looked good, but trails could be deceptive once you actually started walking on them. Lucy prayed she had chosen well. Sometimes there was nothing left to do except pray.

She set the pot of water down behind a large boulder. At this distance from the campfire, only the silver light of the moon and the stars illuminated her actions. *Please God, how about a cloud,* she pleaded. *Even a small one will do.*

As if on cue, the moon's face was momentarily obscured by a thick veil of storm clouds. Drawing in a deep breath, Lucy ran into the welcoming darkness.

CHAPTER TWENTY

Lucy ran until her laboring heart threatened to burst. Then she walked until her lungs seared from the pain of her breathing and the stitch in her side stretched from her knees to her shoulders. Finally, she stopped to rest, leaning against a smooth boulder and closing her eyes as the shuddering gasps of her breath gradually slowed.

She was frighteningly aware of the fact that she hadn't traveled very far—no more than five miles—and that her fatigue was out of proportion to the effort she had expended. She would not even let herself think about the dull ache in the small of her back that had never quite gone away since she fell to the ground after Bruno's beating.

Now that she was no longer deafened by the pounding of her own heartbeat, she strained to detect the sounds of possible pursuit. She heard a man's voice call out somewhere in the far distance, but however hard she listened, she could discern no telltale rattle of pebbles nor see any beam of approaching lantern light. With only four men at his disposal, Bruno was having as hard a time as she had hoped in setting up efficient search parties. At last, she had done something right!

She couldn't afford the luxury of a longer rest. She set off again, drawing her veil across her nose and mouth to lessen the impact of the cutting night wind. Her pace was slowed by the need to walk slightly to the side of the main trail where the going was less sure but where rockfalls and the occasional stunted milk vetch bushes offered the slight hope of concealment. She also didn't want to risk leaving footprints in the sandy stretches of the main path in case, by any remote chance, Bruno wasted time and energy in attempting to track her.

She had no idea how much time Bruno would waste in pursuit, but she suspected that if she could remain free for another couple of hours, he would abandon any hope of catching her. To that extent, Bruno's practical nature worked to her advantage. She didn't think he would waste time on vengeance or wreaking his anger when he still had a mission to accomplish. Assassinating Abdur Rahman Khan and Lord Edward de Beaumont would strike him as much more important than killing a woman who was probably going to die of exposure in the mountains without any help from him.

Fate finally seemed to be on Lucy's side. After about an hour's walking, still without any hint of pursuit, the persistent cloud cover cleared. In the brilliant silver moonlight, the path she had been seeking stood revealed, stretching to her left in sandy, enticing clarity.

She took off her veil and wiped away a trickle of cold sweat, sighing with relief that she had managed to find the trail. With any luck—dear God, with any luck—this was the trail that would take her to Qur'um in less than ten hours of walking.

The surge of elation didn't help her fatigue as much as it should have done. The ache in her back had intensified as she walked, stretching out slow tentacles that settled into her upper thighs and lower abdomen. Gritting her teeth, she pushed her hair out of her eyes and tied the veil back in place as a protection from the continuing bitter cold of the wind. Oddly enough, although she felt chilled to the marrow of her bones, beads of sweat kept dripping off her forehead and into her eyes.

At first, Lucy used a corner of her veil to wipe the sweat away. Soon, she ignored the sweat, as she ignored the cold and the grinding ache in her abdomen. With dogged determination, she put one foot in front of the other, her mind reduced to a machine that permitted her no choice in the endless lift and fall of her steps. Walking was necessary if she planned to survive, and so she walked. Her ears screened the nighttime sounds, filtering out the howl of the jackals and the rare screech of an owl, and allowing her to hear only the few noises that might have indicated human pursuit. Her almost silent world consisted of no more than the yard of path ahead of her and the possibility of Bruno's men behind.

When she finally stopped, it was not from choice but because the exhaustion of her body overcame her willpower. Her steps slowed to a stagger. She righted them, forcing her reluctant body back into the middle of the path. Too late now to worry about tracks in the sand. She staggered again, and again she righted herself, but this time she moved only a few steps forward before she keeled over. Her dazed, fatigue-drugged brain functioned just clearly enough to warn her to pull herself to the side of the path and pillow her head on a boulder, before unconsciousness claimed her.

Her sleep was restless with fear and pain, and she awoke to the unpleasant sensation of being watched. She opened her eyes and found the sun high enough in the clear blue sky to glint with menacing dazzle off the barrels of the three rifles pointed with unerring accuracy at her head, heart and stomach.

She had time for only a single moment of terror before a voice spoke to her in Pashto. "Who are you?" a gruff voice demanded. "Where is your husband and tribe?"

Lucy blinked, disengaging her eyes from the hypnotic glint of the rifles long enough to register that the weapons were held by Afghanis, not Russians. Her immediate feeling of relief was quickly tempered by the realization that waking up to find oneself surrounded by Afridi warriors was scarcely a cause for celebration. Afridis were known for the speed with which they could wield their curved knives to gut their victims.

"I was taken prisoner," she replied truthfully. "I seek my husband, to warn him that enemies pursue him."

"Who is your husband?"

She was too weary to lie and, besides, she seemed to have nothing to lose by telling more or less the truth. "Rashid, the Trader, from the Punjab is my husband," she said.

The men's faces betrayed no reaction to her news, but she knew that they couldn't be operating this close to the village of Qur'um without being aware of the fact that an important meeting was scheduled to take place there shortly between Rashid and Abdur Rahman Khan.

"We will take you to your husband," the leader of the trio said. He gestured with his rifle. "Come, wife of Rashid. We must walk quickly if we are to arrive in Qur'um while it is still light."

She stood, stretching aching muscles, relieved that the heavy ache at the base of her abdomen seemed to have lessened while she slept. The men slung their rifles across their shoulders and set off at what for them was no doubt an easy lope. For Lucy, the pace demanded from her a stamina she just didn't seem to have. The rough cotton of her gown abraded the whip cuts on her back, and the raisins she tried to eat as they walked along did nothing to increase her level of energy.

When the sky started to dance a whirligig around her head, Lucy had no choice but to ask the tribesmen if they would stop for a few minutes. "Honored sirs, could we please rest here and drink?" she asked when they came to a small widening in the trail marked by a thorn bush and the thin trickle of an autumn-dry stream.

The three men stopped, examining her with the unblinking gaze she had learned to expect during her captivity in Kuwar. "We will rest here," the leader announced. "You may sit, wife of Rashid."

She sank onto the sandy ground, too grateful for the rest to question the warrior's generosity. Only when one of the men silently handed her a cup of water he had collected from the stream did she try to pull herself to her feet. Something was wrong, terribly wrong, if these proud fighting men were allowing her—a worthless woman, not of their tribe—to loll around resting while they made preparations to refresh themselves.

"Sit, wife of Rashid." The warrior who had brought her the water gently pushed her back onto the ground.

"I have food to share," she said faintly, reaching into her pockets to find her supply of cheese, raisins and balls of rice.

"Thank you," the warrior said gravely, accepting a piece of cheese and passing her grubby offering to each of his companions. When all three of them had eaten sparingly, they returned the remnants of the meal to her, together with their own offering of *bolani*, a bread baked with leeks at the center.

She couldn't refuse without giving mortal offense. Lucy took the tiniest possible piece of bread, feeling her stomach rise up in protest. The men watched her without expression until the leader finally asked her, "Are you in pain, daughter?"

Their faces might reveal little, but Lucy recognized the sympathy inherent in their decision to address her as "daughter." She closed her eyes, rejecting the implications of their sympathy. She would not think of the grinding pain that had returned to settle in her womb. She would not acknowledge the ache that now turned the whole of her lower body into a single unit of misery. If she didn't acknowledge how she felt, then perhaps the miscarriage she dreaded wouldn't happen.

She hadn't intended to let even the word "miscarriage" slip into her mind. She swallowed the last of her water and sprang to her feet. "No, no, thank you, I'm not in pain. I am very well. I'll come with you now, honored sirs, if you are ready to leave."

"With your permission, daughter." The tribesman did not stop to receive the permission he requested. He simply stepped forward, hitched his rifle out of the way and swung her into his arms. He then resumed his march forward at the same half-running lope he had used all morning, her extra weight seeming of no consequence to his easy progress forward.

She dozed, or perhaps she was unconscious for a while. A shock of sudden jarring pain jolted her awake. She felt the hot trickle of blood between her thighs, and for a minute she thought she must have been shot. When she realized what was happening, she gave a cry of such bitter regret that the warrior who carried her actually deigned to stop and look down at her.

"We are nearly at the house where your husband stays, wife of Rashid. In ten minutes you will see our village of Qur'um."

"Thank you," she whispered through the haze of her pain. *Oh God,* she thought. *What shall I say to Edward? How shall I explain to him that I am losing his child?* Even the need to warn her husband of Bruno's plans no longer seemed so important. The thought uppermost in her mind was that if only she had stayed at home as a wife was supposed to do, their child would still be growing safely in her womb.

"We are here, wife of Rashid," her escort murmured quietly. "We have arrived in the village of Qur'um."

She heard the tribesman give a salutation to the guards posted at the entrance to the village. "I bring the wife of Rashid to safety."

"Looks as if you found her just in time," the guard replied. "Our patrols are busy today," he added, waving Lucy and her three warriors through.

Hearing the guard's words, she wondered how Bruno's band of soldiers had escaped detection. They were following one of the major winter trails off the Khyber Pass. If men from Qur'um were scouring the countryside, it was strange that Bruno hadn't been spotted. It was even stranger that he had been able to buy off the only patrol which accosted him with nothing more than a few rifles and a couple of tins of biscuits.

Coherent reasoning was too difficult to sustain for long, and her mind wandered off at a tangent, imagining what was happening back in Peshawar and wondering if the body of her poor maid Dira had been discovered. *I hope I live,* Lucy thought, *so that I can see Armand and the count arrested.* Except that Armand would probably escape into Russian territory long before she could get back to Peshawar. She sighed with disappointment, but the disappointment soon vanished. Her mind floated off into another memory, this time of her childhood and her English home. Hallerton. She wished her nanny would bring her some hot milk. She was tired and wanted to go to sleep.

"Here is the house where your husband stays, wife of Rashid." The tribesman who carried her stopped in the courtyard of a typical Afghani hut. Walls of sun-dried brick, covered with mud and straw plaster, supported—more or less—a flat roof of rammed earth, interlaced with twigs. A woven mat tied to four poles sheltered the entrance way, and beneath this mat a group of women sat spinning wool.

One of the women jumped up as soon as she saw the tribesman and his burden. "What do you bring us, Khushal?"

"Greetings, Homaira, honored first wife of Yakub. I bring one who claims to be the wife of Rashid. I fear she loses the son she carried for her husband."

"No!" Lucy cried out. "No, I'm not losing my baby!"

"Bring her inside to her husband. Allah have mercy, but her babbles make no sense. The fever must have taken her already."

With her last remaining strength, Lucy disciplined her brain so that she would not speak English, would not betray Edward by using his English name. Khushal carried her inside the dark hut, and in the corner she saw her husband. Her heart leaped with joy, and then contracted with bitter sorrow because she had failed him. She was losing their baby.

"Rashid," she muttered through parched, cracked lips, trying to marshal her straying thoughts into coherent Pashto. "Rashid, Monsieur Armand is a spy and so is the count."

He sprang to his feet, knocking over his stool. "*Lucy!* God in heaven, what have they done to you! My heart, what's happened?"

"Monsieur Bruno, the man who pretended to be Monsieur Armand's colleague—I don't know if you met him while you were in Peshawar—he is really the Russian captain we saw on the pass. And he has orders to kill you, along with Abdur Rahman Khan. The count saw us when I came to your other house to say good-bye, so it's all my fault you are being followed. They took me prisoner, or I would have stayed at home like you said, truly I would. And I think Bruno has sent his men to join forces with the Khan of Kuwar. The Khan must have patched up his quarrel with the Amir. Or maybe Bruno is paying him to fight."

Edward took her into his arms and brushed his cheek against hers. "Lucy, my dearest, thank you for bringing me this information, but now you must rest."

"You don't understand! You must send warriors to the trail that leads to Qim Koh. They'll find Bruno and the Russian soldiers and maybe the Khan's men, too. He must be stopped. He plans to ambush Abdur Rahman, I'm sure of it."

"Lucy, don't worry, my heart. Abdur Rahman Khan is safely on his way back to Tashkent. Everything is under control."

A burning contraction of her womb robbed Lucy of breath. She bit her lip to keep in the cry of anguish as she felt the uncontrollable gush of blood spurt between her thighs, seeping through her skirts, leaving the cloth clammy and wet. Dear God, her poor baby! "I'm sorry," she whispered. "I'm so sorry."

"Get me water!" Edward yelled. He sounded unbearably angry, and yet his arms around her seemed gentle enough. "Homaira, for pity's sake, we need boiling water, salt and clean rags!"

"Right away, Master, they come."

Rashid looked down at Lucy, his eyes dark with emotion. "You will be all right, my heart. I swear that you will be all right."

The pain ripped at her again, but this time she scarcely felt it. She touched her fingers to the tears that ran wet and cold against the hotness of her cheeks. "I thought I could be strong enough," she said.

"Lucy, no one could have been stronger. Now rest, please, my love."

Edward pushed aside the tattered leather curtain that separated the sleeping room from the living quarters and placed Lucy carefully on the rope-and-wood bed with its thin cotton mattress. Her face was white, her cheeks sunken and her lips blue from loss of blood. Looking at her, he experienced fear such as he had never before known, not even in the fiercest battle or at those moments when his own death had seemed most certain.

Yakub, the owner of the hut and the chief of the village, took one look at the unconscious woman in Rashid's arms and tactfully prepared to leave. The approach of death could be watched in solitude. The community support would come later, after the woman was dead.

"I will dispatch some of my warriors to Qim Koh," he said. "The time has come, I think."

"Yes. Bruno serves no useful purpose now that we know the names of his fellow conspirators in Peshawar."

"Your wife has brought us valuable information," Yakub said. He patted Edward on the arm. "Remember, my friend, Allah is merciful."

He walked quietly from the room, and a few moments later his senior wife, Homaira, bustled in carrying the requested hot water. Much more important to her way of thinking, she also carried the goodluck charm of honey, sesame seed and ground toadskin that might possibly scare away the evil *jinns* waiting to steal the soul of Rashid's wife, along with the soul of the baby they had already claimed.

Seeing the snow-white face of the woman and the pool of bright scarlet blood in which she lay, Homaira didn't have much hope, but she dutifully tied the charm around the woman's head. She then bent and whispered "Allah is great" four times into each ear, hopefully terrifying the *jinns* with the mystical power of the incantation.

Glancing up from her efforts to save the woman, she was alarmed to see Rashid dipping his hands into almost boiling water, then rubbing salt all over them and dipping them again into the same jug.

"You may leave us now, Master." Homaira spoke kindly, containing her irritation at the waste of heated water that could have made perfectly good tea. At this time of year, cooking fuel was scarce. "I will give your wife every attention."

"No, I cannot leave her!" Rashid spoke sharply, and seemed to recover his composure with difficulty. He drew in a deep breath, his smile obviously strained when he turned to speak.

"Thank you, Homaira. I am indebted to you for your care and your kind offer to help, but I must stay with my wife and tend to her myself."

"Master, with all humility I tell you that this is woman's work. The sights that follow upon the loss of a babe are not suitable for a man to cast his gaze upon."

Rashid took a clean rag, dipped it in the hot water, then leaned over and wiped away the sweat and dirt from his wife's face and hands. Thank heaven, he at least didn't disturb the all-important charm. "Homaira, what I need more than anything in the world is clean cloth, preferably white cloth, and more boiling water."

"But, Master, you have an entire jug full of hot water at your elbow."

"I know, bit it's dirty now."

Well, of course it was dirty, because he'd just dumped salt into it! Homaira shrugged, deciding with true nobility of spirit to humor the poor man. She'd known other men before Rashid to go crazy when a favorite wife hovered on the point of death. It seemed that the prouder and stronger a man was in battle, the more a favorite woman could render him weak. She supposed that if it made Rashid happy to pour water on his wife, he couldn't do too much harm. The woman was going to die anyway, despite Homaira's generous loan of the most powerful health charm she possessed. Women who miscarried nearly always did, once the fever set in.

"Very well, Master," she replied indulgently. "I will bring you hot water."

"Boiling," he said, not looking at her. "It must be boiling. And a bridal sheet, one that has never been used."

Homaira had always considered Rashid a man of amazing good sense, but this suggestion was too much for her. "A bridal sheet, Master!" she exclaimed. "But what in the world do you want with that?"

He didn't explain, merely turned back to his wife and began to remove her layers of filthy, blood-soaked clothing, thus giving the *jinns* all the access they needed to her fragile body. "Homaira, I beg of you. The water and the clean bridal sheet."

She couldn't bear to stay and watch the *jinns* take possession of the poor woman's body. Besides, with all the *jinns* who must be circling around, hoping for a share in the bloody spoils, there might be one with nothing better to do than hop over onto Homaira's shoulder. The elderly woman made hasty tracks toward the door.

"I will return with the water and the sheet soon, Master." But not before she'd drunken a potent brew of garlic and sour milk to protect herself from the *jinns*, who must be dancing with glee at the unexpected opportunities being offered to them by Rashid's bizarre behavior.

"Lucy, my love, my darling, you must not die. Life wouldn't be worth living without you to tease me, without the sight of your smile. Most beautiful of women, find the strength to fight for your life, I beg of you."

Homaira returned in time to hear Rashid's murmured incantation. She couldn't understand what he was saying, but she was relieved that he had stopped doing dangerous things like exposing his wife to overheated water and fresh air and had started doing something useful like whispering spells. The fact that he spoke words in a tongue she couldn't understand seemed especially promising. *Jinns* were notorious for their inability to understand straight speaking, and it was very wise of Rashid to try all the languages he knew in order to scare them away.

"Here is the boiling water, Master, and the bridal sheet." Homaira spoke with new respect.

"Thank you. Could you bring them here? I want to keep my wife's hips elevated. It seems to help in controlling the bleeding."

These were not promising remarks, and Homaira's optimism suffered a further blow when she approached the bed and saw what Rashid had done—apart from recite spells—during her brief absence from the sleeping room. He had taken off all his wife's clothes and washed her completely, removing the entire protective layer of dried blood. Then, instead of binding her arms to her body with cotton strips, he had covered her loosely with a knitted shawl that had enough holes in the design for a hundred *jinns* to creep through.

As if all that weren't sufficient, Homaira watched in disbelief as he soaked a cloth in the fresh pot of boiling water, waved it a few times in the air to cool it off, then gently wiped away the little bit of blood still encrusted between his wife's thighs.

Homaira wasn't sure whether she was more outraged by the incredible immodesty of this performance or by the danger Rashid was inflicting on a helpless woman. Although his poor wife was so close to death it scarcely mattered, Homaira felt obliged to offer a protest.

"Master, everybody knows that at the time of her flux, hot water is dangerous to a woman, and since your wife has just lost a babe, the danger to her is increased tenfold."

Rashid turned to Homaira, his eyes unseeing. Then he blinked, as if dragging himself back to the reality of his surroundings. "Homaira, don't worry," he said finally. "The spells I use are very powerful, but to make them work properly I need boiling water."

"I've never heard of any such spells, Master."

"These are spells given me by a powerful *khwajah* from across the ocean. He—um—lives on an island surrounded by sea, which is why his spells need water. He is so powerful that he was called in to help deliver the babes of the Queen Empress Victoria."

Homaira was impressed despite herself and agreed to help Rashid lift up his wife and place the large bridal sheet beneath her limp body. To her relief, Rashid brought the ends of the sheet up over his wife, so that she was neatly packaged in white cotton, every inch of her vulnerable skin covered except for her face and neck. But those parts of her, praise Allah, had the protection of Homaira's goodluck charm. A *khwajah*'s spells from across the ocean were all very well, but Homaira placed far greater reliance on her own charm. She had proof it worked. Hadn't she given birth to ten children and lost only three of them, not one of the dead infants a boy?

"I will bring you tea, Master," she said kindly. It was obvious this would be a deathbed vigil, and Homaira wanted to ease Rashid's suffering as much as she could.

"Thank you, Homaira. I'm grateful for all you've done."

"It was nothing," she said truthfully, not anxious to have her reputation as a competent woman-of-medicine ruined by the stories that were bound to circulate about this disastrously mismanaged affair. "You did everything, Master. The responsibility is yours."

For a moment, Rashid actually smiled. "Don't worry, Homaira," he said softly. "I won't tell anybody what you helped me do, if you won't. My wife is going to get better, you know."

She hid her pity as best she could. "Yes, Master, I'm sure she is. I'll bring you that tea right away."

CHAPTER TWENTY-ONE

To the astonishment of the entire village, at dawn the next morning Yakub's youngest concubine reported the amazing news that the wife of Rashid, the Trader, still lived.

Homaira loudly attributed this miracle to her goodluck charm. What else could have proven powerful enough to overcome the trader's reckless addiction to boiling water? Edward wisely remained silent, but mentally attributed the miracle to his copious use of boiled water and sterile cloths. What else could have been powerful enough to overcome the disastrous effects of a toadskin charm, sticky with congealed honey, and a bed literally hopping with fleas?

Edward waited with some anxiety for his wife to return to consciousness. His vigil was not a solitary one. He couldn't remember another occasion in his life when he had so heartily cursed the Afghani custom of community living. Neither Yakub nor Yakub's wives nor any of his sons and daughters seemed to think there was a reason in the world for them to leave the room and allow Rashid time alone with his wife. Lucy had been brought back from the brink of death. This was a moment of triumphant community celebration. Yakub's family crowded forward, eager to hear the first exchange of words between the reunited couple.

Lucy finally stirred, her head shifting restlessly on the pillow.

Edward's throat constricted when her eyes opened. They looked too big for her white, thin face, their size underlined by smudges of fatigue and their brown depths shadowed with remembered pain. He wanted to take her into his arms and kiss away the shadows, kiss away the hurt. Instead, he could do nothing save smile encouragingly.

"Welcome back, my heart," he said in Pashto.

Even after all she had endured, she realized she should not speak in English. "Rashid?" she whispered, looking at the throng of faces surrounding her bed. "Is everything all right?"

"Everything is very well now that you are feeling better." He took her hand, wondering what in God's name he was supposed to say to the woman he loved so much and had caused to suffer so terribly. He noticed her cracked and bleeding lips and said the first thing that came into his head.

"Would you like a cup of tea? Homaira has prepared some specially for you." *Wonderful,* he cursed himself silently. *That was a truly meaningful remark to make a woman who has almost killed herself in her effort to save your life.*

"Some tea would be welcome. My throat feels like the sand of the desert." Her voice rasped with the effort of speaking, but at least she hadn't told him to go away and never come back. He helped her into a sitting position, then took the prized china bowl from Homaira and held it to Lucy's lips.

She sipped the steaming brew gratefully. The tea had been heavily laced with sugar, and she closed her eyes as she drank, obviously feeling better as the hot liquid seeped into her veins, restoring her energy and bringing a trace of color to her cheeks.

Then, much too soon, Edward saw that she remembered. Her hands pressed against her stomach, and immediately the momentary flush of color left her face.

She pushed away the tea bowl and sat up straighter in the bed. To Edward, it seemed that she had the greatest difficulty in forcing herself to meet his eyes. Did she blame him that much for what had happened? he wondered.

"The baby," she said, and her voice sounded harsh, grating. "There is no baby anymore, is there? I lost it."

Yakub and his family drew in a collective breath. This was the discussion they had been waiting for. They turned expectantly toward the trader. Men had been known to divorce their wives for the crime of losing a first-born son, although Rashid seemed altogether too besotted with his wife to consider such a drastic step.

At that moment, Edward would have ransomed his entire fortune to be able to take Lucy into his arms and pour out his confused, tumultuous feelings of sorrow and guilt and love. Instead, for the sake of the documents that burned in his inner pocket, he was forced to maintain his role as Rashid and abide by the customs of the Afridi. Even the fact that he was holding his wife's hand in public was stretching the boundaries of Afridi tolerance to the absolute limit.

"My dear," he said softly, trying to tell her with the pressure of his fingers all that he could not say in words. "Our son is lost, but there will be other sons for us, I'm sure. And daughters, too. We have long years ahead of us to know the joy of having children."

Yakub and his family murmured their approval of this courteously expressed sentiment, but Edward could feel the waves of Lucy's resistance. He knew exactly what she was thinking. As far as she was concerned, the fact that there might be other children was no reason to dismiss the loss of this particular baby. In her physically exhausted state, it was useless to expect her to remember that Edward would lose stature before the Afridi if he entered into the feminine ritual of mourning for a miscarriage. Anger with his wife was a permitted emotion. Grief for the babe was not. And, at this point in time, the fate of an entire nation might hang on Yakub's willingness to ensure Edward's safe passage back to India. Edward couldn't afford to appear a weakling.

Gently, trying to convey by gesture all the apologies he couldn't make, and the words of love he couldn't speak, Edward stroked the hair out of Lucy's eyes.

"You need to regain your strength, my dear, and then we will have time alone to talk of many difficult matters. Homaira, first wife of Yakub, the chief of this village, has prepared some mutton broth for you. Will you please drink it?"

To his relief, she didn't refuse, although from the listlessness of her manner he had little hope that she would eat enough to see her firmly on the road to recovery. Ignoring the cluckings from Homaira that indicated exactly what she thought of a man performing this womanly task, he adjusted the cushion behind Lucy's head and spooned bread soaked in mutton broth into her mouth until she murmured, "No more, please."

"Now it is time for your wife to sleep, Master." Homaira

obviously felt that her position of authority in the sickroom had been usurped long enough. Bowing low to Yakub, she spoke with unmistakable firmness. "You and your sons will wish to leave us, honored husband. I know how many matters of urgent business await your wise attention."

Yakub had been married long enough to know when he was being told to get out of his wife's way. Gathering his sons and sons-in-law about him, he nodded with great dignity toward Edward. "You, Master Rashid, will wish to join us in waiting for the return of our warriors from Qim Koh. The women will take good care of your wife."

Edward had no choice, unless he wished to insult Homaira's domestic skills and impugn his own standing as a brave fighter. "I join you with pleasure, Yakub." With a final frustrated squeeze of Lucy's hand, he followed the chieftain from the sleeping room.

Lucy awoke late in the afternoon to the sound of drums, whistles and hoarse cheers of triumphant laughter. The noise, she realized, came from outside the hut, where some sort of celebration was obviously going on.

"Harumph, so you are awake. Just in time for my *kichri*. Shiri, get the Wife-of-Rashid a bowl of *kichri*."

Shiri, a young girl of about thirteen or fourteen, departed obediently, and Homaira shook her head. "I'm never going to get that one trained. She hasn't the brains of a stillborn camel."

"She is your daughter?" Lucy inquired politely. "She is very pretty."

"Daughter! She is the latest concubine of my husband." Homaira snorted her disgust, then leaned toward the bed, one married woman confiding in another. "My husband has all the pleasure and I have all the training. Anybody who knows her mother would have realized the girl wouldn't have a lick of sense nor a bit of domestic knowledge. But men, you know how they are, and we women simply have to put up with them. At least your husband is still crazy about you. Is he planning to take another wife, do you know?"

Lucy cleared her throat. "Not as far as I know."

"Hurry up and give your husband his son, that's my advice. You may feel weak now and not wanting to think about any more babies, but that's a woman's lot, isn't it? Give him a son, Wife-of-Rashid, and you will have his respect forever."

It sounded like a very simple equation, and for an Afghani

husband and wife no doubt it held true. Lucy had a lowering suspicion, however, that although Edward might be furious with her for losing their baby, simply presenting him with a substitute son and heir would not make all right with their relationship. Lucy sighed. Afghani marriages, despite the number of wives involved, seemed a great deal more straightforward than their European counterparts.

An especially loud cheer coincided with the return of Shiri, carrying the bowl of mushed rice and shredded lamb. "What is happening out there?" Lucy asked, accepting her meal with a smile of thanks.

"They are bringing home the dead bodies of the murderers," Homaira explained before Shiri could speak.

"Which particular murderers are these?" Lucy inquired. Any wayfarer killed by the Afridi was immediately transformed by popular acclaim into a *murderer* or *slaughterer of the innocent*.

"Russian murderers," Homaira reported laconically. Since she considered a villager from across the valley a distant foreigner, Russians were so remote from her frame of reference that she could work up little enthusiasm for these particular dead bodies.

"Russians!"

"Yes. My husband explained that these Russians are very wicked. They planned to murder Abdur Rahman Khan, and Yakub says that years of fighting would follow upon Abdur Rahman's death. Personally, I can't see what difference it makes whether Abdur Rahman lives or dies, since the men fight all the time, anyway. What matter if they fight the Kohistani, or the Kirghiz, or the British, or some other foreigners?"

With masterly inconsistency, she took Lucy's empty bowl and smiled. "But, there, a woman never understands these things, does she? Would you like me to help you walk across to the porch door, so that you can see the dead bodies? The warriors have them tied to their saddles."

Lucy managed to conceal her shudder. "Thank you very much, but I don't think I'm quite in the mood for viewing dead bodies."

"That's understandable," Homaira nodded. "Besides, better that you wait until tomorrow to get dressed."

A sudden thought struck Lucy. "I'm sure I must be sleeping in your husband's bed. Shouldn't I come with you to the women's quarters?"

Homaira appeared gratified that Lucy realized the enormity of the privilege that had been accorded her. "Yes, it's true that you spent the past hours in my husband's bed. If you can walk, Wife-of-Rashid, it would be better if you sleep tonight with the other women." She broke off irritably. "Shiri, what in the world are you doing, darting about all over the place like that?"

Shiri reluctantly stood up, abandoning the chink in the mud brick walls that had been her peephole to the outside world. "They have another prisoner," she said. "A live one, and he is not a Russian. He wears very fine clothes."

"Humph, wrap yourself in the bridal sheet and one of those blankets Wife-of-Rashid, and let's check out what this fool of a girl says. Here, Shiri, take the other arm of the trader's wife and help her into the living room."

Lucy was soon ensconsed on a stool next to the window. Despite all the noise of drums and cheering, there were no more than twenty men and an equivalent number of women and children lined up to salute the returning warriors. From her position behind the tiny, screened window, Lucy could at first discern nothing through the milling throng of strutting small boys, giggling girls and black-veiled women. Finally, the random movement of the crowd permitted her to view a row of tethered horses bearing horrible, limp burdens. She turned her gaze quickly in the opposite direction and saw a somewhat ramshackle palisade, some ten feet square, within which was confined no less astonishing a personage than the Khan of Kuwar.

Lucy gasped. "Hashim Khan!" she exclaimed. "What in the world is he doing here?"

"He was taken prisoner," Shiri said, her knowledge apparently coming from the mysterious network that seemed to inform all villagers simultaneously as soon as one of them possessed a piece of information. "A lot of the Khan's warriors were killed, and the rest fled into the mountains, but the Khan wasn't killed because Yakub has decided to ransom him back to his people."

Homaira cuffed the girl lightly on the ear. "You refer to the master of this household as *my lord*," she said. "Do you have no manners? How many times do I need to tell you the same thing?"

"I don't know," Shiri replied saucily. "Whatever I call him, *his lordship* seems quite content with what I do when I am in his bed. He likes it when I call him Yakub."

"Go and prepare a sleeping mat for the Wife-of-Rashid, and get her something to wear," Homaira ordered sharply. "And remember your place in this family!"

Shiri left the room, her mouth fixed in a sullen pout. Homaira's shoulders drooped dispiritedly as she watched the girl's departure. "Sometimes I worry that I am getting too old," she said. "Shiri causes so much trouble with the other wives, and we were such a merry household before she came."

"She'll probably settle down once she gets pregnant," Lucy said encouragingly, wondering if perhaps Afghani marriages were not quite as simple as she had blithely assumed. Perhaps, when you loved someone, no system was easy.

"But can you imagine what sort of children she'll have, that one?" Homaira turned away from the window where the Afridi warriors were now engaged in the game of extending a leather bottle of *sharbat* to the Khan of Kuwar on the end of a long pole and then snatching it away before he could drink any of the contents.

"Children," she sniffed disgustedly. "Men are nothing but overgrown children. Enjoy your life now, Wife-of-Rashid, while you are still the only woman in his *zenana*."

Lucy rewrapped herself in the blanket and walked toward the women's quarters at the back of the hut. "That sounds like excellent advice, Homaira. I think I shall do my best to follow it."

For five frustrating days, Lucy was confined to the women's quarters of Yakub's hut, and Edward saw her only once each day when she emerged, surrounded by an assortment of Yakub's wives and daughters, to breathe in fresh air and sunshine on the porch and to help with the spinning.

From these brief glimpses, Edward was able to conclude that her physical health was no longer cause for much worry. She had, by some miracle, avoided puerperal fever, and her terrible loss of blood didn't seem to have weakened her as much as it might have done. Her overall constitution remained strong, Edward concluded, in spite of the rigors she had subjected herself to. He watched with relief as her dreadful pallor receded more each day and the frightening fragility of her appearance altered rapidly as plentiful food and adequate rest filled in the hollows of her cheeks.

Unfortunately, Lucy's mental state didn't seem to show similar improvement, and the state of their relationship could only be described as disastrous. Edward worried about the listlessness of Lucy's manner and the heavy shadows that continued to bruise her eyes. Homaira reported that she slept twelve and fourteen hours a day, but an aura of weariness clung to her, and surrounded by listeners as they always were, it was impossible to broach any of the subjects that cried out for discussion between the two of them.

Only on the sixth day did they speak together at any length, and then it was the practicalities of their situation that were discussed. Still, as far as Edward was concerned, even this was a giant stride forward over the courteous nothings which they had exchanged for the past five days.

"My dear, I have ask if you feel you might soon be strong enough to face the journey back across the pass to India."

"We would have to walk?" she asked, not meeting his eyes.

"No, Yakub is more than willing to sell me a horse for you, if you feel able to control one, or a donkey if you cannot."

"I think the horse might be more comfortable, and certainly a lot swifter. When do you want to leave?"

"You must tell me that. Whenever you feel fit enough."

"You've been waiting for me?"

A bellow of rage came from the palisade where the Khan of Kuwar remained confined. He was not proving a courageous prisoner, and the Afridi children had turned him into a favorite source of entertainment. Lucy winced as she heard the patter of falling stones and realized that the village boys were pelting him with pebbles. "I never thought I would actually feel sorry for Hashim Khan," she murmured.

"Don't waste your sympathy. His ransom will arrive soon, and he will return home and avenge himself for this humiliation by beating all his wives. Not to mention his slaves and dancing boys."

She actually smiled. Almost the first smile he had seen since she realized she had lost the baby. "I'm sure you're right. In some ways, I'm surprised the Kuwari elders are willing to send the ransom price."

"They will do it because they feel the honor of the Kuwari tribe is at stake, not because they want the return of Hashim Khan. In fact, I suspect when he reaches Kuwar he will find one of his sons firmly entrenched as the new Khan, with the village elders acting as regents."

"Is it very ignoble of me to say that I can't help being rather glad that he has spent the past few days living in a palisade?"

"Certainly it's ignoble. However, it's also quite understandable. Would you like me to walk by and demand that he kiss my toe?"

This time she laughed out loud. "You needn't bother. I think the small boys are punishment enough to satisfy my thirst for vengeance."

"Hmm. I think I might just ask him how his Enfield rifles are working. I lack your essential kindness. In the meantime, Lucy, could you tell me how you feel? When do you think you might be able to travel, remembering that the journey over the pass is never easy at this time of year."

"Is it urgent for you to return to India? I suppose it must be."

"I won't lie to you, Lucy. I should leave as soon as I can. I have documents and reports, signed by Abdur Rahman Khan and by his followers, that should be seen at once by the British authorities. But your health is far more important to me than anything else. We won't leave here if you feel you wouldn't be able to endure the strains of the journey."

"Do we travel alone?" Lucy glanced self-consciously at the group of women gathered around them. "Is there no danger that the documents you carry might be—stolen?"

"We are to be honored with an escort of Yakub's most experienced warriors," Edward replied, understanding at once her unspoken question. "Yakub is a staunch supporter of Abdur Rahman Khan. They are cousins both on the paternal and maternal side of their family tree, and they consider themselves blood brothers. The men of this village have been monitoring every party that crosses the Khyber Pass ever since Abdur Rahman Khan set out from his temporary home in Tashkent."

"You mean that Bruno and his soldiers were under observation all the time? I wondered why we encountered so little opposition."

"You were very much under observation. The party that actually stopped Bruno reported back at once at Yakub. They brought word that a woman traveled with the group, but your disguise was too good and they assumed you were . . . ahem—"

"A camp follower?" she inquired politely.

"Something of the sort." For a moment he allowed his amusement to show. "I should have been smart enough to realize who you were the moment I heard there was a woman with Bruno's band of assassins. Lord knows, there aren't many camp followers prepared to pursue their profession across the Khyber Pass at the start of winter."

"I didn't willfully disobey you, Ed-Rashid," she murmured. "I didn't intend to follow you here."

"We will talk of it later," he said, touching her warningly on the hand. "But you still haven't answered me, my dear. Can you give me a day when might you be ready to travel? Next week? In five days?"

"Tomorrow?" she said, looking at him questioningly. "Do you think we could leave tomorrow?"

Insofar as any journey across a treacherous mountain pass at the start of winter could be considered tedious, that was how Lucy found the return to Peshawar. Accompanied by a troop of Afridi warriors some twenty-strong, Edward and Yakub saw no reason for excessive caution, and the pace they set was fast. A scout rode out a couple of hours ahead of the main party as a precaution, but since this territory was all controlled by Yakub's kinsmen, the danger was almost nonexistent.

From Lucy's point of view, she really had nothing to do save sit on her horse and, at night, collapse onto her blanket and wait for Edward to bring her food and hot tea. Even this relatively undemanding regime left her more fatigued than she wanted to acknowledge, partly because she found it difficult to sleep at night in the bitter cold.

She wished Edward would share his blanket with her. Each night, she visualized lying in his arms, curling against his warm body and feeling protected from the bite of the winter winds. Each night, Edward politely bade her goodnight and spread out his blanket next to Yakub. In the village, when she slept with the women, she had hoped his avoidance of any personal discussion might be a reflection on their lack of privacy. Now she began to fear that he was so angered by her disobedience that he couldn't forgive her for the loss of their baby.

Yakub and his warriors, in a break with their normal custom of never crossing into British territory, accompanied Lucy and Edward to within five miles of the city of Peshawar. Their entire journey home had been completed in less than six days, record time for this season of the year and for the distance they had traveled.

The parting between Yakub and Rashid was emotional. "Go with Allah, my friend." Yakub kissed Edward on both cheeks and embraced him in a bear hug. Public physical contact between sexes was considered scandalous by all Afghanis, but passionate embraces between those of the same sex were perfectly accept-able. "Your work means much for the people of my tribe and of my country. My cousin Abdur Rahman is a strong and a wise man.

With his guidance, perhaps my countrymen will learn to think of themselves as members of the Afghan nation as well as members of their own individual tribe."

"That is what I work for, with Abdur Rahman Khan's help," Edward said. "Word will be sent to you as soon as I have spoken with the officers of the British government."

Yakub bestowed a final smacking kiss. "May the Prophet, peace be upon him, guide your steps home to safety." Very much as an afterthought, he nodded his head toward Lucy and added, "Blessings rain upon you and your future sons, Wife-of-Rashid."

She bowed suitably low. "May Allah, in his wisdom, reward you for the kindnesses shown to me, Lord Yakub."

After another ten minutes or so of exchanging courtesies, duty was done, and the Afridi tribesmen cantered back toward the pass. Lucy and Edward were alone together for the first time since their parting in the marketplace nearly three weeks earlier.

The sudden isolation didn't cause any softening in Edward's manner. If anything, the tension vibrating between them increased noticeably.

"Lucy, I will have to leave for Mr. Carradin's lodgings as soon as I have seen you safely returned to our bungalow. I apologize, but the documents I carry from Abdur Rahman Khan cannot wait for delivery."

"I understand, Edward. Will you be able to order the arrest of the count and Monsieur Armand?"

"I certainly hope so. It is one of the reasons I feel so pressed for time." He turned to her, his face a mask that even months of marriage didn't permit her to penetrate. "Lucy, why did you risk your life following me into Afghanistan?"

It was as she feared. His coldness wasn't imagined. It was a direct consequence of her flagrant disobedience. "I'm sorry," she said. "But I had no choice. I wanted to speak to Mr. Carradin, to give him the information that Monsieur Armand and Monsieur Bruno were both spies, and possibly the count as well. I had only just realized, you see, that Bruno was not a sheep skin trader as he claimed to be, but the Russian captain we had encountered during our escape from Kuwar. I wanted my visit to Mr. Carradin to remain unobserved, so I made the mistake of dressing in some of my *ayah*'s clothes and going to his house on foot with only my maid for escort. By sheer mischance, Bruno and Armand discovered us and murdered poor Dira. The only way I could think of to bargain for my life and to warn you that your mission was in jeopardy was to persuade Bruno that I could guide him to your meeting place with Abdur Rahman Khan."

"Crossing a mountain pass in Central Asia with winter biting at your heels would strike most women as a bargain likely to save anybody's life."

"I know," she said humbly," and I am very sorry, Edward. I promise that in the future I will be a better, more obedient wife."

She wasn't looking at him, so she failed to see the rueful, crooked smile that stole across his mouth. "That, my heart, seems a promise you are most unlikely to keep."

CHAPTER TWENTY-TWO

The servants greeted Edward's and Lucy's return with storms of uninhibited, joyous weeping. Although their wildly confused milling and shrieking would have driven any British butler to distraction, in actual fact the servants performed their duties with surprising efficiency. A young girl, who tearfully announced herself to be the sister of the dead Dira, supervised the preparation of a warm bath for Lucy. The senior houseboy dispatched messengers to the Rutherspoons, the vicar, and Mr. Carradin, and the cook immediately departed to his kitchen to begin the preparation of a feast worthy of so momentous an occasion.

Edward, still wearing the clothing and skin-stain of his disguise, appeared at their bedroom door just as Lucy was preparing to step into the steaming, ambergris-scented tub. Oddly enough, despite the clothes, he no longer looked like Rashid, although Lucy couldn't define the subtle change that she observed in his appearance.

He crossed the room and took her hands into his. Recently, that was as close as they had come to intimacy. "My dear, please rest and take great care of yourself whilst I am away. You do understand why I must leave at once?"

"Yes, of course. You have a mission to complete that is of great significance. I wish you every possible success, Edward."

"Thank you." He carried her hands to his lips, kissing the knuckles gently. "We will have time to talk when I return, Lucy."

"Yes." She managed to produce a laugh that sounded almost natural. "It's amazing how little time alone together a married couple sometimes has."

"We will make time when I return," he said. He turned abruptly, dropping her hand. "Lucy, I must go. I have an obligation to get these documents into safe keeping and to inform Mr. Carradin of how matters stand in Afghanistan."

"Edward, don't worry, I understand the urgency." She added one final question: "Shouldn't you change your clothes? Doesn't it matter that our servants must have realized that Rashid and Lord Edward de Beaumont are one and the same person?"

"No, it doesn't matter in the least," he said. "Rashid the Trader has just completed his final assignment."

She realized then what the subtle difference was in her husband's appearance. Before, when wearing the clothes of Rashid, he had always *been* Rashid. Now he was merely Edward playing a role. During their recent exchange, he hadn't even bothered to speak in Pashto. His walk, the carriage of his head, the very way in which he held his body, was entirely different. Her heart gave a little lurch as she accepted that Rashid was gone forever.

"Wait!" she exclaimed, hurrying to the door. He swung around to confront her and she reached up to stroke her fingers across his wind-hardened cheeks. His eyes gleamed dark in the candlelight and his teeth seemed extra white against the mahogany brown of his skin. She brushed her thumb over his mouth.

"I would like to say goodbye to Rashid," she said softly, deliberately switching from English to Pashto. "I shall miss him. He taught me many important things."

Edward caught her hand, stilling the questing movement of her thumb, but he replied in Pashto. "He could teach only what you were ready to learn, Englishwoman."

"Then I must have been ready to learn a most important lesson. Rashid taught me how to love—not like an English lady but like a woman. I am most grateful to my teacher."

For a split second she thought she saw passion blaze in the darkness of Edward's eyes. He opened her hand and pressed a hot, hard kiss against the palm of her hand. She swayed instinctively toward him, but he held her away and the momentary passion vanished from his gaze as if it had never been.

"My duty awaits, Englishwoman. There is no acceptable excuse for delay when so many crucial decisions hang upon my presence." Without looking at her again, he pushed her gently back into the bedroom and closed the door. Seconds later, she heard him stride down the hallway, calling for his horse.

She had never felt so alone.

When she awoke the next morning, a letter from Edward already waited by her bedside. She ripped open the thick cream envelope with trembling fingers, needing to read the message twice before she absorbed the simple contents.

My dear Lucy,

Mr. Carradin has persuaded me that I must speak to Lord Lytton in person, since only the Viceroy has the power and authority to put the information I have gleaned from Abdur Rahman Khan to its maximum use. I swear to you that I am indeed comfortably en route for Delhi by train, and not for any other more obscure or more dangerous point of the globe. My manservant has brought me a supply of respectable British suits and ties. I therefore travel to Delhi as Edward de Beaumont, a dull Englishman who hopes that he, as well as Rashid, has played some small part in showing you what it can mean to be a woman. I love you, Lucy. Your devoted husband.

Edward

However many times she re-read this missive, Lucy could not find any hidden message of reproach for her disobedient behavior in pursuing Rashid into Afghanistan. The mystery therefore remained to plague her. If Edward loved her, why had he avoided sleeping next to her on the journey home from Qur'um? Why had he never mentioned the loss of their baby? Why had he never taken her into her arms and kissed away her aching sense of loss? Why did she feel this worrisome sense of estrangement? True, for much of the time since her miscarriage they had been surrounded by members of Yakub's family, but Edward was a man who routinely achieved the impossible. Surely he could have found five minutes when he could have been alone with his wife?

Lucy would have liked to indulge herself in the luxury of lying in bed for several days brooding over the state of her marriage. Unfortunately, the residents of Peshawar were not prepared to cooperate with her wish. By ten o'clock on the morning after her return, Mrs. Rutherspoon had rushed to the bungalow, anxious to assure herself that dear Lady de Beaumont was indeed safely returned to Peshawar. Lucy, who hadn't thought to discuss with Edward what she should say about her adventures, simply told her palpitating visitor that she had been abducted, but that Edward and his colleagues had rescued her.

"Oh, my dear Lady de Beaumont! Abducted! *Again.* Some people really do seem prone to get themselves into the most awkward situations, do they not?"

"I was thinking much the same thing myself," Lucy agreed wryly.

"Who would believe that such villainous abductors are free to roam the streets here in Peshawar? Of course, I have told Mr. Rutherspoon repeatedly that this is a frontier town and we might as well be living in the Wild West of America for all the control the authorities exercise! When we heard that your *ayah* had been found horribly murdered, her throat sl—"

"Yes," Lucy interrupted hastily, before Mrs. Rutherspoon's lamentations could become too graphic. "Fortunately, I know who my abductors were and I expect arrests will be made shortly. They may even already have been made."

"Perhaps the natives will learn their lesson at last—"

"But I wasn't abducted by natives, Mrs. Rutherspoon. I was abducted by respected members of the European community."

"Impossible!" Mrs. Rutherspoon breathed, her eyes gleaming with delight. "My dear, *dear* Lady de Beaumont, you simply must tell me the names of these . . . these monsters!"

"I think perhaps I had better wait for Mr. Carradin to announce the arrests. Would you care for some more tea, Mrs. Rutherspoon?"

Mrs. Rutherspoon weighed the possible advantage of staying to glean further details, against the definite advantage of being the first to carry forth the news that Lady de Beaumont had returned safely from her latest abduction. The glory of acting as town crier won out. She rose to her feet, and delivered her most gushing smile.

"Thank you, Lady de Beaumont, but I wouldn't dream of keeping you. After all the turmoil of the past few days, you must be sorely in need of rest. I will leave you now, but I shall certainly call again tomorrow to see how you go on!"

Lucy's smile stretched to match Mrs. Rutherspoon's. "What a treat for me to look forward to!"

Mrs. Rutherspoon was merely the first in an endless stream of callers, which culminated shortly before dinner in a visit from Mr. Carradin himself.

He greeted Lucy with a warm handshake and a searching scrutiny. "Well, my dear, Edward told me of the sad loss you suffered during your time in Afghanistan. You have my deepest sympathy, although I am glad to see you looking so well recovered."

"My stepmother always tells me that I have the constitution of an ox," Lucy replied, trying to make light of her grief.

"Perhaps so. I suspect, however, that it is your spirit which is so unquenchably strong rather than your physical constitution. When I heard that Edward had married, I confess I was troubled. I have known him for years, you understand, and it seemed to me that he was a man who would demand so much from a lifelong companion that it might be better if he remained single. My brief acquaintance with you, my dear, convinces me that I was wrong. I am sure Edward has found his soul-mate at last."

Lucy's smile was a touch rueful. "Let us hope, dear sir, that my husband reaches the same conclusion. I fear that he is very angry with me at the moment, and rightly so. Any normal wife would have stayed at home to wait quietly for her husband, instead of bounding off on some hare-brained scheme and getting herself abducted."

"I'm sure you mistake your husband's feelings, Lady de Beaumont."

"I wish you were right, but you didn't see his expression when I arrived in Qur'um. I can assure you he was not pleased to glance up from his crucial international negotiations to find his wife swaying on the doorstep, surrounded by Afridi warriors."

"Think of the scene from his point of view! Can you imagine the panic he must have felt? The guilt, that his work and his activities had dragged you into a position of such danger?"

Lucy had never considered the interesting possibility that Edward might feel guilty. Mr. Carradin's words opened up a whole new perspective on her husband's behavior over the past few days.

"When do you think Edward may return from Delhi?" she asked thoughtfully.

"I'm afraid he's likely to be gone for at least a week, probably longer. I'm revealing no state secrets when I tell you that he has an uphill task ahead of him. Lord Lytton feels we should take care of the messy situation in Afghanistan by sending in sufficient troops to conquer the country and annex it to British India. Edward, at the very least, hopes to convey to the Viceroy the message that Afghanistan is unconquerable by a traditional invading army. Our troops would win any pitched battle, of course, but the Afghanis are never going to stand and fight a pitched battle. Our soldiers will advance, and the Afghani enemy will disappear into the mountains. If we do pursue a strategy of more or less traditional invasion, the Afghanis will simply wait until we're far enough from our supply lines to be in trouble. Then they will massacre us."

"It is tragic that our imperial policy so often seems to be formed by men who have no idea what is actually going on in the territories they play with on their maps."

Mr. Carradin snorted. "Sometimes I wonder if they can *read* a map. Otherwise they would surely realize that an area which consists mainly of mountains and deserts—liberally sprinkled with tribesmen who are brought up to fight to the death as a way of life—is not an ideal country for launching picturesque cavalry attacks!"

Lucy visualized a battalion of scarlet-coated British troops, marching in set formation into a valley. She visualized the Afghani warriors, perched safely in their mountain eyries, raining down bullets on the British soldiers with absolute impunity. She shivered. If Edward could prevent such a massacre, his work and his efforts would certainly have been worthwhile.

Mr. Carradin reached out and patted her hand. "Edward is a persuasive man, my dear. I have a lot of hope. The documents he has succeeded in obtaining from Abdur Rahman Khan should convince the most determined of sceptics. Anyway, enough of this grumbling about politics. I came, my dear, to bring you good news. Count Andrei de Karpovich from the Russian city of St. Petersburg, otherwise known as Monsieur Armand, sheep skin trader, has been arrested on charges of murdering your maid, Dira; of complicity in your abduction; and of conducting espionage against the British Empire."

"Oh, you caught him! I'm so glad he wasn't warned in time to escape."

"He seemed to have no suspicion that all was not well with his various schemes. His informers were recruited mostly from among the Kuwari tribesmen, and I understand from Edward that many of the Kuwari warriors were killed by Yakub and his men, which may explain why 'Monsieur Armand' had no warning."

"I'm glad he is to stand trial. Poor Dira! I feel such a great responsibility for her death."

"Your sentiments do you honor, my dear, but sometimes it is better if we acquire a little of the Eastern fatalism. What happens is meant to be. Such a philosophy can help to make the intolerable more bearable." He hurried on, before she could speak. "I also have news for you about Count Guido."

"Oh, the count! You were able to arrest him, too?"

"We arrested him, but have decided to lay no charges, because his complicity might have been difficult to prove. He has been ordered to leave the country under military escort."

"Is he also Russian?"

"No. He truly is Count Guido of Tuscany, but we have discovered that his mother is an impoverished member of the Russian nobility, which may explain the count's willingness to throw in his lot with the Russian cause. I gathered from what he revealed under questioning that he suffered a bitter personal rejection recently, and took himself off to India in some misguided fit of romanticism. I think this brush with the unpleasant realities of espionage has tempered his enthusiasm for the life of a spy. He didn't anticipate that you, Lady de Beaumont, would end up being abducted, and he certainly wasn't at all comfortable about the fate of your maid. He had never considered the possibility that innocent bystanders might get hurt in the course of his adventures."

"I confess to being rather glad that some of what the count told me about himself was actually the truth. He was an engaging young man."

"He was indeed. A great success with the ladies." Mr. Carradin rose to his feet, smiling. "Well, my dear Lady de Beaumont, I will bid you good evening. But please, if by any chance you should acquire some startling information which you feel I must share immediately, I beg you will *not* attempt to deliver it in person. Send one of the servants to me with a note. I assure you I will come running. Edward has left me with strict instructions to see that you do not vanish back into Afghanistan while he is gone." Mr. Carradin laughed. "Although why he expects me to tame you when he has so signally failed in the task, I have not the slightest idea."

The elderly diplomat did not intend to criticize, Lucy realized, as she mulled over their conversation during the next few days. However, it was obvious that she had been a most unsatisfactory wife, and she resolved that when Edward finally returned from Delhi, he would find a reformed creature waiting to greet him. She would use the period of Edward's absence to transform herself into a perfect English wife.

Since she had spent most of her formative years trailing around outlandish parts of the globe in the wake of her father, she had only a nebulous idea of how proper English wives conducted themselves. This, she decided, should not be an impossible hurdle for a determined woman like herself to overcome. From her observations, she already knew that aristocratic wives spent a great deal of time at home doing nothing in particular. They also gave explicit orders each morning to the cook, embroidered slippers for their menfolk, and nurtured the moral welfare of their households.

Lucy was optimistic that she could eventually train herself to be quite as good at these task as any other lady, despite the fact that she abhorred doing nothing, that the cook cooked wonderfully without any instructions from her, and Edward never wore slippers.

These trivial obstacles could not be allowed to deter her. Lucy braved the wrath of the cook and entered the kitchen each morning to inquire into his plans for the day. She was wise enough to make no attempt to change his menus, and the cook nobly refrained from handing in his notice. The problem of the slippers was less easy to resolve, but necessity is the mother of invention. Lucy paid an afternoon call on Mrs. Rutherspoons and returned triumphant, clutching a splendid pattern for a rose-decorated, satin tea cozy.

A visit to the vicar's wife produced an equally promising book of the Reverend Jowett's collected sermons. Judging from the extreme tediousness of the sermons, Lucy could only assume they were exceptionally uplifting. She intended to improve her mind and the moral tone of the servants by reading Mr. Jowett's strictures aloud during dinner, but since she was invited out almost every night, this aspect of her wifely improvement programme didn't progress very far. The servants, at least, were very relieved by their narrow escape.

Work on the tea cozy fared better. Bullied by her maid into retiring for a nap every afternoon, Lucy wiled away the boring hours by stitching at the hideous pink cabbage blossoms that Mrs. Rutherspoon's pattern indicated. Lucy couldn't imagine actually covering one of her exquisite china teapots with something so ugly, but she supposed that wifely virtue was acquired more in the execution of the task than in the usefulness of the object produced. Come to think of it, she could never actually remember seeing a man wear a pair of embroidered slippers.

By the happiest of coincidences, she was seated in the drawing room industriously stabbing at a virulent green leaf when Edward finally returned to Peshawar after a ten-day absence. She heard his carriage pull up on the gravel driveway, then the swift stride of his footsteps in the hallway. With superhuman control, she refrained from hurtling out of the door and throwing herself into his arms. Her programme of self-improvement was already paying dividends.

"Lucy!" Edward strode into the drawing room. He slammed the door behind him and pulled her to her feet, crushing the cabbage-pink evidence of her reformed character as he swept her into his arms.

"You look wonderful, my heart." He crooked his finger under her chin and tipped her face gently upward. "The color has come back to your cheeks, thank God. You must have been resting and taking proper care of yourself for once."

"Yes, Edward," she said meekly. "I have done exactly as you instructed. I have not been abducted, I have rested every afternoon, and I am making a tea cozy."

Edward looked puzzled. "A tea cozy? How—um—domestic."

"I have also been reading Mr. Jowett's Collected Sermons. They are most . . . They are very . . ."

"Boring?" Edward suggested politely.

"Oh yes, terminally so! That is to say, they are no doubt very improving."

"So are cold baths and hair shirts, but I have always tried to avoid both. Lucy, why the blazes are we discussing Mr. Jowett's sermons?"

"It's Sunday," Lucy suggested. "A very proper day for us to turn our thoughts to consideration of higher . . . Edward, what in the world are you doing?"

"My heart, something seems to have seriously addled your wits since I left here last week. Isn't it obvious that I am undoing the buttons of your gown?"

"But Edward, we are in the drawing room!"

He looked around, feigning astonishment. "Good heavens, so we are! How splendid that I can rely upon you to keep me informed of such vital matters." He resumed undoing her buttons and nibbling at her skin.

Lucy ignored the insidious heat rioting through her veins. "Edward, the servants—"

"Are far too well trained to interrupt."

"I hope your trip to Delhi was successful," she said primly, pretending not to notice that her dress was now gaping open all the way to her waist, and that her knees were in the process of turning to water.

"A qualified success at best. Lord Lytton listened with half an ear. I spoke with a few colonels who seemed to grasp the concept that marching cavalry regiments in line formation into a mountain valley wasn't likely to produce very desirable results. At least the people in Delhi finally recognize the name of Abdur Rahman Khan. I told them that one day soon he will be Amir of Afghanistan."

Lucy's dress and camisole were now sliding gently to the floor and her knees had completed the process of dissolution. She collapsed against her husband's chest. "Edward," she said, searching desperately for a few remnants of ladylike virtue. "I have turned over a new leaf while you were gone. I have learned to be a proper wife, just like Mrs. Rutherspoon."

"God forbid! Besides, I was rather fond of the old leaf myself." Edward bent his head toward her breast. "Mmm, indeed, you taste as wonderful as ever. Entirely proper for a wife."

His tongue licked teasingly between her breasts and she gasped. "Dear heaven, Edward!"

"Heaven, my heart, is exactly where I plan to take us. The sofa, I think, is the first step on the way."

He picked her up before she could protest—not that she had the faintest desire to object—and deposited her tenderly against the cushions. "How convenient that you are wearing so few petticoats," he murmured. "I'm not sure that I would have lasted through more than three layers of enticement."

Lucy abandoned the useless struggle for virtue. "I've missed you so much, Edward," she whispered. "After I lost the baby I thought you would never feel able to forgive me."

"Forgive *you*?" Edward's teasing smile faded. "How could you dream that I would blame you for something that was entirely my fault? It was my activities as Rashid that led you into danger. It was my selfishness in bringing you back to India that placed you at risk. I should have insisted that you stay in England where you were safe, but I needed you too much. I wanted you by my side, and I brought you to India, knowing the dangers."

"I'm glad I came. I'm afraid I shall never be a good wife who remains contentedly in the drawing room while her husband departs for exotic foreign places. I make simply terrible tea cozies."

Edward raised himself on one elbow and looked at her in astonishment. "My love, what is this sudden obsession with tea cozies?"

"Well, wives are supposed to embroider slippers for their husbands, but you don't wear slippers, so Mrs. Rutherspoon suggested— "

"Ah-ha! At last we reach the root of the problem! My heart, Mrs. Rutherspoon may satisfy her husband by sewing tea cozies. I, on the other hand, have very different methods of achieving satisfaction. Like this, for example."

He bent his head swiftly and covered her mouth in a deep, endless kiss. Lucy sighed with the pleasure of a joy rediscovered. Her hands crept up to twine luxuriously in Edward's hair while his hands brushed over her body, reacquainting himself with the curves and hollows he already knew so intimately. Then, with the assurance of a man confident his lovemaking was wanted, he wrapped her legs around his hips and locked her ankles behind his back.

"I love you, Edward," she murmured, feeling her entire body flood with pleasure as he slowly entered her.

"Then kiss me again, my heart, my love."

She felt him tremble beneath her kiss, felt the heat of his breath in her mouth and understood suddenly that for this man she would never need to disguise her true personality, or pretend to be a woman she was not. Edward loved *her*, the woman she was. For him, she was already the perfect wife.

"I *hate* tea cozies," she declared as their kiss momentarily ended. "I shall never make one again."

For a stunned moment, Edward stopped his passionate caresses, then he looked down at his wife and laughed softly. "My love, for the sake of my masculine pride, not to mention my intense state of masculine arousal, do you think we could refrain from discussing tea cozies for the next half hour or so?"

Lucy framed his face with her hands, pulling his mouth down to meet hers. "We could certainly try," she whispered.

Success was theirs.

EPILOGUE

On November 21, 1878, a combined army of British and Indian troops crossed into Afghanistan in a three-pronged attack against the faltering rule of Amir Sher Ali. The ostensible reason for the British attack was the Amir's failure to respond satisfactorily to a diplomatic note submitted by the British government in India. The real reason for the invasion was to prevent the Amir from entering into an alliance with Imperial Russia, whose representatives were conferring at that very moment with the Amir in Kabul.

Thanks to the wonderful British-built telegraph system, news of this attack reached England promptly. Lord and Lady de Beaumont, at home in Ridgeholm Hall, greeted the news with surprising indifference, possibly due to the fact that Lady de Beaumont had chosen that very day to go into labor.

Her twins were born at dawn the next morning after what the doctor termed an easy first labor. Lady de Beaumont snorted and told him that if he had spent the past twelve hours enduring what she had endured, words like "easy" would not escape his lips.

The doctor patted her indulgently on the arm, told her that both babies weighed more than six pounds and asked what she planned to name them.

"Our son is to be called Peter," Edward said. "After my wife's late father. Peter Edward Gervaise de Beaumont."

Lucy smiled at him, love and gratitude in her eyes. "And our daughter is to be called Miryam, which is how the people of Afghanistan say *Mary*. Miryam Lucinda Elizabeth de Beaumont."

"A very fine choice of names." The doctor snapped the locks on his black leather bag and took a final glance into the cradles where the Honorable Peter and the Honorable Miryam lay sleeping peacefully. "Amazingly healthy babies, Lady de Beaumont. It's rare to deliver twins who are so sturdy. Congratulations to all of you."

Lucy and Edward beamed with besotted parental pride. "They are beautiful, aren't they?" Lucy said.

The doctor was old enough to understand the merit of addressing spiritual truth rather than physical reality. He ignored his vivid inner picture of two red-faced, bald-headed, wrinkled and pugnacious-looking babies. "They're very beautiful," he said. "Indeed, they are."

Over the next twenty-four hours, the telegraph system not only buzzed with news of Amir Sher Ali's desperate attempts to raise a Russian army to fight the British invaders, it also buzzed with telegrams informing various members of Lucy's and Edward's family of the double happy event.

Lady Margaret, surprisingly mellowed, telegraphed a message of congratulations and added that she would deliver the traditional gift of silver christening mugs in person over the Christmas holidays. She was pleased to hear that the Bishop of Cirencester planned to be on hand for the baptismal ceremony.

Penelope, not to be outdone, sent an express letter from her home in Paris, announcing that she was immediately freighting her own gift: two paintings by her beloved husband Peregrine, one for each lucky de Beaumont baby. Her dearest Peregrine, her letter went on to say, was *much* influenced by the new Impressionist style, although the jealous French critics had quite failed so far to recognize his genius.

On a snowy day in January, Fletcher came to the drawing room door and announced, in his most sepulchral tones, that a carrier had arrived with two wooden crates. "Large wooden crates, my lady. Sent from France."

"Peregrine's pictures for the babies!" Lucy exclaimed. "Have somebody uncrate them and then carry them up to the nursery, will you, Fletcher?"

"Certainly, my lady."

The two paintings were carried in state to the day nursery. Peter and Miryam, awoken for the momentous occasion, stared with interest at the bright splotches of primary color unveiled before their somewhat unfocused eyes. The remainder of the assembled group stared in mingled dismay and incredulity.

Edward was the first to break the stunned silence. "Do you think Peregrine has been helpful enough to provide arrows to indicate which way is up?"

Lucy examined the pictures with care. "No arrows," she said. "And the hanging cord is exactly across the middle."

Edward, ever a man of initiative, positioned a painting randomly on a wall. "How about this?" he asked.

"Coo," said the Honorable Peter. It was the first time he had ever made any sound other than a bellow of rage when a supply of milk was not instantly forthcoming.

"He likes it!" Lucy exclaimed, her maternal powers of translation brought instantly into play. "Peter likes his Uncle Peregrine's painting!"

Edward grinned. "My heart, don't despair. Our son has several more years in which to acquire some discrimination."

The footman held up the second painting, a vivid portrayal either of a dubiously colored fried egg or possibly a sunset.

"Coo," said the Honorable Miryam. "Coo, coo."

In February, 1880, Abdur Rahman Khan, supported by a small army of about one hundred followers, crossed the Amu Darya from Russia into Afghanistan. Joined by most of the northern tribes, he marched toward Kabul. On July 20, 1880, at the town of Charikar, some twenty miles north of the capital city, he proclaimed himself Amir.

The history of an independent, unified Afghanistan had begun.